ROARING

ROARING

LINDSEY DUGA

Entangled Publishing, LLC
10940 S Parker Rd
Suite 327
Parker, CO 80134
rights@entangledpublishing.com

Entangled Teen is an imprint of Entangled Publishing, LLC.

Edited by Lydia Sharp
Cover design by Mayhem Cover Creations
Cover photography by moorsky/GettyImages

Manufactured in the United States of America

First Edition August 2020

To Bridget,
With whom I wrote my first stories

Glossary of 1920s Terminology

Ankle – to walk

Applesauce – drat; darn

Bank's closed! – stop making out!

Bird/cat – referring to a man

Blouse – take off; leave

Bluenose – term for a prude or individual deemed to be a killjoy

Bubs – breasts

Burning powder – firing a gun

Bushwa – bullshit

Cabbage – money

Cheaters – glasses

Choice bit of calico – pretty; attractive

Corn – bourbon

Darb – lovely

Dewdropper – slacker; someone who is often unemployed

Dizzy with the dame – in love

Drum – speakeasy

Duck soup – easy; no problem

Dumb Dora – a girl who is not too bright

Egg man – the money man; the man with the bankroll

Flapper – young modern girl in the 1920s

Flaming youth – young modern man in the 1920s

Gasper – cigarette

Grifter – con man

Go chase yourself – get out

Gooseberry lay – Stealing clothes from a clothesline

Gumshoe – detective

Half-seas over – drunk

Have the bees – to be rich

Hayburner – car with poor gas mileage; a guzzler

Iron my shoelaces – excuse one's self for the restroom

Jake – easy

Jane – a term for a woman

Jingle-brained – addled

Mazuma – cash

Manacle – wedding ring

Oliver twist – an extremely good dancer

Oyster fruit – pearls

Panther piss – cheap, homemade liquor

Phonus balonus – nonsense; horseshit

Pug – boxer

Rattler – train

Rhatz – darn; bummer

Rub – a dance party for college or high school students

Sheba – someone's girlfriend

Sockdollager – someone or something which is truly

remarkable or impressive; a humdinger

Spinach – cash

Trigger men – men whose job it is to use a gun

Whoopee – have a good time

William "The Lion" Smith – famous jazz pianist of the 1920s

Yegg – safecracker who can only open cheap and easy safes

You're on the trolley – now you're catching on

Zounds – expressing surprise or admiration

Zozzled – drunk

Under this single spotlight, I am an angel.
The song flows out of me, free and beautiful and haunting. Rich and smooth as a glass of whiskey. Not that I know what whiskey tastes like. But that's what more than a few patrons have said before.
"Eris, babe, you's got a voice as rich and smooth as a glass o' whiskey."
I smile and dip my head in thanks, not speaking. Not ever saying a word.
Their glazed, inebriated eyes tell me they want to hear my voice, but that they don't care what words I utter. And so I utter nothing as I serve them their drinks.
Don't say a word.
Don't.
Ever.
Speak.

Chapter One

The Singer

Applause met my ears as I finished my set. It wasn't earth-shaking, wall-trembling applause, but the small number of clappers were enthusiastic. They always were. Even if dawn was just around the corner, six or seven empty glasses by their elbows, sleep and moonshine pulling them toward a state of dark but blissful ignorance, they always managed to show appreciation for my songs.

I plastered on a timid smile and blinked in the glow of the spotlight on the tiny stage of The Blind Dragon. Actually, "stage" was a slight exaggeration. It was a six-inch raised platform made from old whiskey crates that Stanley had crudely painted black.

The clapping tapered off, one whistle piercing the smoky air as I stepped off the makeshift stage, eager to vanish into the dark corners of the bar once more.

Because there was usually at least one. One intoxicated fool that approached me and asked me to run away with him.

My reaction was always the same. I would shake my head

and retreat to the back where Stan would glare at the man if he got too close again. Still, the plea would linger. *Run away with me.*

As if I could.

And even if it *were* possible, I'd never want to run away with the fella who was asking. Most of the gentlemen who sauntered into my quiet life probably wouldn't mind a girl who never said a word. But what kind of person would want to have a partner who never cared about what they had to say? Not me, that was for certain.

"Eris," a voice said to my left, and I recognized its husky tone like the harmony of a chord—familiar and reliable. I turned to meet David, our saxophonist, stepping out from the band area. His scruff was growing out nicely along his jaw, now no longer a shadow but the beginnings of a full beard. His white shirt was clean and ironed, sleeves rolled up to his elbows, and burgundy suspenders cutting parallel lines up and down his torso. Even his hair was somewhat combed. He looked like a fancy gentleman.

But the night was still young.

"Stan needs you to mix a few cocktails." David lifted his chin toward the main bar. With its sleek mahogany wood, it was the nicest thing in The Blind Dragon. Everyone said so. New patrons would saunter up to a stool, take a look at the deep red lumber, see their reflection in the shiny surface, and rub their grubby hands across, smearing it.

I hadn't seen Stan make the telltale sign of raising his hand and spinning his index finger in a circle from the stage, but the spotlight prevented me from seeing most things. David's dark eyes roamed my face, scanning as he usually did for any acknowledgment of his words, and any hint at mine.

I nodded to let him know I'd heard, then turned toward the bar dutifully, even though I'd have loved nothing more than to lose myself to another song. The lyrics, melody, and harmony of "Am I Blue" were already waltzing through my head. It was a new piece, popular from the pictures, and the whole country was already in love with it. But I was confident that no person could love it more than me.

I'd barely taken another step before a large hand wrapped around my arm above my elbow, drawing circles on my skin with the pad of its thumb. "Ah, Eris, my love," cooed Marvin, sliding his empty glass along the top of the piano to the edge. "Top me off there, would ya, doll?"

I frowned and held up two fingers.

He supplied an easy, suave smile. "Eris, Eris, don't worry so much. We're gettin' paid tonight, according to Madame, so let's keep 'em coming, eh? 'Sides, she ain't payin' me to bore the folks to tears."

Marvin was a brilliant clarinetist, but a drunk. It was only ten thirty p.m.—The Blind Dragon had been open a mere hour and a half—and he'd already consumed two bourbons. I'd often heard Madame Maldu say to Stanley that he was basically paid in liquor. Almost every penny of his check went back to the Dragon. A dream employee, really. It also helped that he was somehow an even better musician when he was intoxicated.

"Besides, I can hold my booze just fine. Cain't I, Francis?" Marvin said, tapping our pianist lightly on the shoulder and resting his hip against the piano itself.

With a noncommittal grunt, Francis dipped his bowler hat and reached for his own drink.

"See?" Marvin said, smirking like Francis had just delivered a long speech of shining compliments to Marv's long-standing sobriety.

With a smile, I shook my head and held out my hand to take his empty glass. He placed it into my palm, and my fingers curled around it, disrupting the beads of sweat trickling down its sides. Maneuvering past the chairs and instruments of my little band, I skirted around the tables, heading quickly to the bar, hoping that my brief interaction with the band members had allowed the effects of my song to fade.

"Thank ya, my love," Marv called after me as he sat and picked up his clarinet. In a few short seconds, the beautiful notes trickled through the air, and David's sax followed, their combined duet permeating my skin and dousing my soul.

I reached the bar and ducked behind it, avoiding the gaze of anyone and everyone who tried to catch my eye, and then edged up to Stanley. He was pouring three shots of whiskey for some hoity-toity lookin' fellas. The pressed lines in their shirts and slacks, their clean-shaven youthful faces, their rowdiness…if I had to guess, they were Harvard boys. Most men around Boston claimed association to the uni in some way or another, but it wasn't often we got students themselves.

If you asked me, they had a good bit of courage to risk their prestigious law career futures on a few rounds of giggle water.

Turning to the back of the bar, I glanced at the cocktail list Stan had written down for me. A gin rickey, a mary pickford, and a sidecar. Stanley claimed he was bad at the measuring and the garnishes, so most of the cocktails he left to me. I didn't mind, because when I measured ingredients, I pretended I was baking. *Maybe a pie.* I squeezed the lemon juice into the cognac and orange liqueur and twirled the peel with a knife and my thumb. *A lemon meringue pie.*

"Good set there, Eris," Stanley said from the corner of his mouth.

I didn't have to nod or dip my head. He knew I'd heard him even if I didn't respond. Stanley didn't need constant assurance of his worth or kindness.

He was a good man. And I respected the dickens out of him.

"Lookit, gents," a rough, low voice said, the words digging

into my back like a kitten heel.

"It's the angelic sheba herself. Where'd you get such a voice from, doll?"

I didn't reply. It was nothing personal to the fellas—I just didn't speak. All the regulars had come to know this about me. In time, if they kept coming back, they would catch on, too.

Instead, I set aside the finished cocktails, then uncorked the lid of Marv's favorite bourbon and tipped it into the clear glass, already smudged with his fingerprints, greased from the oil in his slicked-back curls.

"Oy, you heard me, bitch?"

My hands flinched at the harsh tone and some of the precious bourbon splashed onto the mahogany.

Stanley's imposing form sidled up behind me.

"Now, I thought you was gentlemen," Stanley said to the stranger. "Was I mistaken?" The rumble of his voice sent vibrations from his back to mine, and I stayed turned around.

Silence from the other side of the bar. I listened hard, my hand still frozen on the bottle of bourbon.

"Those words don't have a very gentlemanly feel to them." Stanley's muscles brushed against my back as he folded his whiskey-barrel sized arms.

"You're right, ole sport," the Harvard boy said, his high-society Bostonian accent dripping off every syllable. "We are gentlemen, and we deserve to be treated as such. It's rightfully rude to ignore gentlemen. Tell the sheba to answer my question." The more he talked, the thicker his accent got and the more slurred his words became.

I lifted my gaze, meeting the Harvard boy's eye in the thin strip of mirror that ran along the back of the bar. He was a might red in the face, irritated at being ignored. Not used to it. Handsome fella like him, I doubt he'd been ignored a moment in his life. From his mother's lap to his girl's arms, he'd been coddled and adored.

When our eyes locked, the boy slowly sat back on the stool, smoothing a piece of dark hair that had fallen out of perfect placement. A smile crept up on his thin lips, and it was like I could read his mind. He imagined us in the alley, wrapped in each other's arms, him pulling me back to his dorm...

Dropping my gaze back to Marv's drink, I carefully placed the bottle of bourbon back on the shelf next to my right knee. That way, I wouldn't be tempted to smash the Harvard boy over the head with it.

"Eris don't speak," Stanley told them, his voice low and edgy. Maybe most people couldn't hear the danger there, but the difference to me was like night and day. The subtle tonal shift from one octave to the next, the tightness in his vocal cords.

Careful, boyos, better run and hide.

"Bushwa," the lad cursed. "The dame isn't mute. She sings!"

"But she don't speak."

A laugh bubbled up from one of the boys, the one in the plaid flat cap that was much too big for him. It made him look too young.

"You telling me, sir," he continued through thick, drunken laughs, "that she don't speak in a *speak*easy? A little ironic, wouldn't you say?"

"Why don't you gentlemen get back to your drinks? Next round on the house," Stanley said, every word wrapped in a swaddling blanket of tight restraint.

Turning back toward the bar to face the Harvard boys, I placed a warning hand on Stanley's large bicep. It relaxed ever so slightly under my touch, and I smiled to the fellas.

My smile was sometimes enough. Enough to quiet the loud ones, let them sit back and fantasize about me on their arm or in their bed. Let them fantasize. After all, I knew the power of fantasy very well myself.

I fantasized every night about getting out, running to the rails and following them far away, out of Boston. Most flappers my age would head for New York. But I didn't want a city that never slept. I wanted sleepy towns, with golden fields and farmhouses and big blue skies and purple mountain majesties. I longed for wholesome communities where they sang at church, worked on farms, brought soup to each other when they were sick. Where kids played in the grass and under shady trees with big yellow dogs named Sunny.

I was maybe the only eighteen-year-old girl in 1929 who fantasized of such things.

In fact, most nights, on Stanley's painted whiskey crates, I imagined I was singing sweetly in a small choir. Singing because *I* wanted to, not because it sold drinks.

Lifting the tray of cocktails, I started to move out from around the bar. But I barely took two steps before a strong hand snapped over my thin wrist, startling me so bad that the drinks teetered and spilled drops of liquor on the tray.

"We're not done chattin', doll."

This fella was persistent. Madame Maldu had always told me under no circumstances should I speak, but these moments were the hardest. How I longed to tell him just a few choice words.

He leaned over the bar, light green eyes—eyes I was sure had ensnared females in the recent past—boring into mine. "Say, doll, let's blouse. There's a rub going on tonight in just an hour or so. We could sneak away and dance 'til we drop."

My song must've really done a number on him, or the more likely explanation was just that he hated rejection.

I tried to twist my wrist from his locked grip, but he held on. Then, before I knew what was happening, Stanley had leaned across the bar and grabbed the Harvard boy by his collar.

The two other fellas stood so fast that their stools fell to the floor with a resounding *bang*, and the flimsy wood cracked against the hard surface. Silence swept through the bar, every dull-eyed patron looking up from their drinks. Even my little band stopped playing, David and Marvin lowering the instruments from their parted lips.

The Blind Dragon was small, as were most speakeasies, room for no more than ten tables, the corner for the band, and the wraparound mahogany bar that could seat about fifteen souls. And it was still early for the night, so it wasn't packed. But busy enough. One gentleman off in the corner, sipping at his drink, was the only one who hadn't moved a muscle at the ruckus. He stood out because of his perfectly tailored pinstriped two-button suit and his distinct lack of company. You got plenty of fancy-dressed men at The Blind Dragon, but not usually sitting alone.

"You want to walk away, ole sport," the Harvard fella said to Stanley. "It's just me and the dame talking."

"I think you're hard of hearing, sir. Let go of the lady's arm," Stanley rumbled as he hooked a foot under the bar and climbed over.

The Harvard boy's eyes widened and his grip on my wrist loosened. I gave one hard yank and stumbled back into the wall of liquor bottles, several of them shaking on the thin wooden shelves. I sent up a silent prayer to the Good Lord to not let any bottles fall. Madame Maldu paid a pretty penny to several bootleggers for the finer stock—they cost more than my life.

"Now I'll ask you to leave, sir." Stanley towered over them, all six foot two of him, broad shoulders and bulging biceps.

But the boy didn't budge. He might've been surprised at Stanley's actions at first, but he was quickly building up his courage and indignation.

Without warning, the boy lunged forward with a right hook, punching Stanley square in the jaw.

I clapped my hands to my mouth, forgetting about the tray of cocktails and Marv's bourbon. They fell to the floor in a crash of glass, alcohol, and lemon garnishes. Gasps traveled around the speakeasy as Stanley's head whipped to the side. But the blow didn't even make him stagger. In fact, the boy's knuckles were probably hurt worse.

Even so, the punch was enough to break the thin cables of Stanley's restraint. He grabbed the boy by the neck and lifted him off his feet. His eyes grew wide as saucers, his face coloring to a shade of pink as Stanley increased the pressure on his neck.

"If you won't go, then I'll remove you," Stanley said through gritted teeth.

Perhaps three drinks ago, the college boys might've just walked out and left in peace, but they were drunk. And drunk men liked to fight even if they were up against an ex-army MP who boxed for fun on the weekends.

The one in the oversize flat cap pivoted and swung a right punch into Stanley's gut. Our bartender barely blinked and backhanded the boy, just hard enough to make him stagger and trip over the exposed legs of their stools and bang his head against the bar's edge.

The third boy let out a roar and rammed himself against Stanley's stomach. Stan grunted and dropped the boy he'd been holding up by the neck to wrap his beefy arms around the charging boy's chest. He lifted him up and slammed him on the ground. Meanwhile the first fella, the one who'd started it all, stumbled backward, rubbing his throat, silky strands of hair falling in his face as he pulled out a revolver from his pocket.

My heart stuttered in time with the panted, agitated

breaths of the boy—no, he was no longer a boy. He was a man with a gun. An angry one.

"You'll pay for that." His thumb reached back and pulled on the hammer.

He was maybe two feet from Stanley. He couldn't miss at that distance.

The silver of the small Remington revolver glinted in the dim copper lights of the speakeasy. I imagined the ruby-orange flare from the sparking flint, smoke puffing around the leather grip, as the bullet burst from its chamber in an explosion of gunpowder and found its home in Stanley's gut.

I couldn't let that happen.

Listen to me, Eris.

Stanley wouldn't get shot. I wouldn't let him.

Don't speak, Eris.

I lunged across the bar just as the man pulled the trigger.

Don't. Ever. Speak.

My scream echoed through the Dragon. "*STOP!*"

The next moment, the whole world did just that.

Chapter Two

The Agent

The heated porcelain of the mug warmed my hands. Rather, it was the still-steaming joe inside it that did the trick. Inhaling slowly, I took in the rich scent of the Ethiopian coffee. That smell that clung to coats, soft shirt collars, and the drab office walls of the Bureau of Investigation. I loved that smell—so thick and black you could taste it without the risk of burning your tongue.

But I didn't take a sip. I only drank coffee if I needed to, which wasn't often. Being an insomniac, my brain was just wired that way. Helpful for stakeouts.

"How is it, Mr. Clemmons?"

I looked up to see Miss Lowensky watching me with baby-blue eyes and an eager smile, leaning on the edge of her chair. She had rolled away from the desk a bit, freeing her dark mid-calf skirt and stocking legs from their prison. The typewriter in front of her was untouched—and had remained untouched since I walked through the door.

Lifting the mug in a cheers-like motion, I returned her

smile. "Best cup o' joe in all of DC, ma'am."

Miss Lowensky flushed with happiness, her pale cheeks coloring under her cheaters, and she leaned forward a bit more, her blonde bob brushing her jaw. "Well, you just let me know if I can get you anything else." As she spoke, her voice dropped an octave in an almost purr.

While most nineteen-year-old men would jump at the chance to neck an older, attractive broad like Miss Lowensky—which was surely what her body language and tone were implying she wanted from me—I knew better.

You don't neck your boss's secretary.

I'd been going on my own assignments for a year now, and Barbara Lowensky, secretary to Matthew McCarney, head of the BOI's Specialized Organized Crime Division—SOCD for short—had been making me coffee for only two months. She still had yet to realize that I never drank any of it.

I raised the mug to my lips and pretended to take a sip of the coffee I hated. It would be too awkward to correct her after all this time. "Thank you, Miss Lowensky."

"We've known each other long enough. Call me Barb," she insisted, tucking a tress of gold hair behind her ear and looking up at me from under long, mascara-covered lashes. I tried not to blush like a schoolboy and cleared my throat before replying, "Well, um, Barb, call me Colt."

Barb seemed to almost hop in place with excitement. She leaned further over the arm of her chair, scanning me up and down. "I've always thought Colt is a swell name. It's so… *strong*. You know, like the gun."

That seemed to be everyone's first thought. I preferred to connect my name to its origin, which was the term for a young male horse. But then, maybe my mother had named me after the gun. I'd never known her to ask.

"Is Mr. McCarney free yet?" I set the mug down on the side table and glanced up at the simple clock hanging on the opposite wall. It was coming close to forty minutes. I'd waited for longer before, but today I was antsy. I'd arrived at the BOI at six o'clock in the morning, a mere thirty minutes after I received the call.

It was unusual for me, a junior agent, to be called in so early in the morning. I had no idea what to expect once I stepped through McCarney's door.

I rubbed my sweating palms on my thighs—blaming them on the steaming mug of joe.

Barb blinked and looked up at the clock on the wall, as if she'd remembered why I was here in the first place.

"I'm sure it won't be too much longer. Mr. Sawyer is in there with him. They should be wrapping up their meeting."

"Sawyer? As in Jimmy Sawyer?"

"Yes, that Mr. Sawyer. They've been in there since I got here at five thirty." She leaned further still, this time a conspiratorial lean instead of a flirtatious lean. "Something *big* happened, Colt. A real sockdollager."

"You don't say." I edged up in my chair. Maybe Barb could give me a clue as to what to expect. Preparation was the mark of a good agent.

"Oh, yes. It's got Mr. McCarney all in a tizzy. Never had so many calls in and out of the switchboards during the night. I don't know the details, but something has the SOCD by the storm."

"Where did it happen?"

Jimmy Sawyer was a field agent. If he was the one debriefing McCarney, it likely happened outside of Washington.

"Boston," Barb said, her voice a hush as a doorknob rattled.

The office door swung open, revealing the head of the SOCD, Mr. Matthew McCarney, my boss. My legal guardian.

McCarney wore the same clothes from yesterday. In

fact, I doubt he'd even left the office. His gray suit was a little rumpled, and a faded coffee stain peeked out from under his vest. Unlike most modern men, McCarney chose to keep with the three-piece suits and starched collars.

"Clemmons," he addressed me wearily, running a hand over his trimmed brown hair peppered with silver. He loosened his tie with two fingers. "Let's get this over with."

"Yessir." I stood and nodded toward Barb. "Thanks for the cup o' joe."

She gave a close-lipped smile, her finger tapping the side of her jaw as she scanned me up and down.

My cheeks heated uncomfortably.

McCarney raised an eyebrow at his secretary, and Barb ducked her head, scooting her chair back under her desk and returning to her pile of papers. Her fingers danced over the keys in an almost blur, and I realized why she hadn't bothered to type with me around. She could afford to dawdle—she was the fastest typist I'd ever seen.

McCarney's office was dim, probably due to the field agent who sat in one of the chairs opposite the big, cheap desk in the center of the room. A ficus plant stood in the corner, the only color brought to the place. The rest of the furniture and walls were shades of gray—the stapler, typewriter, papers, fountain pens, paper clips, and used coffee mugs all blending together in dull government-standard tones.

"Take a seat, Clemmons," he ordered, walking around his desk then sitting in his own chair that creaked as he leaned backward. "You remember Sawyer." McCarney nodded to the man in the pinstriped suit.

Like McCarney, Sawyer's clothes looked a day old. Which was odd. Jimmy Sawyer was a creature of refined taste and expensive fashion, who never skipped out on grooming. What could've possibly had him driving from Boston all the way to DC in the middle of the night?

"I do. Good to see you again, sir." I reached for Sawyer's hand.

His lip curled, but he extended his gloved hand and shook mine. "I really can't say the same, Clemmons."

Not surprising considering most agents hated me. Yes, I was technically too young to be working for the BOI, but here I was, every other week, getting a new assignment, collecting my checks, all thanks to…extenuating circumstances.

In my opinion, there was nothing for Sawyer to be jealous or bitter about. He had the better deal. He was free to roam the country.

But they kept me on a tight leash.

For good reason.

McCarney rested his elbows on his desk, rubbing his temples. "Just brief him, Sawyer."

"I really think you're making a mistake, sir. This is too important to let Clemmons take care of it. I mean, this is the biggest threat to national security we've had since the war, and you're going to just entrust her capture to—"

"Clemmons is the strongest hunter we've got," McCarney interrupted, "and we need our strongest to resist her voice."

I straightened. "Her voice, sir?" Every muscle in my body was wound tight like a coiled spring. Like a bullet the split second before it escaped the chamber. Pressure built up insurmountably inside me.

I glanced at Sawyer. The agent's jaw was clenched, hating my involvement. Hating that the Bureau relied on me so heavily. They would never give *him* my responsibilities.

For good reason.

McCarney's blue eyes narrowed. "Tell him what you saw, Sawyer."

The senior agent let out a frustrated sigh, then he started his story, slow at first, then gaining speed.

"I was in Boston, at some drum called The Blind Dragon."

Neither McCarney nor I blinked at a BOI agent visiting a speakeasy. Whether Sawyer was there to do his job—locating any hints of organized crime within the illegal establishment—or partake in some hooch didn't matter. Prohibition meant little to the BOI. In all honesty, we hated it. All the bootlegging and secrets had paved the way for organized crime to take over. For mob bosses to infest cities and fill the streets with blood.

"And there was this canary. A real looker. Her voice…I ain't never heard nothing like it before. She sang and no one moved. I forgot where I was. I forgot *who* I was. Everything. When she stopped singing, the next thing I knew she was over at the bar, pouring a drink. Then these three uni boys start tryin' to get her to leave with them. The bartender hops over the bar and the leader of the fellas hooks him right in the jaw. The bartender doesn't even blink until the lad pulls out a revolver."

"Were you packing heat?" I asked.

Sawyer shot me an annoyed look. "Course I was. Had a Remington in my coat. Didn't even have time to get to it, though, before the little shit pulled the trigger. Only the bullet didn't hit. It stopped. Midair. And then just…fell to the ground."

McCarney and I stared at Sawyer, hanging on every word. My pulse was pounding. My palms were now *seriously* sweating.

This is it.

"My heart stopped, too," Sawyer continued, moving a trembling hand to wipe his mouth and rub the day-old scruff on his jaw. "Everything just…*stopped.* Because of her."

"The singer?" My voice was barely above a whisper.

Sawyer nodded. "She yelled '*stop!*' and everything did. The bullet, the patrons in the bar, my own damn breathing."

Sounds magnified. Barb clacked away on her typewriter

through the thin office door. The clock hanging on the gray wall ticked and the ceiling fan whirred above our heads.

McCarney slid his gaze back to me. "We found her, Clemmons. We found the lost siren."

Chapter Three

The Singer

Folding the rag over for the cleaner side, I approached the next table and wiped it down, putting in a little more elbow to buff up the shine. The previous occupants of the table had been rowdy, splashing their drinks all over the place, laughing and carrying on. But these were regulars, and they left a decent tip most nights, so I didn't mind cleaning up their mess.

"Eris, a little help over here?" Stanley called from behind the bar.

I held up a finger to let him know I'd be there in a moment, then wiped off the seats, tucked the rag into my apron, and hurried back around the bar. It wasn't ten seconds before I'd left the table that another group of young folks slid into the seats with their cocktails.

Stanley was working as fast as he could, multiple bottles by his elbows, switching from one to another and topping off drinks. He was much faster than I was, but slack had to be picked up. We were jam-packed.

The "mishap" last night had enticed more than a few

flappers and flaming youths to come to the place where their friends had been beaten to a pulp by a bartender.

Luckily, no one seemed to be coming round to see *me* anyway. When the bullet had dropped to the floor, I wasn't sure what I'd been expecting. The tinkling sound of brass hitting wood had seemed roaring within the silence of everything coming to a grinding halt. I thought maybe they would drive me out of town and I really *would* have to hit the rails. Then I'd have the excuse I needed to leave Boston and find the sleepy little town I'd always dreamed of.

Instead, everyone chalked it off to the gun misfiring. As if a bullet could stop *midair* from the misfire of a gun. But there was no other logical explanation for what they witnessed. *People believe what they want to believe,* Madame Maldu had told me long ago, when I first discovered my little gift—or curse, depending on how you looked at it.

I had been eleven, maybe, when I experienced the full power of this strange magic inside me. There had been other times—slips, as Madame called them—but none such as this one. Madame had just bought The Blind Dragon and was hiring contractors to fix up the place. They were working inside and I had been tucked in a corner, reading a book of fairytales with breathtaking illustrations. One of the men had encouraged me to read them out loud for their entertainment. At first, I had shaken my head. Madame Maldu had told me never to say a word.

Then I thought they would be someone else's words, not even mine. So surely it couldn't hurt anything. At the time, all I knew was that when I spoke, people did what I told them to. What harm could I do in reading a story?

So I had started reading *Little Red Riding Hood* to the workers. I should've noticed the abnormality at the beginning. I should've noticed that when I read how the wolf talked to Little Red in the woods, the workers would stop and look around warily. But it wasn't until I got to the part where the wolf eats Little Red and I was trembling with fear at the mention of his big scary teeth that I realized…the grown men were as scared as I was.

So scared, in fact, that one ran outside. Ran right out into the middle of traffic.

He was badly injured.

The men couldn't understand why they had been so frightened. Why had a child's fairytale caused them such distress? But it had been *me.*

My emotions. My fault.

After that, Madame never had to remind me not to speak.

"Eris, what's got you so distracted, hon?" Madame Maldu asked as I squeezed behind her to get into the back corner of the bar. "I've watched you remake drinks twice, and you're moving slower than molasses tonight."

Stanley and I had both agreed not to tell Madame about the incident with the Harvard boys. If she'd known I'd opened my mouth, she'd have a conniption. And since people were blaming it on a gun misfiring, she thought it was as simple as that. While saving Stanley's life had been a noble cause, Madame wasn't known to be very reasonable, especially when it came to keeping my secret.

Besides, I had the feeling that Madame had other reasons to hide me away in this tiny bar tucked into the middle of this growing, bustling metropolis. When we left New York—the night itself fuzzy from my young, childish memories—we'd gone to several tiny townships and small cities. But then I'd have one of my "slips," like asking the store clerk for candy and he'd give me ten pieces, and then more. Every time something like that happened, Madame would purchase two tickets for the next train out of town. She was always looking over her shoulder.

As if we were running from something or *someone.*

I got hints from time to time. Madame would often say things like, "*There are greedy, fearful people in this world. People that want to use your power for themselves. Or people that would be so scared of you that they would loop a rope around your neck and watch you hang. You mustn't speak, Eris. Don't ever let them know what you can do.*"

But any time I got close to asking who might be after us, Madame would place her fingers over my lips and say to me, "*Please don't make me say his name, little angel. He's a powerful man and he has ears everywhere. Let him stay in the past.*"

It was those words—*don't make me*—that clamped my jaw shut. Just because I had the power to get what I wanted didn't mean I should. I had seen enough people bend to my will to be truly frightened of what I could do.

I didn't like looking into Madame's eyes and not telling her the truth of what happened last night. And I certainly didn't like betraying the trust of someone who worked so hard to protect me, but if I did tell her the truth, wouldn't she just pick us up and leave the Dragon? Just like all those other towns, we'd have to disappear and start over.

Though I wasn't partial to the city itself, we'd made a home in Boston. Madame loved this little drum and worked so hard at it. Stan was practically an uncle to me. And Marv, David, and Francis? They were my silly older brothers. We were like a little family. I didn't want to see Madame have to leave a place she'd come to love.

Even if I wanted to most nights. Even if I wanted to run away from the booze, the smoke, and the drunks…

Brushing a strand of hair from my face, I took a deep breath as I swiped two glasses from the top shelf. Madame had already moved on to pour another drink, not bothering to wait for an answer she didn't expect to get. Sometimes I wondered why she bothered asking. Probably just her way of telling me I needed to pick up the pace.

I lifted my gaze to the two gentlemen waiting to be served and gave them a smile. They were older fellas with beards and stained work shirts. Probably worked in the docks—they reeked of fish.

"Panther piss, ma'am. The cheap stuff, if you don't mind."

Nodding, I ducked down, pulled out the brown glass jug, and poured the homemade whiskey into the two glasses. While Madame stocked the real, expensive liquor, some men just wanted to get drunk. The cheapest homemade hooch would do. As long as it tasted a *little* like whiskey going down.

"Thank ya, babe. You have a nice night." The fella who ordered winked at me and tipped his glass in my direction.

Again, I smiled in response and went on to the next patron. Meanwhile, Marvin, Francis, and David played in their little corner, their jazz stylings weaving through the bar in a soft, smooth melody coupled with a light but spicy harmony. None of them had a particular song they were playing, they just…played. Listening to them improvise, to hear the time changes and the movements up and down the scale, was magical. And it was all because they let the music move them.

"Are you not going to sing tonight?" Madame asked me as she leaned her hip against the bar and folded her arms, fixing me with her knowing, piercing gaze.

No, maybe never again, I wanted to say. My singing almost got Stan killed.

I continued cleaning, avoiding her question. The midnight rush had died down and it was coming up on one o'clock in the morning.

I could picture Madame standing before me while I focused on a glass that was already smudge free. Her auburn hair, streaks of gray woven in, pulled up in a colorful wrap, a dress of geometric design that fell down her body attempting, but failing, to hide hourglass curves underneath. Those green eyes lined with black coal—like a chorus girl's—searching my silence for the answer she wanted.

She was a beauty, even at an older age, but it wasn't her physicality that made her a looker. It was her air of mystery. Painted eyes and lips, long curls bound up, big costume jewelry, a shawl hanging around her elbows. She looked like a fortune teller.

"Eris?" she asked again, softer this time.

I shook my head. I was not going to sing tonight. Nor tomorrow night, or maybe even the night after. Last night had not been the first *incident*. But it had been the first one with a gun.

Madame wouldn't force me to sing. The speakeasy did well enough without my songs, but she also knew how much I loved it up there. Even if it was for a bunch of drunkards, I still loved the music. Still loved the thrill that a perfect melody brought. So she probably thought my sudden stage fright was odd at the very least.

"Hmm. Well, all right." She took the glass from my hands and tipped her chin toward a lone man in a corner. "Go get his order. He came in thirty minutes ago but hasn't ordered a damn thing. My drum is not for dewdroppers."

Still with Madame Maldu's gaze at my back, I slipped around the bar and headed for the young man sitting by himself, his fedora pulled low over his eyes. His sleeves had been rolled up to his elbows, showing off pale but muscular hands, wrists, and arms. It was a warm autumn for Boston, so his lack of coat wasn't odd, but it stood out. In fact, he was the kind of fella who seemed like he could do whatever he wanted. If his goal was to blend in and not be seen, he could throw on his coat and sit with a drink and not talk to anyone, becoming one with the furniture. If he preferred to stand out, he could tip his hat back and lift his face and smile, but if he wanted just the right *kind* of attention, all he needed to do was roll up his sleeves.

Walking up to his table, I pulled out my waitressing tools and poised my pencil on my pad of paper, awaiting his order.

It was then that he looked up and I got a peek at the face below the hat.

His eyes were dark. It was the first thing I noticed. Eyes where you could barely tell if there were pupils at all.

He was attractive, but not in a pretty, hotsy-totsy sort of way. His face was geometric. Perfect square jaw, a straight nose, high, triangular cheekbones, and a rectangular forehead. His light brown hair, practically blond, was mostly hidden under his hat. But, like Madame Maldu, he was not handsome solely because of his looks. It was his air. His... competence.

A strange way to describe a stranger, perhaps, but it seemed to me that this was a fella who knew his place in life. His past. His present. Maybe even his future.

It wasn't until he cleared his throat that I realized I was staring. Redirecting my gaze to the pad of paper, I waited for his order, heat creeping up my neck and into my cheeks, and a small shiver going down my spine.

He said nothing.

Glancing up from my pad, I caught him staring as well.

Oh. He's waiting for me. Now, with even my ears growing hot, I tapped my pad with my pencil and gestured it toward him, showing him what I couldn't say in words.

His brow furrowed, and for a moment I worried that he didn't talk, either.

After a few long, silent, and awkward seconds, he asked, "You want to take my order?"

Relieved, I nodded vigorously.

His brow dented deeper, more into a right angle. "Do you not speak?"

I couldn't help but admire the quality of his voice. It was a low timbre, a combination of the strings of a cello, the pluck of a bass, and the lingering bottom note of a sax.

Again, I nodded.

The stranger's brow was now a straight V, as if this angered or frustrated him somehow. An aura of hostility exuded from him.

Tentatively, I took a step back.

At my retreat, his face cleared and he gave me an easy smile, completely changing the lines of his face into something real handsome.

I'd been right. This man was a chameleon. He wore a rugged grin that would make most gals swoon. Maybe me included, if I hadn't felt that anger coming off him like heat from a radiator in the dead of winter.

"Not a chatter, eh? That's all right. I can talk enough for the two of us." He leaned forward, folding his arms and resting his elbows on the table as his grin widened. I noticed his feet shift, hooking his ankles around the legs of the spindle chair.

With this small movement, I caught a whiff of his scent. It was not thick, musky cologne like most gentlemen wore. It was the smell of smoke. Not gasper smoke that made my throat burn and my lungs shrivel if I inhaled too much of it. It was that of a hearth. Of coals and burning wood.

Growing hotter still, I cast a furtive glance back at the bar. Stanley was watching me—he'd kept a close eye on me since last night—and I wasn't sure if that made me feel better or worse. Madame Maldu and Stan were the only ones who knew my secret. While I was relieved to have someone watch over me, I hated that I made him worry so much.

The night Stan learned my secret, I was fourteen—almost four full years ago. Some gentlemen had cornered me in an alley, tried to hold me down and unbutton my dress. For the first time in three years, I spoke. Told them to *let me go and leave.* They did, but not after falling over themselves to get away, scrambling like a bunch of raccoons caught going through the trash. Stan had witnessed the last few seconds of the attack.

Instead of being scared or confused, he'd wrapped me up—while I was trembling and weeping—in a big hug and told me, "*You should've made them do worse.*"

I looked back at the stranger now, and his gaze kept to my face. Straight into my eyes like he was searching for something.

"If you don't speak, I guess you can't tell me your name," he said, his head cocking. "Which is a pity. Lovely dame like you, I bet you've got a name to match. Do you mind if I take a few guesses?"

He wanted to guess my name? I merely stared at him, not sure how to handle this one. Maybe I should back away and let Stanley take his order.

But I had to admit, the stranger intrigued me. It was a thrilling sort of intrigue. Like hearing a scary story. Nerves heightened, bated breath, terrified and yet captivated, thrilled and yet wary.

He was the kind of thrill a person would want to be brave for.

I gave him a subtle nod. Rather, my chin jerked downward in a stiff, awkward motion.

"Let's see...what about..." He pretended to think, his lips twisted to the side as he stared up at me. "Helen?"

I shook my head.

"Mary?"

Again, I shook my head.

"Hmm, those are too common. You seem like a unique creature. Am I right about that?" He tilted his head again, a small smile tugging at the corner of his lips.

Perceptive fella.

I tapped my pencil on my pad of paper, and he chuckled at the impatient gesture. "You have to get back to work?"

I nodded.

"I s'pose I'll get it another night, then."

To my surprise, he stood. Grabbing his jacket from the back of his chair, he hooked it on the index finger of his left hand and tossed it over his shoulder. Then he dipped his fedora at me, that cheeky smile tugging at the corner of his mouth.

"Goodnight to you, miss."

And he left, leaving me with an empty order ticket, the smell of fire smoke, and a lingering feeling of desperate curiosity. Out of my sight, but not out of my thoughts.

Chapter Four

The Agent

The moment I saw the girl behind the bar in The Blind Dragon, I'd had my doubts. *She* was the lost siren?

The most dangerous threat to our country since trench warfare?

It was hard to believe.

She was a looker, to be sure. Sawyer hadn't been exaggerating about that, but what he *hadn't* mentioned was that she seemed more like a girl from another era. Her eyes were big and blue and she had chestnut hair with tones of auburn in thick curls, done in the style of a woman before the turn of the century. The dress she wore was typical flapper design—loose—falling past her curves, but no hint of makeup. Not even painted lips. If it hadn't been for the dress, she looked like she might belong at a farmhouse, milking cows, not nursing drunks on a binge.

When I'd first heard of the monster who'd escaped the detection of the BOI twelve years ago, I'd imagined a sensual, enigmatic vixen with bobbed hair, kohl-lined lashes, a string of pearls, ruby lips, and an aura of vibrant charm.

Not this small, timid doe.

Could Sawyer have been wrong?

And yet she was exactly as he'd described her. From the hair color and the eyes to the fact that she really was mute. Apparently Sawyer had inquired about her to some of the regulars before he'd left. None of them knew her name, only that she was the canary at The Blind Dragon who sang but never spoke.

It was actually smart as hell. But irritating that we were only now realizing how she'd stayed hidden for so long. If she didn't speak, then she couldn't use her powers. If she didn't use her powers, then how could she ever be found?

Smart.

But even so...what if it really *had* been a gun misfiring? What if she really was mute? What if I took in an innocent citizen and the BOI did...well, I didn't know what they'd do exactly.

But I could guess. And it likely wouldn't be pretty.

So I wasn't bringing her in until I was one hundred percent sure. And because she hadn't sung last night, because she hadn't talked to me while trying to take my order, I had to be patient.

McCarney had taught me the mark of a good agent was patience. Follow every lead, no matter how exhausting. Stay awake on every stakeout, no matter how boring. And don't rush to make an arrest when you don't have enough evidence.

Well, her voice would be my evidence. I'd been trained for years to listen for a siren's magic. I would know it when I heard it. I just had to get her to talk to me, and the only way I could think of doing that was to charm her. But charming took time.

Brute force might be faster, but that wasn't an option. I tried not to be a monster, I just hunted them.

• • •

The second night I came back, I could feel her eyes on me almost immediately. As if she'd been waiting for me to walk back into her speakeasy. *Good.*

Taking a seat at the same small table in the corner, I waited. She didn't come to me. She poured drinks, she smiled at customers, she wiped down tables, she lingered next to the bartender—one of the biggest men I'd ever seen in my life.

She avoided me.

That's going to be a problem.

If she was already wary of me, how was I going to get her comfortable enough to speak? While the back of my mind played out possible scenarios of engaging her, I listened to the jazz band. The chaps were talented. Their improvisation and the way they played off one another was at a professional level—good enough to play in the big leagues up in New York or Chicago.

But they seemed content to be *here*, in this tiny speakeasy just like a thousand others. They knew the people. Laughed and talked and joked with the regulars.

For the second night in a row, the siren did not sing. Instead, she merely looked out at the band longingly as she wiped down the glasses.

Not too long before closing time, I left my table and approached her. I'd waited until the giant bartender was in the back and the siren was the only one pouring drinks. There were few people left anyway, and those that had lingered were all half-seas over.

As I sat on an empty stool, she paused her wiping, looking up at me under her eyelashes.

"Evening, Miss Adele," I said.

For the first time, the smallest smile touched her lips. It was barely there, but I counted it as one. Then, slowly, subtly, she shook her head.

"No dice, eh? And I really thought I had it with that one."

She set down the glass she'd been cleaning, fixed me with those big blues, and waited, still not saying a word.

"Delta? Clarice? Millie? Dorothy?" I fired off in rapid succession.

Four shakes of her head, but she was smiling fully now. *That's good*, I thought, then, *she has a beautiful smile.*

I leaned forward, dropping my voice a tad lower and said, "You can't give me a hint, Harriet?"

While her blue eyes locked with mine, her lips peeled back to show her straight white teeth in a smile. Again, she shook her head.

"No to the hint? Or no to Harriet?"

She covered her mouth to mask what I suspected was a giggle. I felt hope stir in my chest. *Come on, siren, talk to me.*

Then she gestured to the rows of bottles behind her, still silent as the grave.

Disappointed, I glanced up at the liquor on thin wood shelves, then met her eyes once more. "No, thank you, I don't drink."

She frowned deeply and tilted her head, looking at me in utter perplexity.

C'mon, just ask me.

When I knew she wasn't going to, I asked for her. "What am I doing in a drum, then?"

She nodded.

Placing my elbow on the shiny red wood surface, I leaned forward just a smidge more—close enough that I could see the few light moles across her clavicle and trailing up her neck. "I heard news of a canary singing in *this* speakeasy that I just had to hear. You heard tell of such a creature?"

Her big eyes widened and her hands twitched on the edge of the bar.

Great. That probably scared her. Good going, Clemmons.

I needed to take off before she got *too* skittish. With a rap of my knuckles on the wood, I gave her a smile. "Well, if you know of her, will you tell her this cat would dearly love to hear her sing?" Then I reached into my pocket and dropped a quarter onto the bar. The coin spun, whirring round and round until it finally rested. Heads up.

Tipping my hat to her, I grabbed my jacket and flipped it over my shoulder, heading out into the crisp fall air.

I let the chill ripple over the exposed skin of my neck and forearms. My skin was always hot to the touch so autumn and winter were my favorite times of the year. The cold chased out the muddy scents of summer in the city and left a sort of freshness—for at least a brief time— before smoke from chimneys and fires would thicken the air.

Agitation stirred in my chest like I'd swallowed three shots of burning fire whiskey. I was leaving empty-handed yet again. But the girl was good. It would take more than a few suave smiles and charming words to get anything out of her.

For a moment, I considered going back inside. Just taking my chances and grabbing her then and there. But…I remembered the serene look on her face as she listened to the jazz, and her full smile and rosy cheeks.

The spots between my shoulder blades ached and my throat seared with a burning itch.

Don't bring her into this world if you don't have to.

Be sure. Be one hundred percent. Find proof.

McCarney would want that, I told myself.

I moved away from The Blind Dragon's door and kept walking.

The street that the speakeasy resided on was nondescript, as were the streets of most. Under an unmarked door, to the left of the fire escape and to the right of the tall pile of crates that never moved. The entrance was a storage room of the pharmacy storefront off the main thoroughfare, but a hidden lever opened the narrow wall, allowing passage to the land of gin and rebellion.

There were a hundred more like it. The fact that Sawyer had found this one, had chosen to wander into *this* drum where the lost siren worked, was nothing short of a God-ordained miracle.

Or it would be, if I believed in Him.

Strolling down the street, two blocks over, I stopped. The sound of my footsteps halted, but the whisper of leaves on the pavement traveled on in a continuous shuffle.

Turning my head to the side, my chin brushing my shirt collar, I asked the empty street, "You going to just follow me all night, Sawyer?"

A sharp-dressed man in a navy-blue suit, trench coat, and fedora stepped out from the alley behind me, his gloved hands in his pockets.

"If you knew I was here you could've mentioned something earlier and saved me the trouble of tryin' to be discreet."

"Maybe I just realized you was there." I tried mocking his Brooklyn accent to make me sound more confident than I was. The truth was I *hadn't* noticed he was there until half a block ago.

Sawyer closed the distance between us, his green eyes boring into mine. "Cut the shite, Colt." His fury was evident, punctuated by the way his black pupils narrowed to slits. "Let'sss just get to your hotel. I'm freezing out here."

The *hiss* in his words was just barely detectable. He hid it less when he was cold. Basilisks, like any other snake, hated the cold—even though locals would call the night *warm* for an October in Massachusetts.

We walked in silence for the next few blocks. The hotel I'd chosen the day before wasn't as bad as a flophouse, where transient men stayed and fleas permanently took up residence, but it wasn't the Ritz Carlton, neither. The hotel was three stories, wedged on the outskirts of the financial district, just a hop, skip, and a jump from Cambridge and Harvard. It was all red brick, so indicative of Boston.

We passed the sleeping doorman and crossed the oak wood floors, recently waxed and shined from a cleaning company I'd seen the day I'd checked in. The color palette of the interior was dark hues—crimson and plum—highlighted only by gilded gold handrails up the banister. The chandelier hung to the right of the staircase—glass, not crystal. Pretty, but cheap.

My room was at the end of a red-carpeted hall with the brass number 207 affixed to the door. I withdrew my key from my pocket and unlocked the door while Sawyer hung back. The door swung open with a click. The scent of freshly washed sheets, must, and coal hung thick in the air, and I was tempted to open the window. But Sawyer would snap at me if I did.

As I tossed my coat onto the one empty chair, I turned around to find Sawyer already pulling off his gloves, flexing his hands. The scales on the back of his hands shone in the dim light of the ceiling fixture. Golden glimmer on green and blue tones made his skin look like an evening gown.

He would slug me if he knew I often compared his scales to sequins on a woman's dress.

Even more, I couldn't imagine the discomfort he had, wearing those gloves day in and day out, having the leather or cotton rub against his scales. But he kept his coat and hat on. Clearly the stuffy room was still too cold for his reptilian body.

"What's taking ya so long?" Sawyer asked, his eyes back to their normal round pupils as he rubbed his hands together and blew on his aquamarine fingers. "Don't tell me just because this kitten is a choice bit of calico that you're hesitating—"

"Take it easy," I said, throwing myself down on the bed and stretching out my muscles. I ached from sitting in the small, rickety chair all night. "I don't care *what* her face looks like. She could be Clara Bow herself and I'd still haul her in. I've gotta confirm it's really her."

"It's *her.*" He *tsked*, forked tongue flickering behind sharp teeth. "You don't believe me."

"I believe you saw something," I said quietly, staring up at the water-stained ceiling, "but I'm not taking her in until I've seen for myself what she can do."

"Dammit, Colt," Sawyer growled. "This isn't some werewolf or manticore you can fill with a bunch of lead and call it a day, this is *the* siren. The only creature capable of—"

"You don't have to tell me what monsters are capable of." I glared across the room at the snake leaning against the wall, fedora tipped back to reveal his pale face. "Now, if all you're gonna do is stand there and nag me, go chase yourself. I'm tired."

"I thought you don't sleep."

"There's a difference between needing sleep and needing rest. Get out." When Sawyer still didn't move, I sat up on my bed and sighed. "What are you doing here anyway? Don't tell me you're ignoring an assignment from McCarney to follow me?"

"It just so happensss I had a job here in Boston before I found the siren." Sawyer's pupils narrowed to slits again. "And I'm back to finish it."

"What job?" I asked, curious despite myself. It could've been literally anything for an SOCD agent, but tracking down another monster was the most likely.

The world of underground, organized crime was filled with more than just tommy guns, dope peddlers, and booze.

It had real, honest-to-God monsters.

It all started nine years ago with the Ninth Amendment. Prohibition had given birth to mob bosses. Mob bosses wanted hatchet men—their own personal armies to protect territories and neighborhoods—but somewhere down the line they decided that wasn't enough.

It was hard to pinpoint the origin of the monster trade. Where it started, who had started it, and *how* it started was all a mystery.

Oh, there were rumors, of course. The BOI had spent a lot of cash and manpower to try to locate the origin and stop the monster trade at its source. Some claimed it started overseas, smuggled in through the docks, in the birthplace of the myths themselves. Greece, Transylvania, England…but the countries were too old, too vast, too ancient to follow any solid leads.

All we could do was hunt the ones we knew existed. The ones that went *bump, chomp, roar* in the night.

Shortly after J. Edgar Hoover took over the Bureau, the SOCD was set up to specifically hunt these monsters. But many—*too* many—stiffs washed up on the shores of the Potomac, the Hudson, and Lake Michigan, all with special kinds of markings—the supernatural kind.

Soon, the Bureau found that the best way to hunt monsters was *with* monsters.

Sawyer was one such hunter. A monster himself, burdened with the scales of a basilisk, he was able to kill a person with a single gaze, if he held it long enough.

Sawyer nudged his hat up, fixing me with those deadly eyes, and answered in a low tone, "A bootlegger I'm after is smuggling vamp fangs into the docks, unloading them in some speakeasy. Just have to find out which one. Then I'm off to New York."

I perked up. "What for?"

"Apparently kids are disappearing off the streets and from orphanages. The BOI doesn't know if it's monster-related, but they need some extra eyes and ears to keep low to the ground."

Kids missing? That wasn't abnormal. So it had to be *a lot* of kids to get the BOI's attention. "Sounds important," I muttered.

"It is," he snapped.

"Then I won't keep you," I said drily. Sawyer acted tough, but in reality he was one of the softer agents. He'd escaped a mob boss in Brooklyn at twelve because he hadn't had the stomach or desire to use his curse. He didn't want to kill anyone.

Well, that wasn't entirely true. There was *one*—the bastard that buried the basilisk's scales into his arms at the age of seventeen. Jimmy Sawyer's only goal in life was to find the mob boss that turned him. Find him and stare him in the eyes.

Sawyer crossed to the bed and used his scaly hand to grip my collar, forcing my face to meet his. "I know what I saw. I know what I *heard*. And *felt*. She stopped that bullet. She stopped everything. All at once. Don't wait for her to speak, Colt, because if she does, it may be the last thing you ever hear."

Chapter Five

The Singer

The third night the stranger came around I'd already been looking for him for a couple hours. It seemed like every time the door opened and Stan would check on the number of patrons in the Dragon, either letting them in or turning them away, I would look up.

And hope.

It was so odd. I'd never been intrigued by someone quite like this before. True, I was still a little scared, but more scared of myself around him. Several times I almost slipped, desperate to answer his questions and to ask him mine in return.

He was unique—unlike any man I'd ever encountered before. He'd never heard me sing, so there was no effect of my gift whatsoever on him. His interest in me was just that of a guy to a gal. And it made me feel…special.

Like when he told me he wanted to hear me sing. For the first time, I *wanted* to sing for someone else.

It was then I knew that he was a story I desperately

wanted to finish.

But the hour crept on later, and I began to wonder if he was ever going to come again. That frustrated me. Would I never get to know the story's ending?

"Eris."

I jumped at my name and turned sharply to the left, abandoning the glass that was already clean three times over. I'd been watching the door again. For the eighth time that night.

David stood across the bar, staring at me with his eyebrow quirked inquisitively. He retrieved a folded *Time* magazine out of his back pocket and laid it on the bar. The cover was a portrait of a dark-haired man in a fancy suit with the words, "*American Royalty: Stocks, the New Gold.*" David flipped past the profile on the important businessman to an article with a picture of rolling gold hills. The title read, "*California, the Paradise Found.*"

Unable to stop myself, I grabbed the magazine and scanned the text. I already couldn't wait to read it. If there was one state I'd dreamed of seeing, it was California.

I peeked up from the top of the magazine to give David my most imploring look.

The saxophonist just laughed and drummed his fingers on the bar. "Yes, you can keep it. I got it for *you*, you know."

I let out a happy squeal and leaned across the bar to deliver a swift kiss to his cheek in thanks.

On my shopping trips I was never allowed to dawdle around newsstands, so David and Stanley often brought me magazines with articles they knew I'd like. I'd never told them of my fascination with the West and the rural areas of the country, but then again, I didn't have to. They'd caught me reading and admiring magazines and newspapers left behind by patrons on more than one occasion.

Making sure that Madame was nowhere around, I

slipped the magazine behind the row of bourbon bottles. I'd add it to my stash later and learn as much as I could about the state, and maybe, *maybe*, I could work up the courage to ask Madame to go on a trip there. Because there would be no going without her or Stan. They were as much my jailers as they were my protectors. I was kept hidden and locked in this cage that masqueraded as a speakeasy, but they kept me safe. I owed them so much.

Smiling, David tipped an imaginary hat to me and left to return to his music. Part of me was tempted to join him, but still I stayed safely behind the bar. I told myself this was for the patrons, that they wouldn't have to feel drunk on my songs in addition to drunk on their giggle water. But in my heart I knew it was an excuse.

Simply put, I was a coward.

Just when I thought I'd never see the stranger again, he walked into the bar, same as the night before. Relaxed. Confident. Handsome.

To the right of me, Madame let out an irritated hiss. I startled at the sound, having not realized the woman had snuck in behind the bar.

"If he doesn't order something within the first ten minutes, I want him gone. And you let Stanley handle him, Eris. I don't like the way he looks at you."

Helena Maldu's voice was low and raspy, hoarse after the few cigs she'd smoked earlier in the evening. It somehow made her sound more powerful and more mysterious than usual, and gooseflesh erupted across my skin.

I jerked a nod but had never wanted so deeply to disobey.

Madame Maldu knew what was best for me. So if she didn't like the way a man looked at me, I should listen to her.

And yet this stranger didn't look at me like others did. His dark eyes, mysterious as they were, were clear, not magicked, nor entranced. Seeing me simply as I was.

So it was painful, more than I thought it'd be, to turn away as he approached the bar. Stanley stepped up to take my place.

"What'll it be, sir?" Stan asked, gripping the edge of the bar and subsequently showing off his rippling muscles.

"How about some orange pekoe?" the stranger replied casually.

Stanley paused, caught off guard. "Orange…you want tea?"

"Yessir."

Stanley said nothing. Didn't even move.

"Do you…not sell that here? I s'pose I could do a cola instead."

"We have it," Stanley grumbled, his words tumbling out like boulders.

"That'd be swell, sir."

I couldn't help it—I cast a glance over my shoulder to see the fella smiling up at Stan, all innocent and gentlemanly like. Ordering tea in a speakeasy.

Stanley turned to me, fixing me with a hard gaze. "Eris, would you—" He paused when he saw I was in the middle of counting change for a table's tab.

He scowled at the stranger. "I'll be *right* back," Stanley said, his voice dropping an octave. Then he turned and headed through the curtain, toward the kitchen of Madame Maldu's home to warm up the kettle and get the tea leaves out.

After counting the change, I dropped it off at the table of a couple wrapped up in each other. They were a little zozzled, but more drunk on love than anything else.

I returned to the bar where the stranger sat. My heart pounded wildly.

"So..." he began in his low timbre as I took up my spot from before, my attention fixed on the tray of dirty glasses I'd just picked up. "Your name is Eris."

Reflexively, my gaze lifted to find him watching me with that same half grin. I swallowed and looked down at the glass with the lipstick smudged across the rim.

There was part of me that was disappointed that our game had been ruined. How silly.

"It's a beautiful name," he said quietly. Gently. "Suits you."

Tingles ran down my spine, and I struggled to keep my expression neutral. If I wasn't mistaken, this stranger had just called me beautiful. Something I'd been called before, but by drunken and often enchanted men.

"Do you know where it comes from?"

The question caught me off guard and I *almost* asked, "*where?*" but just in time I pursed my lips and shook my head.

"It's the name of a Greek goddess."

Until then, I'd been dumping the drinks into the small sink, running hot water over the empty glasses. Now I couldn't help but look up, too fascinated to pretend to be anything but.

I never knew my name had been derived from anything. Not surprising considering I never knew my real parents. It was just the name I'd had at the orphanage.

The stranger's eyes fixed on mine, his dark irises nearly swallowing his pupils so I seemed to be staring into shining plates of obsidian. "You didn't know?" he asked.

I shook my head.

"Then you probably don't know the origin of the word itself."

Again, I shook my head.

"Some linguists believe it comes from the Greek verb *orinein*. It means 'to stir, to invoke action.'" He paused and looked away. "That's swell, ain't it? To know your name means something so powerful?" His gaze jumped back to me.

A shock went through my system—like a low bulb had just buzzed with an electric current while I'd been trying to unscrew it. My hands slipped on the soapy glass I'd been washing.

"Careful." Quick like an alley cat, the stranger leaned over, catching the glass before it fell and shattered in the sink.

We both looked up, and our faces were mere inches away from each other. He had the same scent as two nights ago—fire and smoke. A little sweet, too, like burning wood.

His mouth hooked into a smirk, and he took my hands, gently placing the glass securely into my palms. He didn't let go. "It's not fair, is it?"

My lips were two seconds away from forming words. I was so close that I had to bite my lip to stop them. I'd never had so much trouble keeping quiet before.

What's not fair? The fact that I can't talk to you? No matter how much I want to?

"That I know your name and you don't know mine?" His hands were warm, almost hot, and a little rough with calluses on his thumb and palm.

I nodded. Maybe a little too enthusiastically.

"Here you go." Stanley all but slammed the mug down in front of the stranger, the hot tea sloshing down the sides to form a ring.

The stranger let go of my hands and gave Stan a full-tooth white smile. "Thank you, sir."

Stan folded his arms, sporting his best military stare-down. "That'll be thirty cents."

While most men would cower like a scared pup under the size of Stanley, this stranger merely reached into his pocket and pulled out two bits. But instead of setting the coins on the wood surface of the bar, he reached across once more and took my hand to drop the coins into my palm. As he did this, he leaned in close and whispered in my ear, "It's Colt, by the way."

Then Colt gave me a wink, took his orange pekoe, and headed back to his usual table in the corner. For a moment, we stared at each other from across the bar, then his gaze slid to the band and my little stage.

He was waiting for me to sing.

• • •

The whole next hour, I worked up my courage. Between mixing drinks and waiting on tables, I wrote out a quick set sheet. Just a few of my favorites.

After the band had their fourth break for the night, I walked up to David and handed him the paper. He set aside his sax and scanned it, then looked up at me, grinning from ear to ear. And David didn't grin often. "You going to sing for them tonight, Eris?"

Just for one.

I smiled politely and nodded, my hands twisting in front of my stomach.

If I didn't sing for Colt tonight, he might get bored and leave forever. Since he'd sauntered into my life, I'd had something to look forward to, more than just a dream of escaping this drum that I knew, deep down, would never become a reality. I wasn't ready to let him go yet. I wasn't ready to let this excitement die.

Except I was nervous. I'd never been nervous about singing before. I simply let the song flow out of me and followed its whims. I'd never tried to control it, because I'd never needed to. But this time, I *wanted* to. Maintaining some semblance of control of my voice and this magic inside made me feel like it was *my* voice, not my gift, that Colt would hear.

Was there even a difference?

"Oy, Eris is singing?" Marv's voice interrupted my thoughts, and I turned to my left to find him tossing back his fourth drink for the night. "Good to see you got over that... unpleasantness from the night before. Some cats are just bad eggs," he said kindly, patting my shoulder. "No such reason to keep a sweet canary like you all caged up."

Marv's mention of the *unpleasantness* made me second-guess. What if Colt heard my song and became just like all the rest? He might not resort to gun-slinging, but would it be different because he'd been interested in me *before* he heard my voice?

What naive thinking. I may hardly venture outside of this speakeasy, but I *wasn't* a Dumb Dora. This power didn't consider such things as feelings. It controlled people. It was a *curse*.

Swallowing hard, I yanked the set sheet from David's hands and both men blinked at me, surprised. Quickly I folded the sheet into fourths and then into eighths, my fingers trembling with nerves and regret.

How could I even have considered this?

If I wanted to keep Colt looking at me in *that* way, in a way that made me feel like a real person, and not some enchantress witch, I needed to keep my voice to myself.

And then he would get bored of our little games and my silence, and he would leave.

But it was better than the alternative.

"You changed your mind?" David asked, disappointment coating his voice.

In answer, I turned away, back toward the bar, but stopped in my tracks when I found Colt blocking my path.

Somewhat startled, or maybe it was just my jumpy nerves, I took a couple steps back—right into a chair. It wobbled dangerously as my knee smarted from the ensuing bang.

Colt reached around me and steadied the chair before

it fell to the floor. It reminded me of the moment with the glass just an hour ago, and my chest flushed with heat. "My apologies," he said softly, his breath tickling my collarbone.

Then he stooped and swiped a piece of paper from the floor.

My heart stopped its jazz-tapping movements and beat hard like a big marching drum. That one loud *thump*.

The set sheet. I hadn't realized I'd dropped it—sometime between him walking over and me hitting the chair, I had let go of it.

Colt unfolded the paper and scanned it, his gaze jumping from song to song as my heart did with it.

"I love these songs," he said softly. Then he lifted his gaze, a new smile stretching across his face that was hard to place—eager, but almost...triumphant? "Will I get to hear you sing them?" His voice was calm and low, but I heard the hope there.

Maybe it's better to end this on my terms. After all, if he became like all the others it might be easier to watch him go. *Besides*—I looked back at him mournfully—*it's not as if you'll stay forever.*

I held out my hand, and he placed the folded sheet on my palm. His fingertips brushed my exposed wrist, and I steeled myself against the thrill that small touch brought.

Soon, he'd have the same stare, the same eyes, and the same slurred words as all the rest, and I would feel all alone again.

Let's get this over with.

I turned on my heel, back to the band, and shoved the set sheet against David's chest. He caught it with a fumble, and the band glanced around in confusion as I pulled out the mic and nudged my little "stage" into the bright lights with the tip of my shoe.

I straightened the mic, wrapping my fingers around the

cool metal of its stand and looked out at the crowd. All folks were silent, their eyes on me, holding their breath. Many came to hear my voice, and my silence the last few nights had probably been disappointing.

But I wasn't singing for them.

My blood rushed in my ears as I was highly aware of my every move being followed by the gaze of the elusive, mysterious, and handsome Mr. Colt.

I would sing for *him*.

Sing, and then move on.

As the piano began to play the beginning few notes of the first song from my set sheet, I found Colt had returned to his usual table, watching me. Waiting. His dark eyes were so focused and intense that they seemed to heat my skin.

I knew the melody by heart—it wove through my veins and thrummed in my muscles like the strings of a harp—and yet I let the intro pass, missing my entrance.

My pulse was loud and my knees were shaking. *I can't do this.*

Quickly, Marv and David began to play, although it wasn't technically their time to come in. Their brass wove in the melody where my voice should be. They were saving me, and I was grateful for it.

With wobbly legs, I got down from my whiskey crate and looped around for the bar, hoping to slip into the kitchens and storeroom. I tried not to imagine the disappointment on Colt's face.

"Eris?" Stan said gently as I edged behind him and hurried past the rows of bottles, parting the curtain and ducking behind the wall.

Sliding down the cold brick, I pressed my hands over my mouth and attempted to breathe normally, my pulse still trying to jump from my skin.

Stage fright. That had never happened to me before.

Shame and embarrassment wrapped around me like a python, squeezing out what little courage I had. I wanted to stay there forever, but I only managed ten minutes before Stanley poked his head around the door.

"Eris, hon, I hate to ask, but it's pretty busy up here?"

Without a word, *always without a word*, I stood from my crouched position on the floor and dusted off my apron.

Careful to keep my gaze away from Colt's corner, I went to a table, taking out a pad of paper and pencil from my apron and giving them a pleasant smile...which fell away instantly.

The table held a couple, but not a happy one. Not like the one earlier where they'd been so wrapped in each other's arms they barely knew anyone else existed. This one had a brute of a man and his girlfriend. A brute not because of *his* appearance—a clean white work shirt, gray pants, and a jacket—but because of his girlfriend's. *She* was covered head to foot in bruises. Her thick makeup attempted to cover a black eye. Dangling bracelets hung over dark purple patches on her thin wrists. Cherry-red lipstick tried to hide her busted lip.

This girl was a walking punching bag.

"Excuse me?" the man drawled, raising an eyebrow.

The girl flinched at his words—and they weren't even directed at her.

"Are you going to take my order?"

The girl looked up at me, pleading with me, as if to say, *please don't make him angry.*

The lead of my pencil broke with a snap against my pad of paper.

Over the years I'd seen signs of abuse and mistreatment. Working at a bar showed you a side of people you wished you could unsee. But you couldn't, and tonight...there was something about seeing this girl that made my restraint just... *snap.*

All thoughts of Colt, my songs, and my own curse flew

out of my mind, and a seed of justice took its place.

The man slapped the table, and the girl recoiled. "*Excuse* me, miss!"

I returned my gaze to the monster and smiled prettily, disarming him entirely.

Leaning down, I placed my hand on his chest and it stilled him, maybe with surprise, maybe with excitement. Moving close, I whispered in his ear. I whispered actual, real, purposeful words. Words I would not regret.

"*You will never touch another woman, ever again.*"

The man reared back. His eyes flashed in a moment of glazed confusion, then they cleared, and his brow furrowed. "I'll do whatever I damn well please, you bitch. C'mon, Margaret." He stood, grabbing his girlfriend's wrist and yanking her to her feet.

But for once, it was not she who cried out in pain.

The man stumbled backward, letting out a shriek of agony—an inhuman sound that cut through the music of my little band and the dull murmur of the patrons' conversations.

Twisting his wrist like he'd just touched fire, he stared at his hand in confusion and disturbance. But there was no burn on his hand. It looked completely normal.

I hugged myself, glaring at the man.

His gaze returned to me, eyes widening as if he was just realizing what I'd done to him.

He reached for me and grabbed my arm.

I let him.

He roared in pain, his whole body twisting and recoiling against the mental agony of this torture. Of touching another woman when I specifically told him he never would. Cradling his hand as if he had just broken every bone in it, he practically ran out of The Blind Dragon.

The girl stared at me in wonder and then a slow smile formed on her busted lip. She picked up her coat and made her way out of my speakeasy, head held high.

I'd made the mistake of watching her, because it was then, out of the corner of my eye, that I noticed...Colt was gone.

The Blind Dragon closed early in the morning, or late at night, depending on how you looked at it. Around three thirty a.m., I carried the final crate of empty bottles out into the darkened alley, reflecting on that night.

I was sure I'd never see Colt again.

He must've been disappointed that I'd chickened out and then left as soon as I'd rushed from the spotlight. I didn't blame him. What reason had he to stay? It wasn't as if I was the most stimulating conversationalist.

Sighing, I tilted my head back to look up at the moon. It was full. Just a few wispy clouds passing in front of it. Blowing out a breath, a cloud of steam issued from my mouth caught in the cold air like I'd just taken a drag from a gasper.

I didn't regret what I'd done. Telling the man *that*. Forcing him to live without ever being able to lay his detestable hands on another woman.

What I did regret was not telling Colt my own name. To even just say...

"Hello, I'm—" A cloth pressed over my mouth and nose.

Lungs shriveling in shock and fear, I sucked in, and a strange scent caught me in the face. A chemical, evil scent.

A strong arm wrapped around my waist, clamping me against his body, and I tilted my head back, my hair dragging down the attacker's chest.

Just as my vision grew dark, I managed to make out his face against the backdrop of the full Boston moon.

It was Colt.

Chapter Six

The Agent

When she had run away from the mic and the music, I suspected then that Sawyer was wrong. A siren resistant to a song? It wasn't just strange, it was practically unheard of. What little we knew of sirens, we knew that music always drew them in. Like moths to a flame. So more than likely Sawyer had made a mistake.

I'd come to Boston for nothing.

But I didn't leave. I stayed. I told myself it was because there could still be a sliver of a chance. If I was being truly honest, though, I stayed because I was—maybe just a little—*worried* about her. She'd seemed so distraught up there.

When she emerged, I watched her carefully, looking for signs of tears. Wondering if there was some way to cheer her up. As she moved to her first table, I ran through jokes in my head. Little flirtatious anecdotes to bring out that radiant smile again. Maybe even get her to laugh. If she laughed loud enough and rich enough, would I be able to detect siren magic?

I was wondering just that as I watched her lean down to the customer at the table. Watched her press her hand against the chest of the man. Watched her *whisper* in his ear.

And then the man screamed, and screamed.

She looked on at him with no remorse.

Dear God. I'd found the lost siren.

From there, it was as easy as waiting for closing time. She'd bring out the empty bottles like she'd done the night before, and the night before last. It seemed to be her small reprieve from the smoky bar to get a breath of fresh air. Or as fresh as the air was in Boston.

From the shadows, I'd watched her lean against the brick wall, sigh, and then slip her feet from her heels and massage her toes. Her curls would fall in a curtain around her face as she'd bend down. After a few minutes, she'd go back inside.

But not tonight.

Tonight I moved behind her, slipping from my hiding place in the adjacent alley, and pressed the cloth to her face. She struggled for only a few seconds—which made my stomach twist—and managed to lean her head back to give me a look of terror...and betrayal.

My jaw hardened as I gritted my teeth, her body falling limp against mine.

I couldn't feel sorry for her. If anything, I felt just a little betrayed. She'd seemed so sweet and gentle that even without her voice I had begun to fall under her spell. But then her true nature came out. She had tortured that man. She could do worse with her powers.

It was my *job* to take her in, but more than anything else, my conscience wouldn't let me leave her unchecked.

Bending down, I easily scooped her up into my arms. She felt like she hardly weighed a pound, small thing that she was. Her head rolled back, exposing her thin white neck wherein lay her deadly, monstrous vocal cords. Where, with just a whisper, she'd ruined a man's life forever.

Shifting her so that her head rested against my shoulder, making it look like she was some dame half-seas over and I was a concerned boyfriend, I set off into the dark, empty streets.

When I came to the alley behind my hotel, I slung her over my shoulder and climbed the fire escape. I didn't need anyone, not even the most likely asleep bellman, to see me carting an unconscious girl to my room. I opened the window and hoisted her inside, laying her on the bed. Then I bound her hands and feet with rope. The area between my shoulder blades ached with that familiar, haunting pain as I tightened the knots. But, as usual, I ignored the feeling and left the room, locking it behind me.

Downstairs, I used the desk phone to make a call. Then a cool female voice said over the receiver, "Hello, operator, how may I direct your call?"

"Andromache epsilon five-zero-twenty-two."

The female voice paused, then, "One moment please."

There was a dial switch, a tone, and then more ringing. I waited, rather impatiently, until I heard the other end pick up and my boss's groggy voice answer, "McCarney."

"Sir, I've got her."

Instantly the sleepiness was gone. There was a bang and some shuffling. "Her, as in…?"

"The siren. I've got her in my hotel room now, knocked out."

There was a sigh, a crackling over the phone. "Well done, Colt."

My spine straightened slightly. I'd known McCarney since I was twelve and he rarely used my first name. It was either "boy" or "Clemmons."

"Thank you, sir."

"Tell me where you are."

I gave him the address of the hotel and even the room number.

McCarney was silent for a few long seconds, before I finally said, "Sir?"

"I'm worried about you, Colt. I realize this is what you've been trained for. But doing this on your own..."

For a few moments, I was too stunned to reply. I never thought I'd hear something so sentimental from McCarney. Even if he practically raised me, the man was a soldier through and through. Tough. He put his country and its people first. Not his feelings for a boy he'd molded to be a weapon.

I swallowed. Shook my head. "It'll be fine, sir. There's a rattler I can get her on at seven this morning back to DC. Besides, you know that if she somehow managed to get her gag loose, she could turn any one of the agents against me. It's better if I do this solo." I could almost see her cloth slipping from her mouth, her muttering a few words, and all the men slowly putting their pistols up to their own heads...

"Yes...yes, you're right. I'll at least get a car sent to the hotel. You'll likely have to sign for it, so make sure you leave the siren tied up and gagged before you go down to get it. Am I clear?"

"Crystal, sir."

"Good."

At that, the line went dead and I hung up the phone, slipping around the desk of the clerk who was now snoring loudly.

Reentering my room and seeing her there, sleeping still, I walked over to the bed and looked down at her.

She had seemed so good and innocent...until she had used her voice on that man. Had he done something to make her seek retribution? Or had she been operating under someone else's orders? How often did she use her power like that?

I had so many questions, but one was much more desperate than all the others: *what does her voice sound like?*

I tried to rationalize it. True, I could keep her gagged, but if she knew I could resist her, it might make this whole ordeal easier. If she was powerless, she might even cooperate.

Except none of that was the *real* reason. I *wanted* to hear it. I *wanted* to test my abilities. I wanted to know that everything I'd gone through to get to this point was worth it.

So I took a seat in the corner chair, and waited.

She woke only two hours later, which was impressive for a girl her size and that amount of chloroform. Resting my elbows on my knees, I steepled my fingers and watched her come to.

She blinked her big blue eyes and shook her head as if she was trying to shake out the drug. After testing her restraints, she started taking deep breaths like she was trying, but failing, not to panic.

"And so it wakes," I said, my voice low.

Immediately her head jerked to the side, eyes widening. I saw myself reflected in them, so wide with horror and fear.

Her neck craned and her body twisted as she parted her lips. "*Let me go.*"

The magic in those words was incredible. I was halfway to the bed, reaching for her restraints when my instinct roared to life, halting my steps. I took just a moment to revel in my strength, to feel a rare sense of pride in what I was, when I so often resorted to self-loathing every damn day.

Rubbing my temples to get rid of the magical effects of her words, I growled, "That's not going to work."

She said nothing, her eyes narrowing in confusion and disbelief. Surely no one had ever been able to resist her before. Perhaps she was wondering what I was.

Your worst nightmare, siren.

I couldn't bring myself to even think her actual name. The special name I'd tried to guess over the course of a few nights. Even though the interactions had been brief and one-sided, I'd enjoyed them. Too much, in fact.

She tried a different command. "*Untie me.*"

My fingers twitched with want to obey her. To obey the magic flowing through the air and into me, but I clenched my fists and shook my head. "You can keep trying, siren, but you won't control me."

Her brow furrowed. Slowly she sat up in bed, her warm autumn hair falling around her shoulders. Her fear was tangible, thick in the room like a fog, but curiosity was there, too.

"If you have a question, you can ask," I told her, not liking her fear, like *I* was the bad guy here, not the girl who'd caused a man twice her size to scream bloody murder. "Your voice doesn't work on me, siren."

Her wrists twisted in her restraints, and she slowly moved her legs to hang over the bed, toes brushing the carpet. "Why do you keep calling me that?"

The magic within it aside, her voice was nice, lilting, and not so abnormal. If I had to place it, she sounded a bit like a chorus girl. Melodic, but not too airy—strong and clear.

"Because that's what you are," I answered evenly. Did she not know? Or was she just trying to fool me? No...she couldn't be that good of an actress. The fear and confusion in her eyes were real. So maybe she understood *what* she was able to do, but not *why* she was able to do it.

Shit. This was going to be hard to explain.

Why do you need to tell her anything? a little voice in my head said. *She's a monster.*

"I don't know what that is," she said finally.

I scanned her form, trying to determine what she was

thinking. Her hands were shaking and her skin was pale. If she were completely innocent, she might be demanding why she'd been taken like this, but she seemed to know why. She definitely knew her own power.

"A siren is a creature with powers that allow them to exert their will over others using just their voice. In old texts, they were monsters that lured sailors to their death."

She sucked in a small breath as she tried to yank her bound hands apart. The rope bristling against her skin was loud in the quiet room, while the sounds from the waking city were deadened by the window glass.

"You're saying I'm a…"

"Monster, yes." The faster she accepted this as truth, the easier it would be.

Her brow furrowed in anger, fingers curling into fists. "*I am not a monster.*"

The magic pouring into her words was thick and powerful and it threatened to overtake me. To make me believe her. After years of "practice," I was immune to the powers of most monsters. But withstanding hers wasn't so much immunity as it was a constant battle. I had to shield my mind against her magic in a way that felt like it was testing me.

Her wrists kept pulling against the rope as she stared at the floor. Her eyes roamed from floorboard to floorboard like she was searching for some hidden answer.

"I'm not a monster," she repeated, the magic in her voice weaker. Less sure.

"Would you like me to prove it to you?" I asked, standing. She lifted her gaze to meet mine as I loomed over her.

She glanced away, to the corner, and then back to me. "How would you do that?"

I took her chin in my hand and she tried to rip her head away. "Relax," I sighed. "I'm not going to hurt you. Not like you hurt that man."

At that, her jaw clenched, but her eyes lowered, as if in shame.

I glanced at my watch. The next train was due to leave in an hour, plus I wasn't sure when the BOI car was supposed to arrive. But perhaps I could convince her to come to the Bureau willingly. Maybe if she realized the harm she could put people in—the whole country in—she would want to cross to the good side.

And if she proved to be useful and loyal, then maybe she could live a life under a tight leash. Like me. It wasn't much of a life, but it was better than the afterlife.

I had to imagine.

"Just let me prove it to you. Open your mouth," I said.

She regarded me skeptically, her nose wrinkling rather cutely.

"If I'm wrong, I'll let you go."

That did the trick. She parted her lips and then, without waiting to see if she'd change her mind, I pushed two fingers into the roof of her mouth—finding what I knew would be there.

The smooth surface of a pearl. It was embedded deep so only a portion of it could be felt, but it was easy to tell the difference between flesh and the smooth crystalline calcium carbonate.

The siren's pearl.

There was a small part of me that had hoped I wouldn't feel it.

I retracted my hand quickly as she raised her bound hands to wipe at her lips.

"See?" I said.

"See what?"

"You feel it, don't you?"

"Feel what?"

"Your pearl. It's what's in the roof of your mouth. It gives you your powers. Your ability to speak and have people do whatever you tell them to."

At that, her lips parted once more, this time in shock. "It's a...pearl? Madame always told me it was left over from tonsillitis surgery when I was younger."

To me, it seemed like a pretty flimsy excuse. But if you didn't know much about surgeries or medicine, then it might be easy to hear something like that and simply believe it.

"Madame is the woman who runs the speakeasy. Is she your mother? Does she know what you are?"

The siren's lips pursed, her gaze shooting downward again. Retreating. I suppose I couldn't blame her for not trusting her kidnapper with any information about people close to her.

I checked my watch again. Fifty-five minutes to the train. "Look, whether or not you believe me, I have to get you to the Bureau. They'll decide what to do with you."

"What to *do* with me?" she squeaked. "Waitaminute." Her voice climbed an octave and she began to speak fast. "This is just...too wild. You're telling me I'm some mythical creature and now you're *kidnapping* me?"

"I'm taking you in," I snapped, my patience stretching thin. I was used to fighting against claws and fangs and horns—big burly monsters that controlled the streets. But with her, I felt like the bad guy here.

I shook myself and steeled my resolve against the fear in her eyes. *Evil takes different forms.* "You're the property of the United States government now."

Her mouth opened and closed several times, her eyes huge. "The...the government? Bushwa!"

I let out a humorless laugh. "It's true. I work for a specialized division of the BOI."

"A specialized division for what? Monsters?"

"Yes. You're not the only monster, but you're the only

one of your kind. The only siren."

"What does that mean?"

I sighed, rubbing the back of my neck. "It means the monsters that you've heard stories about—werewolves, gorgons, vampires, cyclops, all of them—they're real. And common, mostly because their magical parts are easy to come by, but a siren's pearl is impossibly rare. Thank God. Imagine if there were more of you. Creatures who would use their voice to make people do whatever they wanted?"

Her wrists twisted again, and a shiver passed through her. I frowned at the redness blooming on her skin.

"This doesn't have to be hard. You can work with the BOI and be under their supervision to make sure you don't—"

Now it was *her* turn to laugh. It was harsh and fake, followed by a bitter smile. "Who's to say that what they would make me do wouldn't be just as monstrous? Colt, do you really think that the government would use me only for good? And I thought *I* was naive."

I flinched at her use of my name. I'd given it to her against my better judgment. I told myself I'd still been trying to seduce her at the time, hoping to get her to talk to me. Now that I'd heard her use it, I wasn't so sure.

She rose from the bed and shuffled two steps, as much as she could with her ankles tied, and placed her bound hands on my arm.

"Please, let me go. I promise I won't do anything else. I'll never say anything ever again. You saw that I don't speak—it's because I don't want to *control* people, and if you take me to the BOI, they'll either kill me or use me. Earlier you asked me who Madame was...she's my foster mother—she rescued me from some bad man who wanted to use me for this power. We spent months on the run. I don't want to be used, Colt. *Please.*"

Even if she hadn't been a siren with magic woven into

every word—whether she intended it or not—she would've been hard to resist.

I met her blue gaze and then, with my own, traced the round curve of her cheeks, remembering my first thought of her—that she belonged to a different time. A softer world without organized crime, tommy guns, dope, and monsters on every dirty street.

If she truly was as innocent as she claimed, then I didn't believe that she should be killed *or* used, but I also knew the damage and destruction she could bring.

I knew all too well.

I had to take her in. Let the BOI figure out what to do with her. Her fate was in *their* hands. So was mine.

And it wasn't all bad.

"You're too dangerous," I said in a low voice. As I removed my arm from her touch, the man's screams reverberated in my head.

Her fingers curled inward and she drew her hands back, bowing her head. Her thin shoulders shook, and I wondered if she was crying.

But then she suddenly froze and lifted her head, revealing her dry face and sharpened, narrowed eyes. "Were you expecting company?" she asked.

The car. Shit.

I didn't have a gag on her yet.

I clapped my hand down on her mouth and she let out a muffled cry.

A knock sounded at the door. "Sir?"

"Yes?" I called back as the siren tried to pull my hand down from her mouth.

"A car's here for you, sir," the voice said, not tired at all. Awake and alert even at six in the morning.

"Swell. Be right down."

Footsteps echoed off to the right.

When I was sure the bellhop was gone, I dropped my hand from her mouth and she glared at me in return. "You didn't need to do that."

I shook my head. "I wish I could believe you." After pulling out the handkerchief from my pocket, I folded it and quickly pressed it across her lips, looping it around to tie it behind her head. She didn't fight it, but her eyes followed me, and with every movement my chest got tighter and tighter, burning with an uncomfortable heat, and the ache between my shoulder blades was back.

I left her on my bed, bound and gagged, just as McCarney had instructed, and headed into the hall. As I emerged, I caught sight of a maid with long dark hair plaited down her back coming out of the staff entrance on my left.

Wait…the staff entrance was to the left? Then why had the bellhop's footsteps gone off to the right?

A small, insignificant detail that could be nothing and yet…my instinct nagged me.

I stepped back inside my room and locked the door. The siren made a small, confused sound behind me, but I ignored her. Listening to my gut, I stayed where I was…waiting. For what, I wasn't exactly sure, but then I heard footsteps outside. More than one pair. Three, maybe four.

What's going on? Did McCarney send backup even though he said he wouldn't?

I crossed to the bed in three long strides and tugged the handkerchief out of her mouth.

"What is it?" she asked me.

While my mind jumped from possibility to possibility, something, multiple somethings, *clicked* beyond the thin hotel walls. A bad feeling crept into my bones and I took out my pocket knife, cutting through her hand restraints in one quick slice.

If it's not the BOI, who else knows we're here?

We had to leave. Now.

"Something's not right. I need you to—"

My order was cut off by a new yet familiar sound: *rat-tat-tat-tat.*

A sound I knew all too well. So I did the only thing I had time for—I wrapped my arm around the siren's lower back and tucked her into my chest just as the first bullet exploded through the wall.

Chapter Seven

THE SINGER

Dry wall and bits of plaster burst outward in a clean radius as a round of bullets flew through the room. One hit the mattress. The piece of deadly lead made a *poof* noise as feathers and fluff erupted from the blankets and pillows.

Another cascade followed, raining down upon us while debris of all kinds blasted through the room, each bullet hitting a new target.

I couldn't see much through the gap between Colt's arm and his chest, but I didn't have to see it to know. This was one of those legendary tommy guns I'd heard of. The machine guns and their ability to fire multiple rounds at once lived up to its reputation.

My breath was loud in my ears as Colt's arms tightened around me and yet I felt like I'd go deaf in the next minute. Having only heard stories about it, I finally understood why gunfire was nicknamed Chicago lightning—it was thunderous with flashes of light caused by the gun's flare. But apparently it wasn't just in Chicago.

At first, I was too scared and too stunned that I was *here* in the middle of a shootout to do anything. Then Colt jerked back, letting out a cry of pain.

The warm liquid running down his arm onto my own skin jarred me, and I screamed. I didn't even realize the words I'd said, but then they echoed through my brain, my magic clinging to the air around us and traveling through splintered wood and ripped plaster.

"*GO AWAY.*"

Immediately, all gunfire stopped, and then footsteps, maybe four separate pairs of feet that I counted, pounded down the hallway, running *away.* As I commanded them to.

Colt slumped against me, a soft moan escaping his chest. He was too heavy to support, but the rope that he'd cut through fell away as I wrapped my arms around his middle and helped him to lie on the torn-apart bed. Feathers, puffs of cotton, and dislodged springs were everywhere, but I didn't care. The white of it all was quickly colored red by the bullet wound coming from Colt's left shoulder.

My shaking hands moved across the blood blossoming on his white shirt. Quickly I took a ripped pillow and applied as much pressure as I could. "*Please, please, please stop bleeding.*"

Unbelievably, it did. I wasn't able to tell at first, but when the pillow didn't immediately soak in crimson I realized that the flow of blood must have slowed…significantly.

Colt's face was still deathly pale. He mumbled a few words I couldn't catch and then groaned.

When my adrenaline finally slowed, my mind started working again. Processing what had just happened, what was *currently* happening.

Did I do that? Did I somehow stop his blood flow? Was Colt…listening to me?

I thought back to when he'd almost crossed the room to

untie me and then how he'd been able to stop himself. Had his will been strong enough to resist my voice, but now, since he was barely conscious, my strange power was working on him?

It was a lot to assume, but it was the only thing I could come up with. What was more, his *body* seemed to be listening to my voice, not just his mind.

As his head turned to the side, his eyes squeezed tight in unfathomable pain, I realized that I was still pressing hard on his wound.

What am I doing?

I was now saving the life of a man who had just tried to haul me into a special monster prison operated by the government, where the nicest thing they would probably do is kill me.

If I wanted to remain free, I would tell the blood to start flowing again. Let him bleed out on the bed that I'd woken up on—stiff, bound, and terribly betrayed.

Of course his betrayal stung. More than anything else. More than even discovering that I was a *monster*. I knew it was stupid. Very, very stupid to be so upset by the fact that this young man had tricked me.

But, on some level, I'd known what I was. A witch or sorceress, or siren—whatever. I knew that my power was not supposed to exist and that it was unnatural and *dangerous*.

I'd known all that.

What I hadn't known was what it felt like to *hope*, and then have someone shatter it to the point of desolation.

Colt turned his head the other way with a grunt, his breathing growing shallow. Every moment, his face seemed to get paler.

In that split second, I made my decision, really the only possible one to make—I would not let him die. He might have betrayed me, but he'd also shielded me from the rain of bullets, and he had kidnapped me because he thought he was doing *good*. He believed he was protecting people from a monster who had the power to hurt others.

I thought back to the workers who'd run into the street during my story.

I thought of the evil man who'd beat on his girlfriend.

How I'd hurt them all.

Maybe Colt was right.

I'd tried so hard for seven years to be good and safe. But maybe that wasn't enough. Maybe it would never be enough.

I didn't believe the government would use me for good as Colt claimed, and I didn't want to go with him, but I also didn't want to see a good person die in front of me. Not because of me. Not when I could stop it.

Removing the pillow, I took a decimated sheet and ripped from bullet hole to bullet hole to create a long strip of fabric. Gingerly, I eased him up into a folded position and tied the sheet tightly around the wound and whispered more commands. "*Stop flowing. Stop. Stop. Stop.*"

Surely everyone would've heard the tommy guns and evacuated the building, calling for help. It seemed simple enough to wait for help to arrive. Coppers could get Colt to a hospital, but then, what if the mystery shooters were among the crowd of onlookers that always gathered around these kinds of things? Or, for all I knew, it might even *be* coppers that had shot at us. From working at the Dragon I'd seen how corrupt policemen could be. The law didn't seem to exist for the ones that enforced it. Plus, having lived and worked at an illegal establishment, there was now just a natural disposition to avoid the law at all costs.

But in all likelihood, it hadn't been coppers. It had to have been the people that Madame had always warned me about. The ones who wanted my power. Though, if that were true, their shootout could've killed me, which seemed to be the exact opposite of their goal. Unless they wanted to just kill me and take my siren's pearl from my corpse, and do what with it, I could only imagine.

No use dwelling on that. Instead, I had to think of a way to avoid anyone who could find out about my power.

C'mon, Eris. Think! What would Stan do?

Stan had been in plenty of illegal boxing matches before and needed a doctor who could stitch him up and not ask any questions. I'd been with him once before when he'd broken his nose for the second time, and again when I'd wanted him to take care of a stray sick kitten I'd found. I remembered the address of the place.

I could leave Colt with the doctor and then escape. No police or hospital staff to dodge and weave. Less chance of drawing attention to a girl who had powers.

If I could pull this off, I'd save Colt *and* save myself. It was the best chance I had.

But I couldn't get Colt out of here by myself. I needed *someone* to help me.

Glancing around the room, I caught sight of a fire escape out the window. *Maybe…*

I moved toward the window and the rope around my ankles made me trip. Luckily, I managed to catch myself on the edge of the bed before falling flat on my face, and luckier still I caught sight of the knife Colt used to cut my ropes on the floor. Grabbing it, I quickly sawed through my binds and crawled out the window.

Out on the cold metal plating, I looked down at the alley below. Sure enough, a few people were gathered on the street corner, waiting for the scream of police sirens and the coppers to roll up and save the day. There was one young fella who seemed around my age, leaning against the building. He wore a uniform that made me think he worked at the hotel. His back was to me and his shoulder pressed against the brick, one foot tucked behind the other.

His stance appeared bored—as if shootouts happened every day. Maybe they did. I didn't know much beyond The Blind Dragon.

Leaning over the railing, I cupped my hands around my mouth and called, "*Yoohoo.*"

I'd heard other women use that before in my speakeasy. One or two birds always looked up. Thankfully, this one did, too.

He saw me three stories up and turned toward the main street as if to get help, but quickly I called, "*Come up here.*"

The man stiffened, and I imagined the brief flash of confusion across his face as my power took hold. Then he raced over and began climbing up the fire escape, taking the metal steps two at a time in his haste to obey.

As soon as the man reached the landing, I pointed into the room. "*Help me carry him outside.*"

The young bellhop looped Colt's arm around his shoulders while I took the other arm and urged Colt to try his best to walk. Once again, the magic that he'd claimed this pearl gave me seemed to propel his body forward, down the hall, and into the staff entrance staircase with our help. At least, that's what I assumed. I wasn't sure how a man who'd lost so much blood would be able to walk otherwise. It had to be by sheer strength of will that he'd resisted my voice before, because it now seemed to work when he was all but passed out.

The question was, how had he developed this willpower? Could any normal human with practice achieve it, or did he also have supernatural abilities? Whatever the case, part of me loved that he could resist—even if it put me in more trouble. Maybe it made me a masochist, but the fact that we could carry on a conversation without his gaze going blank made me happy. *Finally, I'm heard.*

Shaking my head, I focused on the task at hand—making sure my kidnapper didn't die.

The staff entrance led us out the back of the hotel, and we emerged into the alley just as sirens wailed from down the road. I instructed the bellhop to hang back with Colt, and then I ran out to the street corner. The sun had begun to rise and the city was just waking from its booze-induced sleep. A few people made their way over the crosswalk, running to make sure they met the streetlights, while cars zipped along, their drivers on their way to a long day at the office.

Out of the corner of my eye, I noticed a maid with her dark hair plaited down her back standing on the opposite side of the street, watching the police cruisers head for the hotel. Her gaze darted to me, then she hurried around toward the front entrance, as if she could sense I was trouble.

Well, she was definitely right.

I stepped off the curb and lifted my fingers to my lips, letting out a piercing whistle.

A car screeched to a halt a foot away. The driver stared blankly from behind the windshield, then blinked his confusion.

He hadn't been meaning to stop at all. He wasn't a taxi.

I leaned into the open window and told him, "*Stay here.*"

The driver nodded.

I hurried back to the bellhop who'd remained hidden in the alley with Colt and together we helped the wounded agent into the backseat of the jalopy.

"*Never speak of this to anyone,*" I told the bellhop as I slid into the car next to Colt.

With a blank, dazed look, the young man nodded, closed the door, and backed up on the street corner.

I instructed the driver to take us to the address of Dr. Boursaw, a veterinarian who moonlighted as a sort of emergency hospital for illegal happenings. The place was only a seven-minute drive, but it felt like a lifetime with Colt breathing shallow and his head leaning back on the leather seat, the warmth of his body pressed against my side. His shirt was damp with perspiration and the other half of it was coated in blood. We couldn't get there fast enough.

At last, the jalopy parked on a shadowed side street and I recognized the alley to the left as the basement entrance to Dr. Boursaw's office. The driver took my instructions just as readily as the bellhop had, and practically lifted Colt out of the car, supporting him all the way down the steps to the office door. On what felt like my twentieth knock, the door swung inward swiftly and my fist grazed the white jacket of a grizzled old man. His beard was trimmed finely, but his silver hair and eyebrows were wild. Cheaters sat on the tip of his nose, and gnarled, white-knuckled hands gripped the door. "What the devil do you think you're doing beating on my back door at six in the morning?" he barked.

I winced, but said, "*I need you to take care of my…friend.*"

Colt was far from my friend, but "kidnapper" just didn't have the right ring to it.

Stepping back, Dr. Boursaw let the driver inside, who was still supporting a pale and stumbling Colt. The BOI agent was nearly gone. His skin was coated in sweat, and fresh blood was shining through the bedsheet I had hastily tied around him.

"This way," Dr. Boursaw said in a clipped tone, as though he was annoyed with himself for complying.

The old vet led us through a small hallway and into the main basement. The room was about one-third the size of The Blind Dragon and held tall stainless-steel cabinets, while white tiles covered the floor. There was a metal sink in the corner and a shiny metal table in the center of the room, floating like its own little island in a sea of white. Everything appeared sterile and polished, much nicer than a back-alley hospital and vet clinic should've been.

"Lay him on the table," Dr. Boursaw ordered, crossing to the sink and rolling up his sleeves.

The driver didn't move, and I realized he was waiting for orders from *me*. Licking my lips, I said, "*Please do everything the doctor says.*"

I moved around to help the anonymous driver lift Colt onto the long table and as we did so, I noticed the man's clothes and hands were covered in red. Guilt gave me a powerful kick to the gut. I had just *used* this man against his will. Roped him into something dangerous and unknown, and now he had a stranger's blood all over his clothes.

I felt sick.

Positioning Colt's arms on either side of him, keeping an eye on the rising and falling of his chest, I told the driver, "*Wash your hands, leave this place, get a new shirt and jacket, go to work, and never tell anyone of this for as long as you live.*" I swallowed hard as the man moved to the sink.

"I'm sorry," I whispered under my breath as the driver lumbered away.

"This wound should've killed him," Dr. Boursaw said.

I jumped to find him so close—on the other side of Colt, gingerly peeling away the linen I'd wrapped around his wound. Dr. Boursaw clucked his tongue and shook his head. "It hit a critical artery."

That explains all the blood.

The air in the small basement was now thick with the coppery scent of it, overpowering the antiseptic smell that had already been there.

"I'm assuming this is a gunshot? Ah, yes…there's the bullet," the vet muttered as he used a long metal tweezer-like tool to dig into Colt's flesh.

My stomach rolling, I quickly looked away, clamping my jaw shut. Then fingers brushed mine, and I glanced at

Colt's face. He was in agony, his neck straining, muscles and veins pronounced against his sickly pale, sweaty skin. Eyes squeezed closed, his lower back arched and his fingers flexed.

The doctor swore. "I thought the chap was passed out. Hold him down for a minute."

But Colt wasn't going anywhere. He panted, his breathing shallow and rasping, and his eyes rolled back into his head.

Heart jumping into my throat, I grabbed his fingers and squeezed them. Then I bent down to put my lips near his ear and whispered,

"*Shh, Colt. Everything is going to be okay. The pain isn't real. The pain isn't there. You feel nice and relaxed, like having a cup of orange pekoe.*"

His muscles stopped straining, and his breathing grew deep and easy—like he had just drifted off into nothing more than a light nap.

Had I tricked his body into believing it was no longer in any harm?

Suddenly a dizzy spell hit me, and I swayed, my knees strangely shaky and the room twirling so fast that my vision struggled to catch it. Gripping the edge of the table, I closed my eyes and waited for the feeling to pass. Meanwhile I tried to diagnose my sudden weakness. I wasn't squeamish—the blood would've gotten to me way before now. I didn't feel feverish or ill, nor was it my lady cycle.

When it finally passed, my hand strayed to my throat. It was a little sore. Was this my magic at its limits? I'd never used it so much. Could it be giving me this nauseating feeling?

"Just leave," Dr. Boursaw said without looking up as he stuck a needle into Colt's shoulder. "I don't want to have to clean up your mess."

Just leave. Why hadn't I thought of that?

After all, that had been my plan. Get Colt to Dr. Boursaw and then escape. At this point, I'd done all I could.

Live or die, his life was no longer in my hands. It was in God's.

My thoughts were calm, yet my hands shook as I crossed to the sink and washed the sticky blood off my fingers. Then I left the white-and-silver, sterilized basement and shut the door behind me.

But I didn't walk down the hall, up the steps, and out into the alley. I couldn't even take a step forward.

Move. Go!

Instead, I pressed my back against the door, slid down until I was on the cold floor, and laced my fingers together, lifting them to my chin in prayer.

Live. Live. Live. Live. Live.

I didn't even realize I was chanting the word, or how long I had been chanting it, until the door at the end of the hall opened. A large silhouette of a man filled the doorway. As he shut the door behind him to block out the morning sun that backlit him, I could make out features. Big, broad shoulders, a gray jacket with matching trousers and a large bowler hat.

The man was a giant. He had to stoop so his head didn't brush the ceiling.

Now even more nauseated and weaker than before, I struggled to my feet and said, "*Sir, you need to leave.*"

But the big man didn't stop or turn around, he just kept moving down the hall toward me.

Bushwa! Could this man be like Colt? Able to resist my voice?

In four long strides, the man's big, beefy fingers locked both my wrists in only his right hand without any trouble. With his left, he pulled rope from his coat pocket.

A glimpse of white in my peripheral vision made me look up, and I noticed two pieces of fluffy cotton wedged into the man's ears. He couldn't hear me. *He knows.*

The man's strength felt inhuman. No matter how hard I

pulled or twisted, he held on as if I was nothing more than a fussy puppy on a leash. In one feeble attempt, I kicked out at his shin, and my kitten heel dug into his skin. With a grunt, he reared his head back in pain and his bowler hat fluttered to the floor...revealing two white bull horns protruding from his temples.

Chapter Eight

The Agent

Blurry shapes moved around me, shadows in and out of focus ankling through my vision like sludge. I tried to move my limbs and I tried to speak, but I couldn't. My tongue felt thick in my mouth and for once in my life, I was cold. Really, really cold. Freezing and shivering. All except for my left shoulder, which burned like the flames of hellfire.

I'd been shot once before—it hadn't been fun—but it had only been a graze on my side. Not a full bullet tearing apart muscle and flesh.

Then I heard that voice. Soft, soothing, instructive. I let myself listen. Let myself lower my walls and allow the magic to seep through. I didn't have enough strength to resist.

It told me to stand and put one foot in front of the other. I obeyed. Anything for that voice. Absolutely anything. I'd run across the Sahara. Swim through the Pacific. Climb the Chrysler Building for it.

My first lucid moment was in a stark white room with a strange man looming over me. Agony ripped through my body as sharpened metal poked tender flesh.

I just wanted it to end. Just end. End. End. End.

But there was that voice again. Telling me the pain wasn't real. Warm, soft fingers gripped mine. Tickling breath on my ear and neck. Words of comfort and encouragement.

I relaxed. It felt good to drift into sweet, blissful nothing.

Then a beat. A blip, really. It grew louder in my chest. My heartbeat? It thrummed through my body. The low notes wove through my blood like a pluck of a big bass string.

Live. Live. Live. Live.

My lungs involuntarily sucked in a breath, and my heart beat harder and harder against my chest in time with the beat.

Live. Live. Live. Live.

White-hot pain ripped my shoulder apart and burned through my nerve endings. Muscles straining and pushing, I felt my pulse racing in my wrists and neck. My whole body was trying to obey the chant.

Breathing hard, I wrenched my eyes open, and the man in the white coat and cheaters gave a yelp and jumped back.

Everything hurt and my shoulder twisted and clenched with unreal pain, but I ignored it, listening only to the chant.

Live. Live. Li—

And then it stopped, too abrupt to be natural. I swung my legs over the table and jumped down, my shoes hitting the floor with an echoing *tap*.

"Wait—I haven't stitched up your wound—" the doctor cried, flustered, his hands grabbing my arms to lead me back to the table.

I jerked away, frantically scanning the room.

Where is she?

The siren, whose name still lay buried within the left side of my chest, was gone. And yet she still felt close. Her magic lingered in the sterile air. With one stride, I crossed to the door and pulled it open.

One of the largest men I'd ever seen—and I'd seen a lot of large men—had her by the wrists. At the sound of the door opening, she twisted her head back to me, eyes wide with shock and fear and *horror.* And I could see why.

Two small ivory horns protruded from the giant's temples, ending in dark, sharpened points.

A minotaur.

Without a second thought, my battle instincts took over. Even though I could feel warm liquid trickling down my arm and chest, I rushed right into the minotaur's personal space and grabbed his arm in a lock. My left armpit came down on the crook of the monster's arm while my right fist rammed into the man's elbow.

There was a *crack* as his bones popped out of their socket and the joints bent upward into the opposite angle an elbow should bend.

He roared and let go of the siren.

She stumbled backward into the corner between the door and the hall, her hands clamped over her mouth, staring at the two of us in terror.

Turning my attention back to the minotaur, I moved into a boxer's stance and pivoted forward, driving my entire right shoulder into the cavity of his chest just below his sternum. The minotaur stumbled back, probably still recovering from the blinding pain in his elbow.

But then my own wound caught up with me. My shoulder seized, like knives digging into my muscles, and my knees buckled. I fell against the wall, smearing blood down the brick. The minotaur snorted—actually snorted like a bull—and lunged for me. I dodged out of the way, throwing myself to the side and ducking behind him. I made a grab for my shoulder holster when I realized…I wasn't wearing it.

Of course I wasn't. I'd been safe in my hotel room before the shootout happened. And the siren naturally hadn't thought to grab my gun before leaving.

Shit.

The minotaur twisted around and swung his fist at my head.

I ducked just in time, and his wrist grazed the tips of my hair. I aimed a punch straight into his gut. The giant's top half folded over, a deep groan spilling from his throat.

That was a wrecked elbow and two blows to the solar plexus. A normal man would collapse. But this man was a monster. Grabbing his shoulders, I pulled him to me and kneed him hard in the groin. Repeatedly.

Shouts of pain came from the minotaur, and his hands grappled for me—for my throat, my head—anything. He found my shoulders.

As he pressed his thumb into my wound, deeper and deeper, I fell back and screamed, trying to wrench away.

Agony carved its way through my shoulder and down my spine, into all my nerves so they spasmed and locked. My vision tunneled as my adrenaline waged war with the rest of my body to keep me conscious. I couldn't think, I couldn't—

And suddenly the minotaur was off me. His eyes were clear and frightened as his hands and fingers twitched…not on their own. He had both hands on his horns, pulling on them—hard.

Spots of light danced before me and my fingers dripped with blood that continually rolled down my arm. With the wall for support, I blinked blearily at the siren who stood behind the minotaur, two pieces of balled-up cotton in her palms.

Her lips were moving fast. She was whispering something and staring intently up at the monster.

The minotaur let out a roar that seemed to shake the whole building, and turned into the brick wall, ramming his head against it. His horns splintered, and his eyes rolled back into his bloody forehead as he fell back and dropped to the floor. Unconscious.

For a long moment, the only sound in the small hallway was our labored breathing. My spotty vision grew dark and I staggered forward, unable to even hold myself up against the wall.

A smaller, warm hand pressed against my chest, steadying me, as her other hand gripped my arm. "Doctor!" she called. "Doctor, please!"

The old doctor emerged into the hallway. Apparently he had been either a coward or very wise to stay out of a fight he wouldn't have been able to help win anyway. He took one look at the minotaur on the floor and sniffed. "Oh, that's going to be fun to clean up."

The siren stiffened against me as she helped to hold me up. Dimly, I wondered why the hell she was still here. If she had any sense of self-preservation, she'd have been on a train out of here by now.

"You know about…about…" she stammered.

The doctor took off his cheaters and cleaned the lenses on his coat with a sigh. "Monsters? Oh yes, my dear girl. You can't moonlight as a doctor for mob bosses and not be able to treat claw wounds. But if a minotaur is after you"—he eyed the monster on the floor with disgust—"then I'd rather be left out of whatever mess you've gotten yourself into. Please leave."

The siren's parted lips tightened as her brows pulled together in distress. "*You have to help Colt first.*"

A strange feeling emanating from her gentle hand on my chest seemed to chase away the pain. But with it came discomfort. Why was…*this monster* trying to help me? Why had she even taken me here and saved my life when I'd just tried to steal hers?

The name that made her more of a girl and less of a

monster almost broke free. But I pushed it back down.

I still had a job to do.

Summoning all my strength, I pushed away the old vet's helping hands and grabbed the siren's wrist. Ignoring the inhuman amounts of pain careening through my left side, I stepped over the minotaur's body, pulling her behind me. I didn't want her to suddenly come to her senses and vanish when I was in no shape to follow.

"Where do you keep your meds, doc? And needle and thread." The words came through like eating rocks.

"You can't do that yourself. You can barely stand!" Shock tainted her pretty, irresistible voice.

"The bullet's out. I can do the rest. Meds, *now*," I demanded, glancing around the clean, well-kept operating room and looking for the instruments I needed.

"Fine by me," the doctor snapped, striding through the room, opening a couple drawers, grabbing the medical instruments and dropping them, along with a syringe of some kind, on the stainless-steel table. On reflex, I stuck the syringe into the crook of my elbow and injected the painkiller right into my vein.

"Alright, let's go." I grabbed the instruments and shoved them into my pocket.

"Whoa there, stallion." She planted a strong hand on my chest for the second time.

I looked directly into her eyes—a task that had been difficult to do since I'd found out the truth about her. Maybe because her true nature had felt like a betrayal to me. I hadn't realized just how much I had wanted Sawyer to be wrong. Talking with her, even one-sidedly, had been cleansing. As if everything that was dark and evil in my life was somehow washed away by her animated gestures and open expressions.

Now, as I stood here alive, still feeling her magic chanting of *live, live, live* in my heart, I wanted so badly to look into her eyes. I wanted to see the girl who had spoken to me so clearly, without ever saying a word. I wanted that girl back, even for just a moment.

"Don't," I ground out, feeling both weaker and stronger under her blue gaze.

"Don't call you that? Stallion is a good nickname for Colt. I thought it was clever."

She might've been the only person in existence who hadn't immediately linked my name to a deadly weapon. I liked that more than I'd ever want to admit.

"I meant don't stop me," I clarified. "We've got to go, *now.*"

She shook her head, autumn curls swaying from her shoulders. "If we go, we won't get far. You'll bleed out. Just let the doctor stitch you up. Then we'll go."

I leaned against the table, exhaustion seeping in as the adrenaline ran out. "Why aren't you halfway across Boston by now?"

"Because." She took a step toward me, lowering her voice. It became smooth as silk sheets. "I don't want to see you die, Colt. And if you walk out of here without stitching that up, you will."

More blood trickled down my chest. *She might be right.* My head drooped, and my eyelids lowered, allowing me to see only her shoes. "You won't try to run?"

There was a pause from above, then—"Doctor?" Her voice sounded a million miles away. Dimly, I was aware of another person moving closer and of a needle piercing my skin. Thread pulling through muscle and flesh.

That's when I realized…the injection I had taken hadn't just been a painkiller. It was making me drowsy. Weak.

My grip on her wrist slackened and I felt her pull away. "*Take care of him, Doctor.*"

The clatter of heels across the linoleum floors resounded

in my ears as the door creaked open and swung shut with a *snap*.

So she did run—despite me asking her not to. Not that I really blamed her for taking the opportunity.

I tried to push through the drowsiness, but the injection was getting the better of me. I barely held myself up, most of my weight against the table, as the doctor stitched me up. The needle pulled thread through my skin, and despite the occasional wince, I focused on that power inside me.

This was why I didn't drink. I hated the way it made me feel out of control. Foggy. But unlike most men, I could quite literally burn through it.

The heat rose in my chest, blazing through the drug's effects like flames on a cocktail. It chased away the drowsiness and seared through the pain. As the doctor clipped the thread and pressed a bandage over my fresh stitches, smoke curled out of my nostrils and my fingers pressed into the table, leaving dents.

Without a word to the entranced veterinarian, I grabbed a makeshift weapon and left him to the mess of my blood smeared throughout his operating room. The siren couldn't have gotten far, and I had a hunch she wouldn't be returning to The Blind Dragon. A smart girl like her would head to the train station to lose herself in the wilds of America. She'd know that once she was out of Boston, she could disappear again.

I couldn't let that happen.

But first…

I stooped over the body of the minotaur and rummaged through his pockets. He had no I.D. on him. Had he been a part of the shootout from the hotel? No, that didn't add up. He hadn't been trying to kill the siren, while those who shot out the hotel room had clearly been out for blood. It was too much to consider at once, and I had to sort out my priorities.

Priority number one was locating the siren. Later I could figure out who had tried to kill us and why, and whether the minotaur was working with them.

After peeling off the minotaur's jacket, I threaded my arms through it. I was drowning in the material, but at least it covered all the blood. As I stepped over him, I noticed his bowler hat on the ground. The gold lettering patched into the inside rim caught my eye.

Picking up the hat, I inspected the logo. The letters *BKH* were embroidered in shiny gold thread, and I stared at it for longer than I should have—there was something familiar about those letters.

I dropped the bowler hat as I ran down the hall and up the basement steps. Emerging from the alley, I hailed a taxi. I would not let the siren disappear again.

Chapter Nine

The Siren

I wasn't used to talking so much. Ever.

There were the special occasions where I would say a sentence or two out of necessity, but they were few and far between. Each time I spoke, I was grateful to find that I hadn't forgotten how.

I wasn't scared about forgetting to sing, though. Singing was different. You didn't necessarily need words. Just a melody and a harmony and a soul.

But if I was a monster, did I even have a soul?

Leaning my head against the backseat of the jalopy I'd commandeered, I sighed deeply. After another wave of nausea had passed, fatigue overwhelmed my whole body, but the adrenaline seemed to keep me awake just fine.

Like I'd done in getting Colt to the vet, I'd forced a car to stop and hijacked some poor driver into taking me to the train station. Rubbing my hands down my face, I stared out the grimy window. Boston passed in a blur of brick-red, beige, and gray tones of building after building. Awnings and produce stands outside storefronts gave color to the otherwise neutral cityscape. I didn't venture out into the city often, but whenever I did, it never impressed me much. Instead, I would imagine rolling green hilltops, fields of gold wheat, meadows of yellow, white, and red wildflowers, sparkling blue lakes, and distant purple mountains...all that I longed for.

Perhaps I should have thanked Colt. He had given me an excuse to leave the speakeasy life and venture out into the countryside. I could disappear into the Midwest. Into a small town with farms and quiet folk and live peacefully.

I might be alone, I might never speak to another soul again, but I'd be in a place that filled my heart with music.

It was the silver lining in being on the run for the rest of my life.

I had no luggage, no clothes or belongings, and certainly no money. But that didn't matter. I could either persuade someone into giving me money like some low-life grifter, or command the train conductor to just allow me on board.

Escaping was going to be easy, *so easy*, with this power I had. Then, once I was far enough away, I'd fall into silence again. Disappear. If the people who were after me could find me by my voice, I would just stop talking. It was possible. After all, I'd done it for seven years.

But manipulating people to gain my freedom made me sick. I was forcing them to bend to my will and do my bidding.

Any decent person would find such a thing deplorable. It was a wonder Colt didn't just gun me down in the alley under the cover of darkness.

You're too dangerous.

That's what he'd said to me, right before he protected me from a rain of bullets.

Why hadn't he just let me die if he thought I was so dangerous?

Why had I saved his life when he was trying to rob me of

my freedom?

The answer should have been simple—neither of us were killers. And yet, with the way Colt fought the man with the horns, I could see that he'd slain these…these *monsters* before. Killing was not a new concept to him.

What about me? I couldn't remember what exactly I'd muttered under my breath to the horned man, but somehow I'd made him beat himself into unconsciousness. And the man who'd abused that poor sister? I'd turned his body against him any time he touched a woman, now and forever.

I was no angel.

Colt was right. I was a monster.

The jalopy screeched to a sudden halt and I slid forward, my knees hitting the passenger seat. The driver stared blankly ahead at the car-lined street in front of the station. A big brass bell tolled behind a clock tower, and a shrill whistle pierced the air. Columns of white smoke from the locomotives billowed above the station, and the sound of hundreds of voices rose with it.

My ticket out of this life was just a few steps away, but my hand on the door just wouldn't stop shaking. I still had Colt's blood under my fingernails, while my dress was stained maroon with it.

Run, run, run. Live, live, live.

I muttered, "Stop shaking," to my own hands. It didn't work.

Summoning what resolve I could, I cracked open the door and called to the driver, "*You never saw me.*" The driver blinked and glanced around as if he'd somehow been brought out of a trance, but I was gone from the car before he could say a word.

I pulled the coat I'd stolen from the doctor's office tightly around me as I hurried across the street, my heels clicking on the concrete. The oversize coat swished against my calves almost like a second dress. At least it covered up the stained blood.

Squeezing through the throngs of people, I approached the ticket counter to "purchase" my ticket.

"Excuse me, what's the next outbound train?"

The ticket man was a round-faced older gentleman with equally round cheaters sitting upon a small nose. Without looking up, he answered, "Eight o'clock train to Philly."

I glanced at the big station clock. Less than fifteen minutes. Hopefully that wouldn't be too long to wait, not that I had much of a choice. Trying to get out of the city using hijacked cars during this hour in the morning would take just shy of an hour. I wasn't willing to risk being found in Boston's outskirts. To begin with, I didn't know *how many* were after me. Clearly it wasn't just Colt. There were the trigger men at the hotel, and the minotaur wearing the bowler hat, and God knew who else.

Best to take the first train and get out of the city as quickly as possible. From Philly, I could jump on another train and truly disappear.

"*Please give me one ticket.*"

The ticket man's hands hastened to print out the ticket, rip it, and pass it to me under the glass. Before he had time to realize what he'd done, I'd slipped out of line and headed for the right platform. With every step and every person whose gaze I avoided, my anxiety mounted. It clawed and chewed through my stomach like a hungry stray.

Perching myself on a lone bench, I threaded my fingers through my waves to hide my face behind them and tried to be as inconspicuous as possible. A newsie strolled by, hollering about the upcoming mayoral election with some Irish fella as the front-runner. I tuned out the boy's voice—it was easy with all the worries running through my head.

What if there were more monsters among this very crowd? Could they smell other monsters? Were they searching for me?

Then there was the fact that I was leaving the only home I'd ever known. Although I hated the booze and spirits, the drunks on a bender, and the men who'd ask me to run away with them while flashing their fancy suits and pocket watches—as if wealth was the only thing a girl could want in a husband—I would miss The Blind Dragon. Madame Maldu's special brand of gaspers whose smoke I'd come to know so well, or Stan's strong, quiet presence, or David's sax, Marv's laughter, and Francis's dependable piano accompaniment—the best little band a canary could ask for.

Quickly, I wiped a few tears from my lashes with the back of my hand and took a deep breath. The whistle went off—the signal to board.

A flood of people converged toward the train and I was almost swept off with them as I stood. The sheer amount of people heading for one small door was overwhelming. I'd only been on a train once in my life, and many years ago, so I'd forgotten what it was like—the feeling of drowning in a sea of bodies.

With my ticket clenched tightly in one hand, I fell into step behind a woman who reeked of fancy perfume. A man with a fedora and dark gray coat shouldered past me, squeezing in front while another man came right up behind me, pressing against my backside.

My vision flashed red with anger, and I started to twist around, to tell him to back off when his hand came around and grabbed my mouth, covering my lips with his sweaty fingers. Pure shock had me frozen, and before I could try and wrestle myself away, his other hand grasped my arm and tightened me to his chest. Then the man in front pivoted around, pressing a blade against my belly, and grabbing my free wrist. I let out a muffled whimper while tears sprang to my eyes thanks to a combination of fear, panic, and sheer exhaustion. *Not again.*

Meanwhile, people shuffled past us, absorbed in their papers and their own belongings, trying to heave them on board. Completely oblivious to the knife at my stomach.

"Don't say a word, siren," the man with the knife leaned in and hissed, his breath carrying the acrid stench of an ashtray. "Be a good girl and come back to our boss. Do what we say and you won't get a scratch on you. Keep her lid shut, Robby."

I sniffled under the hand of the man named Robby. It was so tight I couldn't even move my jaw.

"Now back up slowly. Nice and easy, that's it..." As they forced me to inch back on the train platform, I considered dropping to my knees, but with the way the man had the knife pressed up against my stomach, I worried about falling into the blade, gutting myself.

Taking another tiny step, I tripped over Robby's feet. He had slowed for some reason, his hand limp and sliding down my chin. The man with the knife stared at me, lips parted, terrified. For a moment I thought his fear was due to the fact that I could now instruct him to do whatever I wished, but then I saw that he was actually staring just past my shoulder where Robby had been.

Robby had backed away, clutching his side. Red was now blooming on his shirt, and his face was the color of fresh snow. Colt stood behind him, panting, covered in sweat and remnants of his own blood. Something silver glinted in his right hand but it vanished into his sleeve and, in one quick movement, Colt wrapped an arm around my waist, pinning me to his side, and twisted the man's wrist to plunge his own knife into his own stomach.

Then, side-stepping the two stabbed men like it was the most natural thing in the world, Colt guided me up to the train door behind a young family, and slipped the train ticket out of my hand. I was in such shock that I could only watch as he passed it to the conductor with a smile that said he *hadn't* just left two men to bleed to death.

"Apologies, ole sport," Colt said in a dead-on imitation of a high-society egg man. "The missus here seems to have misplaced her ticket."

I gritted my teeth. I didn't lose anything—the rat bastard stole my ticket. Though, it's not like I had purchased mine, either.

"Ain't that right, doll? Tell the gentleman you'd dearly love to get on the train with your husband." Colt's eyes bored into mine, a clear warning of what was to come if I said anything that made the conductor turn on him.

Maybe, with just a shout, I could have the entire crowd turn on Colt. But I didn't know what would happen after that. Surely other innocent bystanders could get hurt because of me. And then there was the possibility that my siren magic was zapping energy from me like a car on a tank of gasoline. If I tried to use my voice on so many people at once I could just pass out then and there.

Licking my lips, I moved my gaze to the conductor, who regarded me skeptically. Dark brows furrowed under his cap and his mustache twitched with annoyance.

"Yessir, mister," I said, then layered on sweetly, "*please let me on through.*"

The man stepped aside immediately. He was still blinking in confusion as Colt half-pushed, half-carried me through the train door and into the first spare compartment.

I fell into one of the seats after Colt released me and locked the door behind us. He had dropped something onto the opposite compartment seat—a silver scalpel, shiny red with blood. It was that instrument of healing that I'd seen flash in his palm earlier when he gutted the man.

Pressing himself against the door, Colt looked down at me with wild, furious eyes. "Just who the devil is after you?"

Chapter Ten

The Agent

"You mean besides you?"

The siren scowled up at me, one hand against the glass compartment window while the other gripped the edge of the seat. Her knees and toes were turned inward, and her shoulders were hunched as she regarded me warily.

"What's that supposed to mean?" I asked.

She shrugged. "For as long as I've been in hiding only the BOI has been able to find me. Perhaps it's possible your supervisor doesn't have as much faith in you as you thought."

"You think I'd stab men on my side?" I growled. Given the goons on the platform, I was actually glad I'd snagged the scalpel from the doc's place when I'd had the chance.

She stared at the thick crimson liquid that dripped from the blade into the fabric of the seat. "Frankly, I don't know *what* you'd do."

That shouldn't have affected me, but it did. My fingers curled into fists, and I felt that heat inside my chest billow through me like the clouds of steam from the trains. "I've saved your life three times now. So trust me when I say that me bringing you in isn't personal. You're just my job."

"*Just your job*," she echoed, and, for the first time, I detected a hint of tears. Her eyes turned glassy and her chin trembled, but then she straightened her spine and pushed her feet together into a proper position. "So it was your job to... to flirt with me, then?"

I hated how easily I could detect hurt in her voice. She was not good at masking her emotions. They were all as clear as day. For any grifter that was one of the first things you learned. Hide your real emotions and put on fake ones. But with her, from the very beginning, I'd been able to read her so well. So incredibly easily.

She seems to be as honest as they come.

"Yes," I answered, returning her honesty with my own, "I had to get you to talk. I had to hear your voice to make sure you were the siren."

To that, she said nothing and dropped her gaze.

I took the seat opposite of her inside the small train compartment. "Look, if you know of anyone after you, you need to tell me." Still she didn't reply, and during the silence, I searched through our previous conversations back in my hotel room. "Didn't you mention there had been a bad man after you? Wasn't it why Madame Maldu took you into hiding?"

Once more, I could read her thoughts on her face. She bit her bottom lip and her eyes darted from one side to the other, like she was debating something.

This "bad man" had to be the one who sent those other men after her—the minotaur and the two on the platform.

Just then, the train issued another high-pitched whistle and smoke streams drifted by the window, obscuring the view of the retreating platform. As the rattler lurched forward, she almost toppled off her seat, her knees bumping into mine.

I caught her from falling and winced as a jolt of pain raced down my side.

Immediately, she shrank away from my touch, but her gaze jumped to my left shoulder. "Did you even get yourself sewn up?" she asked.

"I'm fine." I gingerly touched my fresh stitches.

"You don't look it," she said quietly.

Ignoring her, I glanced out the window. Philadelphia. That's where this train was bound. It wasn't *that* far away from DC, but we'd have to switch trains at the station, which meant another opportunity for this girl—this *monster*—to slip through my fingers, whether it was by her own Harry Houdini maneuvers or via these mysterious henchmen that seemed to know her exact location wherever she went. But how? And how had she remained undetected so long if she could now be tracked so easily?

Squeezing the bridge of my nose, I struggled to find clues. This was turning out more complicated than I'd ever imagined. I knew people would be after the lost siren, but so quickly?

I looked up to find her still watching me warily. "So you have no idea who those men on the platform were? What did they say to you?" I asked.

"They wanted the same thing you want," she said, her words coming out in one long sigh. Her gaze went to the window and it stayed there. "They wanted to take me to their boss."

I almost pointed out that *my* boss wasn't a crime lord, unlike theirs who probably was. But to her, I supposed there wasn't much of a difference.

So who was this mystery boss? Could it be her creator?

Mysteries surrounding the lost siren were vast and difficult to unravel. Everything I knew was from the stories McCarney told me. Eight years ago, one year after prohibition began when organized crime escalated, three siren pearls made their way to America. They had to have been smuggled, of course, but the rumors as to *how* were extensive and imaginative. Some claimed that a senator's wife wore the pearls in a necklace on her way back from a European trip. Two of those pearls were located. One had been surgically added into the mouth of a twenty-year-old woman, but she had died shortly following the surgery and the pearl's magic had died with her. The second pearl was recovered during a gunfight between a crime lord who ruled the Bronx and the BOI. But its magic, too, had been lost due to a crack within it. And the third? The third had vanished.

Eight years later, it's sitting across from me.

"Did they mention a name? Anything?"

"The man with the knife—the first one you stabbed…his name was Robby," she said, hugging her arms, keeping her gaze locked outside the window. "Do you think he'll live?" she asked quietly.

I wanted to tell her it didn't matter—that they were the enemy. Who cared if they lived or died? Instead, I said, "I didn't hit any vital organs. And the cuts were shallow."

She nodded, and I pressed, "What about the minotaur? Did he say anything?"

She rubbed her wrists, red from my rope and purple from the minotaur's grip. "No."

I sighed, massaging the corded muscles in my shoulder where the ache was the worst. She wasn't going to be helpful, and I guess I couldn't blame her. But if I could figure out who was after her, I could let McCarney know the name of another crime boss, maybe one whose name and connections weren't even known.

"Are you sure there wasn't *anything* you noticed?"

"I was too busy looking at the horns on his head," she snapped. "And the knife at my stomach. Besides, I don't have to give you anything. Why should I help my kidnapper?"

At that, I leaned forward so close that she was forced to look away from the window and meet my eyes. She smelled of blood. Metallic and coppery. *My* blood.

"Because you're a monster. Don't tell me that man's screams in The Blind Dragon weren't because of you." My gaze drilled into hers, concentrating on her dark pupils and ignoring those soft blue irises. "But what I don't think you understand is that there are men out there who are monsters without horns, or fangs, or claws. There are men who *create* monsters like you, all for the purpose of wealth, status, and power. And blood."

For a long moment, she just stared at me in response. Her hands curled into fists on her thighs. Her eyes were no longer the soft tone of a sky, but the scorching shade of a fire's hottest center.

"*I* don't understand?" Her voice was a fierce whisper. "I *know* men are monsters. I have watched time and again a sister walk into my bar, sit at one of my tables and flinch when her fella raises his hand. I've seen countless bruises pathetically covered by makeup, and busted lips in rouge. Those so-called men aren't just monsters, they're demons. And they need to be punished for it."

Slowly, too slowly, her words became clues, and the clues told a story. A reason.

"The man in the bar," I said, each word tasting a bit more like ash in my mouth, "*that's* why you used your voice on him."

She turned toward the window, pulling her knees to her chest and wrapping her arms around them. All that anger and rage vanished as her slim shoulders seemed to sag with the weight of what she'd done.

It had been out of protection. Not for herself, but for some poor dame from nights and days of abuse—fists, broken bottles, and gin-soaked breath.

"Eris."

Her name broke free as my heart splintered and cracked. *Damn it all.*

At her name, she looked back at me, her eyes soft again.

"That's why, isn't it?"

She didn't reply.

"Eris, had he been hurting another girl? What did you do to stop him?"

Her eyes were shiny, full of unshed tears. Then she glimpsed at the scalpel on the seat, and my hands on the door, and her gaze turned steely.

"Why does it matter? You've decided what I am," she muttered, her words oddly rough. "What does the *why* have to do with it?"

She was absolutely right.

The why *shouldn't* matter. It wouldn't matter to McCarney, or Sawyer, or anyone else at the BOI, but…it mattered to me.

When she had used her voice to torture that man, I'd felt betrayed by this girl with a sweet smile and an honest heart. But now that I knew *why* she'd done it, it didn't seem so monstrous.

"I'll…be right back. *Stay here.*" I stood and fumbled with the door latch, and escaped into the train's narrow hall. I had one more glimpse of Eris's raised brows and parted lips before I closed the door on her.

No, no, no. I wasn't supposed to be having second thoughts about this girl. I wasn't supposed to be questioning this mission. So what if she protected abused women with her powers? So what if she refused to talk to ensure people lived with their free will?

She was a threat to national security. She could convince men to kill themselves, or give up their property, or help smuggle dope, guns, and booze from city to city.

Whether or not she had actually *done* any of those things shouldn't matter, simply because she had the power to do them. At least, that's what I'd been trained to think.

Grimacing, I leaned against the wall and felt it vibrate under my wounded shoulder as tons of coal propelled the train forward. Pinpricks of pain danced down my arm and spiraled through my chest and spine. I breathed out long and slow.

The heat inside my chest burned its way through my lungs and nose. The escaping air came out in a column of white smoke and my mouth tasted like ash. I tried to push it down, but the inferno was damn near impossible to restrain.

Unable to stop myself, I looked back at the door that blocked Eris from my view.

Dammit. The name I'd tried so hard to get, and then tried so hard to dismiss, was branded into my mind. Singed on my tongue.

The name of a goddess, not a monster.

Chapter Eleven

The Siren

There were two possibilities. One, Colt thought I was submissive enough to just sit in this compartment and wait for him to return, or, two, he was arrogant enough to believe he'd be able to catch me again if I escaped.

Whichever one was correct didn't matter. What *did* matter was that I had another chance to get away from *him*.

Colt made me feel drunk. I'd never had a drop of liquor in my life, but surely it had to feel something like this—lightheaded and woozy. Feverish.

Was it because of the way his expression had changed? And the way he'd said my name so tenderly?

It hadn't escaped my notice that he'd refrained from calling me by name since The Blind Dragon. Instead, he'd just called me "siren," so cold and so distant-like. And yet, when he'd guessed my reason for using my powers on that man, he'd looked confused, then troubled, then frustrated.

Then he'd left.

Now it was my turn.

I stood and opened the door latch. The hallway was empty. Colt was gone. For now.

After I closed the door behind me and checked the hall, I made a left, heading for the front of the train. Most passengers were still settling inside their compartments, and it would be a few hours before they got restless and wandered around to stretch their legs.

As I neared the end of my car, I gasped and ducked below the window of the door to the next car. Colt was a few feet ahead, chatting happily with a middle-aged woman. The way he smiled and laughed made me *truly* realize that our moments at The Blind Dragon had not been genuine. It had been an act. He'd been playing a role, like one of those fancy boyos on the silver screen or on the theater stages. I'd been nothing more than another prop. He charmed everyone—I was no exception.

The middle-aged woman laughed while affectionately stroking Colt's arm. Then she beckoned him inside her compartment.

Even though I felt sick and angry, I was strangely glad I'd seen this. It reinforced my decision to leave. I waited until he'd stepped inside and then, holding my breath, sped down the hall of the next car. Two cars later, I paused and spared myself a moment to glance out the window.

The passing scenery made my heart fill with song. Rolling gold, rustic orange, and lime green fields. The mountainous hills were like an old painting, but faded by distance instead of time. Which mountain was Mount Greylock? Were we even close to it? I didn't know the route the Boston train took to Philly, but I hoped it would continue to show this beauty.

Refocusing, I turned to duck into the dining car. As I'd predicted, there were few patrons. Just a couple men sipping coffee and puffing on cigs. A young flapper sat next to an older gentleman. Her elegant cloche hat, complete with feathers and a scarlet ribbon, covered her golden bobbed hair, and the feathers trembled as she took a large pull on her gasper and blew a trail of smoke into the air. Her decorated eyes cut to me then quickly looked away. No doubt I looked terribly strange with my disheveled waves and oversize doctor's coat covering my stained dress.

"Darling," she said, turning to the older gentleman who could've been her father, "let's go back to our first-class car. This one is getting too..." She glanced back at me and wrinkled her nose. "Stuffy."

I stepped to the side as the girl and her egg man hooked arms and exited the dining car.

Their departure on my account reminded me of the maid on the street corner outside Colt's hotel. I didn't blame them. It was human nature to avoid trouble, and I was certainly a whole mess of it.

"Can I get you something?" a small voice said to my left. I nearly jumped to find a girl in a uniform, probably no more than fifteen or fourteen, clearing dishes from an empty table. Her bobbed hair was pinned back, showing a face full of freckles.

I took in her simple uniform and glanced around the rest of the dining car. She was a maid on a train. What a novel life that had to be! How she could be in one city one hour and then another the next. Had she seen the flat, windy plains of Kansas, or the infamous swamps and bayous of New Orleans?

Maybe I couldn't apply to work at *this* train, but there were others. Other depots. America was growing and I could see all of it on a train. Except at the moment, I just needed a way to blend in.

"Um, miss?"

Realizing I'd been staring, I blushed then gave the girl a friendly smile and shook my head no. The maid just shrugged and picked up the tray she'd been using to clear away dishes and headed through a staff-only door.

With an idea forming, I waited a few minutes then followed her into a plain, somewhat grimy hall that led to several more doors. One by one, I began trying out each. The first led to a pantry full of food, boxes of coffee and tubs of sugar and flour, and the second was a bathroom. By the third door—a laundry room—I was getting antsy. Colt was probably still cozying up with that woman, but in the event that he wasn't, then he would've noticed I was missing by now and would hunt me down yet again.

Was it possible that he could sniff me out?

After all, there were several moments where he'd seemed to be…more than human. Whether or not he was a monster like me, I wasn't sure. But he had defeated a man twice his size, mortally injured, and lived. And he could somehow resist my voice.

He had to be…*something.*

Finally, I found what appeared to be a locker room. And, miracle of miracles, a small closet in the corner held a few clean maids' uniforms. Locking the door behind me, I quickly exchanged my stained dress for the uniform. I left my old dress on the floor of the closet and hurried out, down the narrow staff hall, and back into the dining car.

There were two middle-aged men at the bar—one reading a copy of *The Boston Globe*, and the other nursing a hangover with a cup of coffee. And a third older gentleman sat at a small table, a pipe between his lips, cheaters on his nose, dressed in a tweed suit with elbow pads. He was busy scribbling on a docket of papers spread out before him, while a fancy leather briefcase leaned against his chair.

Moving past the three men, I headed into the next car. If I roamed all over the train, maybe it would make it harder for Colt to find me.

Feeling hopeful, I hurried down the hall of the car and

past sliding compartment doors. I was just coming upon one when it suddenly slid open and a woman appeared in the doorway. She was older, over sixty, but she had the bees to be sure. Her dress was top-of-the-line, decked with embroidered sparkles and ending in silk swatches. She wore a headband with a feather around her gray hair. Her outfit looked more like she was going to a Broadway show, not traveling on a train for hours.

She shoved a bundle of clothes that smelled like gasper smoke and whiskey into my arms.

"Listen, girl, my husband needs these laundered right away. Starched and pressed. No dilly dallying."

Without waiting for me to answer, she slid the compartment door closed in my face.

I stood there for a brief moment, opening and closing my mouth. *Now* what was I supposed to do? Well, I wasn't going to actually launder them. That was for sure.

But my waitress-server habits were hard to break. I couldn't just throw them off the side of the train—though I dearly wanted to. Thinking I'd drop them off in the laundry room I'd found earlier, I headed back the way I'd come.

Just as I was about to step through the door, I caught a glimpse of familiar broad shoulders and light brown hair...

Colt.

"Rhatz!" I hissed, dropping down below the window. Maybe he really could track my scent.

Before I had time to figure out my next move, the dining car door slid open and I winced, shutting both eyes, not yet ready to see Colt standing above me.

"Excuse me, miss?"

I opened one eye, then the other, taking in the appearance of the academic-looking gent from the dining car. He had his briefcase in one hand with his pipe tucked into his coat's breast pocket.

"Did you fall, miss? Let me help you," he said, bending and offering me a hand.

As I shifted the pile of laundry into my other arm, I noticed a faint white scar in the center of his palm. Before I could think anything else of it, he grabbed my outstretched hand and yanked me to my feet. I stumbled and felt something sharp prick my skin.

Gasping, I wrenched away. The center of my palm had a large purple bruise already forming. And in the center of *his* hand protruded an onyx stinger, like a scorpion's. It came right out of his flesh and glistened with a clear liquid. The stinger was covered in blood. My blood.

A wave of nausea hit me like a physical blow and I fell. The man caught me with one arm as all feeling escaped my limbs. The soiled laundry slipped from my grasp. The last thing I saw before my vision went black was white dress shirts and black slacks flapping in the wind, flying into the countryside.

Chapter Twelve

The Agent

Of course she ran. I'd actually expected her to. What I hadn't expected was finding her dress in the closet of a staff laundry room. Had she known I was able to track her by my blood's scent on her dress? And if she knew that, then she had to have realized I wasn't entirely human, either.

It was possible that she'd just wanted to get rid of her bloody dress. But either way, I hadn't been thinking clearly. I shouldn't have stopped by another passenger compartment to smooth-talk my way into getting fresh clothes. I'd been arrogant.

Like a damn sap.

And now it was taking far too long to find her again.

Where in the devil is she?

I closed my eyes and tried to think. I could scour the whole train for her. Surely she couldn't hide forever during the ride. But on the other hand…the girl was resourceful. She'd stolen a maid's uniform to blend in. She was clever. Kind.

Unfortunately, I was used to dealing with the inept.

Foolish. Cruel.

I could try to track *her* scent, but I didn't know it as well as mine. Plus, there were a *hundred thousand* scents on this rattler. I'd never be able to find her sweet, natural smell in the cloud of other perfumes, colognes, coffee, and smoke.

There was no other choice, I had to flex my gumshoe skills and look for her the old-fashioned way.

I left the dining car, that familiar heat in my chest pushing against my rib cage, sizzling my bones and yearning to get out. Pausing outside every compartment, I took deep, long breaths, trying to locate her scent. When one smell I detected overpowered anything else, I made some excuse to knock and look around inside. Some women invited me in, some men offered me a game of cards.

But *none* of them had Eris.

With every car I looked through, the panic got worse and worse and the heat burned hotter and hotter.

On my way through the third-to-last car, I bumped shoulders with an older gentleman in a tweed jacket and a pipe nestled in his breast pocket.

"Pardon me, my good sir," he said with a tip of his chin in my direction.

I said nothing, too consumed in my search, and kept going.

But as I got to the end of the car, I paused. *That* scent… it was familiar. His pipe smoke. I had smelled it in the dining car, and I recognized his tweed jacket. He'd been there right when I'd been looking for Eris.

Coincidence, maybe, but…

BOI training taught me that there were no coincidences.

I stayed where I was until the gentleman had passed through the car and into the next. Then I turned on my heel and followed him.

Waiting outside, I watched as the man in the tweed jacket

made it all the way to the end of the next car. He knocked on the second compartment and another man stepped out. The two shared words and that was when I noticed the old gent's hand was bandaged, a strip of linen wrapped around the palm of his hand. A small dot of crimson against white.

My fingers twitched with the need to claw something.

I knew that particular wound.

Manticores' stingers came out through their hands, breaking their skin whenever they did so. A painful process, but it was very useful when shaking the hand of another mob boss. Poison shot through the stinger, paralyzing its intended victim. Stinging their neck or wrist—anywhere the blood flow was strong—could carry the poison right to their heart and kill them. Because of these talents, manticores were incredibly useful. And somewhat rare.

If this manticore had taken Eris, which I strongly suspected, who was he working for? Who had enough money to employ a manticore?

The manticore and the lackey wrapped up their conversation and exchanged places. The man in the tweed jacket entered the compartment and slid the door closed while the other headed down the hall.

I hung back, weighing my options. Somehow these two men had made it onto the train where the siren was. Which meant there had been more men on the platform than the ones that had attacked her.

Who were these people? How could they track her movements so well now when they had left her alone for seven years?

There was so much more to this assignment than I'd first thought. But it wasn't my job or responsibility to figure out who else was after her. Only to bring her in, back to the BOI. Where she'd be safe—I mean, for *the whole country* to be safe.

Clenching my fists, I took a step away from the door and

glanced to my left. Wrought-iron rungs climbed the side up to the top of the train. The wheels click-clacked over the rails and I could smell the coal fires in the air and taste the humidity of the billowing steam.

Reconnaissance. I needed to know what I was protecting her *from*. And if it could help McCarney locate the mob boss who wanted her, and who probably created her in the first place, then that was just the icing on the cake.

Decision made, I headed down the length of the train car, following the lackey. I'd take him out and get as much information as I could, then I would double back and confront the manticore. But I couldn't afford to waste too much time. I didn't want them hurting Eris.

As I was about to step out onto the platform, I got a backward elbow to the face.

My neck snapped back on impact as sharp pain stabbed through my nose, cheeks, and into my spine. The blow wasn't hard enough to break my nose but definitely enough to make the world tilt, spin, and grow hazy. A hand grabbed my shirt collar and yanked me forward, out the door. On the attacker's second swing, I ducked and drove my shoulder into the man's gut. His hands fisted my shirt and his feet tried to gain purchase as I started to throw him over my shoulder, and over the train, into the passing countryside.

I was one thrust away from achieving my goal when he boxed my ear. My ears rang and rang with incessant stinging, forcing me to drop my arms. The man went for me again, and I just managed to swerve to the side, his fist catching only air. He came after me, pummeling my stomach with hard blows until he had me pressed up against the railing. One fist after the other, each punch knocked precious air from my lungs and I folded over, hacking and coughing while instinctively trying to shield my organs from internal bleeding. Another blow to my stomach and my vision jumped into double-view.

Head throbbing and blood pounding, I reached around and found what I was looking for—the iron rungs.

I needed a reprieve or my body would never be able to bounce back. Climbing to the top of a moving train would not have been my first choice, but it was my only option.

As I pulled myself onto the rungs, the man grabbed hold of my pant leg. I kicked him in the face and continued upward, not waiting to see if I'd been able to break *his* nose. Rung by rung, I climbed the side of the train and heaved myself to the top. The wind whistled through my hair and batted my clothes against my body. Judging from the scenery, we'd left Massachusetts and entered the Connecticut Shoreline. Waves crashed against the rocky coast as the rattler slowed to maneuver around the terrain. But even slow, it ran close to sixty miles per hour.

If I fell, I was a goner.

The lackey was nearly on top of me, but the crisp wind helped to clear my mind, and when he held up his fists like a professional pug in a boxing ring, I was ready. First came a jab, jab, with his right then a cross with his left. I jerked my head to the left twice and on his cross, I ducked and threw an uppercut to his stomach. As he doubled over, I drove my elbow downward into the back of his neck. The blow was too hard for him to stay standing, and he dropped to the hard metallic surface.

As I bent to grab the back of his shirt to heave him up and drive a knee into his gut, he rammed into my shins. I lost my balance and rolled across the top of the train, the wind blowing over me like a tidal wave, pushing me further and further toward the edge. My foot slipped and the sole of my shoe hit only air. My pulse skittered as my heart leaped into my throat. I kicked against the side and started to heave myself forward. But my opponent was already there. Waiting for me.

He ground his heel into my bad shoulder. I cried out as warm blood blossomed under my new shirt. Agony rippled through me and my strength waned, my body slipping further toward the edge. He pressed harder until my legs swung off and my hands gripped the top of the train car.

I was now dangling over the sharp rocks of the Connecticut coast.

This man wasn't a monster. He would've used his powers by now. Even so, he was a good fighter.

But there was no way I was losing.

With a growl, I relinquished my grip on the side and grabbed the man's ankle. He teetered as I squeezed my fingers harder and harder into his Achilles heel. Howling with pain, he bent down to try and pry me off. Seizing my chance, I hauled myself up and head-butted him, driving my forehead up into his nose with a movement that rivaled the speed of the train. I earned a satisfying crunch from above and the man jerked back with a muffled groan.

My whole body was on fire, burning with heat and fighting spirit. My blood felt like it was boiling under my skin. The raging wind helped to cool it, but not my temper.

The lackey held his face, blood oozing over his fingers.

"Who sent you?" I roared. I tasted the salt spray on my tongue as my words rode the wind and waves.

The man just spat blood and bent at the hips, as if preparing for another attack.

But this fight was over. In three short steps, I stormed at him and aimed a front push-kick, driving my own heel into the man's groin. He stumbled back and back, disappearing over the edge with a scream.

I took careful steps to the edge, arriving just in time to catch a glimpse of his broken body against the clay-colored rocks. The saltwater of the Atlantic mixed with the iron crimson of his blood. It became smaller and smaller as the train carried us further down the coast.

My chest and skin hummed with energy.

Eris.

I needed to get to her *now.*

Glancing to each side, I estimated the location of the compartment I'd seen the man in the tweed jacket enter. Fighting the raging wind, I made my way to the second window from the end.

Summoning both the human and *in*human strength I possessed, I hurled myself off the train. At the last moment, I grabbed the edge of the train's roof before it was too late and, using my body's momentum, thrust my legs, feet first, through the glass.

Chapter Thirteen

The Siren

I woke up unable to move my arms, my legs, or my jaw. Unable to move anything except my eyes. Judging from the ceiling I was staring at, we were still on the train, but was it the same train? How long had I been out?

"Awake already?"

A calm, sophisticated tenor, a tone of an educated man. Without even looking, I knew it was the man in the tweed jacket, the one who had pricked me with some odd stinger coming right out of his palm.

"And I gave you a hefty dose of poison, too."

His face came into view as he leaned over me, giving me a cruel, taunting smile.

My skin crawled, tingling with disgust as the man's hand drew up my leg, his fingers fiddling with the hem of the maid's uniform. I made a sound in the back of my throat—a cross between a whimper and a growl.

With raised eyebrows, he withdrew a large handkerchief from his jacket. "Well, we can't have you talking, now can we?" He pried my lips open and threaded the cloth through my mouth so my tongue pressed against the fabric. He finished it with a knot on the back of my head.

"Your hunter seems to be looking for you. Lucky for us you managed to slip away so we needn't have engaged in a brawl right in the middle of the train. Now my…er…colleague can just take him out quietly," the academic said, patting my knee. "No one shall be the wiser."

The handkerchief in my mouth tasted like cologne. The thick scent gave me a terrible headache, and the poison from the stinger made my body sluggish and heavy.

God, are you punishing me? Maybe I deserved whatever fate the BOI had in store for me.

I couldn't stand the idea of them finding Colt and killing him. And Colt wouldn't go down without a fight. There would be nothing "quiet" about it—that much I knew. What if any of the other innocent passengers got hurt in whatever fight broke out?

Colt was right. I was a danger to society. Not for what *I'd* do, but for what others could make me do, or what others would do to get to me.

Tears swam in my eyes, but I suppressed them. I was good at that. It would be terrible to bawl while I was gagged, and completely unhelpful. I had to find a way to get rid of this paralyzing poison.

But to my horror, the monster—for that was the only thing he could be—bent over and grabbed a length of rope, beginning to tie me up quickly and expertly.

As he looped the rope around my ankles, I looked around the compartment, now just barely able to move my neck. Was there something I could use? It was pretty bare, except for the suitcase that I'd seen in the dining car resting against his chair. It lay on the bench across from me, and I could very clearly read the upside-down gold letters of *BKH.*

I stared at the letters for a long time, thinking I might've seen that sequence before, in that typeface. But I couldn't be sure. It played with a memory from so long ago.

Jerked from my thoughts by rough fingers skimming down the side of my face, I looked back in horror to find the monster staring at me intently. There was a gleam in his eyes I'd seen many times from my nights in The Blind Dragon.

It seemed those were the only words I ever uttered: *stay away.*

Except now I couldn't.

I whimpered again, twisting my face away from his touch, and a shadow passed across his expression. At my movement, he held up his hand to show his bandage with the small amount of blood where his stinger had been. "Keep moving like that and I'll sting you again."

Just then, a giant *thud* came from above. The both of us glanced up at the ceiling, following the heavy banging noises with our eyes, even though we couldn't, of course, see through the metal.

What is happening?

The sounds stopped for a spell, while my pulse pounded harder than ever.

Then the window exploded.

Glass shattered, hitting the walls and raining down on my skin like tiny sharp pebbles. Heavy feet hit the carpet next to me and the monster backed up against the compartment door, his eyes wide with shock. I craned my neck back to catch a glimpse of Colt standing with one hand braced on the window frame, backlit against the morning sun. The wind whistled through like we were trapped in a tunnel.

Colt took a step forward and his gaze homed in on his opponent, glass crunching under his shoes. At the sound, my captor seemed to snap out of it. He ripped off his bandage and thrust out his palm. The stinger emerged, breaking through bloody skin and shooting out tiny stingers like darts. Colt threw up an arm and blocked a few from his face, the little needles embedding into the bare skin of his arm.

Colt then twisted back with his right hand like a pitcher and threw a large shard of glass like a throwing dagger. Distracted by the deadly sharp edges heading for him, the monster dropped his stinger hand and Colt lunged forward with a right cross to his face.

Dead center.

He went down, groaning in agony. Colt picked him up by the collar and held another shard in his hand, pressing it against the monster's neck.

"Tell me who sent you," Colt growled.

I twisted my hands again and again, the binding around them loosening. Maybe the monster had been too obsessed with other thoughts to do his job well. It also helped that the adrenaline pumping through me seemed to be overcoming the paralyzing poison. I could feel my aching muscles scream into consciousness.

"Her creator," the monster in the tweed jacket choked out under Colt's tight hold.

The strange term caught me off guard. My *creator*? How had someone *created* me?

"I need a name, old man." The muscles in Colt's back tightened as his grip grew stronger.

The monster just turned his head to the side, coughing.

"Tell me!" Colt shook the monster again, this time so hard that his head banged against the door.

I got the gag off, twisting and wrenching at the rope around my wrists until it had finally earned me freedom and a harsh rope burn. At last, I had some semblance of power. I could speak.

"He'll kill me," he moaned.

"*I'll* kill you," Colt growled, sounding like a feral beast.

"*Colt!*"

He turned at his name. Turned to look at me with wild, almost *red* eyes. Maybe I should've tried to use my voice on the monster who'd poisoned me—who had information about the people who were after me—but right now he wasn't the one who was scaring me.

I licked my lips and spoke words that I believed to be true. "*You're not a killer.*"

The magic in my voice permeated the air, thickening it with persuasion and conviction.

Colt stared at me for a long moment, then wrenched his hands away. His gaze, clear and angry, made me sure that it was not my magic that had stopped him. What had?

The monster slid down to the floor, gasping and wheezing. His wild gaze then focused on me. Absolute terror was there. Then, before either one of us could stop him, he pressed his stinger into his own neck. His eyes rolled back into his head and tiny bubbles frothed at the corner of his mouth.

Another tense moment passed as Colt ran his hands through his hair and jerked his shirt collar straight, sending another spray of glass tinkling to the ground. He glared at me over his shoulder. "You don't know *what* I am."

It was true. I didn't. He was something, but *what*, I couldn't hope to guess. Not yet. I knew nothing about him. Even what little traits I'd been able to glean at The Blind Dragon could be fake. All part of an act he'd been assigned to play.

Even so…I didn't think he *wanted* to be a killer.

I said nothing as Colt crouched and checked the monster's pulse. He shook his head and dropped his wrist. "Dead."

Shocked, I stared at the corpse on the floor. "He killed himself?" Had he been that scared of…of me? Of my power?

Colt shrugged. "Many men choose death over being captured. That way they escape torture, and the possibility of giving up information to their enemies."

I was still replaying the man's death over in my mind while Colt knelt before me and began untying the rest of my bindings.

"What are you doing?" I asked.

"I'd rather not cut the rope. Might be useful later, and it's not like the manticore needs it anymore."

"Is *that* what he was?"

Colt just nodded.

"Are you sure you *want* to untie me?" I muttered. I'd tried to escape him twice already.

He froze, then lifted his gaze to me. "Are you going to run away again?"

I glanced at the manticore, who'd seemingly been a nice gentleman trying to help me to my feet, but then turned out to have a stinger in his palm. I thought about the stabbed men on the platform, and the minotaur left at Dr. Boursaw's office. Destruction and death followed me like a trail of gasoline. What would be the match that ignited everything in my wake?

Colt was right. I needed to be brought in.

I'd sacrificed my voice for seven years for the independence and integrity of others. Sacrificing my freedom for their safety did not seem like such a bad deal.

Slowly, I shook my head. I wouldn't try to run again.

Colt held my gaze for another long moment, then he continued working on the ropes at my feet. Eventually, he got them unraveled and they slid off my ankles. I rubbed at the marks on my wrists. I was so tired of being bound.

"There's another one," I suddenly remembered with a gasp. The manticore had mentioned his "colleague" going after Colt. I moved to get up, but Colt raised his hand to stop me.

"Don't worry about him."

Slowly, I lowered myself back on the seat. “Why? What happened to him?”

Colt didn’t answer.

You’re not a killer.

You don’t know what I am.

Chapter Fourteen

The Agent

We left the dead manticore and headed back to our compartment. I took his briefcase with me, unsure whether or not anything useful would be in it. But I figured at this point, any clue could help. I also stole his hat. I'd lost mine back at the hotel when I was shot and moving around without one made me feel naked.

True to her word, Eris did not try to escape. She sat by the window, still as a statue, and watched the world pass by.

We didn't say a word to each other, but inside, I was burning.

Nothing could stop this incessant heat in my chest. This need to get rid of it. Every breath was difficult and I almost *wanted* her to try and run away again. It would give me something to do, something to chase, anything other than watch her sit there, resigned to a miserable, lonely fate. I tried to tell myself that the BOI would be the safest place for her, and for everyone, but I couldn't help but remember her words: "*Who's to say that what they would make me do wouldn't be just as monstrous?*"

Her words rang with a seed of truth. My own past with the BOI was proof enough.

Still...

I dug my knuckles into my temple and gritted my teeth. The old scars between my shoulder blades ached and I shifted in my seat to try to find a more comfortable position, even though I knew there wasn't one.

Since the beginning, nothing had sat right with this girl. Everything I'd come to learn about her was the exact opposite of what she was *supposed* to have been.

"*You're not a killer.*"

The broken body on the Connecticut coastline said different.

"Are you feeling all right?" Her soft voice pulled me out of my frustrations and I let loose a curse from under my breath.

And then she kept asking me things like *that.*

I lifted my head and met her eyes. It was the first time she looked at me since she'd asked what had happened to the other man—the one whose lifeless body lay miles and miles away.

"Not remotely." The words were out before I could take them back. I was finding it harder and harder to put on a show around this girl. To con and manipulate her like I'd done at The Blind Dragon, before I'd known her character.

The character of a girl who tried to save a person who had kidnapped her—not just myself but the manticore as well.

Christ, I was so confused.

So wrapped up in my own head, I didn't even notice she'd taken the seat next to me and was dabbing my cheek with a handkerchief. I leaned back, away from her gentle touch.

She frowned. "A piece of glass cut your cheek. You're bleeding."

Sure enough, my fingers came away red when I touched my face. It stung a little, but it didn't hurt. The injury was so minor, the idea of tending to it made me almost laugh.

"I'm fine."

"Then is it your shoulder? Did you open your stitches?"

I thought back to my fight and the man's heel digging into my wounded shoulder. "Probably," I answered with a sigh.

Her gaze dropped to my shirt collar and her fingers squeezed around the cloth. "Then we should check on it."

"I'm fine," I repeated.

"It could get infected, Colt."

At my name, my gaze cut to her and I suddenly felt *angry* seeing her there with concern on her innocent face. Why was she so nice? So compliant and caring? I'd stolen her away. Taken her from her home. Forced her to leave everyone she loved and everything she cared for behind. She should feel angry…she should feel…disgust.

It's what I felt.

All the time.

"It's not going to get infected," I replied, each word gruffer than the last.

"Oh, are you a doctor, too, then?" she said, placing one hand on her hip.

I suddenly leaned in so that our faces were close enough for our breaths to mingle. "I told you before, you don't know *what* I am."

Eris didn't move away. Instead, her eyes searched mine.

"I don't have to know what you are to know what you're not."

I'd never felt more disoriented. Even when I'd had seven straight shots of whiskey when McCarney took me out on my nineteenth birthday.

I sighed. "Eris, I have to take you in. I don't know what you're doing to me…pretending to care, or saying what I…"

My mouth was running wild. I shook my head. “But I *have* to. You’re too—”

“Dangerous. I know.” Her gaze was directed at her lap and the handkerchief that was wrinkled to hell now, her shoulders hunched. “I have to… I’ve gotta hope that the government will be a better choice than whoever is sending all these monsters after me.”

Ah. So that was it.

I leaned my head back against the wall, closing my eyes, feeling the rattle of the train as it continued onward to Philadelphia.

For the first time in a few years, I wished sleep would come easy to me. I’d grown used to stakeouts, to traveling all night, to staying awake while others slept, but all I wanted now was a way to quiet my mind. To slip into blissful ignorance.

I’d used to dream of doing just that every night for four years after that day…

“Colt?” Eris’s sweet voice asked.

“It won’t get infected,” I croaked. “I swear.”

I felt her get up from the seat next to me and heard her sit back down on the opposite bench.

We rode in silence the rest of the way.

The moment the train pulled into Philadelphia, I ushered Eris out of the compartment and down into the throng of passengers waiting to depart. She stuck close.

It was what I’d wanted, right?

Then why the hell did I feel like such shit?

Gritting my teeth, I pushed my way through the crowds on the train platform, still holding the briefcase from the manticore. I’d noticed the letters *BKH* in gold on the edge, and recognized them immediately. They were the exact same letters inside the rim of the minotaur's bowler hat. The briefcase had been locked, but I broke it easily and looked inside. There was nothing except academic papers.

So he'd been a professor of some sort. But he'd been employed by someone else…who? What mob boss had their hands in a university?

Any one of them I supposed. They had their connections to seemingly everyone and everything.

Broad Street Station of Philadelphia wasn't unlike the Boston depot with its crowds of people carting luggage and billows of smoke and train conductors yelling at the top of their lungs. Though the architecture was different with its gothic spires and arched windows, making the whole structure look more like a cathedral in Europe than a railway station in America.

Despite its massive size, it felt too small for the amount of people it held.

Without a word, I offered Eris my elbow, and she tucked her hand into the crook of it. Her fingers pressed into my arm through the fabric, and I felt the heat of her touch as much as the burn inside my chest and throat.

I wanted to make sure I didn't lose her again.

"Where are we going?" Eris asked as we stepped off the curb, leaving the train depot behind and crossing the streets milling with people in the early evening hours.

My stomach growled. Hell, I was hungry.

Just across the street was a deli and my mouth watered, imagining the smoked meat, the vinegar tang of mustard, and thick bread garnished with sesame seeds.

"Hungry?" I asked Eris.

"Starving," she answered.

Together, we waited amidst the commuters at the streetlight, and at the signal we crossed. Upon entering the deli, Eris dropped my arm and raced to the counter, immediately examining the fresh cut meat on display.

I joined her, watching how her gaze jumped from one meat to the next, her excited breath fogging up the clean glass.

Behind the counter stood a burly man with a thick black beard, who seemed absolutely delighted at Eris's entranced look. "Look and drool as much as you want, miss. More drooling tends to mean more cabbage in the register. Right, my young man?" he said, giving me a wink.

"Absolutely," I said.

"You two take your time," the man said as he went to help an older woman with her order.

"Have you never been to a deli before?" I asked Eris as she turned to the row of cheeses, her silky hair slipping over her shoulders.

She shook her head. "No, Stanley or Madame were the ones who ran errands most of the time. I wasn't allowed out too much."

Another dull ache traveled down my back, but I only shifted my stance and said nothing. What could I say? So I stayed silent as we looked at the menu, pretending to read the words in chalk.

"Settled on anything?"

The owner's voice made us both flinch—Eris more so than I. Seeming to understand Eris's timid nature, he leaned forward, his elbow on the counter, and started to weave a tale about his honey hams and smoked turkeys, describing each one like he would an old friend. Enthralled, Eris listened, her eyes widening as each sandwich was illustrated in delectable detail.

With her distracted, I decided now was a good time to plan our next move. Besides, I had to report to McCarney. The man was probably pulling his salt-and-pepper hair out. "Excuse me, sir? Might I be able to use your phone? I'll tip extra," I offered.

The owner waved his assent without even breaking stride in his storytelling.

Quickly, I looped around his counter and into the back where a phone hung on the wall next to a washroom. I waited impatiently for the operator.

"Hello, operator, how may I direct your call?" a smooth female voice said.

"Andromache epsilon five-zero-twenty-two," I said.

A pause, then, "One moment please."

"McCarney."

The man's voice was as close as I'd ever heard it to hysterics. He sounded breathless, wounded.

"Sir, it's Colt."

"Colt. *Jesus*. Where in the Jersey Devil have you been?" he hissed through the phone. "I've got half the team in Boston scouring the city."

"It would take too long to debrief you, sir, but I'm in Philly now."

"Philadelphia? The hell are you doing there?"

"Long story, sir. But I'm with the siren. She's agreed to come in." The words tasted like an ashtray for some reason.

"Has she now?" I heard a chair creak and pictured him leaning back in his dull gray desk chair. Pictured Barb clacking away on her typewriter. It felt like a lifetime ago and three continents away.

"Yes, sir."

"Then I'm sending backup to you. And, Colt? This is not up for debate. The last time you said you didn't need backup a goddamn hotel got shot up and I've had to clean up your mess all over Boston."

With all the other attempted kidnappings of Eris, I'd almost written off the shootout as the same as the rest. But the MO didn't match. For one, the shootout had intended to *kill* her, not kidnap her.

Something didn't sit right, but I didn't have enough evidence to tell McCarney that we might be dealing with *two* different groups after the siren. One who wanted her dead, and one who wanted her alive.

"Now," McCarney continued, "I can have two agents meet you within the hour. Where are you?"

I glanced out the window of the deli, saw the massive structure loom not so far in the distance. "Tell them to meet us under the Delaware Bridge."

"You got it. Be careful, Clemmons."

"Sir." I hung up and found Eris where I'd left her. She was laughing at a joke the owner must've told, her fingers gripping a toothpick with a sample of pastrami.

She looked happy. Carefree.

My chest burned hotter, so much that sweat broke out on the back of my neck.

I didn't want to do this.

But I have to.

Twenty minutes later and Eris had finished her whole sandwich—pastrami on rye—and was licking her fingertips of any rogue mustard.

I'd forced myself to eat half of mine and left the rest to the pigeons. Knowing what was to come, I'd lost my appetite, even as hungry as I'd been.

Now, we were on the side of the street, hailing a taxi to take us to Camden where we could wait under the Delaware River Bridge.

"Is your back all right? Did you hit it on the train?" she asked out of the blue.

I glanced away from the taxi emerging from the line of traffic and looked back at her, my pulse jumping. "It's fine.

Why do you ask?"

She shrugged. "You just keep shifting your weight. Like it's bothering you or something."

"It's fine," I said shortly.

"If you say so. You still haven't told me where we're going," she said as the taxi rolled to a stop, brakes squealing loudly. "DC?"

"We're meeting with some other agents. They'll help us get back to DC," I answered with a hard swallow as I pulled the door open for her.

She slipped inside and I followed, instructing the driver to take us to Fourth and Pearl Streets in Camden.

"Do you think once we get there I can call Madame?" she asked as the taxi turned down a congested street. "Just to tell her I'm okay?"

My throat scorched as I replied, "I'm sure that's possible."

The taxi continued its journey through the streets of Philly while Eris stared out the window. Sometimes, she leaned forward to look up at the three-story buildings—nothing she hadn't encountered in Boston—but when we got to the Delaware River Bridge, she bounced a little in her seat.

"That's the biggest bridge I've ever seen," she said with a *whoosh* of breath.

I gave a short laugh. "You should see the Brooklyn Bridge."

"Where's that?"

"New York City."

Eris scooted away from the window, back into the cushion of her seat.

I frowned. "You don't remember what happened to you in New York, do you?"

She shrugged. "Bits and pieces. I remember staying at this Catholic orphanage. The nuns took good care of us. I remember singing in a choir. But then this man…" She furrowed her brow, scowling out at the bridge as it loomed closer. "He was a benefactor of the orphanage. He came and took me away and then…then I really don't remember much… at least not until Madame Maldu took me into hiding." She shivered.

"It's okay, you don't have to try," I said quickly, not surprised at her discomfort, but shaken by it. It sounded so similar to my own experience.

An orphanage…then McCarney arriving and telling me that my country needed me. That I could be a soldier…

I hunched forward, resting my head in my hands and my elbows on my knees.

Then, a tentative hand on my back. Delicate fingers through the fabric of my jacket. "What's wrong?"

"Didn't you ever want to go back there?" I asked. My breath was like steam coming out, every word coated in smoke.

"Go back where?"

"New York. Find out who did this to you?"

She was quiet for so long that I finally turned to look at her. She'd pressed herself against the corner, her face half hidden in the shadow of the cab and her gaze fixed out the window.

"I don't like big cities."

"Why? All the flappers want to go there."

Eris hugged her arms, her hands rubbing up and down her skin and trailing over the sleeves of her maid's uniform. "Do I look like a flapper to you?"

No, she didn't. I'd thought that of her the first time I saw her. That she belonged in a different era. Maybe I'd seen her exactly how she wanted me to.

"I want to live in the country. In a small town where you know everyone's name and you bring soup to people when they're sick and pies to picnics." She gazed longingly outside as if she could see this little town of her dreams. "It's odd, I know. And I seem a bit of a bluenose but I've lived my whole life in cities. Speakeasies and high-rises and giggle water every night. *For so long, I feel like I've lived in the night. I just want to live in the sun.*"

She hadn't meant it to, but I felt her magic weave through the air of the cab. Felt the desire in her voice like a tangible thing.

Then she turned away from the window and fixed me with her blue-eyed stare. "All right, Mr. Agent. I've answered all your questions. It's time to be honest with me now. When I get to the capital, what are they going to do to me?"

I stared back at her, lost for words. I wanted to say that McCarney would take her in and we'd train her—for good. To work for the United States of America. To help her country. But now we knew for sure that there were people after her who knew her power. Was it safer for the country to kill her? Was it possible I'd been told to bring her in only to have her executed in the name of freedom?

And then...what if they experimented on her like they did on me for two years? Needles and tests and gallons of blood drawn...

Clasping my hands tight together, I opened my mouth to respond when the taxi came to a stop. "We're here, sir."

"Thank you," I said, dropping a fair amount of coins into the driver's outstretched palm.

I was turning to open my door when I noticed Eris thread her handkerchief between her teeth and tie it behind her head. Her movements were fluid and calm. Resolved.

Beyond the glass, under the massive concrete columns of the Delaware River Bridge I could see the two BOI agents we were to meet, standing outside their jalopy.

My stomach twisted and another puff of smoke came out through my labored breath.

Eris was gagging herself. She knew they wouldn't let her speak, knew they wouldn't trust her not to use her voice against them.

She shifted in her seat and held out her wrists.

Mechanically, like I wasn't in operation of my own limbs, I threaded the rope I'd taken from the manticore around her wrists and helped her out of the car, taking the briefcase with me.

As soon as we were out of the cab, the taxi driver peeled away, leaving a puff of smoke in his wake. Naturally, once he saw a girl gag herself, he knew something had to be amiss. Likely some kind of mob warfare he didn't want to be a part of.

Eris walked forward. She reminded me of a damsel walking the plank in a pirate story I'd heard once.

I followed, every step feeling like I was walking through once wet and now drying concrete. Pulling at my shoes and pants legs and yanking me down, and down, and down into the depths of hell itself.

"You got her!" a rough Brooklyn accent called from the jalopy. "Ace work, Clemmons!"

On the right was an Irish man with the signature red hair and pale skin—an agent named O'Connor. He was well known for his work as a yegg. He broke into mob dens and took everything from their safes then was gone in three minutes flat. On one occasion he used nitroglycerin and the ensuing mess almost got him chucked out of the BOI. The man on the left was a fella from Brooklyn, Frank Foster, once a gumshoe, now a recruited agent.

Neither of them were monsters. That I was aware of.

Foster let out a low whistle, bending slightly at the waist to peer beyond the curtains of chestnut and auburn waves to get a look at the lost siren's face. "Hoo boy. She's quite the dish, ain't she?"

"Did she give you a lot of trouble, Clemmons? What put you in Philly?" O'Connor asked in his thick Irish brogue.

I was too busy watching Eris. She was completely still. Frozen like a statue with…fear? Resolve? I ached to know.

"Clemmons?"

"She came willingly," I finally choked out. It was hard to breathe through the inferno in my chest.

Foster's thick brows rose clear into his forehead, almost touching his hairline. "Did she? Not according to some copper reports from Boston."

"We ran into some trouble. Her creator is trying to get her back."

O'Connor scratched his chin. "How'd he find her?"

"Don't know yet," I grumbled, my gaze shooting to the briefcase in my hand. *BKH* was my only clue right now.

"Well, doesn't matter now. We'll get her to the Bureau." Foster grabbed Eris's arm, but she went without any encouragement, her short heels clicking and shuffling over the concrete.

O'Connor opened the back door of their jalopy. I was staring, while my whole body remained stiff. The heat still burned inside, relentless.

As Eris slid into the back, I noticed a violin case tucked halfway under the seats.

The *rat-a-tat-tat* sound of the tommy guns clicking and lead firing through the walls of the hotel echoed through my head.

We fought gangsters to make America a better, safer place.

But tainting another innocent soul with blood…was that truly doing good?

It felt wrong. Turning her in felt *wrong*.

My mind flashed with old memories. Of my time at the BOI. Those years of "training." I'd committed my first murders there. Learned to kill or be killed.

How could I bring Eris into this?

She was a girl whose dream was bringing pies to a neighborly picnic out in the country, under the shade of sassafras trees.

Before the door could close on her, I caught the edge with my left hand.

"Clemmons?" Foster's voice came from far, far away.

Eris stared up at me, the handkerchief still between her lips and her brow furrowed in confusion. Her eyes searched mine, and I could see her trying to understand who I was. I'd tricked her before, then showed her my real self. And now... now what was I doing?

"Clemmons, what's wrong? Speak up, man." O'Connor's strong hand came down on my shoulder.

My grip tightened on the briefcase I still held.

Behind me, I heard O'Connor thread his other hand into his jacket. I knew he was reaching for his BOI-issued Savage.

I closed my eyes and took one long, cool breath. The heat in my chest...gone.

I'd made my choice.

Then I twisted, the briefcase following, its gold-plated corner smashing into the cheek of my fellow BOI agent.

Chapter Fifteen

The Siren

I winced as the briefcase made contact with the agent's face and an awful cracking sound ensued. Something heavy dropped to the ground as a nasty curse word rang through the air.

The wind whistled under the gargantuan bridge as two men grappled against the car's side, their movements shaking its interior. A gun fired once—twice. Three times.

A body slid against the window with a soft squealing sound. And a groan.

When I opened my eyes again, Colt was kneeling on the ground in the doorway of the jalopy, his chest rising and falling rapidly.

After catching his breath, he finally moved in to untie the gag around my mouth. It loosened and fell to my lap.

"Are you ready, Eris?" he asked, still breathless from the fight he'd just initiated.

My hands shook. "Ready for what?"

"To fight for your freedom."

As I stared at him, attempting to process each word, he pulled out a switchblade he must've stolen from one of the agents and quickly cut through the ropes around my wrists. They slid from my hands like snakes and dropped to the floor of the jalopy.

"But you said I was too dangerous," I said, my voice hoarse.

"You are," Colt said with a jerky nod, his expression more troubled than I'd ever seen it—even when he'd been shot and was bleeding out on the veterinarian's steel table.

I didn't understand. "Then…why?"

He gripped my hands, pulling me near, gently. The pebbles under his knee crunched as he shifted closer. The rim of his hat nudged my forehead and pushed the fedora up slightly so I could see more of his dark brown irises.

"When I went to The Blind Dragon, I was expecting to find a monster. What I found…was you."

Without a second thought, I threw my arms around his neck, burying my face in his good shoulder. Tears leaked out and dampened his soft collar. They'd been threatening to fall for some time. Through everything, I'd held them back, but now I no longer could.

Surprisingly, he was incredibly stiff under my arms. With his handsome face, I would've taken him as used to having women throw themselves at him.

Embarrassed, I drew back, wiping my tears with the back of my hand. With a soft chuckle, he picked up the handkerchief that had been looped around my neck.

"Here, doll."

I took the cloth and wiped at my eyes and runny nose. My neck flushed from the affectionate tone. Had he even noticed it himself?

"We should get going," he said, turning businesslike once more. "Before they wake up."

One of the reasons I'd decided to go along with the BOI was because I had agreed with them. I was dangerous to the people around me. But...but I didn't *want* to be. Didn't that count for something?

And maybe I could change. Maybe I could finally learn how to control this power in a way I'd never dreamed.

Obviously Colt had to believe it was possible, otherwise he wouldn't be helping me.

I owed it to myself to at least try.

"I'm ready," I said, my voice muffled behind the handkerchief. Then I lifted my puffy eyes up to Colt's and lowered the cloth. "To fight."

A small smile tugged at the corner of his lips. "Let's hit the road, then."

We left the BOI agents untied and leaning against one of the giant pillars of the Delaware River Bridge, a hundred cars and however many more tons hanging above their heads. But we took their black jalopy.

Colt was a good driver. He expertly shifted the stick and peeled out onto the road, a cloud of dust flying up behind us. In no time, the great city of Philadelphia was only a small dot in the mirrors. Like on the train, we rode in silence, a new uncharted territory stretched between us.

While Colt had been maneuvering through the complicated streets of Philly, I'd kept quiet, knowing he had to concentrate on driving. But now that we were on the open road, driving past fields and rolling hills, shifting from a summer green to an autumn gold, I had to know his plan. When he asked if I was ready to fight, what had he truly meant? Did it mean he actually wanted me to use my voice?

"So where are we headed?" I asked over the rumble of

the jalopy's engine and the whistle of wind through cracked windows.

"Chicago."

The name of the Windy City gave me chills. I shrank back in my seat, pressing myself against the door as if I suddenly wanted to jump out...and I greatly considered it.

Chicago was New York City's twin in crime and nightlife. In gangsters and rum-running. In murder and most assuredly, now that I knew they existed, monsters.

Colt cast me a sideways glance and frowned. "I know you don't like large cities, but there's someone who might be able to help us figure out who's after you."

"So you're...you're really planning to find out who put my pearl in?" I swallowed, feeling the magical object in question on my tongue.

"If we ran, they'd find us. Somehow they've been able to track you ever since you left The Blind Dragon. It's only a matter of time before they send someone to Philly. We need to stay one step ahead. If you *really* want to be free, we have to stop whoever's after you."

"Maybe they found me like you found me and just followed us around Boston."

A muscle ticked in Colt's jaw as he pressed the gas a little harder, and the engine roared beneath. "Maybe. But if they found you at the Dragon then why didn't they make their move sooner? They wouldn't have cared if they captured an innocent girl, and they also could've recognized you. Instead, they wait until you're in the hands of a BOI agent? No, I think they didn't know where you were until you started speaking at the hotel."

"Is that why they shot up the room? Because they wanted to get to me?"

"That doesn't make much sense, either. They don't want to kill you, they want to kidnap you. Call me paranoid, but I think there might be two groups after you."

"Three. You're forgetting about the BOI."

Colt didn't say anything for a long while. Finally, he replied, "McCarney's top priority is national security. He'll do whatever it takes."

"McCarney?" I asked.

"Director McCarney of the Specialized Organized Crime Division of the Bureau of Investigation. He's a bit to me like Madame Maldu is to you…a foster parent. He watched out for me when I was recruited by the SOCD."

"And you betrayed him." The words were out before I could take them back. "For me."

Colt's hands clenched on the wheel and he squinted at the road ahead. Silent.

I licked my lips and tucked a loose piece of hair behind my ear. "I'm sorry—"

"*Eris.*" My name was harsh, gruff. Almost like a growl. "Don't apologize. It's my decision. Not yours to bear."

My gaze shifted back to the endless stretch of asphalt leading us to a city of demons and monsters. I wanted, more than anything, to be going in the opposite direction.

I took a deep breath. *Fight.* That's what I was going to do now.

"The point is, once you started speaking and using your power, your creator might have found you through a trace in your magic."

"But I've spoken a few times before."

"How often and how many words?"

I thought back to the incidents over the years. "Maybe five times since being at The Blind Dragon. Never more than a sentence at a time."

"I think that's what's different. At the hotel, you talked for ten minutes, saying over two hundred words. The whole room was full of magic."

A jolt of realization went through me and I whispered, "Does that mean I shouldn't—"

Colt reached over and grabbed my hand, squeezing it.

The gesture was so surprising a wave of shivers went up my arm.

"No, keep talking. What's done is done, and besides, if you have a voice, you should be able to use it. No one should take that from you."

I bit my bottom lip, thinking over his words as he let go of my hand and returned both to the steering wheel. So many silent years...he was right. All along, I'd wanted to be heard.

"But tracing my power...how is that even possible?" I asked.

"Whenever monsters are made there's a special substance used to fuse their human nervous system with that of a monster's properties. They call it the *chimera agent.* It was essentially the piece of the puzzle that allowed humans to survive once monster parts were infused with them."

"Chimera? I don't know that word."

"It's what we are," Colt said with a heavy sigh.

Before I could ask what he meant by *we*, Colt continued, "In the Greek myths, a chimera is a monster that has different animal parts all fused together to make one creature. A lion's head on a goat's body with a serpent's tail."

"Sounds horrific."

He blew out a tired laugh. "It is. But it's also special because of its ability to possess multiple animal genes." His gaze cut to me quickly, then went back to the road. "Do you know what genetics is?"

I lifted my shoulder in a half shrug. "Vaguely. It's what makes up a family tree, right?"

"Yes, parents pass on traits to their children and we call them genes. So all humans have genes like brown hair or blue eyes, but humans with monster parts also contain monster genes. Monster genes make us chimeras because, like the monster itself, it means we possess two kinds of genetics—monster and human."

"That's unbelievable."

"But possible. It's a breakthrough science. Decades ahead of its time, but that's the world we live in. Men with money can buy anything. Even the most brilliant scientists on the planet."

"So what does this have to do with my creator and the fact that he could find me?"

"Right." Colt tapped his fingers on the steering wheel. "Well, when the first experiments to fuse a monster part with a human failed, they realized it was because humans were unable to support both gene types. So they inserted the blood of a monster that can possess different genes—"

"A chimera," I whispered, unable to keep the horror out of my voice.

Colt nodded. "They inserted chimera blood into humans, and if the blood didn't kill them, then they were able to be fused with a monster part."

Rearing back, my gut clenched and rolled with disgust. The pastrami on rye sandwich now seemed like a terrible idea as my poor stomach wanted to reject it. Breathing in through my nose, I tried to sweep the nausea away.

"You're...you're saying I have both a chimera and a siren inside me?"

Colt nodded, his jaw still clenched. He looked just as disgusted as I felt.

"Over the years, scientists have tampered with the chimera's blood, trying to make it more adaptable to humans. There's hundreds of versions of chimera agents out there, so it's possible that *your* agent had been infused with some other monster's genes that allows it to be trackable somehow."

"Trackable by what?"

"I'm not entirely sure. But as long as the BOI have been fighting monsters, we've always been a step behind. Maybe not for every drop or stakeout or mission, but there've been times when..." He trailed off. Then he cleared his throat and his grip twisting on the steering wheel made a squeaking noise. "Regardless, I believe they'll be able to find you, no matter where you go. The only reason the BOI was able to find you was because another agent had been in The Blind Dragon the night you stopped a bullet."

"So we're going to Chicago because someone there might know how my creator is tracking me?"

A corner of his lips quirked into a half smile. "Now you're on the trolley."

America's wilderness, or what I could see of it from the front seat of a car, was everything I'd dreamed it to be. I rode with my face pressed against the glass, staring out at the Pennsylvania countryside and drinking in the view like I was a drunkard off his ten-hour shift tossing back a few rounds of corn.

Fields of color looked like an artist had dropped his paint can and splashed coat upon coat of rich autumn hues. Dark evergreen boughs and brilliant red maple leaves, golden rows of wheat, and pure white wildflowers dotted amidst emerald green. The chill in the autumn air told me they wouldn't last much longer, so I thanked God that I had the chance to see them now.

Colt let me look on, driving in silence. He was a constant presence in my mind, but not an imposing or unwelcome one.

For the first time in seven years I could finally, *finally* talk to someone. The fella next to me was immune to the charms of my voice. I *should* have been talking his ears off.

But I wasn't.

The impulse to stay quiet was deeply ingrained, a part of my bloodstream like the need to sing. For so long I'd resisted the urge to talk, and now that I finally had the chance to, I had no idea what to say.

I wanted to ask him everything—starting with what *he* was, and then questions such as, what was it like to work for the BOI and hunt monsters? Where had he grown up? What places had he been to? How did he become such a good fighter? Did he step into the boxing ring for some extra cash like Stanley?

And yet my tongue seemed glued to the roof of my mouth, resting against my pearl. That blasted thing that everyone wanted so much.

That's when I had a question I *had* to ask.

"Can't I just remove it?"

Colt flinched at the sound of my voice, almost like he'd forgotten I was there. "Remove what?" he asked.

"The pearl. Can we get a dentist to take it out or something?"

A single beat passed, like the beat in a song, before Colt shifted gears and braked, swerving onto the shoulder of the road. It was so sudden, my hands flew to the door to keep me from sliding off the seat and in case I needed a quick escape.

Colt twisted toward me, fixing me with an intense stare. "Never, *ever* get your pearl taken out."

"W-Why? What will happen?"

"Well, you could die, for one," Colt growled. "It's not a tooth extraction, Eris. It's part of you. It would be like removing an organ and trying to ankle your way down Times Square at five o'clock."

"How do you know? Have other monsters had their parts…removed and survived?"

Colt turned back to face the front, then looked out his

driver side window. “Just…trust me on this one. Removing the part won’t stop you from being a monster.”

Scanning him up and down, it hit me. I was like one of the bugs on our windshield. I hadn’t seen it coming.

He’d had his part removed. *Whatever* it had been, on wherever, was gone.

I gaped at him, for an incredibly rude amount of time. Even when he calmly put the car back into drive, checked over his shoulder and pulled onto the road, I was still staring.

He probably guessed I’d more or less figured it out, and I wondered if he was just *waiting* for me to ask all the questions running through my head.

What had he removed? How had he removed it? How had he survived it if it was so terrible?

Balling my hands into fists in my lap, I remained silent. Sometimes, being trained not to speak was a good thing.

We didn’t talk again until a gas station came up on the side of the road and Colt turned into it.

I was relieved we stopped. I had to iron my shoelaces, and my legs were getting antsy with the need to get up and walk a bit.

As he pulled next to a pump and shut off the engine, I opened the door. “I’m going to freshen up.”

Colt merely nodded as the gas attendant who’d been snoozing in the shade perked up and started toward the car.

I was two steps away when he called me back. “Eris.”

I turned and tried to give him a reassuring smile. “I’m not going to go anywhere.”

He was leaning over the car top, and at my words, he shook his head with a chuckle. “I wasn’t worried about that. Here.” He held out a crisp dollar bill. “Get us a couple of

Cokes."

I crossed back to the car and slid the bill from between his fingers and waved it with a small smile. "You don't want some coffee? It's a long drive."

He tipped back his hat, giving me a better view of his face. "The drive'll be duck soup. Besides, you know I prefer tea."

I folded the bill once, twice, then tucked it into the pocket of my apron and met his gaze. "Do I?" I asked. He had been playing a part at The Blind Dragon. Everything I knew about him could be a lie.

Any hint of a smile dropped from his face.

Before I could take it back, I turned on my heel and entered the store. As the door swung shut behind me, the little bell went off. A bored clerk raised his head from his magazine, then returned to reading when he saw me make my way toward the restroom.

After washing my hands and splashing some cool water on my face, I looked at my reflection in the mirror.

The girl who stared back had on a wrinkled maid's uniform, mussed-up waves, and dark circles under her eyes.

I slapped my cheeks and pinched them to give them some color but it was a useless endeavor. I was a right mess. And very tired. I hadn't slept in well over twenty-four hours and on top of that whenever I spoke too much the magic in my voice seemed to double my fatigue. Not by a lot, but noticeably.

It was almost sundown. I couldn't believe that just last night I'd been in the Dragon serving drinks as usual. But with everything that happened since the moment I'd stepped into the alley, it felt like a lifetime.

Threading my damp fingers through my hair, I took one long, deep breath then headed back out into the store. The clerk hadn't moved. Unsurprisingly. But what I hadn't noticed before I walked into the restroom was a phone in the dimly lit hallway to my right.

A phone.

Since I was no longer going to DC, I couldn't very well follow my original plan to call Madame from a BOI cell block.

A powerful force rose inside me that threatened to knock me over. Longing. Since the very beginning of this wild journey, I'd tried hard not to think about Madame, Stanley, and my beloved little band—Marv, Francis, David—because I knew that life was gone. If I went back, I'd endanger all of them. But now that I was here, standing before a phone, knowing that their voices were merely a call away, I missed them more than I'd ever dreamed possible.

Moving quickly, and not second-guessing my impulse decision, I pulled two Cokes out of the cooler and set them on the clerk's counter with a loud *clack, clack* of glass hitting wood.

Almost irritated that I'd interrupted his precious reading time, the older balding man looked up from his copy of *Time* magazine.

"I'd like to purchase these, *please*."

The clerk leaped into action, his hands moving fast to type out numbers in the register and whip out a paper bag for my purchase—all rushed, hurried, almost *panicked* movements.

My own anxiety had forced him to move quickly and desperately. This knowledge churned my insides as he took my dollar and handed me back my change—a pile of coins that felt cold in my hot palm.

With my change in one hand and my paper bag of chilled Cokes in the other, I hurried back to the hallway and inserted two nickels into the old pay phone.

"Hello, operator, how may I direct your call?"

I gave the only number I knew. The phone in Madame Maldu's parlor.

My heart pounded like the short, blaring trumpet blasts

in "Shanghai Shuffle." Would she even answer? I didn't have time to wait around and call again. Colt could be back any moment.

The phone rang and rang through the receiver, and with each ring my heart dropped lower and lower. Just when I thought it was useless, the phone line clicked and there was a deep, "Hello?" on the other end.

Stan.

"Hello, Stan? It's me," I said quickly, then, realizing that he may have heard me talk only once before, I added, "Eris."

"Eris?" The voice was breathless. Shocked. "You…you're talking. Where are you, kid? Are you all right?"

"I'm safe," I answered, giving him the best, shortest answer I could. "I just…I just wanted to let you and Madame know that. So you wouldn't be worried about me."

"Of course we're worried." Each syllable sounded strained. "Tell me where you are. Whatever trouble you're in, we can get you out of it. I'll come get you right now."

My eyes burned and I squeezed the cord between my fingers. I opened my mouth a few times, but only squeaking came out. I missed him so much, but how could I tell him the truth? That I was a monster and on the run with another monster who hunted monsters?

"Eris? You still there, kid? Don't go silent on me now."

Resting my forehead against the top of the phone box, I swallowed. "Stan, I need to speak to Madame. Can you put her on the phone for me?"

"She's…" A long silence on the other end and my heart pounded painfully.

"She's what?"

Across the store, a bell dinged. It was unlikely the lazy clerk had stepped out, so someone must have entered. Colt.

"She…well, she went to New York to look for you, kid."

"*What?*"

"She went to New York to look for you," Stan repeated in an almost mechanical tone, and I realized I'd made him do so.

I cursed the magic in my voice and stamped my foot, just as I noticed Colt's gray fedora move over the tops of the aisles, making its way toward the back.

Sending a silent prayer of forgiveness, to God, to Stan, to whoever might be listening, I magicked my bartender with a purposeful command. "*Stanley, don't try to look for me. Tell Madame that I'm fine and that she should come home. And… be careful. Stay safe.*"

I could imagine Stan in the parlor, the phone to his ear, staring into space, letting my command wash over him and seep into his bones.

Pushing through my sudden wave of exhaustion, I hung up the phone and hurried through the aisles, nearly colliding into Colt. He grabbed me by the elbows as my short heels slipped on the waxed wood floor, just before I twisted an ankle.

"Easy," Colt said as he steadied me. "Worried I'd leave without you? I'm the one always after you, remember?" Before I could respond, he gave a nod toward the restrooms. "Just hang tight. I'll be right back."

Standing there in the aisle, I scrubbed hard at my eyes, turning the dark circles into red blotches.

Talking to Stan had been one of the hardest things I'd ever done in my life, and for as long as I could remember, I'd always wanted to talk to him. The irony was painful.

Leaving him, and Madame, and my band was excruciating. But now Madame wouldn't have to worry about me and she could live her quietly glamorous life of speakeasies and rum-running. Even a life of crime had to be safer than a life with a monster.

With a heavy sigh, I stumbled my way back to the car and

slipped into the passenger seat. Colt came out a few minutes later, but instead of going straight for the driver's side, he looped around the car and opened my door. Kneeling down in the dusty parking lot, he reached into a brown paper bag he'd been carrying and pulled out a clean white roll of gauze and a small tin of ointment. I recognized it as a salve for burns.

My rope burns.

Entranced, I watched as with gentle fingers, Colt took my right wrist and rubbed the salve over my red, raw skin. Then he did the other one, methodically, covering each inch where the binds had made their marks. His thumb brushed over my pulse and I swear it skipped.

I swallowed while he wrapped strips of the gauze around my wrists. My skin tingled from either the salve, or his touch—I honestly couldn't be sure which.

Then, without a word, he stood and moved back around the car to slide behind the wheel. It was only by the time he peeled out onto the highway did I realize I hadn't even thanked him.

But I couldn't somehow. Not because I didn't want to, but because if I spoke I might start crying again. Oddly, the tears wouldn't even be for me, but for Colt. I'd been so obsessed with my own little family, I hadn't even thought of what he was leaving behind as well.

That McCarney cat or whoever he was… Not only would Colt never see him again, but Colt had betrayed someone who was like a father to him. *All for my sake.*

So even though he'd manipulated me in the past, fooled me into thinking he was a nice fella who liked orange pekoe… when someone turns their back on their whole world for you—the people they cared for, their job, and their beliefs…

Then they deserved a second chance.

Chapter Sixteen

The Agent

When we got back on the road, the sun was setting directly ahead. I had to squint and pull my hat lower over my eyes to try and offer some kind of shade against its radiant glow.

Eris sat in the passenger seat, quietly sipping on her cola. The condensation dripped down the bottle and trickled over her fingers, dropping onto her apron in dark water spots.

Over the sound of the tires on asphalt and the wind outside, I kept hearing her voice in my head ask, *Do I?*

Her words stung more than they should've. Given the way I'd conned her, it was natural that she'd be wondering whether anything I'd said at the Dragon was the truth or not.

I wanted to take it all back—make her trust me again. Not just because I wanted to help her survive and get her freedom, but because I wanted to get to know her.

The only problem was that I didn't know how to make her warm up to me again. Unlike before, I couldn't turn on the charm. That worked once, but it wouldn't work a second time. Besides, I didn't *want* to. I wanted to return the open honesty she'd always shown me. But how would I even start?

"How far west have you gone? Have you been to California?"

My pulse jumped at her voice, and I resisted the urge to glance over. I flexed my fingers on the wheel. These seemingly simple questions felt significant somehow. Like an olive branch. Or maybe I was interpreting it wrong. Maybe I was being too hopeful.

"Just once. There aren't many monsters to hunt in California. Smaller cities. Fewer places for crime bosses to really seize control. It's a beautiful state, though, and the California Redwoods are a sight to behold."

"What are those?"

"Huge sequoia trees. It's like the tops of them can touch the sky. I've never seen trees that tall or that wide. And there are whole forests of them up and down the hills along the northern coasts."

I'd ridden, unable to take my eyes off them, through one of the forests with McCarney on horseback, following the trail of a mass killer. The man was a POW from the Spanish–American War who'd escaped the military prison of Alcatraz off the coast of San Francisco. But Eris didn't need to know all that.

"They sound incredible. It would be just darb to go see them," Eris said, her voice full of longing and wonder.

"Maybe you can go one day, after all this is over."

Eris yawned and settled back into her seat. The springs shifted and the leather squeaked, as she said sleepily, "I sure hope so."

We'd barely gone another mile before the rhythm of her breathing changed into something deep and slow. We hadn't gone five before her head rolled onto my shoulder.

My heart roared like the engine of a hayburner in the middle of the Brooklyn Bridge, echoing over the waters of the East River.

We drove through the night until I noticed the gas gauge droop to worrisome levels. So I found a gas station and parked to wait for it to open. There was no point in driving further if we were going to run out of gas.

When I cut the engine I would've thought that the squealing brakes or the lack of the monotonous sound would've awoken Eris, but she slept on. Without driving to concentrate on, I was forced to acknowledge the warmth of her against my side and the smell of her. Back at The Blind Dragon, so much of her scent had been the alcohol and the cigs, and even though she didn't partake in any of them it still painted her skin like fresh varnish.

But now her unique fragrance filled the car until it was all I could breathe. She was unlike anything I'd smelled before. Better than the sweetest treat from my favorite bakery in DC.

Mentally, I groaned. Troublesome thoughts swirled in my head like thick gasper smoke. The desire to wind my arms around her slim shoulders and pull her to my chest—to protect her—was more than just an impulse. It was a need.

But I didn't. I kept still and watched the stars, unmoving, in the black night sky.

At some point, I wasn't sure how much later, she shivered against me. With the utmost care, I leaned to the side, allowing her head and upper torso to fall gently against my chest. From there, I guided her head to rest on my right thigh and slipped my arms out of my jacket. Then I draped the jacket over her sleeping form like a blanket.

Then, like it was the most natural thing in the world, I brushed a piece of hair away from her cheek. I sucked in a breath. *Damn. What am I doing?*

Stretching my arms across the back of the seat, I returned my attention to the stars. They twinkled back at me mockingly, as if to sing, "*You're such a fool.*"

Eris finally woke up when I turned the car engine on after the gas station worker flipped over the OPEN sign. She pulled up so hard and fast that it was a miracle she missed hitting the steering wheel.

"Where are we?" she said blearily, rubbing her eyes.

"A little outside Cleveland," I answered, parking next to the first pump.

"Where's that?"

I got out of the car. "Ohio. About seven hours or so from Chicago."

She followed me out. "Did you sleep at all?" From her tone I could've sworn she was worried about me.

"A few hours. I'm fine."

"We could rest a little more if you needed—"

"No, we shouldn't take any chances. Let's keep moving."

She nodded, then glanced down, holding out my jacket while her cheeks turned a shade of poppy red. "Thank you for your jacket. It was really…swell of you."

I moved my hand down my mouth and across my jaw to get rid of any sort of goofy smile. "Keep it. You'll freeze your mitts off without a real coat."

With gas in the tank and breakfast in our stomachs, we got on the road once more to head for the Windy City.

Mark Twain once said, "*It is hopeless for the occasional visitor to try to keep up with Chicago—she outgrows his prophecies faster than he can make them. She is always a novelty; for she is never the Chicago you saw when you passed through the last time.*"

I understood his words deeply. Chicago was always

changing—it was a twisting menagerie of art, culture, murder, politics, business, crime, and, above all, monsters. It felt like I was here every other month chasing down a freshly made beast dripping blood on the pavement—not to mention a fancy new skyscraper climbing its way toward the heavens as if to touch God Himself.

If He was even up there.

Driving into Chicago, Eris became much more subdued. The last few hours we'd been talking, which felt...precious. Our conversations hadn't been about anything too significant, but then, that's what made them so important. She told me about when her bartender, Stanley, took her to see a Red Sox game. He spent the whole time explaining to her the rules of baseball and while she barely understood them, she recalled it as one of the best times of her life.

She asked me about my favorite cities and what kind of food I'd tried in New York. She asked about Broadway shows like *Show Boat* and *Don Juan* and jazz bands. She even wanted to know about our nation's capital and the Lincoln Memorial, only seven years old but already promising to be one of the most famous.

For a girl who seemed to spend most of her days in a dim speakeasy, she was incredibly knowledgeable. I could almost see her, picking up newspapers left by patrons at closing time, and reading for hours on end about a world just outside that nondescript door.

"Everything is so big," Eris whispered into the corner of the window, craning her neck to view the latest skyscraper going up.

Indeed it all was. The so-called "giants" of the city made sure of it, enlisting famously brilliant architects and drafting great plans, determined to not only meet their former glory before the Great Fire of 1871 but far surpass it. And they'd done it.

Keeping my gaze on the road, I maneuvered us through the hellish traffic. The jalopies and hayburners, men on horseback and people in carriages, newsies dodging in between bumpers, waving their papers.

"So where is this friend of yours?" Eris asked, her gaze on a passing streetcar with red paint and gilded gold trim.

"A drum in the heart of downtown."

Eris blew out a breath. "Of course. A speakeasy. Why couldn't they be a curator in a museum?"

I laughed. "Actually, this specific monster would make a good historian."

"What's that supposed to mean?"

"You'll see." I tried to make it sound teasing because I didn't want to scare her unnecessarily. She had plenty of reason to be scared already.

Eris folded her arms and wrinkled her nose. "Fine, so what now? The drum won't be open till dusk."

It was then that I swerved the car into a space that another had just vacated, angering three other cars behind me that likely wanted the same spot. "We need to get you something else to wear."

"What's wrong with what I'm wearing?" she asked, glancing down at her uniform. "It's rather comfortable."

"Eris, you can't wear a maid's uniform to a speakeasy."

She huffed and rolled her eyes but followed me out of the car anyway. With the manticore's briefcase in hand, I fell into step beside her and we headed down Third Avenue.

Queen Vicky's was a high-end, high-society, high-price, high-everything boutique that had been in Chicago for at least two generations.

I could've taken Eris to a new fancy department store—

like Sears or Macy's—to get her a new dress, but I needed to talk to the tailor. He had old familial connections to one of the head gangsters in East Chicago, and I figured that if anyone in this city would know what *BKH* stood for, it would be him.

As we entered the high-ceiling boutique, Eris inhaled sharply.

It *was* impressive.

The floors were marble imported from Italy, all white and gray and light blue swirls in a sea of soft cream. Moldings lined the corners in extravagant patterns like that from ancient Greece. A crystal chandelier hung in the middle, lit up with bright yellow electricity. Dresses and suits hung on silver racks while a few strategically placed and posed mannequins stood on elevated daises sporting the latest and greatest fashions.

"Colt Clemmons, as I live and breathe," a low, smoky voice said from the back of the store. A thin older woman with string upon string of oyster fruit around her neck and bobbed silver hair emerged from beyond the silk curtain hanging in the back of the store. Belva Murdeena once told me she received that curtain from a sheikh in Arabia who claimed to be in love with her. A bunch of phonus balonus, but Belva Murdeena sold extravagance and embellishment, so it naturally flowed from her like spilled glass bottles on milk day.

I carved a smile onto my face and took off my hat, drawing it to my chest with a slight bend at my waist. "Belva, you look a vision as always."

Belva moved toward us, her dress flowing around her thin frame and the tassels brushing against her calves. "Always," she agreed with a smile on her red lips. Then she slid her painted eyes over to Eris, looking at her from head to toe.

"And who is this unfortunate creature? Your latest

squeeze?" She *tsked* as she plucked at Eris's uniform with long fingernails. "If you were going to pick up the help you could've at least gotten one from the Ritz Carlton. Plenty of girls there looking to join your wild, adventurous lifestyle."

I'd only met Belva once when I'd been shadowing Sawyer, but apparently I'd made an impression on her. How would Sawyer handle this? He'd probably schmooze her up. I didn't like the idea, but I needed her husband's help.

Sometimes the ends justify the means. Another lesson from McCarney.

Unable to stop myself, I glanced down at Eris once more. She was looking at Belva with curiosity as if the shop owner was indeed an artifact in a museum. "She's not joining anything, Belva. She's just a friend in need of your help. Besides, you're the only dame for me," I said, flashing her a white smile.

Belva threw her head back, exposing her wrinkled, swan-like neck. "Oh, Colt. I would believe that if you could both stop gazing at each other like a couple of lovesick fools."

Eris stiffened, dropping my arm.

Dammit. Clearing my throat, I stepped away from Eris. "Belva—"

"Not another word of your so-called flirting, you handsome devil, your *friend* and I have quite a bit of work to do." She grabbed Eris by the shoulders and drew her toward the side of the shop with flapper dresses covered in sequins and sparkles. As they walked, Belva glanced over her shoulder. "Now, do be a dear and go after what you *really* came for. Gus is in the back."

Astute woman.

Eris threw me a shaky smile as she was steered away. After returning her smile, I ducked behind the Arabian sheikh's curtains and followed the sound of a sewing machine.

Gus Murdeena was the second son of one of Chicago's

oldest crime families. They came from Dublin, wanting to make their American fortune, and found it in tailoring and safe-cracking.

Gus was hunched over a sewing machine when I walked into the back room, moving a strip of fabric steadily under the rapid needle, cheaters on and large nose so close that it was in danger of being sewn into the dress.

At my steps, he looked up. His eyes narrowed. "Colt Clemmons," he grumbled.

Unlike his wife, Gus was a practical man with…simpler tastes. He didn't care for my "wild, adventurous lifestyle" and he detested the monster trade. In fact, it was when his brother started using monsters as trigger men that Gus began his role as a BOI informant.

"That fool McCarney still using a *boy* to run his dirty errands?" Gus shook his head and turned off the machine, leaning back in his chair to rub his eyes.

At nineteen, I was hardly a boy. To be honest, I'd stopped being one the moment I woke up a monster on the BOI's operating table.

"I'm not working with the BOI on this one, Gus."

He blinked his watery blue eyes and frowned, running a hand over his thinning hair. "You know I don't approve of what they did to you, lad. But you need their protection. You've still got—"

"There's someone else who needs protection more than me. Someone is after this girl—she's a monster. Made one about eight years ago and she doesn't remember much. Not the name, nor the face of her creator. I figured the only way to keep her safe is to find this creator. At the very least, I need to know who we're running from."

Gus stared at me through his thick lenses for a long time before he blew out a harsh breath. "So what do you need from me?"

"I've got to get in to see Gin tonight. Do you think you can arrange it?"

Gus folded his arms and scowled. "Short notice, but I can make a few calls. Mind you, I can only get you through the door. You'll have to do the rest."

"That's all I'll need."

Gus grunted and returned to his sewing machine, inspecting the stitches he'd just made and their tiny perfect lines. "So why are you still here?" he asked.

I crossed over to his sewing table and set the briefcase next to the half-made dress.

"What's this?" he asked, pulling the briefcase toward him.

"The gold letters on the side: *BKH.* Ring any bells?"

Gus squinted at it for a good thirty seconds before he shook his head. "Can't say that it does. But if it's from New York, that's probably why. Where'd you get this?"

"Pulled it off a manticore after us."

Gus cocked a brow. "A manticore, eh? Nasty piece of work."

"Not for me," I said. It was meant to be honest, not arrogant. A manticore's poison, like so many other magical monster ailments, didn't affect me. I'd…gone through a lot to ensure that.

"You mark my words, young hunter," Gus said, leaning over his work and pointing to me. "You'll be in a ring with a monster that you can't knock down one day. And it will be too late. Then I'll be standing over your cold corpse, saying I told you so."

"Thanks, Gus, I love our little talks."

He waved me out of his back room. "I've got calls to make. Go *buy* something."

Four hours later, I was still waiting on Eris. In that time, I'd used Gus's quarters to bathe and change into a new suit that Gus himself had tailored. Hidden in one of the suit pockets was a slip of paper with the password for the speakeasy I'd need for tonight. Using a government-issued lighter I carried but rarely used, I burned the paper and brushed the ashes off my hands.

The clock on the shop's wall read half past ten when I heard sounds from the stairs behind the side door that led to the Murdeenas' apartments.

"Well come on, child." Belva clicked her tongue, summoning her like she would a pet poodle.

I stood, straightening my suit, about to tell Belva she'd cost us precious time, when Eris emerged from the darkened stairs into the boutique's light, and all words died on my tongue.

Eris's auburn hair had been washed and styled into finger waves and bunched and pinned below her ears and around her neck. Tucked into the folds of her curls was a simple yet elegant feather hairpin and her makeup was light, accentuating her blue eyes and painting her lips in a subtle pink hue. Her flapper dress was a soft cream, closer to white than peach, and it sparkled and shimmered at the slightest movement.

As I'd been waiting I couldn't help but wonder what kind of dress Belva would choose for Eris. I'd imagined the usual fashion—dark, rich colors, like plum or emerald, maybe even a solid slinky black, since that seemed to be popular among young flappers. But I should've known better. Belva was legendary for finding the right attire for anyone—and it involved her seeing beyond the limitations of things like past and present fashions.

She'd looked within Eris.

And what she found was an angel.

Chapter Seventeen

The Siren

"Colt got your tongue?"

Belva chuckling at her own joke made the spell break. Both Colt and I had been staring, speechless, at each other for an unknown amount of time. I wasn't even sure *who* her question had been directed to.

I dipped my head to hide the flush on my cheeks as Colt tilted his upward, rubbing the back of his neck.

Stepping into the light of Belva's boutique had been like stepping onto a stage—I felt woozy, dizzy, and a little blinded. Not blinded by lights, but by the young federal agent standing before me, dressed smartly in a well-cut pinstripe suit and a dark fedora.

He stared at me in a way that made my skin feel warm and tingly like my whole body had just been doused in giggle water.

"Well, my job is done. You two get going before you fog up the windows." Belva pushed me forward, her hands still clamped on my shoulders.

Her push, coupled with the new heels on my feet, made me stumble forward, but Colt caught me by the elbows. "Careful," he murmured. He ducked his head, looking into my eyes from under the rim of his hat. "You look beautiful, Eris."

From my chest to the roots of my hair, I flamed with heat, and sweet jazz pumped through my heart. It was akin to the feelings in The Blind Dragon—only stronger. And when I realized that, I quickly wanted to shut them off.

He's a grifter, Eris. Don't let him con you again.

I dropped my hands and turned toward the storefront window, another part of me fighting valiantly against the advice. *Yes, but one who turned his back on everything for you.*

Looking out into the Chicago night, I saw windows glowing yellow and heard shouts of laughter and blasts of trumpet players on street corners trailing through the corridors of the skyscrapers, carried on by its legendary wind. I imagined the clubs and the smoky rooms hidden within those very tall buildings and wanted nothing to do with them.

Pressing my fingers against the glass, its chill rippled through me, and I shivered. As if in response, a heavy fur coat dropped onto my shoulders. I found Colt in the glass's reflection. Our reflected gazes met and a quiet understanding passed between us.

We were about to enter a drum full of monsters and vodka-soaked chaos, and we needed to rely on each other to get out alive.

"All right, you kids," Belva's voice called from the back of her boutique. "Hurry up now, and make whoopee. The night is still young—but she won't last for long!"

Colt worried about any BOI agents stationed in Chicago noticing and tailing the stolen jalopy so we left the briefcase with Belva and took a taxi further into the heart of downtown Chicago. As the car ducked and wove through the busy nighttime streets, Lake Michigan peeked through buildings. Colt fed the driver directions and, in a matter of minutes, we were standing on a street corner with a single gaslight hanging overhead. The rest of the street was well illuminated, but this one seemed significant somehow—as if it was the first of its kind. Created a century ago, it stood for one hundred years, the product of a different era—no place for it in the modern world. And yet here it still stood.

In my fur coat, I wasn't cold at all, but I couldn't stop the shivers that raced through me every few minutes. Trembles not from the biting wind, but the fear of *real* bites in this seedy Chicago netherworld.

Colt started forward, tugging my arm gently along, and I followed.

He spoke softly under his breath. "The minute we get into the Cerberus Club they'll likely separate us."

My steps faltered and I hurried to keep up with Colt's lengthy stride. "Why?"

"The owner knows me and doesn't trust me. The last time I was here I took out one of her favorite bodyguards—a minotaur by the name of Charlie Wade. I'm sure she'll likely take you as collateral…and you need to let them."

Glancing at the skyscraper that seemed to hold up the ceiling of dark clouds, I licked my lips and forgot that I was wearing lipstick. It tasted waxy. "You want me to use my voice on them."

"I want you to protect yourself. If you use your voice, you can make them think they're in charge while *you* have all the cards."

I tried to fight the scowl on my face. "I'm not very good

at poker."

"That's because you show all your emotions on your face. Eris, listen to me—" Colt stopped, squeezing my arm against the warmth of his chest. "This place will be *crawling* with monsters. The Cerberus Club is like a safe haven for them. Where they can be themselves. You'll see things and you can't let them get to you. But you have to remember, you'll be the most powerful creature there. They can't do anything to you that you don't want them to."

I'll be the most powerful creature.

I almost wanted to laugh at the absurdity of it. I've never felt powerful in my life. Not even when I forbade men from touching other women. I felt vengeful and angry, but not strong. And then later I'd feel disgusted with myself.

If Colt was talking about this like a game of poker—I would drop all the cards.

"You don't believe me," he stated quietly.

I looked up then. Half his face was bathed in shadows, the other half illuminated by the gaslight behind us. His warm breath came out in clouds of steam.

I didn't know what to say.

"Is it because I conned you before? That was a job. I was trying to make sure that the lost siren wasn't...evil. You're not evil. I know that now."

His dark eyes pulled me in, and I almost confessed to him all my insecurities. All my beliefs that I was, in fact, evil. This siren's pearl that made me so powerful, so desirable, made me feel like a walking plague. Like sin personified—lust, envy, pride, wrath, gluttony, sloth, greed.

And yet, here on this cold, dark night, where monsters danced beneath us and drank beyond brick walls, he gave me hope. Just like he had when I'd thrown my arms around his neck and wept.

Don't ever speak.

I swallowed the lump in my throat and pulled my fur tighter around me. "Just tell me what I need to know about this...this Cerberus Club."

I started walking again, and with our arms linked, he followed as a result.

He talked rapidly, his voice low and fast, but I caught every word. Every syllable spoken in his rich baritone.

"A bouncer is going to grant us entrance and then we'll probably be found within the first five minutes. If they take you, it will be to another room away from the rest of the drum's chatter. But once I get the info I need from Gin, I'll come find you and we'll get out of here. In and out. It should be simple."

Should be.

"Who is Gin?"

"She's the owner of the Cerberus Club."

"Is she a monster?"

"She is."

I waited for him to tell me what she was, but silence passed between us, the only sounds the music of Chicago's nightlife and the beat of our footsteps.

"Well, what—"

A metal *clang* from below interrupted me, and I sucked in a breath. To our right, a staircase had descended into darkness, ending with a single red light at the top of a metal door.

It was like the staircase down to hell itself.

A large man wearing suspenders and a bowler hat, his bulging biceps straining against the white fabric of his shirt, leaned against the door. His hat was pulled low over his eyes and he tilted his chin down as Colt and I took the steps toward him.

"Password?" the man grunted in a thick Scottish brogue.

"The Fall of Bellerophon," Colt answered.

The large man stepped to the side, and we were granted entrance. Colt pushed the door open, and we entered the Cerberus Club.

It really was like walking into Lucifer's kingdom. Immediately I wanted to shed my fur coat as the heat of bodies pressing against the dark cement walls of the speakeasy threatened to strangle me. We stood on a balcony looking out over a dance floor littered with oliver twists, swinging their hearts out to the jazz band that played on the extravagant stage directly opposite to us. Dim electric lightbulbs hung from the ceiling, shaking and trembling with the blasts of clarinets and saxes and the pounding keys of the pianist—playing like The Lion himself. A long bar ran the length of the speakeasy, packed with patrons all hanging on the edge, shouting their drink order and waving mazuma in the air for the harried bartenders.

At first glance, it looked like any other city nightclub, extravagant and bigger than most, but normal.

But then I picked up on flashes of *abnormal.*

A woman in a red flapper dress had dark emerald locks of hair, writhing and twisting around her shoulders. It took me a second too long to realize what they were—live serpents. A man with bull horns protruding from his temples sat on a lone barstool, nursing his sixth glass in front of him. Another man danced with a dame whose whole arms and legs were covered in bluish-green scales reflecting the yellowish electric light. The singer up on the stage crooned into his mic and swayed with the beat of his jazz ballad, feathers falling to the floor from his arms like he was a cat shedding hair.

I pressed my hands to my mouth as sweat broke out on the back of my neck.

Monsters. Here, there, everywhere.

I closed my eyes, swallowed, and lowered my shaking hands to my sides. Before I had another moment to collect my wits, a young woman with a black bob came up beside us. I did a double take. Her eyes were feline—yellow irises and black slit pupils. A lion's tail curled around her waist and flicked Colt's elbow, and when she opened her mouth to talk, sharp fangs glistened behind rouge lips.

"Welcome to the Cerberus Club," she purred—quite literally—her eyes darting up and down Colt's tall frame. "May I take your coat and hat?"

As Colt reached for his fedora to hand to the feline-girl, I shrugged out of the fur coat. It had been comforting to keep it around me, almost like a coat of armor, but now it was much too hot and it would be hard to move in.

She handed Colt a token with a number on it in return, gave a little bow, and backed into the darkness.

"What was she?" I asked.

"A sphinx."

I wanted to ask exactly what a sphinx was, but the next song started and it was a loud one. The trumpet gave four short blasts and then the rest of the jazz band swooped in with a tune of their own design, but one the crowd had clearly heard before, because they gave a cheer and started into the Lindy Hop. Some dancers were better than others, but all were passionate—twirling and double-then-triple stepping.

Then there were the darker parts of the dance floor where couples were twisted together in a way that would make Madame Maldu throw them out on the street. One man had a woman pressed against the wall, necking her, while her eyes rolled up into her head and her mouth parted in pleasure. The man tilted his head back and his tongue flicked over his lips—they were blood-red.

Two flaming youths stumbled in front of us, both completely half-seas over. They were singing—if you could call it that—along to the melody of the band's song. The one closest to us winked at me and reached to loop his arm around my neck. In less than a second, Colt had gripped the man's shoulder with white knuckles. The boyo gave a shout of pain and twisted away. He seemed to sober up in that moment and stumbled down the steps, disappearing into the throng of dancers, his compatriot following.

Colt dropped his hand to mine and intertwined our fingers. "C'mon," he said gruffly.

With the sound of the band, no one but myself would've been able to hear him. But I was clued into the timbre of his voice like radio towers tuned into certain frequencies.

"Remember what I told you," Colt said as we descended the stairs into the moving, shifting dance floor, "you're the most powerful monster in this place."

"*You're an abomination, Eris.*"

I gasped suddenly, the words cutting through my mind like a dagger driven through my skull. Were they my own thoughts or the words of someone else from years ago? Darkness consumed my eyesight and I couldn't breathe. My mouth was hot and my arm ached like someone had just injected something into the crook of my elbow.

Then I blinked, brought back to the present by the scent of a smoking hearth. I tilted my head up, my chin brushing the fabric of Colt's suit jacket. His body had melded against mine and we stood, embracing, in the middle of the Charleston dancers. Lightbulbs trembled above us with the steps of a hundred feet swinging. A few women at the bar, all with snake hair, sipped on cocktails and sent curling blue smoke toward the ceiling with their cigarettes.

I fisted his jacket and clung to him like he was a life preserver in the middle of the Atlantic.

He moved his head back, bringing his hands to cup my cheeks, and stared into my eyes. "What happened?" His breath was hot, but not unpleasant—it reminded me of the warmth of a fire in the dead of winter.

What *had* happened? I'd never had a flashback like that before. That missing time between the nuns at the orphanage and when Madame Maldu and I went into hiding—had it been from that time? When I'd gotten my pearl?

Before I could answer, two large men emerged from the shadows and formed a barricade with their bodies between us and the stairs.

The man on the right flexed his hand and his fingernails transformed into steel claws before my very eyes. The hair on his forearms grew until his whole hand, wrist, and up to his elbow was coated in fur. His nose and mouth rippled back into a snarl as they shifted into an elongated snout.

A werewolf.

"Colt Clemmons," the werewolf said, his lips peeling back to reveal fangs as big as my pinky, "Gin would like to see you."

Chapter Eighteen

The Agent

"Good to see you, too, Carl," I replied, forcing a smile. "How have you been?"

"You killed my cousin, so dreaming every night of cutting your throat open." Carl lifted his hand and ran his long wolfish tongue across his front claw. "And if Gin didn't want to see you, I'd gut you right here, right now like a fish."

Eris shivered beside me and another pang of guilt and regret punched me in the gut. What had happened on the dance floor...I'd never seen anyone lose it like that before. She'd frozen and sucked in a breath like a drowning victim, then started shaking from head to foot. I couldn't think of anything else to do other than wrap her in my arms and hold her.

Refocus, you fool. The reason we'd come to this place was to find out who was after Eris, and for that, I had to meet Gin. "You're not on the docks anymore, Carl. You've got to be an upstanding gentleman."

"Are you going to come willingly or can I knock you out

first?" Carl growled. "I wouldn't mind breaking both your legs and dragging you there."

"Easy, easy, ole sport, I'll—"

"*You will not harm Colt Clemmons. You will take him to Gin peacefully.*"

Eris's magic was so thick and powerful it clung to my mind like cobwebs. Had she intended to pour more magic than usual into her voice, or was it just her own emotions bleeding through?

Carl looked down at her in a daze. "I will not harm Colt Clemmons. I will take him to Gin peacefully," he repeated.

Eris turned back to me and gripped my hand with both of hers. "I'll do what's necessary, don't worry about me. Just be careful." She bit her bottom lip as her gaze searched my face. There seemed to be something else she wanted to say, but then the other man stepped forward. He didn't seem to be a monster, but he was big and burly and plenty threatening.

"Carl, what did this dame just do?"

Eris gave me a tight nod then turned back to the second man. "*What were your orders?*"

The man blinked at her then started to talk, quickly, in a thick Chicago accent. "We was supposed to fetch Colt Clemmons and bring him to Gin's room. I was to guard you in the cellar and then kill you in case Clemmons acted up."

Eris paled, but she didn't miss a beat. "*You will guide me to the cellar, but you will not touch me and you will never tell Gin what I've done to you or your friend.*"

The man just nodded dully and then stood there, staring off into space, as if waiting for further instructions.

The jazz band slowed their song and switched to a new melody. Dancers wove around us, heading off the floor for a break and for more booze. Eris turned back to me, the lights catching the white-silver sparkles on her dress. "I'm sorry I've let you take me this far—I wasn't thinking. We don't have to go through with this. Leave me. Go back to DC, and don't worry about me."

The heat in my chest that had been burning since she'd started trembling fizzled out and a cool sense of reason and purpose took its place. I caught her hand and, still staring into those blue eyes that had ensnared me all the way across some tiny Boston bar, I placed a kiss into the center of her palm.

This was why I followed her. This was why I'd smashed that briefcase into the side of my coworker's face and turned my back on the only home I'd ever known. Her goodness. In the midst of all this danger, she kept on sacrificing her own happiness.

With our eyes still locked, I lowered her hand from my lips. "I'm ready, Carl."

I left Eris at the bottom of the stairs, feeling, for the first time in my life, that I was doing something *I* wanted. She wasn't a mission. She wasn't an assignment. She wasn't something I had to protect out of a warped sense of duty.

She was good and precious to me. And maybe if I kept following her, then some of that goodness could rub off on me.

Gin's room was down a brick corridor lit with gaslight lanterns. The cold, dank underground air of Lake Michigan's icy depths played across my hot skin. The temperature between this part of the Cerberus Club and the main dance floor was like night and day.

Carl said nothing as we walked. It was as if he was still captivated by Eris's words and intent on following her instructions to the letter.

She proved, at least, that she understood the importance

of using her voice. Yet the disgust on her face when the two men had bent so easily to her will had not been lost on me.

She detested it.

We arrived at the red door at the end of the corridor, and Carl knocked in a practiced sequence.

A younger man, slimmer, and quite beautiful, opened the door. He was as pale as the moon with dark, unintelligent eyes and seemed to be in a daze, like Carl, but not one of a siren's making. He stepped aside to let us in, and I found the room similar to the last time I'd been there. Memories of that night came back to me in short flashes, and my skin crawled.

It was a large room decorated with velvet furniture—all lounging couches and settees—with a window looking out over the dance floor. A woman with a curtain of black hair and a dark maroon sequin dress lay on the middle couch, her eyes on the window, watching the writhing crowd below. A young flapper with bobbed blonde ringlets sat to her right, straight-backed and stiff, staring ahead.

Another young man and woman lay stretched on the other couches, their eyes half closed, their lips parted, but with euphoric smiles on their faces.

I didn't let a single emotion show through my expression—disgust, or rage, though both flowed through me.

"Colt Clemmons," the woman with the black hair said, her rouge lips transforming into a smile. "You've come back to me at last."

"Gin," I said with a nod, then glanced down at the inebriated couple lounging on the couches, barely breathing. "Did you have a good meal?"

Gin's dark eyes flicked to them and she frowned. "Somewhat disappointing, actually. Too much whiskey and tobacco in their blood. You, however"—she lifted her gaze to me—"would be delectable. A la flambé, if you will."

Hard to imagine that only three years ago I'd been drawn

in by that same magnetic smile and sexuality. That vampiric draw.

The memory of her fangs sinking into my neck, drawing blood, wanting to give her everything and more, was something that kept me up many nights following.

But I was no longer that innocent boy. That sixteen-year-old fool who was angry at the world and everyone in it and desperate to prove his worth. That he didn't have to be a monster—that he could hunt them and be better.

It would've been easier if he'd just accepted his monstrosity. It's always easier that way.

"Not tonight, Gin," I answered.

Gin watched me carefully, tapping her fingers on her lips. "Another night perhaps. So"—she lounged into the velvet cushions, throwing her arms across the back of the sofa—"what brings you to my little club?"

"I need information."

Gin cocked an eyebrow then gestured toward a settee opposite her. "Then take a seat, and let us negotiate, Mr. Clemmons. Anything comes with a price, and why don't you double it, seeing as how you killed one of my men and I've yet to receive any retribution for it."

I sat on the settee and leaned forward, interlacing my fingers. "I can get you some cash, I just need to wire it to you."

Gin threw her head back and laughed. "I don't need any spinach. I want something only *you* can offer me."

Despite my best efforts, I drew away, sitting up taller. "I'm not letting you drain me."

"Yes, Colt, you made that clear." She tucked strands of raven hair behind her ears to show off dangling rubies. "You know I prefer my food to be willing."

"Gin," I said through clenched teeth, "what do you *want*?"

"I want what you want. Information." The vampire tilted

her head to the side, resting her temple on her fist.

I should've guessed that. Gin had been a vampire long before the monster trade made its way to America. Her fortune came from old money, way back when the New World was young and rich with resources—when the first vampires were said to have made it to the port of New Orleans in coffins. Rumors were that she'd been one of them.

"Regarding?"

"The monster trade."

I stared at her. Gin probably knew more about the monster underground than I did. In fact, she was often referred to as the "Queen of Chicago's Netherworld." In times of desperation, even the SOCD had come to *her* for help. What could *I* know that would be useful to her?

"What about it?"

"Any crime lord—any dealer in the trade—knows the most powerful monster in America is seated in this room." Her dark eyes locked on mine, and she smiled a full, white smile, revealing her glistening fangs. "Well...who knows what you are *now*."

My temper spiked as the aching, searing burn in my chest roared to life. "I've told you," I seethed through clenched teeth, "I don't know *where* the BOI got them."

"And I believed you," Gin said with a serene nod. "Few people can lie to me when I have my fangs inside them. We're in a war, young hunter. A free-for-all. Booze. Dope. Cabbage. Bootlegging. Every night is another battle and every night a new player enters the ring, and we all need more hatchet men." She paused and her sharp eyes narrowed with intensity.

Something dark and twisted seeded in my gut as I listened to Gin. I didn't like where this conversation was headed, but if she could give me the name of Eris's creator...then it'd be worth it.

"You see, I used to think you were special merely because

of the rarity of your monster part. But then I realized...why did such a powerful item not kill you? Most men and women barely survive the infusion of the chimera agent. But you were a young boy—how could *you* have survived?"

"How should I know?"

"Maybe you don't, but I do. I've spent a long time studying monster transformations to find the secret of its success," Gin replied.

"What is it?" I asked.

"Youth," came a cold voice from behind.

I flinched. The blonde flapper who sat next to Gin hadn't moved, or barely blinked, but I'd completely forgotten about the other male vampire.

I twisted in my seat to look at him. He leaned against the wall, cleaning his fingernails with a knife, and when he felt my gaze on him, he stared right back.

"Children are much more adaptable to the chimera agent and their minds are so malleable," he said, a smile curling his pale lips.

Every syllable fell cold and hard, like a knife into my back, and the space between my shoulder blades once again began to throb with that same dull pain. I'd live with it forever.

"Frederick," Gin sing-songed, "hush now. Our little agent doesn't need to know the details. Just what I need from him."

I licked my dry lips. "Which is?"

Gin's expression flashed into one I'd seen many times before—greed.

"Your immunity. You are immune to most monsters—a werewolf's bite, a vampire's blood, a manticore's stinger, a basilisk's stare...you've survived it all. Was it the chimera agent they used on you or the monster you are—or *were*?"

My gut clenched. Few crime lords knew of my immunity, and few knew of my monster days...the BOI had made sure their secret weapon was kept *secret*.

My chest burned again and I was reminded of Eris and our goal. The manticore, the minotaur, and the men on the train platform. How many attacks could we survive without knowing who we were up against?

"Okay, you've laid out what *you* want. Now I need to know if you have the information that *I* need," I said. It was highly possible, after all, that she would have no idea who BKH was.

Still smiling, Gin flicked her wrist, gesturing me to continue.

I reached into my coat pocket and pulled out the gold emblem that I'd pried loose from the briefcase. Leaning over, she took it from me and, as she inspected the letters, I caught an almost imperceptible moment of recognition in her gaze. Even one of shock.

"Where did you get this?" she asked calmly.

"I pulled it off a manticore's briefcase. And I saw the letters again embroidered into a minotaur's hat."

"Was this before or after you picked up your latest squeeze?"

She was referring to Eris, of course. I was wondering when Gin would bring up me taking a girl to her club.

"Why should that matter?"

She shrugged. "It doesn't. Not really." Then she shot me a heated gaze. "But I'm a jealous woman. I like to know when my favorites get girls."

"Gin."

She waved her hand dismissively. "Oh, fine. You've gotten boring in your old age, Colt. How about we at least have a drink?" Snapping her fingers, she beckoned the younger vampire over. "Frederick, be a dear and escort Millie to get our guest something to drink." Gin drew her arm around the slender shoulders of the blonde flapper next to her. The flapper shuddered slightly under Gin's touch and her eyes rolled back into her head. Her lashes fluttered and she gave a soft gasp, like a soul possessed.

"I don't need anything," I said. "Let's just get to it. Do you know what BKH stands for? Who's behind it? Is it a crime syndicate?"

"If memory serves me right, you like tea. Orange pekoe, isn't it?" Without waiting for my affirmation, she tilted her chin toward the flapper. "Mildred, my love, go fetch our guest some tea. And I'll have a white Russian. Off with you now."

Mildred stood on shaky legs like a newborn calf and then hurried out the door, Frederick following and shutting it behind him.

"Now," she purred, lounging back into her velvet cushions again, "BKH. Interesting sequence of letters. It's not often you see a crime organization use an acronym, do you?"

"No."

"Which begs the question—is it even crime-related?"

"What do you mean?"

Her fangs gleamed with an even wider smile. "Well, how do you know it has anything to do with rum-running and dope dealing?"

I knew the Socratic method well. McCarney had used it to train me as a gumshoe. Thinking deductively and all that. But why was Gin wasting my time with it? She was stalling.

"Because both the men with this emblem were monsters."

"So?"

"So?" I snapped. "Monsters are used by crime lords."

"But only them?"

My mind blanked. *Only.*

Within the SOCD, all I'd known were the criminals who operated in the netherworld of cities. That was where monsters were engineered, created, born, bred, used, and murdered.

Then, slowly, the wheels started to turn.

"For Godsakes, Colt, it's been nearly a decade into the monster trade," Gin said. "You don't think it would've stayed *just* within the crime world, do you?"

Monsters could be anywhere. Used by anyone. Anyone with power. Resources. Capital.

"A company," I said slowly. "BKH is the acronym of a corporation. What is it?"

Gin smiled, tilting her head, dark eyes glittering. "I think I've supplied plenty of information so far. Now you give me something." She leaned forward, hair cascading down pale, bare shoulders. "Your immunity. How is it possible?"

If I knew BKH was a company that would be enough information. Only truly rich companies could afford something like the siren's pearl.

I stood. "Thanks for your time, Gin. I'll be off now."

Her eyes narrowed. "We had a deal, Clemmons."

"I never agreed to it. And I don't make deals with conniving hags." So maybe I was a little jaded from our last encounter. How she'd taken advantage of my youth and self-hatred.

Anger flashed across her face like a lightning strike, but then it cleared and she smiled once more.

"Wait a moment, sugar. I do have one more piece of information I should share with you. And this is free."

"No, thanks." I turned my back to her when, at that moment, the door opened and in came the flapper named Mildred. In her hands was a tray with a cocktail and a white porcelain teacup.

"Millie, darling. Come set down the drinks. I'd like you to show Mr. Clemmons something."

Mildred obeyed. She set down the tray and faced me, her gaze, for the first time, alive and locked on mine.

Gin stood, draping an arm across Mildred's shoulders like she'd done before, and petted the girl's cheek with two fingers. "Show him, my love."

Mildred pulled off her headband, shaking loose her blonde curls and revealing...a third eye dead center in the middle of her forehead.

The eye was blue, just like her others, but slightly wider and without a lid or eyelashes. It could never blink.

A cyclops.

But I'd never seen a small female one before. Cyclops were known usually to be men—big brutes with super strength like minotaurs.

"Millie, here," Gin said, moving her fingers into Mildred's hair to play with her curls, "is my own special brand of cyclops. Did you know a cyclops eye has untapped potential? Men with no imagination think a cyclops can do nothing but break some bones. But it's a *third eye.* Think about it, Mr. Clemmons. A third eye has always been mythicized to possess mystic abilities. It can see things. *Read* things. For example...seeing across time and space. Hearing words that were never actually said..."

"Gin, what've you done?" I asked, panic coating my voice for the first time.

"Experimenting mostly. Succeeding occasionally. Winning always." Gin twirled another one of Millie's curls, petting her cheek with one long finger topped with one long red nail. "And I've found that telepathy is a winning hand, wouldn't you say, sugar?"

Still trying to unravel her words, the door opened for the third time.

My chest flared with heat and it traveled into my throat and through my nostrils, as real and certain fear held me in a vice-like grip.

Chapter Nineteen

THE SIREN

Was this what it felt like to have five shots of bourbon in one hour? I'd seen many of my patrons slam glass after glass on the mahogany bar and watched them stumble away, out into the Boston night.

I wondered if I looked that way now. My steps swervy, legs like jelly, knees wobbly and my head spinning, while the Cerberus bouncer led me to the cellar steps.

I couldn't remember being kissed before…by anyone. Not my faceless birth parents who abandoned me at an orphanage, not the nuns I spent my childhood with, not Stan, or the bar patrons, or even Madame Maldu. She'd treated me well. Kindly, but distantly. Not a hug or a kiss or any significant, definitive displays of affection. I felt like a charity project to her, one that she liked, cared for, but not necessarily loved.

The touch of Colt's lips on my hand had done something to me. It made me realize how much I'd been living *without*. Without touch, without connection, without the feeling of being wanted or desired. The realization hurt.

The man stopped at the threshold of the cellar. He stayed there like a puppet waiting to be moved. Was the magic in my voice too much? Did he have *any* free will now? Would he always be like this or would it wear off?

The worry of what my voice had done to this man—even if he was a murderer and thug who worked in a monster bar—sobered me, and I was able to shake off the remnants of Colt's unexpected and disarming kiss to my palm.

Gnawing on my lip, I forced myself to look into the man's blank hazel eyes. "What's your name?"

"Raymond. Ray. Raymond Harold Fitzpatrick."

I raised my eyebrows. Would he have just gone on listing names if he had any more? "Rest at ease, Ray."

And he did. He blinked, his shoulders slumping slightly, and he sat back on the steps, tucking his hands in his pockets.

Looking around, I took stock of the cellar. It was just like any other, I supposed. Brick walls and hard-packed floor covered with cheap, smoothed-over cement then stacked to the ceiling with stained whiskey barrels, crates of bootlegged liquor, drums of panther piss, and racks of fancy wine that were surely sold at exorbitant prices.

Unsure of how long we'd be here, and feeling the pinch of my new heels, I picked a sturdy crate and sat on top of it gingerly. It held my weight well with only a slight creak in the wood planks.

Ray still said nothing, looking at me, and then looking at the floor. It was as if his brain seemed to be at war with itself. His desire to watch me and guard me for his boss versus his subconscious need to evade me at any cost.

I could have sat and pondered what was going on inside poor Ray's head for another two hours, but a muffled, troubling sound made me freeze.

I listened hard, barely breathing, and ignoring the sounds of stamping feet, pounding piano keys, shouts and laughter, trumpet and trombone blasts, sax and clarinet harmonies, and bass plucks. It was all still loud, but I could focus past it. I wasn't sure if it was a siren ability or if I'd simply been born with good ears. Regardless of the reason, I could detect sobbing.

Real, aching, heaving sobs.

The heartbreaking sound came from beyond the brick wall. I stood, moving toward the sobbing. Then I stopped and turned on my heel to find Ray, who still sat on the steps.

"Ray," I said gently. "Who's crying?"

Ray answered immediately. "That's just the tykes."

"Tykes?" I repeated, shooting a furtive glance back at the brick wall. "You mean there are children…down here?"

Ray nodded. "Yes, miss. Children."

"Children…why…what are they doing here?"

"Dunno, miss. Gin keeps 'em locked up. Good for her experiments."

My skin crawled, like spiders and centipedes and manticore tails skittering up and down my arms and back. *Experiments?* I didn't want to think about what that meant, and I didn't need to, to decide what to do next.

If there was a child crying in a hidden room within the cellar of an illegal monster nightclub, there was only one thing *to* do.

I closed my eyes, took a deep breath. "Ray…*lead me to them.*" The roof of my mouth where my pearl was embedded heated and tingled. More and more I was beginning to notice how the pearl seemed to respond to the desire in my voice whenever I spoke. It seemed to be less about the words I used, and more about their intent. Was that the trick to controlling this power?

Immediately, Ray stood and crossed to the back of the cellar. There was a pathway of sorts between all the liquor crates, and he wound his way past them and then knelt before the wall. Reaching behind a rack of wine, he gripped some sort of lever and a hiss of air escaped through. Then the brick wall creaked inward, toward whatever contents the secret room held.

Ray pushed the door open further and I hurried past him, slipping under his elbow that propped open the secret passage before I could lose my nerve.

It wasn't a room so much as a bunker. It had the same brick walls, yellow lightbulbs, and cold cement as the cellar. The difference was that instead of whiskey barrels and liquor crates, it held two bunk beds, a shabby curtain where I assumed there was a toilet and sink, a lone cabinet, and three small children.

Two boys and one girl huddled together under one bunk bed. They stared at me with wide eyes. I must've had a similar look of incredulity and awe—and horror.

Slowly, I moved toward them.

They flinched back.

I swallowed and raised my hands in an innocent gesture. "*It's going to be all right. You can trust me.*"

The effect of my words was immediate. The smallest boy, whom I could tell from his tear streaks had been the one crying, gave a hiccup and wiped at his eyes. The older girl and the middle boy edged forward on the bed, their expressions transforming from fear to curiosity.

I turned back to Ray, who still stood in the doorway of the secret passage, looking confused but patiently awaiting further instructions.

"Ray, is there another way out of the club than through the main entrance?" I asked. I couldn't imagine leading out three kids in the middle of the dance floor. I would have to enchant the entire club all at once, which seemed highly impossible.

"Yes, miss."

"Where is it?"

"Up the steps, to the left, through the door into the office closet of the telegraph company next door. It's the front for the club."

"Can you—"

Footsteps came from above. Heavy, solid footsteps, followed by the click of a woman's kitten heels.

I looked back at the children, frozen where they sat, staring at me with trust and…hope.

Someone was coming, likely to the cellar, likely for me. If Gin had ordered Ray to watch over me, I doubted she'd allow bartenders down to refill their stash.

My mind raced through fifty possible scenarios, and all of them ended with the one thought—if the children stayed in the bunker and I didn't come back, they'd be there until only God knew when, but if they hid in the *cellar*, then they could have a chance. Maybe they'd get caught and hauled back to their same fate, but at least there was some slim possibility for them to escape when the partying was at its peak—where monsters and patrons alike were zozzled with drink and weary with dance.

At the sound of a lock sliding out of place and the key turning, I whispered my instructions to the three children.

"*Quick as you can, hide behind the barrels and crates and don't make a sound. Don't leave until I tell you to or if you're sure no one else is in the room. If I don't come by the time you count to one thousand, try to leave the way Mr. Ray described.*" I looked at the girl, who was the oldest. "*Do you understand?*"

She nodded. I placed a hand against the doorway to steady myself as a feeling of fatigue swept through me. So many instructions, and so much magic at once. But I couldn't stop now.

"*Quickly then.*"

The girl grabbed the tiny boy's hand and hurried out of the bunker, the middle boy followed, and in the span of fifteen seconds they were hidden amidst all the bootleg liquor. Hidden well, too.

"*Close the door, hurry,*" I told Ray, hurrying toward the center of the cellar.

The brick wall slid into place just as shoes came into view on the stairs.

No use waiting. Better to use my voice now to make sure the children wouldn't be found.

"*Stop right there. Don't come closer.*"

But the shoes kept coming down the stairs, one by one on the wooden steps, *tap, tap, tap, tap.*

The magic in my voice wasn't working. Why? My intent and desperation was there. Did they have the same mysterious ability as Colt to resist me? Or was it because I was getting tired?

I tried again. "*Stop—stop where you are.*"

People emerged into view. The first was a man, maybe in his mid-twenties, pale with black hair and a sharp black suit with white suspenders. His eyes were dark, practically black, and he was smiling at me. No, smirking.

The second was a young flapper. Maybe my age or a year or two younger. She wore a loose purple dress with a violet beaded headband around her forehead, holding down thick locks of springy gold curls. In her hand was a glass of some sort of liquor I didn't recognize—and I'd seen a lot of liquor.

"*Stop immediately.*" Panic strangled me as they continued across the cellar floor, fast. "*Ray—stop them!*"

Ray took a step forward as the pale man pulled out a revolver from his jacket and fired three rounds into Ray's barrel-sized chest without breaking stride.

Raymond Harold Fitzpatrick went down like a statue.

I screamed, clawing my fingers down my cheeks.

Blood gushed from three open bullet wounds, and I was still staring at them in horror when the pale, slender man grabbed my wrists.

I just got a man killed. I used him like some kind of... shield...or weapon.

I really am a monster.

I barely comprehended the flapper girl gripping my jaw and forcing my lips to pucker. She pushed the glass of brownish liquid to my mouth. I choked and coughed as she poured the concoction down my throat and pinched my lips shut, forcing me to swallow.

It burned like fire. Like I'd chugged real rubbing alcohol.

The pale man released me and tucked his gun into the waistband of his trousers, like I was no longer a threat.

My nails dug into the skin on my throat—it felt like it was being turned inside out. Like sewing needles in a machine punching at my vocal cords and ripping them apart. The pain was too much to handle, and I fell forward on all fours, coughing and hacking, wanting to throw up. To get whatever poison they poured inside me out.

Flecks of blood sprayed onto the floor and down the front of my beautiful white dress.

"That should do it."

I looked up as the pale man plucked out two thick cotton wads from his ears, and the flapper girl did the same.

Cotton in their ears so they couldn't hear my voice...just like the minotaur.

He was smiling as he crouched in front of me and took my chin in his hands. "Hello, little siren. Welcome to the Cerberus Club. Gin would like to meet you."

I tried to speak, to tell him to let me go, but no words came out. Only a small squeak. That liquid had done something to my vocal cords.

I couldn't talk.

For years I'd chosen not to, and now I literally couldn't. If this was permanent, the world was unfair and cruel. Or maybe it had always been.

I thought of the children hiding behind the rum crates and the dead man on the floor. Despair and desperation threatened to swallow me whole.

"Millie, go get their drinks," the pale man told the flapper who had yet to say a word.

Millie mounted the stairs back up to the main level.

I stared at the concrete floor, listening to Millie's heels on the wooden steps and then the click and creak of the cellar door.

A cold hand moved curls from my neck. I recoiled and found the man's face much too close. His irises were tinged with red, and he was looking at me like he was ready to...to eat me.

"I wonder how a siren tastes," he purred, his thumb brushing my collarbone. "I'd dearly love to find out." A tongue slid between his pale lips and then he grinned, and that's when I saw them. Fangs.

"But," he said with a frown, "that man would likely kill me if I drank from you."

Was he talking about Colt? Or someone else?

"Up you get, little siren." The man hoisted me up with only one arm, and I was surprised at his strength. It was deceiving from the look of his slender upper body, but maybe that was one of his monster powers. Paralyzed with fear of what was to come, I let him lead me up the cellar steps.

I sent a prayer to God to keep the children safe. *Help them escape. Please.*

Gin's man marched me across the dance floor, down a long hallway and into a room where he shoved me to the carpeted floor. I fell on all fours again—another coughing fit taking over my lungs and throat making me hack up droplets of blood.

When I lifted my head and saw the man standing before me, I couldn't help but try and say his name.

Colt.

Chapter Twenty

The Agent

"When did you know?" I asked Gin, my gaze still glued to Eris on the floor.

Gin's smooth, delighted tone wove through the air. "As soon as I saw the emblem. The CEO has been looking for this little monster for quite some time."

"How did you know he was looking for her?" As far as I knew, the BOI wasn't aware of any monster trade within the corporate world, so the secrets must be kept locked tight.

A soft laugh from Gin. "Pillow talk. You know how it is, sugar."

I dropped to one knee in front of Eris. Our gazes locked, and while she seemed on the verge of tears, she held them back valiantly with a tight jaw. Gently, I took her chin and lifted it, moving it from side to side to get a full look at her neck and collarbone. Then I rotated her arms, staring at her wrists.

No fang marks.

"Does she pass your inspection?" Frederick sneered.

I stood. "I was just checking if I needed to kill you fast or slow."

There was a long, tense pause. Then, "You've got some balls on you, ole sport," Frederick said. "Let's see how big you talk when I rip them off."

Gin held up her hand as he took a step forward. She was no longer smiling. "Colt, it doesn't have to be this way. There's no need to get violent. You tell me the information you owe me and I'll let you walk away free and clear."

"Will you let me take the girl?"

"Out of the question, I'm afraid. Her creator wants her back *very* badly."

"Then no deal."

I looked back down at Eris to find her staring at me with earnest. As if she was trying to tell me something. Her gaze flicked down to her right hand on the carpet. She had her index finger and thumb outstretched.

Gun.

"I'm sorry to hear that, sugar."

I refocused my attention back on the vampire. She was frowning.

"I wasn't lying. You really were one of my favorites."

In just a subtle motion of Gin's index and middle finger in a *come here* gesture, the conversation was over. No more talking.

In that half second after Gin lifted her fingers, Frederick had two small revolvers out, pulled from the waistband of his trousers, and he was already burning powder. Which meant I had to be moving half a second beforehand.

I dove for his shins, driving my shoulders into his kneecaps and my head through his legs. The guns went off above. I could feel the heat of their flints catching and sparking just over my head. Wrapping my arms around his calves, I twisted, forcing him to the ground. He fell down hard, the gun in his left hand going off accidentally while pointing the other down to fire at me for a third time. But I already had hold of his wrist. With pressure on one side and a jerking motion in the opposite direction, I broke his wrist. He howled in pain, dropping the revolver and twisting around to protect his injury.

"Carl!" Gin screamed over the scuffle and gun. "Carl, *get him, you idiot*!"

But Carl didn't "get me" because Eris had told him not to. He just stayed there, locked in place.

Meanwhile, I drove the base of my palm into Frederick's nose, shattering it and sending bone fragments up into his brain. The vamp rolled his head backward, as dead as the undead could get.

Dimly, I heard heels running across wood and when I looked up, Millie was gone. But Gin still stood there, her hands twisted into Eris's hair and a knife at her throat.

"She did something, didn't she?" Gin hissed through her fangs, the point of the knife digging into Eris's bare throat. "To my Carl?"

I licked my lips, heat searing through my whole body. "You won't kill her, Gin," I said slowly, picking up a gun from Frederick's limp hand.

Her lip curled, eyes dark and full of anger. If there was one thing about Gin it was that she hated when her loyal followers were hurt.

"Are you sure about that?" Gin snarled, pressing the knife tip into Eris's flesh so a bead of blood rolled down its blade.

My chest burned with the truth. No, I wasn't sure. But I had to guess. I had to call her bluff. "Yes, you're scared of him. Of her creator. It's why you don't have your fangs in her right now."

Her eyes flashed with a hint of surprise, and I knew that it was the truth. That in itself was frightening. What kind of person made *Gin*, the Queen of the Netherworld, scared?

She lifted her chin. "I am scared of no man."

"If you weren't scared…" I glanced at the knife at Eris's throat. "Then she'd be dead already."

"She's useful."

"She's an innocent girl. Let her go."

"*Innocent?*" Gin cried. I'd never seen Gin look unkempt before—nothing but calm and sophisticated—except now her voice was shrill and her eyes were wild. "No monster is innocent. We're all condemned to dance with the devil."

A small whimper escaped Eris's lips. Her eyes were lifted to the ceiling and at Gin's words, she closed them. One tear trickled down her cheek.

Strangely enough, Eris's reaction seemed to calm Gin. The vampire queen took comfort in others' weaknesses. Gin shushed Eris, petting her waves almost affectionately. "There, there, baby doll. You're going back to your daddy. Don't you worry."

Eris's blue eyes suddenly snapped open and her grip on Gin tightened. Thrusting her hips back, Eris threw her upper half forward, planting down all her weight and heaving Gin over her back in a solid shoulder-throw.

The knife rolled across the carpet as Gin slammed into the floor on her back.

Eris kicked the weapon away and grabbed my hand. Together we ran out the door, Gin's scream following us. "You can run from him, but you can't hide!"

Our footsteps pounded against the wood floor, the light of the gaslit lanterns bouncing and jumping on the brick walls thanks to our shadows racing across.

As we ran, I let go of Eris's hand and quickly dismantled the gun like I'd been taught at the Bureau, dropping the parts like breadcrumbs in our wake. We came to the entrance of the club, but instead of bolting out the door to the alley, she turned left toward the black-and-white checkered dance floor. Before she could enter the mass of writhing bodies, I grabbed her wrist.

"What are you doing? We have to go!" I yelled over the blaring jazz.

But she couldn't answer. Whatever concoction they'd given her had rendered her voice useless. Instead, she just stared up at me with imploring, big blue eyes.

Trust me.

Easy to read.

Just as I'd made the decision to follow her into the unknown, a howl pierced the air. It broke through the cacophony of piano, sax, laughter, and tapping feet.

Five massive werewolves with ripped shirts and furry faces emerged at the top of the stairs. Millie must've run to fetch them on Gin's telepathic orders. They'd probably be chasing us down the street by now if Eris hadn't continued onto the dance floor. Out there, we might've had a chance in running. In here, I wasn't so sure.

They scrambled over one another to get down the stairs as screams and shouts issued from dancers who ran to make way for Gin's henchmen. Some even jumped behind the bar to hide.

Eris paid the beasts no mind. She seemed to be so focused on her mystery mission that nothing in the world—not even five bloodthirsty werewolves after her—could distract her.

I had to admire her guts.

We took off across the floor, now clear of bodies, and ducked into a back hallway. Eris stopped at the door to the right and grabbed its knob, rattling it.

I pushed her to the side and backed up. In three short but fast steps, I kicked the door. The wood splintered and shook as the lock dislodged and the door vibrated open.

We raced down the cellar steps and when we came to the

tall liquor crates at the back, Eris pulled up short. It was so sudden that I almost lost my balance, but I managed to steady myself with a whiskey barrel that came to my waist.

Out from behind the crates emerged three small children—the oldest being maybe twelve while the others looked to be around nine and six.

The situation hit me like a five o'clock freighter. *Gin's experiments.*

Eris had found them and now wanted to rescue them, because…of course she did.

There was no getting out of here without them, but I didn't know how we could manage it. If Eris had her voice it'd be jake. But she didn't. And as for my own strength…going up against five werewolves was going to be not only difficult, but impossible.

Gin had been right. Maybe *once* I'd been the most powerful monster in America. Now, I didn't know what I was.

Eris beckoned the children to her side, and they hurried to her, clutching her white dress like she was their angelic savior, which she was, really, in more ways than one.

A werewolf howl ripped through the hall, quickly followed by thundering footsteps above.

I turned to Eris. "Did you have an escape plan for these kids?"

She pointed up the steps and then moved her hand to the left in a jerking motion.

The left. Did that lead to another way out? Unfortunately, it was still up the steps through the horde of werewolves.

My mind raced through one hundred possible scenarios and each one of them seemed to end with me dead, the kids back in their cage, and Eris in the hands of her creator.

Growls echoed as feet stamped on wooden planks down toward us.

Before I could make any kind of plan, Eris thrust a child

into my arms. The smallest boy. The kid wrapped his hands around my neck and held on for dear life, as if he knew the plan better than I did. As I held him, Eris opened my jacket and slid her hands into the inside pockets.

I tried to ignore the heat of her arms and the feel of her soft hands skimming down my sides, but even with monsters hitting the middle steps and their claws scraping along the brick wall, she was difficult to ignore.

"Eris—what—"

But then she found what she was looking for. My pocket knife.

The first werewolf hit the floor of the cellar in a crouch, snarling. The two children clung to my jacket, whimpering. The little boy pushed his face into my neck, and I felt dampness spread across my collar.

Eris flipped open the blade, whirled around, and pressed the tip to the hollow of her throat. Threatening.

The werewolves froze, one by one. The last ran into the wolf right in front of him and caused a domino effect as they all edged forward.

I gaped at her. Dammit. She'd gotten the idea from Gin. She was holding her own body hostage and it was *working.*

Gin's henchmen must be under strict orders that no harm come to her. Just how badly did this corporate giant of BKH want her? Enough to pay a fortune. Enough to give the Queen of the Netherworld anything her dark heart desired? Or had he threatened her to the point of true fear?

Eris glanced back at me with wide, urgent eyes. *Go. Take the children. Leave me.*

I shook my head. *Not a chance.*

The first werewolf bent slowly, on all fours. "You wouldn't dare," he said, his words garbled and difficult to understand through his mouthful of razor sharp teeth and long, lolling tongue.

But no one moved.

The little boy hiccupped and let out a sob into my neck. Eris shot me another glance—this one of anger. She was furious I wasn't taking these kids and running while I had the chance.

But how could I live with myself if I left her to these dogs?

The werewolf inched toward her and Eris dug the knife down her skin, from the hollow of her throat to her collarbone, opening a long red cut. Blood trickled down and the werewolf shrank back, eyes wide. She didn't flinch from pain or cry out. She merely raised the blade back to her throat and glared menacingly at them as if to say, *next time it will be deeper.*

My heart stuttered and jumped, then it shattered into a thousand pieces. She was making this decision for me. Whether I liked it or not.

The heat in my chest was building and building...but with the children here, I couldn't let it free. Not now.

There was only one road to take.

Edging around the barrels and crates, holding onto the youngest boy and feeling the other two kids move alongside me, I came to the steps where the werewolves stood. They were unmoving, their attention divided between me, their prey, and the asset, Eris, whom they were supposed to retrieve and protect.

Eris grunted and pressed the blade once again, opening another minor incision. The werewolves stayed immobile while I mounted the steps with the children.

The monsters didn't seem to care much at all. So what if I walked away with some orphans? There were hundreds in the city, and they could get more. But there was only one siren.

Hating myself, cursing God, Gin, and the devil pulling her strings, I made it to the top of the steps while Eris remained in the center of the cellar. She was bleeding all down her pretty cream dress, but she stood strong.

Strong and beautiful and brave.

This couldn't be the end. We still had so much to talk about. So much I felt like I could learn from her.

But how could I go after her with three kids to worry about?

"Mister."

A whisper called to me, and I glanced down at the oldest child, the little girl. She was tugging hard on my jacket.

"The exit." The girl pointed to the left, to a dark door at the end of the hallway, then she wrapped her hand around the small boy's wrist in my arms, as if to show that she would take him and protect him.

This girl was just as easy to read as Eris. She wanted me to save their angel.

And I would, too.

I set down the small boy and met the little girl's intense stare. "Run," I said.

And they did.

Chapter Twenty-One

The Siren

Even after Colt's feet disappeared from view and the smaller footsteps ascended to the ceiling above, I kept the pocket knife to my throat.

My hands were back to shaking. The blade tip pricked my skin again, but I hardly felt it.

Eventually the heat of the werewolf's fur and the stench of his breath—like Dijon mustard mixed with blood—became overpowering. He was so close now.

I swallowed the impulse to run away. *This is working.* If I could save those three children by threatening my own life—which I knew they wouldn't risk—then it was worth my freedom.

A furry claw pried my fingers from the knife's handle. I could no longer hold on. If I'd been stronger, maybe I could've bought them a little more time to get away, but I could feel my own body betraying me. My knees were weak, and every limb I had was trembling.

"All right, bitch," the werewolf growled, gripping my

upper arms. "You've caused us enough trouble."

As I forced myself to meet his piercing yellow pupils, I thought I saw a whole door fly through the air.

No. I hadn't imagined anything.

The large slab of wood came flying down the steps, slamming into the two werewolves standing near the foot of the stairs. They stumbled into the brick wall and shook their heads, disoriented.

Colt barreled down the steps. Hooking his hands on a wooden beam from the ceiling, he swung himself forward, feet first, and landed on the door that lay on top of the smooshed werewolves. Using it as a diving board, he sprang off and went for the next two monsters.

Unfortunately, the other henchmen had managed to quickly recover from their shock and attacked Colt with just as much fervor. Claws and fangs against legs and fists.

But I wasn't able to see much more of the fight.

The werewolf holding my arms picked me up and slung me over his shoulder like a sack of coffee beans, and in the next second, I found myself staring at a stained shirt pulled tight against a bulging back with layers of fur. With a grunt, I was able to lift myself up enough to reach a crate right in front of my face.

It was open.

I threaded my arm through and pulled out a bottle of bourbon—coincidentally, Marv's favorite—and using all my strength, smashed it against the man's head.

He dropped me and I fell to the floor with a squeak of pain.

"Eris!"

I only had enough time to roll out of the way when a great furry body crashed into the spot on the floor where I'd just been.

A hand grabbed my wrist and yanked me to my feet, and

I came eye to eye with Colt.

For a moment, I considered hitting him myself. What had he been *thinking* coming back for me? Where were the children?

But before I could do anything, he tucked my face into his neck and pulled me down with him as gunshots went off overhead.

Not again.

Under his arm, I could see two werewolf bodies—if not dead, then unconscious—lying on the floor.

"Stay down." Colt's voice was gruff and labored and when he moved away from me, I could feel something warm and sticky on my shoulder. My fingers came away red.

He was bleeding.

Again.

I prayed it wasn't the same wound reopened.

Struggling to my feet in a blatant disregard for his orders, I took in the scene. Two werewolves were on the ground and the one I'd smashed with a whiskey bottle leaned heavily against the stack of crates, groaning and blinking, trying to not pass out.

Colt hid behind a pyramid of barrels as gunshots went off right and left. The two werewolves that had been pinned to the wall by the door had freed themselves and now had revolvers, burning powder. A few shots hit the barrels and dark liquid frothed, bubbled, and poured out onto the floor in big splashes. More bullets hit wine bottles and crates, spraying glass, liquid, and flecks of wood into the air. One shot hit a lightbulb and glass and sparks exploded, throwing the cellar into a world of shadows and flashes of light off flints.

I bit my bottom lip and glanced around. How could we get out of here in the midst of all this deadly chaos?

Another stray bullet found a barrel and it trembled and shook, brown, foul-smelling liquid pouring onto the floor.

The whiskey just flowed, gallons and gallons lost… And then an idea hit me.

Praying to God I wouldn't catch lead, I dove from my hiding place toward Colt's, which was still behind the pyramid of whiskey barrels. He looked at me questioningly as I pressed my palms against the barrels. The next second, he caught on, and then the next, we were both pushing. Pushing as hard as we could.

One after the other, the six barrels rolled forward. Without waiting to see the damage of over two thousand pounds of whiskey against the remaining wolves, Colt seized my hand, and we climbed the cellar steps. He swerved us to the left and we ran down the dark hall to the door at the end.

"The kids went this way," Colt panted as we ran.

The kids knew how to get out thanks to Raymond Harold Fitzpatrick. And because of me, Ray was dead.

The guilt made me cringe with physical pain, but Colt held me upright, supporting me as we burst through the door into a small storage closet.

It was as Ray had described, but Colt clearly hadn't been expecting a closet. He fumbled and slammed into the side of the wall. Pushing away left a smear of red on beige. I couldn't tell exactly where he was bleeding, only that the wound wasn't shallow.

I extracted myself from his side and ran my hands along the opposite wall and down the base boards. Feeling something loose, I kicked at it with the toe of my shoe and the hidden door creaked open. Breathing out a sigh of relief, Colt threw his weight against the door and we burst into a dark office space.

The room was fairly large, double the size of the Dragon—or maybe it just felt that way because of the sparse furniture. Laid out on the thin, rough carpet were eight desks lined in four rows, by two columns. Rolling chairs were tucked into each one with filing cabinets towering next to them. There were typewriters and in-and-out cubbies with papers and pens. The lamps on the desks were all dark.

Except one.

At one of the middle desks was a woman leaning against the wooden edge, her silhouette illuminated by the light of that one gold lamp. At her feet were three small figures, and in her hand…was a revolver.

Sniffling came from their dark shadows and I praised God the children were alive. For now.

The woman was blonde with a lavender flapper dress. It was the woman from the cellar. The one who had poured the drink down my throat. Except the only difference now was that there was a third eye in the center of her forehead. Blue and unblinking.

She turned to us, her blue eyes a dark cobalt in the gloom. "Took you long enough."

Colt stepped forward. "Millie, let them go."

The cyclops girl raised her hands, the gun's trigger guard looping around her thumb so the revolver hung loose and dangling.

Colt and I remained where we were, unsure. Was this a trick?

In five quick steps, she crossed to us and flipped over the gun in her palm, holding the muzzle in her hand and extending the grip to where Colt could easily seize it and point it at her.

"Take it. You have maybe two minutes before the rest come."

"The rest?" Colt asked, taking the revolver.

"Of course. Gin always has more," the flapper said calmly. Her gaze was far-off and her third eye stared straight ahead at nothing. It was unnerving. "The werewolves and minotaurs are on their way. I stopped the children because they'd never make it out of the city alone with a horde of monsters combing the streets. But you can lead them to safety. There's a boat. A dingy with a ferryman by the wharf. If you can get there he can take you up the lake to a church. The monsters won't be able to follow you."

"Why are you helping us?" Colt asked just as calmly, though my own heart was beating a mile a minute.

"Because you now owe me a favor."

"A favor? Not likely. How can we even trust you?"

"Why would I lie about this? I could use my eye to communicate to Gin telepathically right now and tell her where you are and it would be all over, but I'm giving you an out."

"But why?"

"Because *I* want an out."

"You want to come with us?" I asked.

"No, I want you to shoot me. With that gun." She pointed to the revolver in Colt's hand.

I lifted my fingers to my mouth as horror washed over me.

"No," Colt said.

"Do it, or I will call them all here now."

"You can just come with us—"

"*No!* That won't stop the pain." It was the first time her voice broke. Her calm exterior fell away as a crazed look entered her eyes. She reached trembling hands into her curls, tugging at their roots. "My head…hurts all the time. It hurts. It hurts. It hurts. It hurts." She dropped to the floor. "I can't stand Gin's voice in my head. And I can hear her all the time. What she thinks about. What blood tastes like. There are others that I can hear, each thought and desire louder than the last. It's like a constant foghorn in my head. Like a train whistle. I can't take it anymore. I can't. I can't. I can't."

She continued to mutter and shake and rock back and

forth as if the clasp on her sanity had finally snapped.

Colt's jaw tightened. "Eris, go take the kids outside. Don't wait for me. Keep walking."

I was reminded of the time I'd found a sick kitten in the alley and took it to Dr. Boursaw. He was a veterinarian. He could help her. But instead, he told me that it had contracted an infection and it was too far gone. It kept mewing and mewing in pain. In the end, he stuck a needle into the kitten and it went quiet.

I cried for a week afterward.

"Make it stop. Make it stop. Make it stop," she whispered over and over again.

Colt leveled the gun at the girl hunched over the office floor, moaning and trembling.

With numb legs, I ankled over to the children and guided them up with gentle hands. I ushered them outside through the front door of the telegraph company.

We got ten steps when the sound of a gun pierced the still night air, and a howl quickly followed.

Chapter Twenty-Two

The Agent

Millie's body fell to the floor. I'd shot her right in the third eye. Right in the spot that had tormented her until her last breath. I promised myself then and there that once I'd gotten through all this mess I would hunt down Gin and drive a stake through her heart.

Even though it was too late to take back what I'd done, I was already asking myself if there had been another way to save her. Yet I knew deep down there wasn't. You can't remove a cyclops eye—it's too close to the brain—and the poor girl had suffered long enough. Even so, I had pulled the trigger. She was another name to add to my list. Another face to haunt my nightmares. Another sin to mark my soul.

This time, I didn't dismantle the gun. I tucked it into my jacket and reached down and closed Millie's eyes with two fingers.

Then I ran out of the telegraph office. Down the street, heading in the direction of Lake Michigan, I could see Eris, her white dress glowing in the gloom, and three smaller figures around her.

I caught up to her just as the third howl ripped through the air.

A pack of ten men—turned monsters—rounded the corner. The gaslight bounced off their coats of brown fur and shiny bull horns.

Reaching down, I picked up the smallest kid and drew out Millie's gun in my other hand. Without a word to each other, Eris and I turned our walk into a run.

The monster horde gave chase.

We were a block and a half ahead, but Navy Pier was still a ways to go and we had two younger children with much smaller strides than the monsters after us.

As we ran down the shadowy, lamp-lit streets, I tried to turn and aim a shot at the oncoming monsters but quickly realized it was too risky. There was a one in a thousand chance I could hit my mark while running.

The office buildings and skyscrapers shifted into steelyards and warehouses and factories. The stench of fish permeated the air, replacing the scents of oil, coal, and the occasional sour dumpster. The pier was well within reach, but the monsters were now so close they were practically on top of us.

The kids were stumbling and exhausted, and when the boy tripped and Eris had to catch him, I knew we wouldn't make it.

Growls, yips, snarls, and howls grew to a dull roar. The alley we were in was wedged between two large warehouses on either side. They were abandoned, or maybe just closed for the incoming winter months. A clang resounded overhead, like feet hitting a fire escape.

They were above us now.

Moonlight stretched down into our little alley, illuminating an open door into the warehouse just ahead on the right.

A block away, there was the pier. We were so close, but we wouldn't last even twenty more yards.

Making a snap decision, I grabbed Eris by the elbow and jerked her into the warehouse. The two kids came after her and I led us toward the massive building's center. The monsters followed like fire ants swarming a piece of cake at a picnic.

Some burst through windows overhead, some leaped onto crates piled ten feet in the air, and some followed in our exact footsteps.

The warehouse looked to be some kind of storage for ship parts. Ropes and cables and big steel contraptions poked out of crates and boxes. Windows made the perimeter of the warehouse, two stories up. Large cranes hung from the ceiling and big trappings dangled above like an abandoned training facility for trapeze artists.

As we ran across the open concrete floor stained with oil, I scanned the back of the warehouse. *Shit, if there isn't…*

But I found it. A back door.

"Kid!" I yelled at the little girl. "See if that's open!" I pointed to the shadowy door nestled in the corner.

Without a word, the girl raced ahead, tired but spurred on by a mission.

The door opened at her touch.

Seeing beyond the doorframe into the dark wharf—the waters of Lake Michigan reflecting the glow of the moon and streetlights scattered along the piers—a sort of calm washed over me.

It was right there. I could get them out.

I stopped and pivoted around, still holding the little boy in my arms. He clung to my neck tightly as I surveyed our pursuers.

They were just feet away. I counted three minotaurs

and seven werewolves. They were more wolves than men at this point. Three had fallen on all fours, their back legs transformed into haunches. Their shirts were gone and rich chocolate-brown fur coated their back, chest, arms, and their elongated snouts. The minotaurs were slower, all on their two feet, panting and stomping, charging ahead.

A tight hand grabbed my arm, yanking me close. *Eris.* I passed the child into her arms and pointed to the door. "Get out of here!"

She looked back at the open door, then at me, and then at a werewolf crouched on a tower of crates just two feet away, mere seconds from pouncing.

I could see the anguish in her eyes. Our roles from ten minutes ago reversed.

The little boy pressed his face into her neck as another howl ripped through the air. She closed her eyes briefly and tears spilled down her beautiful cheeks. *Decision made.* Then she turned for the back door and ran.

The werewolf lunged, his claws scraping against the crates, sending wood chips into the air. I met him dead-on, twerking my hips to punch him square in the throat. With a yip, he flew backward into a rack of steel tools.

That's when they all attacked at once.

I took a deep, deep breath and surrendered to the heat.

The burning in my chest that had begun since I first met the siren had grown insurmountably in the past hour, building and building until I could no longer hold it back. Thankfully, I no longer had to.

Smoke curled out of my nostrils as my shoulders sagged with its release. I took one step, leaned forward, and roared.

A column of flames exploded out of my mouth. Fire, red and angry, and all-consuming blasted into the crates and the oncoming monsters.

Howls and cries bounced off the walls and the ceiling

of the warehouse as the inferno consumed the four nearest werewolves. They fell on their backs, thrashing, as their screams turned into that of men, not monsters. It just went to show—we all burned the same.

The other werewolves and minotaurs hesitated to come after me, especially once they saw how the flames had taken hold and danced across the bodies of their brethren.

But I did not hesitate.

Once I let go of the flames, they were damn near impossible to contain.

The fire poured out, rolling across my tongue and lips, and I tilted my head to angle the flames upward. It traveled up the shipping crates and into the hanging trappings. I swiveled left and right and let the flames roll across every surface until the entire warehouse was ablaze. Glass windows exploded and smoke pressed into each crack and crevice.

And then the burning within me faded, like the light dying on a candle run out of wax. I was spent, the old scars on my back no longer aching, but *roaring* with agony. My body collapsed amidst the flames and I let it take me—I deserved a death of my own making.

The darkness came swift and easy and I welcomed it.

• • •

"Try to use them, Colt. They're just like arms and legs. They're yours to command."

"Get them off. Please."

"Colt, this is what you've been training for. Remember? You wanted to be a soldier. This is how you serve your country."

"No, I never wanted this. Get them off."

"Use your damn wings, boy!"

The bones on my back that did not belong to me...

twitched. A soft shhh *sound filled the air as the red leathery wings trembled then flapped, brushing the clean white linoleum.*

The cold hand of the devil touched my soul. These…these things on my back were mine.

God? If you can hear me, please save me.

• • •

A soft light tickled my eyelids and, for a while, I resisted its pull. The longer I could put off hell, the better.

Because that's where I was. I had to be. I mean, if there *was* an afterlife, then I certainly wasn't in the good place.

Except when I finally opened my eyes, I was proven wrong.

A warm yellow glow backlit the figure of a young woman with delicate features and gentle waves of autumn hues. She was straightening the curtains of white lace, trying to stop the morning sun from getting through.

I moved my head to the side to get a better look and felt the soft cotton of a pillow under my cheek. Blinking, I slowly evaluated the rest of my body. It appeared I still had feet and arms and hands, but every single inch of me *hurt.*

I could count on my hand the number of times I'd released my flames, and it always took a gigantic toll on my body. This time, I hadn't been expecting to deal with it.

Yet, here I was, lying on a fluffy mattress in crisp cotton sheets, watching Eris straighten my curtains.

Alive.

I tried to lift myself onto my elbows, but pain shot through my muscles and they seized, making me fall back into my previous position. At my groan, Eris turned around, and when she saw me awake, her face lit up with a big beautiful smile.

She dropped to her knees next to my bed and took my right hand in both of hers.

"The kids?" I croaked, my voice raw from all the fire and smoke.

She nodded with a smile.

So, she still couldn't talk. I wondered if she'd ever be able to talk again. Then again, if Gin had intended to hand her over to her creator then it couldn't be irreparable.

"Where are we?" I asked.

Eris pointed to something on the wall, and I glanced over at the ornament, quickly recognizing it with a drop in my stomach. A crucifix.

"A church?" That's right—the church Millie mentioned. We must've made it.

Eris nodded, still smiling.

"How did…how did you get us here?"

Her brow furrowed.

"Sorry, no, you don't have to explain. I can wait."

Eris shook her head and held up a finger. Then she turned to the nightstand next to my single bed, grabbed the pad of paper and pen, and started to scribble furiously on it. While she wrote, I shifted just slightly to check my wound. It was bandaged properly, and even though I was naked from the waist up, I felt clean and…safe.

An odd feeling after believing I'd been dead only minutes ago.

Eris drew my attention back to her when she held up her pad of paper.

It explained how Kenneth, Eugene, and Marion—the three kids we'd saved—had found the man with the dingy, while Eris had returned to the burning warehouse and dragged me out. With the old man's help they got into a boat that took them up to St. Agnes Catholic Church. The nuns here promised we could stay until we were back on our feet.

I wondered if that would be true if they knew we were monsters, but I didn't point this out to Eris. She just seemed so pleased to be here. And happy to see me awake.

Which didn't make sense, either.

She had to have seen what I'd done. The truth of what I was, and what I could do. She'd watched me burn down an entire warehouse, and still she looked at me without fear or judgment.

"You shouldn't have gone back to get me. That was dangerous."

She scowled at me, then flipped over a new page in her notebook and wrote in all caps, *WE'RE EVEN*. "Even" was underlined three times.

I couldn't get too mad at her, since I had done the same. But the idea of her running back into a burning building and dragging me out…it made my stomach clench with worry and my skin grow icy with fear.

Eris set down the paper on my sheets and leaned forward, taking my hand again. It was only then that I noticed new bandages on her fingers and palms. I encircled her delicate wrists with my fingers and lifted them closer to my face.

"You burned your hands."

She pulled away, letting loose a small sound of protest in the back of her throat.

Pressing my head back into the pillow, I stared up at the blank white ceiling, picturing her grabbing my coat doused in flames, touching the searing hot doorframe as she dragged me outside…

I felt her gentle touch on my bare arm, just above my elbow.

"You know what I am now?" I asked the ceiling.

I could hear the sound of her picking up the pad of paper and her scribbling again. She held up the paper. The word was in all lowercase script this time. As if she didn't want to yell it. As if she wanted to whisper it.

dragon

The word seemed to taunt me. It was something that I'd been, and still was, in many ways, yet it felt so distant. I'd had my wings for hardly a week before they were removed because they believed me to be too dangerous with them… and they were right.

After what felt like a full minute of staring at the word, I lifted my gaze to meet hers. I fully expected to see fear there, but instead she was staring at me in earnest. Somewhere between pity, empathy, and something…intense. I wasn't quite sure what it was, but it wasn't fear.

"How are you not scared of me?" I asked her in disbelief.

She'd watched me blow flames. I'd turned ten seven-foot-tall monsters into piles of crisp skeletons and flecks of ash.

If the devil ever walked the earth, then maybe I was his cousin.

Her brow furrowed as she looked down at me and her mouth opened and closed, then she shook her head and put her pen to paper.

You saved me. And the children.

I blew out a breath. "You make me sound like a hero. I'm not."

More scribbling.

I know what you are now. You're not a monster.

I'd told her on the train that she didn't know what I was. Now she knew *what* but she didn't know everything.

Eris wasn't a priest or a nun, but we were in a church and there was no one else I wanted to confess my sins to. I closed my eyes and began my confession.

"The Treaty of Versailles ended the Great War, but it didn't end the government's intense paranoia of the next biggest threat. The army went out to orphanages and picked up young boys, telling them they could fight for their country.

For peace." I licked my lips and closed my eyes, seeing that day where the orphanage lady came in and pointed at me and said, *this one is the biggest.* "But that wasn't why we joined. We joined because we wanted a family. Brothers who would watch our backs. I'd had every intention of joining the army, but then the BOI came to my orphanage. They wanted me to be a new kind of soldier. A special operative. I was twelve.

"They taught me how to fight, how to read people, how to fire a gun. But it was more than just agent training, there were medical tests, too. I didn't understand why, but they took samples of my blood and hooked me up to an IV with weird glowing blue liquid that made me feel sick, weak, and very strange. One morning they wheeled me in for a surgery." Wincing, I pushed myself up onto my elbows and gingerly turned to the side. The sheets slipped down, exposing my bare back and the thick, ropelike scars right inside my shoulder blades. There was a sharp intake of breath, then soft fingertips brushing my scars. I shivered from the gentle touch and her skin on mine. It was an area that had never been touched except by a surgeon's hands.

It took me a long couple of minutes to find my voice again. "The next thing I remembered was waking up on my stomach with wings attached to my back." I let myself fall back into the pillows and trained my gaze on the ceiling. "There was clapping and cheering once they saw that I was awake—it was like they hadn't even believed I'd survive the surgery. Maybe there were others before me. I don't know."

"The wings...I didn't handle them well. They were a part of me, like my own arms, but they also felt like they had a mind of their own. I don't know if it was all in my head, or if the wings really were alive, but I swear I could hear them whisper at me. In just a week, I felt like I was going mad."

I thought of Millie, cringing and twisting and crying on the floor. I'd felt the same.

Get them off. Get them off.

It hurts. It hurts.

Kill me.

"And they kept telling me to use them. To try and... and *fly*." The ceiling grew blurry and a new kind of burning started in the back of my throat. It reached my eyes, too. Not wanting her to see, I laid my arm over my eyes and continued, pressing on, "They didn't even know what dragon wings could do, but they wanted to see it. Whatever *it* was. They grew impatient. They wanted to see a *dragon's* power. They pushed and pushed and before I knew it, my chest was so hot. Hot like I'd swallowed a mouthful of burning coals. I opened my mouth and..."

My throat caught, and my words stuttered. For several long moments I said nothing.

You never forget your first kill, McCarney had told me once.

He was right.

"Flames just poured out. Before anyone even realized what was happening, six people lay on the ground, crumbling to ash."

Searing tears rolled down the corners of my eyes, dampening my pillow.

"I killed them. I killed them all. Doesn't matter whether or not I meant to, or wanted it, they died because I wasn't strong enough. Plain and simple. My fault."

My sins.

I was meant to be a soldier. Their deaths should walk with me, not smother me. But they did. Even after they cut off my wings and I felt like limbs were missing...the flames stayed inside me. They came forth in response to emotions of distress, anxiety, anger...panic.

I'd told myself I'd gotten over it all. I was older, certainly stronger, than the thirteen-year-old scared kid on the lab room floor. But had I?

Then I saw myself in Millie, on the office floor, begging to die. It was me who wanted to die then, and instead I killed everyone else.

My sins. My fault.

Monster.

Feather-light fingertips brushed my jaw. Surprised at the touch, I moved my arm slightly above my head to find Eris leaning over me. A curtain of chestnut waves fell across her shoulder while her gaze held mine—strong and unyielding.

Before I could move, or say anything at all, she closed the small distance between us and pressed her lips to mine.

Her kiss was brief, but it was gentle, tentative, and brave—*her* in a kiss. Her hand lay across my jaw, while the base of her palm rested against the pulse in my neck. I was sure she could feel its restless beat—not that I cared if she could. In fact, I hoped she did. I needed her to know how she affected me. How, with one simple, innocent kiss, I was completely *gone.*

It wasn't that her lips were smooth and full, or that she smelled like fresh cotton with just a hint of herbal tea, lemon, and honey, or even that she was so brave and good that she saved children from a den of monsters and pulled people out of warehouse fires...

It was that...in this kiss, I felt forgiven.

Instead of being offered a chance at redemption, she gave redemption to me freely. She was telling me that she saw all of my sins and ugliness but believed I could be saved anyway.

It was everything I didn't know I needed.

Although the kiss was short, she didn't retreat. She met my eyes and her fingers against my jaw seemed to press harder on my skin.

I reached up and parted the curtain of her hair to brush her bottom lip with my thumb. Her eyelashes flickered downward, gaze jumping to my mouth.

Ah. There it is.

Sin replacing virtue. Lust replacing chastity.

And if *this* made us sinners, I wouldn't walk through the gates of hell—I'd run through them.

My hand wove into her hair at the back of her neck and I guided her mouth to mine.

But before we could kiss for a second time, a knock sounded at the door.

Eris practically fell. Pressing her fist to her lips, she stumbled back a few steps. Except she forgot that a chair was there, so her feet got caught in its legs and she fumbled to steady it.

The door opened and an old nun walked in. She looked from Eris's red face to my irritated expression and said, "Ah, he wakes. How are you feeling?"

Before I could answer, Eris bowed her head, lips pressed together, and escaped the room.

I fisted my hands at my sides, frustrated I couldn't just up and chase after her.

The old nun cleared her throat, trying to capture my attention. "Mr. Clemmons, I'm Sister Adaline. I believe we have much to discuss."

I was still staring after Eris when she said, "About having a dragon in my church."

Chapter Twenty-Three

The Siren

An amazing thing happened. Well, many amazing things.

We escaped the Cerberus Club. We rescued three children. Colt breathed fire. I dragged him out of a burning building. Kind nuns took us in and gave us food, aid, and shelter.

And then I kissed Colt.

I wasn't sure how much of it was a moment of weakness and compassion for his horrible past, or just purely because I *wanted* to. Regardless, I was both thrilled and absolutely petrified.

Of course, it wasn't as if we could just talk through what that kiss meant, at least not soon. The nuns had been giving me this herbal tea with lemon and honey that might help my raw throat, but there was no telling exactly when, or if, my voice would come back.

Being unable to talk honestly hadn't bothered me until Colt woke up. Just like in The Blind Dragon, I felt this desperation to answer all his questions and ask hundreds of my own. Did he feel all right? When had his dragon wings been removed? What had the BOI done after he'd accidentally killed those people? I wanted to tell him it wasn't his fault. He'd been a child coping with something wholly supernatural, and far, far too powerful. How could he be expected to control something like dragon flames?

They'd been cruel to force that on a child. Crueler still to let him believe those people's souls should mar his.

When he told me all those things, when he laid his arm across his eyes, I knew I had to do something. *Anything.*

Down the corridor, twenty steps from Colt's room, I stopped and leaned against the cold stone wall, recalling that moment. With a soft groan, I covered my face with my hands.

That first kiss had been innocent, but I knew the second kiss wouldn't have been.

I should call myself lucky that Sister Adaline came in when she did. I should, but God forgive me, I wished she hadn't.

Moving my hands from my eyes to my burning cheeks, I licked my lips, still feeling his.

For over a day, I'd been hovering by Colt's bedside, anxious for him to wake. Despite the nuns' assurances, I'd been so worried that he'd never open his eyes again. That all the smoke in his lungs and the deep scratch on his side had been enough to do him in.

But now that he was awake, perhaps it was time to shift my attention back to the children that I felt somewhat responsible for. I enjoyed being with them and it would give me the chance to clear my head, which still felt very much overheated.

The grounds of St. Agnes were that of a typical Roman

Catholic Church. There was the main sanctuary, with an altar, pews, stained-glass windows and dusty old hymnals. It was connected by stone-covered walkways to the rectory and to the convent where the nuns lived and took care of orphans from time to time.

They didn't have the facilities of a full orphanage, but they housed what kids they could until they became of age to live and work on their own. And from what I could tell, the kids loved St. Agnes. They had a little schoolroom, a vegetable garden, and plenty of space to play and adventure. Just being here for a day made my insides warm. This was what I'd wanted—a quaint life. Tending to gardens, cooking, feeling like I was a part of a community, a family.

It made me miss my own. How were Stan and Madame Maldu and my little band?

Leaves skittered across the walkway to the chapel and batted against the new navy blue dress the nuns had given to me. Their kindness so far had made me realize that I would've been content to stay here and become a nun. To sing and follow the word of God and take care of children…it seemed like a happy enough life to me. But then I'd gone and kissed Colt and, well, now I wasn't so sure.

I opened the door to the narthex and was met with a deep and profound quiet. Sister Louisa had said the kids would be here, but they couldn't be. Not in this silence. Or maybe they actually *were* reading their bibles. Doubtful.

Just to make sure, I creaked open the massive oak doors and peeked inside. Afternoon sunlight streamed through the stained-glass upper windows on either side of the nave. The glass murals told the stories of the three recognized archangels of Roman Catholicism. Raphael was to the left, holding his staff, his right palm outward, with gold sunlight shining through as if he actually was healing someone—like in all the stories. Gabriel was on the right, holding his fabled horn as if to proclaim some prophecy of the birth of a saint or the savior himself.

Then there was Michael. The angel closest to God was in the window behind the altar wearing robes of red and gold, covered in silver armor. In both his hands he held a sword pointing downward, with his eyes cast up to the heavens.

Multicolored lights of the stained glass decorated the dark wood of the pews and hit the gilded gold statues of angels, Mary, and of Christ. Autumn wreaths hung on the doors and on the front of the altar—that one in particular seemed messier than the rest, and I guessed the children had made it.

The sanctuary was mostly empty with the exception of one lone figure sitting up at the steps of the altar. It was a man in a dark coat and fedora, hands tucked into the folds of his jacket and head bent low, the brim of his hat hiding his face.

Is he praying?

Not wanting to interrupt his time with God, I turned to leave when a curtain pulled back to my left, in the north transept area. The curtain of the confessional. A woman came out dressed all in black—mourning clothes.

As she walked up to the man, he looked up at her with a question in his eyes. She shook her head, and then passed through the crossing, down the aisle straight toward me. Realizing this, I quickly opened the door for her, and she went by me with a small nod of thanks. Her black cloche hat was pulled down far enough to cover her forehead and cast shade over light blue eyes. Strangely, it felt as if I'd seen her before. Dark hair, mature features, an enigmatic air…

She probably just had one of those faces that were so striking they seemed memorable.

I started to follow the woman out and let the door close behind me, to leave the man to his prayers, when he called out to me. "Excuse me, miss?"

Rhatz. I can't answer.

But it was incredibly rude to just walk away. So I turned and hurried down the aisle to the man.

He was now standing at the bottom steps of the altar, wearing a sharp, expensive suit and a gentle expression—one that was not quite a smile, but close to one, as if he wanted to smile but couldn't find the strength to do it. He was handsome enough, with brown eyes and brown hair, sides lightly streaked with gray.

"I'm sorry to bother you, Sister, but do you know where Father is?"

He thought I was a nun. Wishing I'd brought my pad of paper with me, I shook my head.

"I see," he said with a sigh, then walked over to the front pew and sat. "I suppose I'll have to come back next week then. I just…" He leaned over, resting his elbows on his knees, and rubbed his brow with another deep, labored sigh.

Even if I could speak, I wasn't sure what I'd say.

The man looked up again, inspecting me. "How long have you been a sister?" he asked.

I waved my hands while shaking my head.

"Oh, you're not?"

I nodded.

"You're mute?"

I gestured to my throat, making a tiny squeaking noise.

"Oh, I see. Throat not feeling well, eh? My apologies."

I shrugged, then, when he still looked troubled, I tried to mime pouring tea and holding a cup to my lips.

At that, he actually smiled. "How clever. My son loved charades."

Loved, as in past tense.

The smile faded from his lips, reading the sadness on my face. "I'm sorry, I didn't mean to make you uncomfortable. You're just easy so talk to, I suppose it's because you can't talk back. If you need to leave, I understand."

When he hung his head again, he felt very much like a man who had just lost everything. Steeling my nerve, I crossed to the pew and sat next to him, placing a gentle hand on his arm.

Glancing up, he gave me a small frown. "Are you sure?"

I was a far cry from a priest, or even a nun, but this man reminded me of the one I'd just left who had also needed his own confession, so I nodded.

The man wrung his hands and then took a deep breath. "My son died because of me."

My eyes widened, but I kept my hand where it was.

"I'm a bad man, and an even worse father. I was a rum-runner, and a damn good one," he continued. "I worked heavily with the mob, but every day it became more dangerous for my family. I tried to leave, but it's practically impossible to get out once you're in. I should've seen the writing on the wall when they were tightening the screws on me. I should've sent my family away. But I was arrogant and wrong. So wrong. They gunned him down in an alley. Left him there for me to find...not even two blocks from our apartment."

The silence stretched inside the chapel. So big and heavy it could carry across a canyon created by the legend Paul Bunyan himself.

I could feel the glares of the archangel Michael, and of Gabriel and Raphael. I could almost hear their holy voices whispering, *You're just like him.*

Colt may have gotten involved with me because of his job, but now he was helping me and staying by my side out of the goodness of his heart. I'd been so relieved to be at St. Agnes, where the world was peaceful and happy, that I'd forgotten how we'd gotten here in the first place. My creator hunting *me* down with guns and monsters. Not Colt. *Me.*

He had almost died in the fire, all because he'd been

helping me.

I was scared that if Colt stayed with me any longer, this stranger's guilt would be my own.

"I'm not asking God for forgiveness," the man said softly, his voice like the lowest note in the church organ. "I don't deserve it. But this might be the best place to talk to Jacob. To tell him how sorry I am and how much I miss him." Then he sighed deeply, placed his hands on his thighs, and stood. I followed as it seemed the right thing to do.

"I'm sorry to take up so much of your time, miss. I do hope your throat feels better."

He started down the aisle, then stopped and turned back toward me. He dug into his coat pocket and pulled out what looked like a hard candy in a red cellophane wrapper. "Here. It's my favorite brand of throat lozenges. As thanks for listening."

He dropped the lozenge into my outstretched palm and walked down the aisle through the giant oak doors into the narthex...leaving me with a sin I hadn't even known I was carrying.

Selfishness.

I was being selfish in keeping Colt with me. True, I'd told him he should leave, but that's the kind of person he was. He helped people, and he didn't abandon them. Leaving the BOI meant he didn't live on blind faith. He decided what was right and what was wrong and, in me, he must've seen something right.

That should've made me feel better, but it didn't. I felt worse. So much worse. Because I was selfishly accepting his help when I should be running away from him. Running away from everyone.

I mounted the steps toward the altar and stood there, looking up into the face of the angel closest to God in his red robes and silver armor and all his glory.

While in The Blind Dragon, I used to imagine I was one of them.

An angel, alone, in the spotlight.

Tell me what to do, Michael.

But I already knew what I had to do. I had to leave Colt, and everyone and everything I cared for and disappear and never speak a word again. I'd run from him for the third time, but it would be the first time that I didn't want to.

The creaking of the giant oak doors echoed through the chapel and I whirled around, expecting to see the man again. I hurriedly unwrapped the lozenge and stuffed it into my mouth—maybe it would soothe my throat enough for me to talk to him. To tell him that his son *was* listening, and then to tell him he shouldn't wear his hat in the sanctuary.

Two small heads poked out from the doors. Marion and Kenneth.

Their faces lit up with great big smiles when they saw me. "Eris!" Kenneth called, running down the aisle. I was nearly knocked over as he flew into my stomach, wrapping his thin arms around my waist. Marion followed her brother, but slower, much more mature for her twelve years of age.

The rest of the kids headed toward the altar as well, holding hymnal books. Sister Edna took up the rear with young Eugene at her side, gripping her hand. He'd really taken a shine to the nun.

"Oh, Eris." Sister Edna greeted me with a smile. "Will you be joining us for choir practice?"

Sucking on the throat lozenge that held a rich cherry flavor, I shook my head. I had a lot of thinking, and planning, to do.

"Please, Eris, please?" Kenneth whined, still holding my waist.

"Leave her alone, Kenny," his older sister admonished. "Her throat still hurts."

But…it didn't, actually. Not anymore. The tasty, soothing lozenge seemed to coat my sore throat and vocal cords in a protective, healing film.

Clearing my throat, I tried to speak.

"It's feeling better," I said, then blinked in surprise. My voice sounded surprisingly normal.

"I would say it's feeling a lot better." Sister Edna chuckled. "Well that's wonderful. Will you be staying then?"

Kenny had reluctantly let go, but looked up at me with pleading eyes. I smiled down at him and ruffled his hair. "For a few songs."

Chapter Twenty-Four

The Dragon

Sister Adaline wore a traditional black habit with a white collar. She *looked* like a kind old woman, the quintessential image of a nun.

But looks were deceiving. Who was this woman and what place had we come to that knew about monsters and dragons?

She smiled at my confusion—it must have been all over my face—and leaned over to pick up the glass of water from my bedside. "Here, drink."

I took the water but didn't drink. My fingers curled around the glass, and I imagined it cracking under the pressure of my hold.

"Who are you?" I asked.

"The abbess of St. Agnes. Mother Superior, if you will—are you familiar with canonical order? Hm, doesn't matter. Either way, you can just call me Sister."

"That doesn't tell me shit." I slammed the glass down on the bedside table. Water sloshed from the rim onto the wood.

The nun didn't even flinch. Only her smile faltered. "You

want to know my connection to the monster trade I suppose."

"Obviously. And how you know what I am." Eris wouldn't have told her. She wasn't like that.

Sister Adaline leaned back, almost like she was settling into a big luxurious armchair. "The Catholic Church has been battling demons for a thousand years, Mr. Clemmons. Just because the demons take on different forms doesn't mean our war has ever stopped."

For a long time, I stared at her. "You're telling me that the Catholic Church hunts down monsters?"

Her green eyes narrowed, the wrinkles around them becoming more pronounced and severe. "Not in the way you do, I'm sure. Not with guns or bombs, but with forgiveness, patience. Virtue. Violence breeds more violence. You of all people should know that."

My fingers curled around my bedsheets. "How do you know about me?"

Her chin tilted downward and her jaw tightened in a way that showed intense disapproval. "We'd been aware of the monster trade for some time, but when the BOI came to us with their idea to fight monsters with monsters, a rift opened within our Order. Many in the church agreed with their tactics to put an end to the monsters being used by the mob, while others, including myself, argued against it. At the end of the day, we couldn't stop the government from their experiment on you. We could only send one of our own there to bless you and ensure it didn't get out of hand. We failed." She folded her hands in her lap and fixed me with a level stare. "As for how I knew that it was *you*… I saw the scars on your back."

My blood seemed to stall in my veins, stopping my heart and pulse, as I remembered the day when I looked into the mirror and saw those leathery devil's wings extending behind my back. It was laughable that the church thought they'd be able to bless something so cursed.

"I'd never thought I'd come to meet you face-to-face, but God works in strange, miraculous ways."

I met her smile with a glare. "Leave God out of this, Sister. The people who put those wings on my back were just that—people. God has nothing to do with anything."

Sister Adaline's smile turned down slightly but didn't vanish entirely. "It's a shame you feel that way, Mr. Clemmons. Because I believe God led that girl to you."

Electric tingles ran up and down the base of my spine at the mention of her.

"Do you know what *she* is?" I asked.

"The siren, of course."

"Then you know that we have to leave. Monsters will be coming for her. Soon."

"Yes, I imagine many people would be after her power."

Thinking back to my revelation with Gin, I asked, "Do you know of a corporation with the acronym BKH? That's who's after her."

Sister Adaline shook her head. "Unfortunately, no. I'm somewhat limited in my knowledge when it comes to business and economics." She gave a rueful smile. "Moves too fast for an old woman like me. Besides, I have other things that take up my attention. Speaking of which, I'd like to show you something." She stood from her chair. "If you feel up for walking, I'd ask that you follow me."

She crossed to the door and paused, waiting. I threw off the covers and got to my feet gingerly. I was wearing slacks, but my chest was bare except for the clean white bandages along my side. Grabbing the shirt draped on the corner of the bed, I threaded my arms through the sleeves and followed Sister Adaline out the door, buttoning as I walked.

My bare feet made little noise across the stone floor as the abbess led me around the corner, down the stairs, and into a side door opposite from the kitchen and laundry.

It was a church office full of books and shelves and papers, and…what looked like a small laboratory.

The sight of a microscope, glass vials, and various scientific instruments on a very clean, stainless-steel table made me pause.

Just who were these nuns?

Sister Adaline closed the door behind me and gestured that I take the seat across from her. I stayed where I was, still staring at the miniature lab.

"I dabbled in biology some years ago," she explained, "before I found the calling of the church. It's actually what I wanted to discuss with you. Please, take a seat."

I stood there while she sat at her desk, and we stared at each other a long while, almost in a stalemate. I wanted to get Eris and leave, especially now that I had a solid clue as to who her creator was. But I was still weak from unleashing my flames and the Mother Superior knew it.

She smiled and steepled her fingers. "There is nothing you can do for Ms. Eris at the moment. You are both safe here, so please, indulge me."

Grudgingly, I took the seat before her.

"Why *are* you keeping us safe?" I asked, unable to stop myself.

"We've been providing sanctuary to refugees for hundreds of years. And if Mildred told you about us, then I trust you."

At the name of the girl I'd just killed, a wave of nausea swept through me.

I can't. I can't. Kill me. Kill me.

"So you knew her."

"Oh, yes. She actually lived here up till a couple years ago. Her parents had been killed during a box job gone wrong. They were gunned down. Innocent store owners. Her mother was one of our parishioners. Millie came to me at thirteen, not sure how to make her way in the world. We hadn't started taking orphans at that time, but we let her stay, thinking maybe she could adopt the way of Christ. But..." Sister Adaline shook her head, hiding what seemed to be tears in her eyes. "She was too full of hate."

"She said the ones who killed her parents were monsters, real ones, and she wouldn't let it go. She found the Cerberus Club, found Gin, and decided to go undercover. I begged her not to, but she wanted to do something. Couldn't live with herself otherwise. So she began feeding information to the BOI and, of course, to me. Gin found out what she was doing, but instead of killing her, she gave Millie a choice—become a monster herself or have everyone here, at this church, murdered.

"So Millie chose to become a cyclops. She knew that Gin had been experimenting with that monster part and its abilities. Once she had the eye, she used its power to wipe all knowledge of St. Agnes from Gin's mind. But it took so much out of her that she started to deteriorate. Her mind's walls crumbled. She worried every day that Gin would find out more of her secrets now that they shared one mind. If Gin remembers our existence here—"

"She won't," I interrupted, my voice hoarse.

Sister Adaline's brow furrowed. "How do you know for sure?"

"Because I killed Millie."

The words felt like Latin. Dead. The language of a distant, strange land.

The blood drained from Sister Adaline's face and her wrinkled lips parted. The two of us stared at each other in silence, until the abbess wiped at her eyes and took one long, slow breath. In and out.

"Why?"

"She asked me to."

"Did she?"

"Begged me."

"I see." The old woman bowed her head. "May God watch over her soul."

I said nothing. The heat in my chest was already back, singeing my heart.

Sister Adaline reached for a handkerchief in her desk to wipe her eyes. "I suppose she felt like her job was done, in a way. She sent me the most important piece of information I've ever discovered in the decade I've spent investigating this trade."

I straightened, sitting forward.

"Who? Eris?"

"No. Those three children."

Now it was my turn to be shocked. "Those…what are you talking about?"

"Gin has been working on experiments—"

"I know, with children and the chimera agent."

"The chimera agent is just part of it."

I frowned. "I'm not following."

"It's better if I show you." Sister Adaline stood from her desk and crossed to the little laboratory desk. She picked up a blood smear—a drop of blood squished between two pieces of glass—and inserted it under the microscope. "This is a sample of my blood."

I looked into the microscope and saw normal blood cells and platelets. McCarney had me study some biology, especially hematology, the study of blood, so I knew enough to see that this seemed to be a healthy, normal drop of blood.

"And this is a sample of your blood." She inserted another blood smear after removing hers. If she thought I'd get angry at her for taking my blood without my permission, she didn't show it.

My blood looked normal, with the exception of tiny,

miniscule floating light blue particles. "That's the chimera agent," I observed.

"Correct. And this"—she slid a third blood smear in place—"is Marion's."

Again, normal blood cells and platelets, then the chimera agent, then a third particle. It was green and shaped like a slug.

"What's that?" I asked.

"Are you familiar with Dr. Rivers' work in virology?"

"The study of viruses?"

"Yes. Dr. Rivers headed the Rockefeller Institute for Medical Research. His research is far more advanced than what the public is aware of. He has helped develop a microscope that allows us to see these particles..." She gestured to the microscope. "A gift from him, if you can believe it. We're old friends. Anyway, all three of these children have what looks like a virus in their bloodstream."

"But they're not sick, or they don't look it."

"No, they're not sick, but they are infectious."

"How can you tell?"

"The morning after those children slept in the same room with the others, the rest of the orphans had a slight fever. It didn't last for more than a few hours. I thought it odd, so I tested their blood. The other children now all have the chimera agent and these particles in their blood stream."

I stepped back, my knees weakening, and almost fell over the chair I'd been sitting in. "You're saying they were infected by a virus that Marion, Kenneth, and Eugene carried and now they *have the chimera agent*?" I thought for a minute and glanced at her other blood smears. "What about blood from other sisters? From adults?"

She shook her head. "Yes, I thought of that. But none of us felt feverish at all. I checked our blood compared to theirs and it all looked normal. It's clear that whatever virus this is only affects children." She looked at me with a grave, stone-face expression. "If my findings are accurate, then every child in Chicago could be turned into a monster if this virus were to spread."

After leaving the office, I went to find Eris. I had to talk to her. She needed to know about this virus Gin had manufactured. I was supposed to be the one with all this experience, but I was beginning to rely on her morality as my own compass. What did *she* think?

When I'd asked Sister Adaline why she was showing me all this, her wrinkled lines had formed into a hard mask of severity. "*Because the BOI can do something about it.*"

While I wasn't a BOI agent anymore, her words had given me a glimmer of hope. Maybe I could convince McCarney that this virus was much more important than the lost siren.

The nun in the kitchen told me Eris was likely to be in the chapel, so I stepped outside into the bright afternoon sunlight—now with shoes on—and walked across the courtyard toward the covered stone walkway that led into the chapel.

Slipping into the shadows of the back of the sanctuary… that's when I saw her.

Heard her.

She was singing. At long last, I was hearing her sing.

I was so captivated that I'd almost forgotten she hadn't been able to speak an hour ago.

"*When the dawn is breaking…*"

Her voice shined through the rest of the little children choir, but it didn't overpower them. If anything, it enhanced them.

"*Words of faith and trusting…*"

When she sang, she smiled the biggest, brightest smile I'd ever seen on her. Ever seen on anyone, really. She was glorious in her song.

"*Angels sent from heaven…*"

There were so many paths laid out before me—go to the BOI and tell them about the virus, go in search of Eris's creator to ensure her safety, or even simply forget it all and live in hiding for the rest of our lives.

Whichever path I took, it'd be with her.

Chapter Twenty-Five

The Siren

"Your song was worth the wait."

I didn't even flinch at Colt's voice so close. Even if I hadn't been watching his progress under the stained glass of Raphael, I'd felt him move closer. And now, with the children gone after our little practice, his presence was even more magnified. My body seemed to be drawn to his like the moon orbiting Earth.

"When did you get your voice back?" he asked.

Finally, I lifted my gaze to him, and my heart launched up into my throat.

He wore a simple white shirt, his first few buttons open, revealing his collarbone and just the beginning of his muscular chest, along with dark slacks, shoes, and that was it. No fedora, or tie, or vest. Like this, he felt barer to me than being in a hospital bed, naked from the waist up.

"One of the parishioners gave me a throat lozenge," I said, fingering the red cellophane wrapper in the pocket of my dress. "It helped a lot."

"That's good, then," he said with a short nod. "That means we can leave soon. Eris, I wanted to talk to you about…"

But I'd stopped listening.

I swallowed. *We* can leave.

How foolish I'd been to kiss him. Kissing him…him about to kiss me back…he wasn't about to let me go easily.

Standing from the altar steps, I avoided Colt's eyes and started down the aisle, my hands twisting nervously in front of my waist. His footsteps fell behind me and my breath grew shallow. Leaving him felt next to impossible. The temptation of…of *him* was too great. Even here, in *church*.

I hadn't even realized I was running until Colt caught my wrist. Our breaths sounded labored under the stone awning. Somehow we'd already made it back outside, under the walkways covered in shadows from the early evening sunlight. The door to the church was only a foot away, and though we were outside it felt more like a closet.

"I scared you." Colt's words were tortured, wedged between heavy pants.

I jerked my gaze up to meet his. The sadness there fractured my heart. Like it had when he told me his story and lifted his arm to cover his tears.

"Of my past. Of what I did. Of what I am. I scared you."

I shook my head violently—almost hurting my neck in the process.

He dropped my wrist. "Then why are you running? Was…it because of…"

Again, I shook my head, but slower this time.

"Eris, *talk* to me. Please. I'm begging you."

I lifted my hands to my eyes so I wouldn't have to look at him, like the coward that I was. "Let me go, Colt."

He was silent for a long minute, then said, "I'm not touching you."

I wrenched my palms from my eyes and glared at him.

"You know what I mean. We should...we should split." I didn't sound like myself. My voice was thick and anguished. "We've run into trouble nonstop together. It'll be safer if we go our separate ways."

His heated blue gaze scanned my face. "You mean safer for me," he said slowly.

I said nothing, biting my bottom lip.

"I thought we were past this. I'm not going anywhere."

Angry, frustrated tears sprang to my eyes and I stepped forward, weakly pounding his chest with the sides of my fists. "Please, I'm trying to save you, Colt. You almost died in that fire and I don't want—"

"You *have* saved me. And not just from the fire." Wrapping his hands around my fists on his chest, he leaned down and brushed his lips against mine. Teasingly, but so, so sweet. "Your kiss was my salvation. Thanks to you, I know what redemption tastes like."

My fingers loosened and then curled around his shirt collar. A button popped under my grip as I tugged him closer, needing to know what my own redemption tasted like.

Our kiss in the shade of the chapel was nothing like the one in the light of the nun's room. It was sinful and destructive, dark and rich. Tempting and testing.

His lips found mine first, knowing what I wanted and giving me what I needed. There was nothing tender in the pressure of the kiss. It was demanding and relentless, and I matched it force for force. A strong hand skated down my side and wrapped around my hip to find its place on my lower back. His other hand cupped my cheek, the base of his palm planted firmly in the line of my jaw.

I was unpracticed and inexperienced, but Colt didn't seem to care or notice. He never let one kiss last too long, kissing me as if each one held a distinct flavor in a new angle of our lips. My legs lost their feeling and I couldn't find the strength to hold myself up. I stumbled backward into the wall, and he followed, never once stopping our embrace except when he removed his hand from my cheek to brace himself against the wall.

And then those kinds of kisses didn't seem to be enough. His tongue swept across my bottom lip, requesting entrance, and I gave it to him. A soft hum vibrated in the back of my throat as my tongue met his, stroke for stroke. Breath for breath.

I was ready to hand my soul to the devil. Perhaps he already had it, what with me being a monster and all that. But if it meant I could take this moment and stretch it on for an eternity, I'd give it up to him.

And will you condemn him, too?

Fear hit me like icy water. Like someone just dropped me into the middle of Lake Michigan. Was that what I was doing? Was my kiss a death sentence or the grace of salvation?

He felt the hesitancy in my kiss. "I won't let you go," he murmured, thumbs ghosting across my cheeks. His hands gently cupped the back of my neck, tilting my mouth for a light, tender kiss.

Reassurance.

My hands released his shirt collar and I wrapped my arms around his neck, deepening our kiss once more. The muscles in his back seized with tension as his fingers traced my spine through the material of the dress the nuns had given me, and then up between my shoulder blades.

I was aware of every touch, sound, and scent…

Sweet woodsmoke and coal—the smell of burning.

Now I knew why he always smelled like that. From the moment I'd approached his table in my little speakeasy, I smelled the dragon on him. *In* him?

The scent enveloped me, taking over my mind and senses as I became wrapped in this moment. Threading my fingers into the hair at the nape of his neck, feeling his whole chest press against mine, and his arms box me in, I felt this ache inside. This desire, and this *need*, to confess.

Confess my sin or confess my love? To God, they might be one and the same.

"*Ahem.*"

Colt ripped away from me, nearly stumbling into the opposite wall. My own hands, left empty with Colt's absence, flew to my mouth as I turned my head to find the priest of St. Agnes standing a foot away, barred entrance to the door because of our...petting.

My whole body flushed with heat—of the embarrassment kind, not the kind that I'd just been feeling ten seconds beforehand.

"Good evening," Father Clarence said kindly, his dark eyes twinkling as he regarded us, hands clasped behind his back.

Oh God, I was mortified, and yet I couldn't find an ounce of guilt inside me. Not shame, regret, or guilt...just this inexplicable *elation* coursing through me.

Colt dipped his head but said nothing. His wide-eyed stare at the ground told me that maybe, for the first time in his life, he was completely speechless.

"What a lovely evening, isn't it, Eris?" Father Clarence said.

I rolled my lips between my teeth. "Yes, Father, it is."

Father Clarence was maybe in his late sixties, with balding brown hair, which he made no attempt to hide. He had small cheaters with thick lenses that magnified dark eyes surrounded by a net of wrinkles, mostly from smile lines, if I were to guess.

"But getting chilly. So do come inside before you catch a cold." He gestured to the door with one hand as if to say, *after you.*

"Of course, Father," I muttered, then took the door handle with a shaky grip and pulled it open. With one more glance at Colt, who was still actively looking anywhere *but* at me, I ducked into the kitchen of the annex, Father Clarence right behind me.

Colt did not follow.

I didn't see him the rest of the evening. He seemed to be avoiding me. I couldn't necessarily blame him after that sockdollager of a kiss.

Or...oh, *applesauce*! What if I was the only one who thought it had been the bee's knees? I'd never been kissed before, and maybe I'd really been no good.

At the time, it had felt perfect. But it was so difficult to tell what he was thinking. He hid his emotions behind thick layers while I wore mine on my sleeve.

Like a coward, I was hiding in the kitchen while Sister Louisa cooked dinner, trying to decide when and how to face him. During my mess of emotions, I'd forgotten that there'd been something he wanted to talk to me about.

The children also proved to be quite distracting. They filed into the kitchen, eager for food, and I helped Sister Louisa dish out her hearty, aromatic stew and cut up fresh bread from the oven. Eugene got his stew everywhere and it was all I could do not to laugh at his horrid table manners.

Eventually, after I'd served dinner, I gathered up my courage and went on a hunt to find Colt. We had to *talk* this time about our next move. I could keep my hands to myself... if he could.

As I was passing Sister Adaline's office, a telephone rang. And rang. And rang. Apparently the abbess was not in her office. Peeking through the open crack, I caught sight of the phone. *A phone.* The last time I'd seen one had been at that gas station, which felt like approximately a lifetime ago. How was Stan? Was Madame Maldu back from New York yet? Before making any decision about it, I was already in the office, at the desk, dialing for the operator.

On the fifth ring, Stanley picked up. "Helena?"

My stomach dropped. "No, Stan, it's me. Eris."

"Eris." My name came out in a whoosh of his breath. I heard a creak through the phone and could picture Stanley dropping himself down onto the chair that Madame took all her calls in. "Eris, where are you?" His voice was tormented, strained, in a way that I'd never heard from Stan before. He was one of the strongest people I knew.

"Someplace safe, I promise. A church. Where's Madame? Were you waiting on her call?" The pounding of my pulse drummed in my ears so loud I could barely even make out his next words.

"For three days. It's not like Helena to not check in, Eris. I think…I think something happened to her in New York."

Chapter Twenty-Six

The Dragon

I'd done it again. Lost control.

True, I may not have murdered five people like before, but I'd burned the both of us.

I could still taste the flames of desire for her in the back of my throat. Still feel her soft skin under my fingers and smell sandalwood and roman candles—the scent of the church all over her. Kissing her was like playing with fire...dangerous, but enthralling.

I just had to hope I hadn't ruined this for good. She didn't *seem* scared when she slid her arms around my neck or pressed her body against mine. But I had, perhaps unwisely, given her time to think about it. Mostly because I had needed to calm myself down.

So what if, in that time, she thought about it and realized how...tumultuous that situation had been and how the matter of *us* wasn't a good idea?

Then you'll just have to convince her otherwise, I told myself.

As much as I wanted to think about Eris and *only* Eris for the rest of the evening, the new information from Sister Adaline kept bugging me like an angry gnat.

This new chimera virus had to be shared with McCarney and the rest of the BOI. I'd meant to tell Eris when I saw her, but we'd obviously become distracted.

On my way to Sister Adaline's office, I passed by the kitchen. Eris was inside with the other children. She was serving them dinner and I watched, unable to stop myself from smiling, as she bent down and wiped one of the boy's mouths—either Kenneth or Eugene—with a napkin. She belonged in this setting much more than a smoky drum. Before she could catch sight of me, I continued on past, slipped into the Mother Superior's office, and picked up her telephone. After giving the code, I waited for the voice of my supervisor.

"Mr. McCarney's office, how may I help you?" a peppy female voice answered.

"Barb? It's Colt."

She squealed so loud I had to rip the phone away from my ear. "I knew it. I just *knew* you'd call. Where *are* you? The whole SOCD is in a downright uproar about you taking out those two agents."

"I didn't take them out."

"You put O'Connor in the hospital."

A twinge of guilt pinched my stomach as I recalled the briefcase smashing into the side of his face. "Is McCarney there? I need to talk to him."

"He's out looking for you in Philly."

I cursed under my breath and pounded the side of my fist on Sister Adaline's desk, making a pot of ink tremble. Eris and I had to get on the road—and soon. Who knew when Gin's monsters or BKH could find us again, and I didn't know the next time I'd be able to get my hands on a phone. But I *needed* to tell McCarney of Gin's experiments on children and this unknown virus that made monster breeding easy as pie. I may have left the SOCD for Eris, and other personal reasons, but they did good for this country. Their methods might be shoddy, but you couldn't argue with the results most of the time.

"I need to talk to him," I repeated. "Can you give me the number of his hotel? Please?"

There was a moment of silence on the other end. "I was ordered to get the operator to tell me the location of this call. You're a wanted criminal by the BOI."

I figured something like that would happen. Once they got my call they'd trace it from the operator's switchboard. It would take them some time, but it wasn't impossible.

My hands curled around the side of the desk, nearly denting the wood.

"But I'll give you a few hours' head start."

My brow furrowed. "Why would you do that?"

There was a tapping of nails on her desk. "Because I don't think you'd hurt anyone without a good reason. Even if that reason is a dame who isn't, sadly, me."

I stared long and hard at the wood patterns of the desk and swallowed.

"It's the Bellevue-Stratford Hotel," Barb said after a few seconds. "I hope you're on our side. Mr. McCarney was mighty upset to hear about...you going rogue."

"Barb?"

"Yes?"

"I won't let you down. And you can tell your boss he's got the best damn secretary in the world."

There was a soft chuckle on the other end of the phone. "You'll have about ten hours before agents are sent to your location. I suggest you use them wisely."

Then the phone went dead. Stomach churning, I dialed

for the operator again and asked for the front desk of the Bellevue-Stratford Hotel. I waited a long time to be patched through to his room.

"McCarney."

His voice sounded tired, but from more than just physical exhaustion. Weariness. Stress.

"Sir? It's me."

Shuffling. Banging. A swear amidst the scuffle, then a deep breath. "Colt. What the devil were you thinking?"

"I was doing what I thought was right," I said, pressing the phone to my ear and licking my lips. Then I wiped them with the back of my hand, remembering hers there not long ago. "But there's something I need to tell you. Please, just listen to me."

"I don't listen to traitors."

Rage hit me like a blow to the chest. Heat traveled through me, and I blew smoke through my nose, the hot steam curling and twisting in the air. I could still see the look on Eris's face when she cupped my cheek. Open, honest, pleading, telling me *it's not your fault*.

All my life I'd carried that guilt with me, and now I wondered, how much of it was really mine to bear? The BOI had forced those wings upon me and even though the deaths of those people weighed on my soul, and maybe always would, should they be mine and mine alone?

I gritted my teeth. *No. Maybe not.*

"And I shouldn't have listened to your bullshit of serving my country, when the reality is you turned me into a *goddamn monster*."

Silence over the phone as I breathed out and breathed in. *Calm down.*

"You will listen to me, *sir*, because I just left Gin at the Cerberus Club and I have information the SOCD needs to know about new advancements in the chimera agent." I paused, lifting my gaze to the ceiling, watching the smoke break apart and disperse. "Just because my country betrayed *me*, doesn't mean I'll turn my back on innocent people."

McCarney snapped his fingers, and I could picture him gesturing to someone for a pad and pencil. "All right, Colt. You have my attention."

I told McCarney almost everything, leaving out that I was still with Eris and that she had played such a large role. He needed to know about the chimera agent, the experiments on children, and this strange virus that seemed to affect only them…not about my growing feelings for a woman he considered to be the enemy.

"We'll look into it," McCarney said once I was finally done and practically hoarse. "But this changes nothing. You're still wanted by the BOI. You and the siren. I know she's still with you. Whatever your plans are, I'm begging you to reconsider. Turn yourself in now and all could be forgiven." His voice had that familiar hard edge—that tone I knew so well and once respected.

"Tell me, what were you really planning to do with Eris?"

There was a pause. "That was never up to me."

"Kill her, lock her up, or use her. Those are the options." I glanced at the door. Pictured her in the dining room with the kids eating their stew for dinner. "But we both know it was only going to be option number three. So, who gets to make that call? Who gets to say how people should be controlled? Was it the people who said putting dragon wings on a thirteen-year-old was a good idea? I'm not bringing her anywhere near you people."

"Colt, don't make this mistake. You'll be on the run your whole life."

I knew the BOI and the SOCD. Knew how they thought and how they hunted. I could hide forever, but we couldn't hide from this mysterious creator after Eris who seemed to know her every step.

So we'd find this man, I'd put a bullet in his head, and then we'd run. And we'd keep running if we had to.

"What's that saying, sir? Catch us if you can."

Then I hung up.

I left Sister Adaline's room and was climbing the stairs when I heard the telephone ring incessantly. Was that McCarney calling me back? But how'd he get my location so fast? I retreated back down a few steps and was surprised to see Eris disappear into the office I'd just left. I frowned. What was she doing in there?

The Blind Dragon.

Of course. It was foolish for me to assume she'd never try to check on the people and the home she left behind.

I started back down the steps to tell her that the SOCD would be scouting The Blind Dragon to see if she came back or contacted them. Knowing McCarney, he had someone casing the joint for good measure.

I very much hated the fact that I had to tell her that. Especially since I'd just convinced her not to run from *me* in an attempt to keep *me* safe. If there was one thing I hoped our…our *tryst* in the hallway had done, it was convince her that there was something between us. Something that I wanted to keep, protect, *grow*.

I'd only just reached the office door when Eris ripped it open with a large *whoosh*. Her eyes were wide and her hair looked wild, like she'd just threaded her fingers into her curls and tugged.

"What's wrong?" I asked immediately.

She didn't even seem surprised to see me at the threshold, she just gripped my forearms tightly, her fingertips digging hard into my skin. "Madame—she's *gone*!" She sucked in a breath which bordered on a gasp and a choked sob.

Dammit. I should've thought about this sooner.

"She's been gone for three days, without a word. Stan said she went to New York to look for me. Oh, Colt, what if something happened to her? What if—"

"Slow down," I said, placing my hand over one of hers on my arm and gently squeezing her fingers. "It's going to be all right. We'll look for her." I wouldn't promise her that we'd *find* her, but we could at least look.

Eris blinked, tears clinging to her lashes. "We will?"

I guess our decision was made. I nodded. "Of course. We have to go to New York anyway. BKH has to be in Manhattan and it's our only clue as to who's after you."

She took a deep breath, wiping at the corners of her eyes. "If…if anything happened to her, I…"

"You can't think that way," I murmured, winding my arm around her waist and pulling her against my chest. Her lips, nose, and cheeks were warm and wet through the soft fabric of my shirt as she pressed her face right near my heart. "We'll leave as soon as possible and we'll look for her there."

"And how will you get there?"

For the second time, Eris and I were interrupted, turning to find Sister Adaline standing at the end of the hall.

"Train is fastest," I said.

"Yes, but to get to the train you'll have to go back through downtown Chicago. The place could be crawling with Gin's minions looking for you."

Damn, she was right. Gin would ensure the odds would be against us. And it wasn't as if Lady Luck had been on our side lately.

"I can get you safe passage across Lake Michigan to Michigan City. There's a train depot there with a rail straight to Manhattan."

It seemed like a solid plan, one with the possibility of fewer monsters, which was extremely attractive.

"How soon can we leave?" Eris asked. I glanced down at her, strengthened by the conviction and the intensity of her voice. She was much stronger than she gave herself credit for.

"Leroy owes me a favor. I just have to make a call, but," Sister Adaline said, glancing between the two of us, "he likely won't want to sail at night. First light is probably the earliest we can make it. It's late tonight already, perhaps we should…"

"*Please call him now*," Eris said.

Sister Adaline's spine straightened, eyes dulled, and then stepped into her office purposefully, the door closing behind her.

"Oh no," Eris whimpered. "I just used my voice on her."

While we waited silently in the hall, I kept her hand in mine, rubbing the back of her knuckles every so often with the pad of my thumb. I couldn't think of anything to say that would offer her any consolation. I wasn't very good at shedding guilt myself.

Finally, Sister Adaline emerged from her office, her face grave. "You leave at dawn's light."

Chapter Twenty-Seven

The Siren

Our departure an hour before dawn was without much ceremony. With the exception of Sister Louisa and Father Clarence, no one saw us out. The children were still in bed, and I wanted to keep it that way. Saying goodbye to Kenneth, Marion, and Eugene would've been too difficult and it wasn't something I could easily explain. Especially when the truth was that I would've loved to stay with them.

I took up my post in the passenger seat while Colt steered the car to the end of the gates. The sound of the tires over pebbles echoed across the empty church grounds and I watched the chapel as we drove slowly by. The stained-glass angels seemed to glow, and I wondered if candles had been lit within the sanctuary.

Folding my hands in my lap, I closed my eyes and sent a silent prayer. *Lord, please forgive me for what I've done. I never meant to manipulate Sister Adaline. And please protect Marion, Kenneth, and Eugene.*

A hand closed around mine on my lap, and I opened my

eyes. Colt glanced at me and gave me a small smile. I twisted my fingers into his and felt the tempest inside me quell a little.

At least he was here with me. And yet it felt like another thing I had to pray for. *I'm sorry, Lord, that I'm not strong enough to do this on my own.*

Perhaps God had sent me the man in the fedora yesterday as a warning. To tell me that if I continued along this path with Colt then he would meet the same end as that man's son.

I was still staring at our entwined hands when Colt stopped at the end of the church driveway. I looked up, expecting to see oncoming traffic from the road, but instead found Sister Adaline striding toward us, clutching an envelope.

Colt shifted into park and rolled down the window as the abbess approached the car.

She handed Colt the envelope, her eyes focused on him and avoiding mine. My heart sank even lower. "I have a contact up in New York. A chemist. His name is Dr. Durwich. He might be able to spin up a vaccine, or maybe even an antidote, for Gin's new chimera agent using the samples I collected. I've included a small vial and the blood smears in here. Be careful with them."

Colt took the envelope, opened his jacket, and slipped it into his inside pocket. "Thank you, Sister."

She turned to leave when I spoke up, not wanting to leave her like this. "I'm sorry, Sister. Please, forgive me, I—"

"God forgives you, Eris, and so does his Son," she said stiffly, her gaze finally meeting mine, "but I am having trouble."

She turned and walked back toward the church. Numb, I pressed myself into the passenger seat as Colt turned onto the main road.

Colt followed the directions that Father Clarence had written down for him, while I just sat there, wallowing in self-hatred and disgust.

All my life, I tried so hard, *so hard*, to not take away people's free will because of that exact look I'd gotten from Sister Adaline. Revulsion.

"You made a mistake."

I glanced at Colt, feeling the red heat of shame tinge my cheeks and neck.

"But you learn from it," he said, his voice clear and sure in the silence of the cab, "and get stronger because of it."

My laugh was dry and harsh. "Isn't that my problem? I don't want to be strong or powerful. I want to be normal. That's why it was easier to not talk. Not talking would prevent me from slipping and from hurting the people I cared about."

And protecting myself.

"It might've been easier, but not better, Eris," Colt said, spinning the wheel left, and turning the car down a road that led toward the docks. The waters of Lake Michigan rippled in liquid gold patches from the streetlights. "Protecting others from yourself is the same as cutting yourself off from others. It hurts everyone. You're good and strong and the world deserves to hear you."

Just like that, the heat of shame turned to the heat of unbelievable happiness.

Cupping my hands over my mouth and nose, I squeezed my eyes shut as the sweet praise washed over me.

I would be better. I would learn how to control this power and speak without hurting anyone.

He swung the car into an eastside parking lot next to the piers. Our ticket out of Chicago had to be one of those tall dark ships silhouetted against the beginnings of sunrise.

"Are you ready?" he asked, cutting the engine and turning in his seat toward me.

"What did Sister Adaline give you? What does she mean by 'Gin's chimera agent'?"

Colt winced. "That's right. I haven't told you yet."

"Told me what?" I asked, my pulse skipping.

"The reason Gin had those kids"—Colt stopped, his gaze concentrating on the docks and the water lapping against the barnacle-crusted wood and ships' underbellies—"Kenneth, Marion, and Eugene, was because she'd...she'd been experimenting on them."

My stomach rolled in disgust. Ray had mentioned something of the sort, but I hadn't had time to give it much thought other than *I need to get them out.* Now that Colt had reminded me I had all sorts of questions.

I swallowed, my throat scratchy. "Experimenting on them how?"

Colt slid his gaze back to me. "How old are you?"

I tilted my chin up a little, meeting his gaze. "Eighteen."

He gave me a quirk of a smile. "And I'm almost twenty. Do you remember when you got your pearl? How old you were?"

Counting back the years from being at The Blind Dragon, I answered, "About ten, I suppose."

"I was thirteen when I got my wings."

I flinched. *Thirteen.*

"My point is, the reason we survived such powerful magical items being attached to us was because of our youth. Maybe it's because children's bodies are still developing so rapidly, but whatever the case, we can accept the chimera agent—the new DNA—into our bodies much easier than an adult can. So our percent rate of survival after those surgeries...is much higher."

I stared at him. Long and hard. Trying to understand what this could mean, or maybe just refusing to. "What exactly are you saying?"

"I'm saying," he said with a sigh, "that children, maybe as young as eight and as old as fifteen, are being used more and more to transform into monsters. And Gin has developed a way to distribute the chimera agent widely—without an injection."

"*H-how?*"

"She's been able to develop a virus that carries the DNA of the chimera. It's incredibly contagious and seems to only infect children."

"A virus? But…but why? Why would she want to infect *so many* children?"

Colt grimaced. "That's what we don't know. And that's what I'm worried about."

"But the blood vial that Sister Adaline gave you…that has the…"

"DNA. This is advanced science. Science that the public doesn't know even exists yet. If the world knew what was possible, there could be widespread panic. That doctor in Manhattan might be able to develop something that could prevent the virus from spreading—or maybe even an antidote."

I bit my bottom lip, terror slicing through me in a way I'd never felt before. "Colt…this is…"

"Not our problem."

I blinked. I hadn't been expecting that.

His stare had returned to the shipyard and the horizon over the waters of Lake Michigan. A muscle jumped in his jaw, and he glared out the window like he was taking aim at something. Some invisible enemy I couldn't see.

"That's a job for the BOI. I'll get the doctor this blood, and I've told McCarney all I know, but then that's in the government's hands. It's their job to protect our country. It's what taxes are for, right?" He glanced at me with a rueful smile. He was trying for a bit of humor, but it fell short in the lengthy silence of Father Clarence's car.

"The government is made of people," I said quietly. "People protect people."

"I'm not going to continue being their pawn." He shook his head. "When I knocked Foster and O'Connor unconscious, I knew there was no going back." His eyes, so dark brown they looked like chocolate, glimmered with the reflection of the surrounding streetlights. "Saving the country is not our responsibility. We're just two people with simple desires."

His gaze lingered on me, dropping from my eyes, to my mouth, to my torso, and then to my legs. I was hot and my skin felt electric. Like a fuse had just blown inside me somewhere.

Then he looked away, leaning his elbow on the window seal. "We should go. We have a boat to catch."

We hadn't yet talked about our moment outside the convent door, up against the stone wall and under the shade of the church itself. I guessed he was thinking about it, because I certainly was...and how I'd like to do it again. But he was right. We had to go.

And I knew what he meant by leaving the problem of the virus to the BOI, but I could see in his tense, coiled posture and his angry gaze that it made him frustrated. Something told me he had loved being an agent, whether he admitted it or not. Stopping criminals and putting down monsters—it was in his blood, right there with the dragon.

We gave each other one parting look and I reveled in the feeling of his eyes ensnaring mine. Then we got out, closing the doors behind us with a *snap* that echoed in the chill quiet of the early morning.

He offered his arm and I took it, the two of us ankling down the docks toward Pier 23, where we were to meet Captain Leroy with his ship. Our steps echoed and creaked across the wooden planks as we started out over the open, frigid waters of Lake Michigan.

I was honestly surprised at the look of our transport. When Sister Adaline had first told us about the captain and his ship, I'd expected a simple fisherman's vessel. But this felt like a much smaller version of a luxury cruise liner. I'd never seen the infamous *Titanic*, but I'd heard of its luxurious decor and superior modeled technology. Of course, the comparison of this boat to the Titanic didn't make me feel any better.

Like most ships, it was an aluminum-bodied craft, but with rich brown wood paneling the main cabin at the top. I didn't know much about boats, but more than a few patrons had talked of them before. One zozzled Harvard boyo spent over two hours describing his uncle's wooden-motor yacht with a schooner bow and fantail hull and how it cut across the Charles River like the ship of Odysseus himself.

"Ahoy, there," a friendly voice called as three figures appeared through the thin morning mist.

Colt squeezed my hand against his side and shot me a tiny smile, then he raised his arm and gave a short wave. "Good morning."

Two gruff-looking sailors with dark trousers and thick leather boots, vests, and frayed jackets came into clear view. One of them pushed an older man in a wheelchair with a plaid blanket draped across his legs, who also wore a captain's hat, a captain's jacket, and the quintessential white beard of a ship captain.

In fact, he looked *so* much like a captain that Colt stepped up to him and extended his hand. "Captain Leroy, I presume?"

"Indeed I am. Welcome to the *Cassiopeia*, Mr. Clemmons," Captain Leroy said with a smile, grasping Colt's hand with a clap and a firm shake. He reminded me of St. Nicholas with his white beard and rosy cheeks. "How do you do?"

"Well. Thank you. And this is Mrs. Clemmons."

I froze at the title, trying, and most likely failing, to keep the shock off my face. *Mrs. Clemmons?* What in the tarnation…

As if to sell the story, he wrapped his arm around my waist and pulled me close, giving the captain a charming smile. *Ah.* There he was again. The con man who had ensnared me so easily.

His thumb swept across my ribs and the intimate touch nearly had me leaping out of my skin. *Zounds.* There was nothing fake about that.

"It's a pleasure to meet you, Mrs. Clemmons," Captain Leroy said, extending his hand.

I was still so jingle-brained that I'd barely heard him. It wasn't until Colt's elbow nudged me in the side that I came to and presented my hand. The man brushed a scratchy kiss over my knuckles with his whiskers.

"The pleasure is all mine, Captain," I said.

Captain Leroy shifted back in his wheelchair and gave the two of us another warm smile. Then he gestured to the men beside him. "This big lug is Frank, my first mate, and then his brother, Billy. If you two need anything or have any questions you can always come to us."

"Thank you, sir," Colt answered.

"So then, shall we shove off? It'll take the better part of the day to cross the lake. But not to worry. *Cassiopeia* will get you there in time for the train," he said with a nod.

"That would be swell, sir." Colt gently guided me forward, following behind as first mate Frank rolled Captain Leroy up the elevated gangplank to the ship's main deck.

"*Mrs.* Clemmons?" I hissed under my breath, as I shot him a look.

Colt's gaze was trained on the backs of the crew. He didn't even look at me as he answered, "A young man and woman traveling alone together? Being hitched is just easier."

My heart dropped a few feet. Disappointment. I couldn't believe I was feeling disappointment for something so logical.

He cleared his throat. "And I'd rather...not risk other

men after you."

My gaze shot up to him, homing in on the slight pink tinge to his cheeks. I had a sudden urge to cover them with kisses.

"No need to get jealous," I replied smoothly.

He grunted, not even denying it.

"I can just tell them to leave me alone and they'll actually do it," I continued, trying to stop my smile from growing. "How do you think I've survived at a speakeasy for so long? I do have *some* self-preservation skills, you know."

Finally, he looked down at me, our eyes meeting. "Could've fooled me, doll. You're always doing *non* self-preservation things...like saving my hide."

At that, I grinned fully. "Maybe I think you're worth saving."

For the first time, Colt stumbled. I'd never seen him lose his gait like that—he was always so sure-footed. When he straightened back up, his cheeks were an even darker pink and his gaze drifted to my lips again. "Yes, you've made that clear."

"Mr. and Mrs. Clemmons? We should really get going for first light."

Colt and I turned toward the voice above us. Captain Leroy and his crew were already up at the top of the gangplank, looking down at where we were—merely halfway up the walkway.

After we reached the top, the two brothers set to work disconnecting the plank and getting ready to shove off. The deck was clean and shining. Wooden walls of the cabin area held a line of circular windows that allowed us to look out at the passing waters. A set of stairs led up to the upper level, where I could see another man looking out of the balcony, his hands folded into his jacket.

Captain Leroy gestured to the door that led into the ship's

main interior. "Right in there you'll find a lounge and a coffee bar with some light refreshments. Please, enjoy yourself."

Colt raised an eyebrow and I wondered if he, too, had expected something more…humble.

The ship shuddered under our feet, and in no time, the dock and the connecting pier grew smaller as our vessel set off. No sooner had we left the shore than dawn finally woke. Over the waters, the sun peeked, spilling gold, lavender, and shades of orange and pink. The lake sparkled and shone like the world's largest gemstone, and before I could stop myself, I was crossing up to the bow of the hull.

The next moment, I felt Colt's presence next to me, standing…close.

The wind whistled and the water lapped against the aluminum, and the motor whirred gently. The sun was difficult to look at and it made me squint, but it was beautiful.

Was this what it was like to cross an entire ocean? No land in sight? Just an endless expanse of glittering blue?

Instinctually, I leaned back against Colt's arm and the sturdiness of his chest. For a moment, he hesitated, then his arms came over me, weighted on my shoulders in more than one meaning.

I closed my eyes.

Stay with me, I thought suddenly, heart-achingly. *Always.*

Since Colt had come into my life, it had been one terrible nightmare after another. Gunmen, monsters, vampires, and viruses, and yet I'd never felt safer or *happier.* And it was all because of this quietly powerful and enigmatic man behind me.

I reached up and threaded my fingers through his, and then placed the palm of my other hand against the side of his cheek and slid it down to cup his jaw. He lowered his mouth to my neck and gave me a lingering kiss. Soft, warm, tender.

"You won't run from me again, will you?" he whispered

against my skin.

I opened my eyes and turned around in his arms to look up into his face, half shielded by the low brim of his hat. "No, only toward you."

He smiled, a small pull at the left corner of his lips, but he said nothing more.

Eventually, we would talk about these feelings, but there was so much else before us and it seemed too distracting to talk about this *thing* between us when our lives were at stake. There was still a whole powerful, mysterious corporation out there with money and influence after me. And this new virus that Colt insisted wasn't our responsibility and yet…

While he'd said that it was the BOI's job to save the country—not ours—I wondered if he could really just walk away. Despite what he'd told me back at St. Agnes, my dragon did have a soul.

And it was beautiful.

A horn's blast from the ship interrupted our moment and the two of us flinched. We separated and our gazes dropped to anywhere but each other—to the deck, the retreating Chicago shoreline, the sunrise, or the gentle lake waters.

After a couple awkward seconds, Colt threaded my arm through his and led me across the deck toward the main cabin.

"So what do we do once we get to New York?" I asked.

"It will take a long time to find this Dr. Durwich. Time we don't have if we want to find Madame Maldu and figure out who the devil is after you. So it's better if we drop off the vial of blood to the BOI satellite office and they can get it to him."

"Where is the office?"

"There's a few. But the operator will tell me the location of the closest one. The BOI is for the public after all, they can't really be hidden from the world."

Colt opened the door to the cabin and we entered an open seating area with low comfy chairs and small tables. A bar area made of the same rich wood sat in the center with no one there, but a small spread of coffee and breakfast had been laid out. Colt and I didn't go near it. It wasn't that I wasn't hungry—it was that it felt prepared for other guests. Reputable guests that weren't fugitives on the run. Instead, we took two seats in the corner by a circular window to watch the waters swallow the distant Chicago shore.

We sat in silence for a while before I decided now was as good a time as any to iron my shoelaces. I certainly wasn't going to make it the whole day without having to use the bathroom at least once.

I excused myself from Colt's company and he looked like he wanted to follow, but I gave his arm a reassuring squeeze. Exiting the main cabin, I emerged into a narrow hallway, and to the left was the restroom. After using it and washing my hands, I was just about to open the door when voices came from beyond the thin wood.

It was mostly nautical speak that I didn't quite understand. Knots, wind speed, and engines—things like that, but as their voices grew a bit further away, I peeked out from the restroom to see if the narrow hallway was free.

Through the crack in the door, I saw Captain Leroy and his first mate. And then I witnessed something that made my heart stop beating.

Something *moved* under the captain's blanket that was draped over his legs.

Not a foot, not something…human. The movement was a slither. A ripple under the blanket.

Sucking in a breath, I jerked backward, pressing myself against the wall of the farthest end of the bathroom.

Oh, God. What was *that? Is he a monster?*

Taking a deep breath, I scooched back up to the crack of

the door. I had to find out.

"Hello, little kitten."

Before I could even scream, a hand shot through the crack—a muscled arm following—and gripped my mouth, squeezing. His hold was so strong and so painful, I couldn't move my jaw. *No, this can't be happening. They found us? Again? How?!*

"Billy!" the man called. It must be the first mate—Frank—who had hold of me.

Thundering footsteps, then the bathroom door was pulled all the way open and, sure enough, Frank stood before me, all six-and-a-half feet of him, gripping me like his life depended on it. "A little help here?" he grunted to his brother, who stood gaping at the two of us.

Billy swore, digging into his pocket and pulling out a little vial of clear liquid. "Tip her neck back."

With great effort, they tipped my neck back while I tried to wrestle away. Billy pried open my teeth just enough to dribble some of the clear liquid on my tongue. I tried to spit, but like at the Cerberus Club, a hand clamped on my mouth, forcing me to swallow.

No, no, no, please. Not again. Please, God!

The liquid burned and scorched my throat and when they dropped their filthy hands from my face, I was no longer a threat to them. Maybe I'd never been, weak thing that I was.

"Are you willing to fight for your freedom?"

Those words roared inside my chest, echoing through my heart and soul and limbs and carrying me into action.

I dropped my head, clenching my fists as I inched my foot backward.

"I'll watch her, you tell the captain that we need to take down the hunter now—"

The tip of my pointed shoe connected with Frank's groin and he folded with a high-pitched groan. As the second brother just stood there, blinking in shock, I shot forward, driving the top of my head into his nose.

It wasn't perfect, not like Colt's headbutts. But it was enough to disorient him and push him into the wall. I wove past their big bodies and dashed out into the hall.

Coming right around the corner, I nearly crashed into the captain in his wheelchair. Captain Leroy took one look at me and the tangle of legs coming from the bathroom and put two and two together.

"GET THE HUNTER!" he shouted.

On instinct, I grabbed the blanket on his lap and ripped it off.

If I could've screamed, all of Chicago would've heard me.

Where the man's legs should've been was a cluster of tentacles. Not like that of an octopus, more like those of a squid. Light blue and silver with red and pink freckles decorating the slimy skin. They writhed and slithered around the wheels and the footrest where his feet should have been. They left patches of dark ink, slick like oil, on the carpet of the hallway.

Turning on my heel, I ran the other direction, bursting through the door at the end onto the stern. Churning bubbles exploded behind the ship, leaving a trail of white water in our wake. I skidded around the corner of the cabin and nearly slipped as my heels struggled to find traction on the well-waxed wood. Racing past the circular windows, I came to the open deck and reared back in horror.

They already had Colt at gunpoint.

Thirteen men stood scattered on the deck, all of them with tommy guns drawn and pointed at his head and heart. Where had all these men come from? Below deck? This was an ambush. A plan in the making far before we stepped onboard.

But I had no time to consider it. I was too consumed with

the vision of bullets ripping through Colt. His gaze frantically combed the ship and when he saw me on the port side, his eyes widened and he shook his head barely perceptibly. I knew immediately he was trying to tell me to run away.

No. Only toward you.

I ran across the deck, my heels clicking on the hard surface. Not stopping—even with the sound of bullets exploding and hitting the waxed floor—until I reached Colt and threw my arms around his middle. His arms wrapped around me and his heartbeat pounded under my cheek.

"HOLD YOUR FIRE, FOOLS!"

The furious voice of Captain Leroy cut through the spray of bullets and everyone froze. I peeked over my shoulder, where I still protected Colt with my own body—the body that was too valuable to shoot at—to see the captain roll himself forward in his chair. His tentacles were going every which way, as if responding to the man's rageful emotions.

"A *kraken*?" Colt hissed above me. I felt the word vibrate in his chest more than heard it.

"Let the girl go," Captain Leroy called across the deck. "She's ours now."

Colt had the gall to laugh. Loud and without humor. "Wrong on both counts! See, it's *she* who won't let go of *me*."

Proving his point, I tightened my hold on his middle, squeezing my eyes shut. *No, they won't take him. Not if I can stop it.*

"And she'll never be anyone's. She's her own woman." At his words, Colt shifted under my embrace. His arm slid into his jacket then threaded into the pocket of my dress.

"Last chance, sonny," the captain called, voice echoing across the expanse of water.

Then Colt's hands clamped down on my waist and he lowered his mouth to my neck. For a moment, I thought he was going to kiss me there again but instead, he whispered something. Before I could comprehend his words, he shoved me backward. Hard.

No sooner had I hit the deck than the rain of bullets went off over my head. Five seconds later, a splash from down below followed.

And he was gone.

Only now, as rough hands grabbed my arms and hauled me to my feet, did I register Colt's parting message to me.

I'll find you.

Chapter Twenty-Eight

The Dragon

Exhaustion would kill me before my bullet wounds did.

Mostly because the wounds weren't that deep. They were merely grazes, skimming across my skin in a comet of heat and lead and deliverance. Painful, but tolerable. When I hit the icy waters of Lake Michigan, my heart stuttered like the engine of a spent hayburner. It began beating again, but sluggishly, fighting against the intense shock to my system.

Trails of blood twirled off me and streaked toward the surface of the water. I held my breath, knowing that if any sign of life came to the surface that I'd have to worry about the henchmen turning their tommy guns to the lake.

As I let my body drift, gathering strength, fighting the cold, letting the boat chug past me, I replayed Eris's look of horror as I shoved her onto the deck and threw myself over the side.

I'd left her. Abandoned her.

The only thing that kept me fighting against the freezing temperature and the knee-jerk reaction to inhale as my lungs screamed was the promise I'd made to her. *I'll find you.*

And I would.

When the ship was far enough away, I kicked to the surface and my head broke free. I inhaled with four sharp gasps before my shriveled lungs reduced to coughing and hacking out a small dose of lake water. Blinking droplets out of my eyes, I watched the boat continue onward just in time to catch the gold letters plated on the side.

Cassiopeia, and then, *BKH*.

Son of a bitch.

The frustration and anger and despair burned my chest, literal flames scorching the back of my throat as I watched the yacht sail far out of my reach.

They had her, but not for long.

Glancing up at the sky, I was able to tell directions thanks to the position of the sun. Because of the distance already traveled from Chicago, going south was my best bet rather than turning around. Unfortunately, thanks to the sluggish October currents, there was hardly any to speak of in the western side of the lake. I'd have to do most of the work myself.

I wrestled out of my clothes so I was left in only my boxer shorts. Everything would only weigh me down, offering no warmth whatsoever.

Luckily, I could produce my own heat.

One of the few benefits to being a dragon was that the cold was merely a minor inconvenience. Giving in to my emotions, the heat in my chest built and built, burning through my body like a spark on dry leaves. I blew into the water, steam rising to the sky as the two extreme temperatures clashed.

But I was careful not to expend too much of my fire breath too quickly. I had a long way to go.

I swam for what felt like days. My muscles groaned and protested with each kick and stroke. Eventually, my toes and fingers grew numb and exhaustion threatened to pull me under.

Just float. Rest your eyes a bit. Would it be so bad?

Each time the traitorous thoughts bit into my mind, I would picture Eris's face, and hidden strength would flow back into my limbs. I had to find her again. I *would* find her again. I jumped over that side so I could live to fight another day. I was no good to her at the bottom of Lake Michigan.

But as the day wore on and the sun dipped behind the horizon, there were brief moments of darkness that I actually wished for my wings back. Maybe I could've flown to shore. Flown to Eris. Gotten us both out of there.

Then I'd remember some of the thoughts that had gone through my head with those wings attached to my back. Truly monstrous thoughts.

Human flesh…what does it taste like?

Burn everything. Destroy. Destroy.

Hunger, hunger, hunger.

I hadn't thought of what those wings had made me think, feel, and yearn for, for a long time. Even as a thirteen-year-old, I'd managed to somehow keep them at bay, but there was that small voice that whispered to me, testing my strength.

Someone was always testing me.

Teeth chattering, I summoned more fire in my chest, but what came out was just a pathetic cloud of steam.

Twilight descended. Stars peeked through the vast, vast sky. Endless. Beautiful. Horrible.

My hands sliced through the full moon beams reflected on the placid surface. I played a game with myself. I picked a star's reflection and tried to catch up to it.

I was swimming, swimming…until I wasn't.

A shrill cry pierced the air and I jerked upward in response. I gasped, hacking up water and mucus, and tried to fight against the sensation of my muscles seizing. Dimly, I blinked the water from my eyes and a bird circling overhead came into focus.

Clarity cut through my mind like a hot knife and I twisted around, the waters thrashing around me.

And there it was. Land. A line of evergreen trees decorated the shore—nature's perfect skyline. The break of dawn made it just visible. Merely a shadow against the lightening sky.

With a surge of strength, I kicked and pulled and swam. The shore didn't seem to get any closer, but then it came up on me fast. To avoid the current pulling me into the sharp rocks, I dove down into the depths, dodging the undertow, and managed to grab hold of an outcrop.

Using what little strength I had left, I climbed up onto the rocky shore, and once I was out of the icy waters, showered occasionally by spray from the wind's restlessness, I passed out.

When I woke again the sun was higher in the sky. My whole body was sore and aching and the bullet grazes itched and burned. I exhaled and the heat of my steam breath warmed the rock.

My fire breath wasn't completely gone yet.

Pulling up my bare limbs, I folded into a ball as tightly as I could. Then I took deep breaths, letting the fire in my chest build and build. I focused my mind on Eris and how I'd been separated from her yet again. Was it Sister Adaline who had betrayed us? After all her work on discovering the virus and helping us, it seemed highly unlikely. It could've been Father Clarence—I was never one to trust a priest. Or perhaps Gin had found the man with the dingy who took us to St. Agnes. There were a dozen different ways we could've been tracked, but in all the scenarios, one thing was bound to be the same—the real Captain Leroy lay at the bottom of Lake Michigan.

Finally, I looked around, seeing nothing but trees and boulders and thick woods stretched out before me.

Swell. I couldn't wait to walk through the wilds in nothing but my boxer shorts. I ran a hand through my wet hair and carefully picked my way across the slippery, rocky shore. With a heavy sigh, I stepped from the rocks to the soft ground covered in dirt, grass, and fallen pine needles and began my trek through the forests.

It was late in the day, nearly sundown, when I saw the smoke. Hope rose inside my chest, following its cloudy gray trajectory. The smoke could mean a lot of things—a hunter starting his campfire for the night, maybe a cabin, or even the outskirts of a small town.

Picking up my pace, I jogged through the woods, desperate not to lose the smoke to the encroaching night sky. By the time I got close enough to see light through the thick trees, I was out of breath and my skin was covered in cold sweat. The perspiration seemed to freeze as it rolled between my shoulder blades and down the ridges of my abdomen.

As I drew nearer, I could make out the shape of a cabin and smell cooking meat. A clothesline bordered the edge of the homestead along with a small stable and shed. Counting my lucky stars, I yanked off a shirt and pants and quickly dressed in the shadows. I'd never dreamed I'd need to pull a gooseberry lay but I also never dreamed I'd fall for the lost siren and follow her all across the Midwest.

After stealing a pair of boots from the shed, I slipped into the stable and was relieved to find a gorgeous steed. I saddled up the horse and set off on the obvious trail leading to a promise of further civilization, the moonlight guiding our way.

• • •

Two days later, I sat in a nondescript speakeasy in Cleveland, Ohio. Outside, I looked almost like my old self, except with darker circles under my eyes. It was quite possible I hadn't slept since I left Eris on that goddamn boat owned by BKH.

She was probably in her creator's hands by now. I hated to think what he was doing with her, and yet I couldn't chase away all the nightmarish, wild thoughts.

If he touches her, I swear to God and all his angels that I'll take him to Hell with me.

As much as I wanted to go after her *now*, to storm whatever corporate palace in Manhattan he was holding her hostage, I had absolutely nothing in my arsenal. No money. No guns. No ammo. And no backup.

After finding a small town a few miles south of the cabin, I'd left the horse at the post office. They'd promised to return it and, with that, I had hitched a ride on the back of a farmer's truck all the way to Cleveland.

In the middle of the bustling streets of the Midwestern metropolis, I placed a call to Gus Murdeena, requesting a loan of a nice suit, and met up with a tailor friend of his. Then I waited until dark.

Like most growing cities between Chicago and the east coast, Cleveland had boomed. Steam car and electric car companies, all pioneers in the biz, had accelerated the growth of the city, and when prohibition took hold, organized crime sank its fangs in as well. Literally.

I remembered one time with McCarney when I'd joined him on a stakeout to watch Little Italy's Mayfield Road Mob undergo a major bootlegging operation in smuggling cases of hooch all the way from Canada. We hadn't made a move that night. Instead, we'd been hoping to catch bigger fish. Maybe even Joe Lonardo himself—but then a minotaur showed up and ruined our plans, nearly taking out an agent's eye in the process.

Needless to say, the BOI was no stranger to Cleveland. So I knew that if I went to enough speakeasies tonight, I'd find at least one agent. One of them watching, waiting...*hunting.*

Ah, the good ole days.

The jazz band in the little speakeasy started up again. It was a song I recognized. A song that had been on the set sheet that Eris had dropped that night in The Blind Dragon. I watched a black woman in a slinky red dress croon into the microphone. It was a song by Victoria Spivey, "How Do They Do It That Way?"

She was good. Real good. Rich and deep and bluesy. She could've been the famous canary herself.

"*I'm no chump but I would jump if I could find someone that's not unlike me, too.*"

I drummed my fingers in time with the piano keys as the cup of orange pekoe I'd ordered grew cold. For a moment, I pictured Eris next to me on the barstool. Pictured her tilting her head and giving me a smile, all teeth this time, showing a small dimple in her left cheek.

I ached to know how she was doing. Her well-being, more than anything, had occupied my thoughts the past two days, but occasionally I would think of the envelope that I slipped into the pocket of her dress before I jumped ship.

It would've been lost once I went overboard. At least with her, there was a chance the blood vial could get to Dr. Durwich. Albeit a very, very small one.

"*Oh when the river runs, flowers are bloomin' in May.*"

A small circle of metal pressed into my lower back. The muzzle of a gun.

"Move your assss an inch, and I'll blow your head off."

For just a split second, I froze at the familiar voice. Then I chuckled.

"Jimmy Sawyer. Always a pleasure."

"I really can't say the same, Clemmonssss."

"*And if you get good business, how do you do it that way?*"

Chapter Twenty-Nine

The Siren

They kept me drugged. Not in the way I'd seen a few girls come into the speakeasy, high on dope or some kind of other malevolent substance that robbed them of their wits. My drug was the clear liquid sprinkled into my water and food. I knew what it was each time I drank or ate and felt the familiar burning sensation in the back of my throat, robbing me of my voice.

Or rather, my siren magic.

It was clever, I had to hand it to them.

After Colt went overboard, everything just...faded into the background. The world became blurry shapes. Rough hands grabbed my arms and dragged me to a small cabin with nothing more than a bed, a bathroom, and a nightstand.

Unable to yell or speak or command, I simply lay on my bed and gave in to my tears.

They fell, hot and salty, down my cheeks and into the pillow and with every thought, I prayed. *Please God, protect him. Save him. Don't let him die.*

But the truth was, I didn't know if anyone was listening. Not that I didn't believe in God. No, my faith in His existence was unshakeable. What I wasn't sure about was whether I deserved to have Him listen at all. To answer any of my prayers.

Monster. Monster. Monster.

Endless scenarios of escaping ran through my mind, but everything I thought of was all pointless. Hopeless.

The only thing I clung to? The vial of blood in my pocket.

Colt had stuffed it into my dress when he'd held me close. I squeezed my eyes shut, cupping the tiny vial of blood in my palms. *Dr. Durwich.* I would find a way to get this to him. If nothing else, I would do this one thing.

Several days passed on the boat. I judged the time by the number of meals I received and how hungry I grew between them. The boat would pause in its journey at least once or twice a day. The motors would cease their whirring and the voices of the sailors would carry throughout the halls, yelling orders. Judging from the muffled words and footsteps, it sounded like things were being loaded off the yacht.

Were they delivering something at each stop? And if so… what?

With these endless questions and the long hours of doing nothing, I grew restless. Finally, on my sixth meal, I gathered up the courage to stop Billy, the brother to the first mate. He was the one who always brought me my meals.

When I placed my hand over his as he set down the tray, he met my eyes with a frown.

I pointed to the door, then threaded my fingers together in a pleading gesture. *Let me go outside, please.*

The man's heavy brow furrowed deeper into a dark V and he turned away, grumbling under his breath. He closed the door and locked it behind him.

• • •

I'd been doing the same exact thing I'd been doing for the past four days—obsessing over the people I cared about—when Billy returned to my cabin in the early evening. Colt was a constant presence in my mind, but so was Madame. Was she still in New York? Had Stanley managed to find her?

Unlike all the other times before, Billy opened the door wider, stepping back as if to allow me past him. Shocked, I stood immediately. He was letting me outside?

Before I could take two steps, though, he gripped my upper arm. With a frown, I took his left arm and placed enough pressure to show him I wanted him to bend it. Once he did, I threaded my right arm through his outstretched elbow.

Billy's eyebrows practically hit the ceiling. He cleared his throat, then we continued walking down the hall and out onto the main deck.

Being arm-in-arm with a man made me think of Colt. He was the last man whose arm I'd…actually, the only man until now.

Please, please be safe.

As soon as the wind hit my face, I felt somewhat rejuvenated. Not stuck in those wood walls with the white bed and the same dishes to stare at…I was so grateful, and I gave Billy a gentle squeeze on the arm to tell him so.

The sun peeked behind the clouds, making the lake shimmer—or was it a river? The shore was surprisingly close on either side. I could see the rocks and heavy fir trees line the coast. Even the water seemed shallower and the current stronger.

"We're in a canal." Billy outstretched his arm as he pointed from the hull of the ship to the bow. "Back there we left Lake Huron, and now we're about to enter Lake Erie.

The Great Lakes are connected, you know."

My mouth popped open in a small surprised *O*. No, I hadn't known that. But why were we traveling through the Great Lakes? Weren't we supposed to be going to Manhattan if that was where my creator was? Seemed like it was a terribly roundabout way to go.

Maybe this man would tell me more. Give me some kind of hint to my fate. I made a continuing gesture with my wrist as if to say, *go on*.

Billy watched me with steady, dark eyes. He seemed around Stan's age. Mid-thirties, if I were to take a gander. His black hair, parted down the middle, brushed his shoulders. A smooth deerskin jacket covered broad shoulders, a barrel-sized chest, and strong arms. Complete with his scruffy beard and tan skin, he looked like a trapper. I imagined him on the frontier, around a fire, fur pelts in the back of a wagon…

I gave him a small smile and made the *go on* gesture a second time.

He tilted his head in thought, then continued, "We went up Lake Michigan and through a small channel into Lake Erie. If this boat was much bigger we wouldn't have made it. Me'n Frank wanted to take our boat, but it would've been too small for the crew, and Mr. Brocker insisted we take a lot of men. Luckily, his yacht turned out to be just small enough."

Mr. Brocker?

"Then we went down Lake Huron and now we're in a canal that'll take us to Lake Erie." He snaked his arm through the air, as if to depict how the waterways would wind. "From there, we'll take the Erie Canal to the Hudson River and that'll shoot us right out into the Hudson Bay. Mark my words, they'll expand these canals and channels to be big enough to move ships like the *Titanic* through. Imagine being able to transport goods all the way from Europe to Chicago without stopping to unload." He chuckled. "That's the future."

I tried to imagine this future Billy painted for me. Big tankers with shipping containers—practically skyscrapers lying on their side—floating down the river. They carried goods from Europe and…

I gripped Billy's arm tightly, my fingernails digging into his thick jacket.

Maybe these canals were how monster parts were being smuggled all the way into the Midwest. They traveled up through the bays and canals, into the Great Lakes. They could smuggle the items in small boats and get away with it because the BOI wasn't guarding and inspecting the shipments in Chicago ports, or at least, not like the ports in Manhattan. During our long drive, Colt had told me quite a bit about the monster trade, and Chicago's mysterious talent in creating the most monsters out of all the cities—even New York. This could be why.

Ripping my hand from Billy's arm, I hurried to the railing and looked down the port side of the yacht. Sure enough, large crates marked "BKH" sat stacked on the deck as if they were waiting for their next delivery.

Is *that* what was happening *now*? If I were to open a crate, would I find werewolf claws, manticore stingers, minotaur horns, or cyclops eyes?

Billy stomped toward me, his brows scrunched together, a harsh scowl on his face, angry as if I just betrayed his trust. I pressed my palms together and mouthed, *sorry.* His gaze softened and he offered me his elbow again.

I was pleasantly surprised. Just goes to show, you attract more flies with honey.

The squeak of the wheelchair came to a stop in front of my door, and my chest tightened with dread. The doorknob rattled and the monster who looked very much like St. Nicholas with a skirt of tentacles sat in the doorway.

"Ms. Eris...Or should I say Mrs. Clemmons?" the so-called "captain" chuckled and leaned forward in his chair a little. "I've come to tell you to freshen up. We're about to arrive at our destination, and Mr. Brocker is mighty eager to see you."

That name again. Mr. Brocker—whoever he was—had to be my creator. The one who had inserted this godforsaken pearl and condemned me to this fate.

The tentacles twitched and curled around the spokes of the wheels and my stomach rolled. Eyes twinkling, he gave me another grin and said, "It's been a pleasure being your captor—I mean *captain*. I do hope you join us on one of our voyages again."

I wanted to chuck my uneaten dinner roll at his head.

Actually, I wanted to do more than that, but I was scared of what this monster might do to me, despite his employer's orders. *I'm such a coward.* The seemingly brave acts of putting a knife to my throat to save the children or throwing myself in front of Colt during a shower of bullets were nothing of the sort. Because I *knew* they wouldn't kill me, it made it easy to be brave.

As the kraken wheeled away, still chuckling, I dropped my head into my arms and didn't look up until Billy came for me.

This time he came with rope. There was an apology in his eyes, but I shook my head as if to tell him, *I understand. You're just doing your job.*

As Billy knelt to tie up my wrists I had a flash of Colt kneeling down before me to rub ointment on my rope burns and cover them with gauze. Such gentle hands, such careful movements. My skin healed only to be rubbed raw again.

With my hands tied at my front I was given a long jacket

to hide my binding. Then I was led to the main deck. We were just docking the yacht in the Manhattan harbor, and the crew scurried around, pulling ropes and dropping anchor. Lady Liberty loomed over the bay in the near distance, as if guarding all the incoming ships tired from their long journey across the Atlantic.

Before the gangplank was lowered, the captain spread the blanket back over his tentacles.

"Walk, siren," he growled behind me as he rode his footrest on the back of my heel.

Wincing, I stumbled forward and headed down the plank to where Frank was waiting. The kraken remained on his yacht while Frank and Billy walked me down the pier. We crossed the docks, rancid with the smell of fish wrapped in old papers, and came to the most luxurious car I'd ever seen. Perhaps Henry Ford had made it himself. It was black with a long white hood and a silver miniature statue on its nose. Two men stepped out of the driver side and the passenger side, and then I was handed off.

Frank took the briefcase one of the men offered, and then he shoved me forward. "Pleasure doing business with you gents," he sneered.

The man who'd handed over the briefcase caught me by the shoulders, then wordlessly guided me inside the car and slammed the door shut. Just like that, the deal was done.

We drove in silence through the "City that never slept." Vaguely I recalled walking through these streets, holding tight to Madame's hand as she whispered to me, *Don't look behind, Eris. Keep walking. Just keep walking.*

If only I could somehow slip away and go look for her. I could turn over the blood vial to Dr. Durwich and maybe even the BOI would help me. I didn't relish the idea of using my voice on agents—whenever my voice returned—but Madame was more important to me than any moral code, or any government sealing me away. I owed her everything, and I would *do* everything to make sure she was safe.

The buildings stretched upward. Some were all dark gray concrete or deep red brick showing off their history rather than the other newer ones cased in silver and chrome steel.

We passed a gaggle of flappers at the street corner and their skirts were the shortest I'd ever seen—almost to their knees. We passed streets with loud vendors and a few jazz players seated on overturned buckets, playing smooth bluesy rhythms to their heart's content.

When we were in the heart of Manhattan, just a skip away from Central Park, the car swung into a scraper's underground drive. The building was perhaps a few floors less than the infamous Woolworth building with its baffling number of fifty-seven. With spires and gothic trimmings, it looked like a modern castle, all the wondrous magic contained in one solid column of glass and steel. The drive sank below the earth and darkness descended upon our car. In just a few short minutes, we were parked and the two brutes practically dragged me into a wrought-iron elevator in the corner of the underground garage.

I stood between them as the elevator rose and tried to stop myself from trembling.

This was it. My creator finally had me. I could almost feel claws around my neck, squeezing and squeezing.

Floor after floor passed us by, and I caught glimpses of marble floors and plush red carpets, of colorful, expressive paintings with gilded frames and velvet furniture. Bouquets of roses in ceramic vases, mahogany wood, and crystal chandeliers.

The elevator stopped at one of the top floors—thirty-four. The men opened the grating, pushed me out, and then closed the grate. The elevator rose again, my silent guards going with it.

They'd dropped me off in a suite. I was in a living area of some kind with a bedroom and bathroom visible from my vantage point.

I was still standing there, in my dress from the nuns, which I hadn't washed or changed out of in nine days, when two maids scurried out from the bedroom.

"We are to give you a bath and dress you up, miss."

I looked from one maid to the other and heaved a great sigh. Of course I'd be expected to be gussied up first. A man who'd paid so much to possess the world's finest jewel wouldn't leave it on a pedestal with smudges on it.

Nearly three hours later, I sat on the light pink settee, my back ramrod straight and my scalp still smarting from the way the maids had attacked my hair. Between my breasts rested the vial of blood. I had been cooperative enough with my maids that they'd let me undress and redress myself. I'd been stealthy in hiding the vial during my bath and tucking it into the fold of my clothes while they'd done my hair in silky, smooth finger waves.

My dress was sapphire blue with bold geometric designs in sequins. It was easily the fanciest thing I'd ever worn—or seen. Even the dress that Belva Murdeena had given me didn't seem to compare. The fabric *smelled* like money. Like gold. And around my neck was a string of pearls because… of course.

The maids were off in the bathroom, cleaning after the storm that had been my hair and makeup, and I was just sitting…trying not to hurl into the potted ficus.

For nine days I'd been stuck on an awful boat, unable to do anything at all, and now all this anxiety and restlessness was about to boil over. Wringing my hands, I moved from the bedroom into the living area and stopped short when I came upon a dainty coffee table with a vase full of daffodils and a framed issue of *Time* magazine. I recognized the issue immediately. It was the one with the California article that David had brought to me that night at the Dragon. But why was it here? Framed of all things?

My gaze narrowed at the cover of the dark-haired businessman in the sharp suit and the title, "American Royalty: Stocks, the New Gold." Underneath the title it read, "A look into James G. Brocker's roaring success."

Lunging for the magazine, I knocked it to the floor, almost cracking the glass in the frame. With trembling fingers, I undid the latches and pulled out the magazine that held an entire profile on the man who'd ruined my life—and who I was just minutes away from meeting.

Mr. Brocker.

His portrait on the cover showed merely part of his profile, so I was unable to get a good look at him—but it was very artistically done. It was as if the editor of the magazine had wanted to make him like a king, or a president on a coin.

Sitting on the carpeted floor of my suite, the pages of the magazine shaking with the continual tremors of my hands, I read about "a hard-working American man with insight and experience." The article went on to explain James G. Brocker's humble beginnings as a young office clerk, and then his almost clairvoyant ability to foresee the potential in the stock trade.

Stocks, the article read, *are pieces of investments into fledgling businesses that don't have the money to be funded on their own. Once the new business starts making money, owners of stocks are able to earn back their investment and then some, growing their investment along with the company.* But Mr. Brocker had decided to build his empire on the stocks, rather than the businesses themselves. By purchasing and controlling a multitude of shares in other companies, he made his fortune off the success of other businesses.

With every sentence about Brocker's wealth and power and ingenuity, I grew more and more intimidated. How could I hope to escape such a man?

I was so consumed in the article that I nearly jumped when the elevator doors opened and a woman stepped out. A beautiful woman with raven-black hair, a fashionable rose-gold evening dress and *three* dark, glittering eyes.

Somehow I didn't recoil at the cyclops. With a stab in my heart, she reminded me of Millie. She even looked somewhat familiar, but I couldn't place her.

"Here at last," she said softly, taking a step from the elevator and onto the carpet. "I've been looking for you for some time."

I must've been staring too intently at her cyclops eye, because she frowned. "If you're wondering whether or not I will go mad as well, the answer is no."

Something clicked in the back of my mind. Millie's ability to read minds was unique to a cyclops' third eye. What if this cyclops also had a unique ability with her third eye?

Like Colt had told me more than once, my thoughts were easy to read on my face, because the cyclops answered, "My eye finds things. Specifically, powers of monsters. It's how I was able to find you."

Just like Colt had suspected. Now it made sense how this Mr. Brocker had been able to track me everywhere.

She watched me expectantly, as if waiting for some kind of reaction.

When I gave her nothing, the cyclops woman shook her head. "You really don't recognize me, then."

I blinked, confused. Was I supposed to remember her? From when? My time here when I got my pearl? But I barely remembered any of that.

She turned on her heel, back toward the elevator, flicking her wrist toward me. "Come, I'm supposed to take you to him."

Unable to ask her anything, I stood and followed her into the elevator. We were silent as I watched the buttons for each floor light up, and outwardly, I tried my best to look calm.

But I wasn't. My breaths grew more and more shallow with each foot we climbed into the air. Higher and higher until...we stopped.

The cyclops woman opened the elevator door and gestured that I step out. She avoided my gaze as she pulled the door closed. "He'll be right with you." As the elevator dropped down, the last thing I managed to catch before she disappeared was one glistening tear rolling down her perfect cheek.

Who was that woman? Why was she crying?

I was left alone in a long office. Almost ten yards of nothing but carpet and floor-to-ceiling windows. At the end were two large leather chairs and a massive oak desk with a winged chair that looked fit for a king. A king of industry maybe.

Tentatively, I crossed the ocean of carpet to approach the desk and leather chairs. Between the chairs was a little end table with a glass bowl full of hard candy.

Candy that was covered in a red cellophane wrapper.

My breath caught.

With trembling fingers, I reached down and picked up a piece of candy. Or what could be referred to as a throat lozenge. It crinkled in my fingertips.

At the far end of the office, the elevator door opened and out stepped the man from St. Agnes—the one who'd sat in the sanctuary and confessed his sins to me. The man who gave me the cherry lozenge.

He smiled. "Hello, Eris."

Chapter Thirty

The Dragon

I kept still. After all, I didn't want to get my head blown off, and Jimmy Sawyer was a monster of his word.

"You've got a lot of guts showing your ugly mug around here, Clemmons. In one of the most frequented speakeasies of the BOI?" He *tsked* with his forked tongue, which came out more like a hiss. "You were just asking to be caught."

"Very intuitive. But let's be honest."

"Regarding?"

"Not one inch of my mug is ugly."

The muzzle of his gun pressed tighter against the muscles in my lower back. "You trying to be funny?"

"A little."

"You took out two of our own. How dare you make jokes when you've pulled a Benedict Arnold, you rat bastard," he growled.

I sighed. "Just trying to defuse the tension… I didn't kill them, Sawyer."

"Doesn't matter. You put them both in the hospital, then

you eloped with the world's most dangerous weapon."

"We didn't..." I sighed again. "Listen, I have something McCarney will want to hear—"

"I don't give a damn what McCarney wants to hear. You're talking to *me*. And I want to know why you betrayed us for a pair of big goo-goo eyes and some nice bubs."

At that, I whirled around, *done* playing Mr. Nice Guy. Grabbing the muzzle of the gun in my left hand, I pointed it down toward the floor, twisting Sawyer's wrist in the process. With my right hand, I slid my fingers under his left sleeve and pinched at one of his scales. He winced. Tearing off a basilisk's scales was the equivalent of pulling fingernails.

"*Don't talk about her like that*," I growled, a tendril of steam escaping my mouth.

Sawyer stared at me with wide eyes, then his brow furrowed. "You really are dizzy with the dame, aren't you?"

"And if I am?"

"Then you're a goddamn fool." He jerked his arm away and tucked the gun inside his jacket. "She's bewitched you, ole sport."

I shook my head. "Not in the way you think."

He grunted and rolled his eyes, gesturing "two fingers" to the bartender. The bartender returned with two fingers of scotch in a crystal glass. Tossing back a large gulp, Sawyer leaned forward and rested his elbows on the bar.

"It's exactly the way I think. No man in his right mind would betray his countrymen and his whole life for a pair of..." I glared at him, and he finished hastily, "for a pretty Jane."

I took off my hat and set it on the stool beside me, running my fingers through my already messy hair. "I'm not here to argue with you about whether or not Eris cast some sort of spell on me."

"Then what *are* you here for? Clearly you're turning

yourself in, but why? You couldn't possibly be changing your mind, not when you keep on defending the little witch."

I gnashed my teeth together, trying to keep my anger in check. He didn't know her like I did. In fact, I'd been like him once, too.

"You're right. I haven't changed my mind. She's still the only thing I..."

The only thing I care about.

The words almost slipped out so easily. The truth was I tried to think of something else that I cared about more than her, but I couldn't think of a single thing. When I'd walked away from the BOI, I walked away from *everything* I'd had. I'd chosen to believe in someone who had stayed silent her whole life to ensure she never robbed anyone of their free will. Someone who stood up for women who were abused and battered.

I'd found something in Eris that I hadn't realized I'd been looking for...light. A window of beautiful gold light in the dark, dark netherworld I'd been drowning in for so long.

"The only thing you what?" Sawyer asked, the glass almost to his lips as he gave me a sideways look over his shoulder.

"Care about," I finished. If I couldn't say it out loud, then I didn't deserve to think it. I needed to start being more honest, like her.

"Jesus, Colt." He slammed down the glass so hard I was surprised it didn't crack. "You've known her for what? A stinking week? The BOI has been your life since you were twelve! McCarney practically raised you as his son—we took you in from a hellish orphanage. They gave you everything—"

"Stop."

There was something in my voice that made Sawyer halt in his rant.

"Half truths."

"What?" Sawyer asked.

"I'm tired of living my life on half truths. Yes, the BOI rescued me from an orphanage. Yes, they gave me a home. But it all came at a cost."

"What the devil are you talking about?"

I lowered my voice and looked into his serpent-like eyes. Pupils that were slits when he was distressed. "Do you know what I am?"

He shrugged, gaze darting away. "Most hunters are monsters. The good ones at least. But I've never seen any part on you. What does this have to do with—"

"Just listen," I cut in, my eyes keeping hold of his. "I was an experiment, Jimmy."

My ex-senior agent stared back at me, eyes narrowed, his fingers curling around the side of his glass. A muscle in his jaw ticked and he nodded slowly. He believed me. "What are you?"

"Well," I said, taking a sip of my tea, "I *was* a dragon."

"A DRAGON?"

Half the folks in the speakeasy turned to look at us. Jimmy cleared his throat and took a drink. When they turned back to their conversations, he ducked his head and whispered, "A *dragon*? You're shitting me."

I shook my head. "I can show you the scars on my back where they took off my wings."

Jimmy sucked in a breath. "Well…damn. I didn't even know dragon wings existed." He took a long pause, then looked back at me. "Did they do that to any other agents?"

"I don't think there are any other wings out there. At least not in America. Besides, I was such a failure, I don't think they did."

Jimmy frowned. "What do you mean?"

"The wings took, but I couldn't control them. I accidentally killed five people. They removed them after that."

"*Shit.*"

"There's more," I said.

"More?" Jimmy groaned, wiping a gloved hand down the side of his face. "Why are you telling me all this, Colt?"

It was a fair question. Jimmy Sawyer had always been a grouchy, judgmental thorn in my side, but he'd been one of the only agents who'd truly taken the time to train me. He cared about the right things. He went after evil. Honestly, I was glad he'd found me first and not anyone else.

"Because I want you to know why I did what I did. Why I'm making *her* a priority instead of the people who turned me into a monster. Because I want…no, I *need* your help."

He gave me another long sideways look and then dipped his head in a gesture for me to continue.

"There's a reason why I'm the strongest hunter the BOI has."

"Yes, you're a bloody dragon, I get it."

"Not just that."

He cocked an eyebrow at me.

I gnawed on the inside of my cheek, studying him. I'd come this far, I had to tell him the rest of what the BOI had done to me—what I'd never even told Eris, because I hadn't wanted to see the pain in her gaze.

And what Gin had tried to bargain for.

"Try staring at me, Jimmy."

He blinked. "What? No. I'm trying to turn you in, not kill you, you idiot."

"You can't kill me. Try it."

"Look here, you arrogant son of a—"

"Jimmy. *Do it.*"

He hissed, rage coloring his face red at my arrogance. His pupils became full slits as a yellow substance glossed over his eyes.

His basilisk stare. One look into his eyes and death should

come to me if he held the stare long enough. My insides should shrivel and my heartrate should slow, my blood should burn and the oxygen should freeze in my lungs. My body was supposed to shut down, organ by organ.

I didn't even flinch.

Jimmy blinked, his eyes clearing of their yellow glow as his gaze roamed over me. "What in the…"

"Do you remember when McCarney had you stare through two eyeholes every week for three months?"

Jimmy nodded, something like fear and disgust creeping into his expression.

I took a deep breath. "I was on the other side of that wall. I stared into your eyes every week for three months and built up an immunity to a basilisk stare. It was the same with manticore poison, or a gorgon's stare, or a kraken's ink, or…" I shook my head. "A dozen other wounds and effects from some monster. I'm immune because I *built up* an immunity. It's not my dragon genes, though I'm sure that might be how I survived it all. It's why McCarney wanted *me* to go after the siren. I listened to recordings of a siren's voice for hours on end so I could resist its magic."

"You were tortured," Jimmy muttered under his breath. He let out a slow, deep exhale. "Good God, Colt."

Tortured. Huh. I'd never used that word before to describe what I'd gone through. The general had called it "training," but now that felt naive.

"Call it whatever you want, I guess." I leaned closer, enough to smell the expensive cologne he liked to wear. "I'm not telling you this to get your pity. I'm telling you how I could become a traitor. It's not like they did right by me, Jimmy. And at any rate, I'm ready to follow someone I *really* believe in."

Jimmy looked at me long and hard, and then, with two fingers, scooted back the cuff of his shirt to reveal his wristwatch. "Then you better chase yourself."

The skin on the back of my neck prickled. Should've figured he'd already called for backup. "How long do I have?"

"A minute. Maybe two."

I slipped off the barstool before Jimmy had even finished talking. Snaking through the tables, I ducked out of the speakeasy and into the back alley behind the automobile warehouse owned by White Motor Company. The place smelled of copper and oil, and it seeped through the brick walls into the surrounding dark streets.

As I turned the corner, I nearly poked my eye out on a long pistol muzzle.

Rubbing my cheek where the metal had hit, I stepped back to find three suits holding their BOI-issued guns at me.

With an inward groan, I raised my hands.

• • •

I spat on the floor. It was a gross mixture of blood and spit, and I hoped to God not a tooth. I ran my tongue along my upper right molars and felt them all intact then let out a relieved sigh.

Above me towered a hunter who seldom did *hunting.* He was more the muscle. Our ace-in-the-hole in field work. It wasn't that he couldn't hunt well, or be the gumshoe you needed to be as an agent, but he was too conspicuous. People would remember a man almost seven feet tall with hands the size of trash can lids and the color of dark red clay.

Norman Rodgers was a golem. They were rare, mostly because the skin of a golem was incredibly hard to surgically place and grow. Only people with a lot of...body landscape could adjust to new skin literally made of clay—hence the monstrous size of golems.

Usually his punches were like wrecking balls, but at

this point they were starting to feel more like gnats. After almost a week at the special BOI holding prison in DC, I was beginning to crumble. Mentally and emotionally. Physically, I felt okay, as good as I could feel getting beat up every other hour under their so-called "interrogation."

It was my worries over Eris that was the true torturer. She was in New York with her creator, and God only knew what he was doing to her, or *forcing* her to do and *say*.

I shuddered. Norman cracked his knuckles—crumbling bits of clay flaked off and fluttered to the ground—and grinned. "Ready to give it up yet, Clemmons?"

"I've already given you everything," I said wearily. "It's not my fault you assholes don't believe me."

It wasn't under the pain of interrogation that I'd given it up, either. The minute I stepped inside the BOI office, I'd given them everything. Even the parts I'd left out when talking to McCarney in Sister Adaline's office. The story about Eris and how she wasn't evil, and then about BKH and the other monsters after her, even about Madame Maldu being missing in New York, and then finally the mysterious virus that Gin and her goons had been working on.

McCarney had glared at me from across a silver table like I was a criminal—no, worse than that. A traitor.

I tried *not* to care, but after years of doing anything to win this man's approval, I still did somehow.

After talking till my throat was raw, McCarney had stood, tapped the spine of the file folder on the table, and said, "We'll look into it."

That was six days ago, and what had followed were sleepless nights, crap meals, and Norman using me as a punching bag. It was all clearly revenge for thinking I could turn my back on them without consequences.

My eyes and chest burned with the helplessness of it all. Maybe I should've gone to New York alone and taken my chances in rescuing her. Maybe they were figuring out ways to find her and take her out instead. If she was in the hands of anyone who wasn't the US government, then she was a weapon ready to terrorize the country. Had I condemned her to a swifter death?

The muscles in my stomach and arms seized in agony, and I folded inward, wheezing with something that felt like panic.

What have I done? What did I expect? That the BOI would actually take a traitor's word and help me rescue the girl I love?

Yes, *love.* After over a week of being away from her, worrying about her constantly, picturing her smile, and wishing I could hold her in my arms again, I was ready to admit it.

The creak of a door parted the storm of thoughts spinning through my head. I lifted my chin and blinked through a black eye.

Jimmy Sawyer sauntered into the stark white room and nodded to Norman. "How's he holding up?"

Norman smiled, rolling down his sleeves to cover his clay arms. "He'll break soon."

If I haven't already.

Jimmy nodded. "Good. Well, McCarney's ordered me to take him back to his cell. Some of the big wigs are coming tonight and they wanna ask him some more questions."

Norman shrugged. "I think we're done here anyway. You need help?"

The basilisk sneered. "I think I can handle a broken monster."

Chuckling, Norman left, dusting off his hands, leaving a trail of dirt in his wake.

I tilted my head back to stretch my neck and aching shoulders and sighed. I had nothing to say to Jimmy Sawyer.

For a minute there, I felt like he was finally beginning to see me for who I was. And see the BOI for what it was. Greedy. Not perfect. Human.

Then I felt the ropes binding my wrists slacken as Jimmy cut through them. He tossed me a black hood and a pair of cuffs. "Here. Put those on."

Dumbfounded, I stared at him as he crossed to the door and looked out the window.

"McCarney believes you, dummy. But his bosses don't. We've been watching the building of Brocker and Kurtz Holdings."

BKH.

"He's found your dame. She arrived at the New York Harbor this morning." He glanced back at me. I was still sitting in the chair, holding the cuffs and the hood. "What the hell are you waiting for?" he snapped. "Let's get moving!"

Chapter Thirty-One

The Siren

When the shock wore off, I dropped the throat lozenge onto the carpet and crushed it under my heel. The hard candy snapped and popped, and the cellophane wrapper crinkled. It was all muffled to my ears.

So. It had been him all along. At least now I knew why the cyclops woman had looked so familiar. She had been his so-called "wife" back at St. Agnes—the woman coming out of the confessional. And come to think of it, I could've sworn I saw her dressed as a maid outside Colt's hotel in Boston, too. Had that been when she first confirmed it was me? The first of Brocker's monster attacks had been at the vet, just after I'd seen her.

Brocker walked down the long stretch of carpet, tucking a hand into his pocket and arching an eyebrow. "You're angry," he commented.

He came to a stop five feet in front of me, and I returned his amused expression with a blank one. Keeping my face as neutral as possible, I clapped slowly.

Well done for figuring out that one, ole sport.

He chuckled. "So expressive. Even without words, I know exactly what you're saying."

I dropped my hands, curling them into fists at my sides, and stomped the broken throat lozenge deeper into his expensive carpet.

He stopped smiling and returned my glare with an even, steady gaze. Then he dipped his head and gestured to one of the fancy leather chairs. "Take a seat."

I remained immobile as he strode past me and looped around his gigantic oak desk to sit on the kingly chair. His actual appearance hadn't changed at all since seeing him at St. Agnes, but now his entire...*essence* exuded power. It wasn't just the fact that he wore a finely tailored suit, or that he was surrounded by extravagance, it was in the way he carried himself. In his stare and cadence of words.

Mr. Brocker nodded toward the bowl of hard candy. "Please, take one. I'd prefer if this conversation wasn't quite so one-sided."

Folding my arms, I stared right back at him. If he thought I was going to roll over and take a treat like a dog, he had another think coming. Besides, if he was comfortable enough to offer me a candy to give back my voice and my powers, he had a trick up his sleeve.

I had no desire to give this man what he wanted.

"Eris, I will only warn you once. I don't tolerate disobedience." He leaned forward and steepled his fingers together. "I'm generally an understanding man. I even abided by the rules of the sanctuary and left you in peace at St. Agnes."

He regarded me for a moment, observing every line of hatred and distress on my face. I wanted to be stronger, to hide how deeply he frightened me, but I was weak. *Always will be, too.*

"You've grown into quite the young woman, Eris. One of the things I regret most in life is letting that woman take you away from me."

Madame.

He stood and crossed to me and I struggled to stand my ground. To not move an inch. With his left hand, he tucked a piece of hair behind my ear. By some miracle, I resisted the urge I to jerk away.

"She's not your mother, my dear. She's nothing but a kidnapper. And it hurts my heart to see you make that face on her behalf. If she hadn't taken you from here, we'd be working together to pull off my plan. We'd be standing side by side."

My eyes narrowed up at him. *What plan?* I'd known all along my creator wanted me back in his clutches to use my power, but I'd never given any thought as to *what*, exactly, he needed my power for.

His gaze shot to the bowl with all the red cellophane candy wrappers. "Take a lozenge, Eris. I won't tell you again."

I shook my head. He'd have to force me. Stuff it down my throat. God, I never hated anyone before like I hated this man.

His chin tilted downward to glare into my eyes. A dark aura seemed to surround him, consuming the powerful essence into something terribly sinister. "You're disappointing me," he ground out.

Mr. Brocker turned to the left wall where the subtle outline of a door stood out among the panels of oak. He hooked his fingers into an indention and the wall glided over the carpet without a sound.

The long sliding door opened up to another room with three people in it.

I gasped, hands flying to my mouth. My whole body gave one violent shudder.

Madame Maldu sat tied to a chair in the center of this hidden room. Her wrists and ankles were each bound with thick, coarse rope and a handkerchief gagged her mouth. Blood trickled down her hairline over the cloth threaded through her lips, and she sported a black eye. Two men in suits—I recognized them as the men who'd brought me here—stood on either side of her, hands clasped behind their backs.

Mr. Brocker strode over to her, and automatically the man on the left drew out a pistol and handed it to his boss.

Mr. Brocker cocked the gun and raised the muzzle to Madame Maldu's temple. "Do I need to repeat myself now?"

I lunged for the candy so hard and fast that it knocked the delicate glass bowl to the carpet. It shattered, sending stray pieces everywhere. Scrambling for one, and feeling shards of glass prick my hands, I grabbed a stray lozenge and unwrapped it with trembling fingers. I stuck it in my mouth and sucked hard until the cherry flavor burst through my taste buds and soothed the rawness in the back of my throat.

Mr. Brocker waited, his expression blank, as I sucked on the candy. Madame Maldu stared at me all the while, imploringly. Her big green eyes were rimmed with old mascara, and streaks of it stained her cheeks.

I cracked the lozenge with my back molar and tried to chew it, to get it down faster.

Oh God, oh God, oh God.

Mr. Brocker gave me a cold smile. "That's my girl."

Madame squeezed her eyes shut.

Just as I was swallowing the last few morsels of the candy and could feel my voice rise up in my throat, the pistol went off.

Madame Maldu's head dropped to her shoulders as red and pink sprayed across the carpet and the wall.

My scream pierced the air and I wailed like a banshee.

The floor-to-ceiling windows cracked. Several spider-webbed, the rest of the glass exploded from its frames. The two men stumbled backward, holding their heads, while blood oozed from their ears.

Brocker didn't even flinch. He simply handed the gun to his henchman.

I slumped onto the carpet, the glass and the cellophane candy sticking to my damp, sweaty skin like red and silver sparkles. Footsteps padded their way across the carpet toward me. A hand moved my hair away from my cheeks and stroked my skin with cold fingertips. "Don't disobey me again, Eris."

Shaking violently, Madame's execution replaying in my head over and over, I turned and threw up, barely missing Brocker's shoes.

He took a step back.

While I collapsed on the carpet away from my sick, voices carried on overhead. Orders. More orders.

"Get her up and cleaned. Don't let her touch the body. I don't want any blood on that dress. It's expensive. And for godsakes, call the damn window company. I want those windows replaced before tomorrow night."

The other men hoisted me up and shoved me around like a limp doll.

Time still went on. The earth still rotated around the sun…

…as if my world hadn't just ended.

For a long time, I couldn't comprehend much. It was like my brain had just turned off. Like a lightbulb, it had flickered and died. Useless. Broken.

At some point I remember being taken back to…*my* suite, I supposed. The maids dabbed away sick and made me rinse my mouth. They washed away blood from my shallow cuts from the glass and applied some antiseptic that stung.

Then they left me on the bed for a long while.

My mind had changed from a burned-out lightbulb to a film reel. Flips of scenes from The Blind Dragon flickered through my vision. I could remember every detail.

Madame teaching me how to pour drinks.

Madame tucking me back into bed when I was still young and I had a nightmare.

Madame taking me to the market to buy groceries.

Then Madame shaking my wrist, her eyes wide and frightened, as she told me not to speak. Warned me. Many times.

Don't speak, Eris. Don't ever speak.

All along I'd hoped that maybe one day I could talk to someone. Tell them my wants and fears, and hopes and desires. Share my heart with them.

But a monster didn't deserve that.

I thought of Colt, then—and his own past. People had died because of him. Madame Maldu had died because of me.

I'd tried to tell him it wasn't his fault—but could the same be said for me?

I could've saved Madame. I could've been stronger somehow. Eaten the candy sooner, commanded him to stop. But I'd been weak and indecisive and stubborn and now she was dead because of me.

Some unmeasurable amount of time later, a voice raised me from my self-loathing. "You should do what he wants."

Jerking up, I twisted around to find the cyclops woman standing in the doorway. Her long dark hair fell around her shoulders in silky waves, and her clothes and makeup were as perfect as before, but her expression was tired. Weary.

I glared at her, fisting the sheets as overwhelming rage

boiled inside me. "*You will help me escape from here.*"

The woman's delicate eyebrows pulled together in sympathy. "Oh, Eris, my sister, I wish I could."

In answer to the shock written on my face, she pushed back her dark hair to reveal a cream foam-like substance wedged into her ears. "Ear plugs. Mr. Brocker had them made specially for all of us. And many of us have been trained to read lips." She shook her head. "There has been so much preparation for your return."

Dammit. Dammit. I wanted to scream again. I knew he had a trick up his sleeve. There's no way he'd give me back my voice when I could turn this whole building against him.

"Listen to me." In three long strides, she was at my bedside, looking down at me. "There is more at stake than just your life. You have to agree to his heist. For all of them."

Her words made no sense. "His heist?" I asked. "What is he planning to steal?"

Before she could answer, the sound of the elevator opening echoed through the suite. She grabbed my hands and pulled me off the bed, guiding me back into the living room just as the two large henchmen stepped into my suite.

"She'll go willingly," she told the men.

Wordlessly, I followed them to the elevator, noting the plugs in their ears as well.

Its iron bars unfolded to cover us in the ornate cage-like contraption and we left the cyclops behind in my suite, descending to the thirteenth floor. Compared to the rest of the building, this hallway was downright dull. It had simple thin carpet and bare walls, no expensive vases with rare flowers or Impressionist paintings.

The two men walked me down the hallway to the door at the end. The first one opened the door and stepped back to let me pass through first.

I wasn't sure what I'd been expecting in this building of

horrors, but it hadn't been a room like this. The floor was shiny white with white walls and stainless-steel tables, and it reminded me of Dr. Boursaw's veterinarian office. A glass window panel spanned across the three walls of the strange room that faced *inside* the building, showing concrete walls straight across.

Brocker stood at the glass, his head tilted downward like he was watching something below. He turned at our entrance and his expression held nothing—no remorse, no emotion. Just cold, businesslike indifference.

"Come here, Eris."

I didn't move. I was disobeying him again, but I didn't care. *Just kill me. At this point, you've taken not one but two people I cared about most in the world.*

He regarded me for a long minute while no one else moved. No one even breathed. Then he turned fully toward me, tucking both hands into his pockets. "Helena's real name was Helena Kurtz. She was the wife of my partner, Robert Kurtz. When she found out I had the pearl embedded in your mouth, she escaped with you into the night, and her husband helped her. I killed him that very night." His hard, cold gaze locked with mine. "You see, Eris, *no one steals from me.*"

I glared back at him, hatred pouring through my veins like molten lava. It ignited life inside me again, not healing what had been broken with Madame's death, but making it hurt worse. Inflicting pain upon pain until I could do nothing but try to breathe fire through it.

Brocker's mustache quivered as his lips pulled to a smirk. "You think you have nothing left to live for. That there's no other way I can control you. Oh, but how wrong you are, my dear. I have one hundred and twenty ways to control you."

What the hell did he mean—one hundred and twenty ways?

He tilted his head toward the glass. "Come here, and I

will show you."

Something told me not to go anywhere near that window. That whatever was down there could break me into even tinier pieces.

"*Why?*" I rasped.

His smile stretched wider. "Words at last. Good. Now more. Why *what*, Eris?"

I wrapped my arms around myself, trying to stop my whole body from quivering with rage and pain. "Why are you doing this? What do you want to use me for?"

Watching Brocker, my stomach clenched and my blood pumped faster in my ears. He didn't give any indication that he felt my magic, even though I knew the air had to be thick with it. There was too much raw emotion in my words. Too much anger and fear.

Still, he gave no response to my words affecting him. He didn't have ear plugs, either—I would've noticed. Was he like Colt, too? A dragon but with no wings?

Instead, his smile merely grew wider. "Such power in your voice. I can feel its call in my very blood." He dropped his gaze to look down at his hands, then he clenched them into fists. "With you, this will work."

"*What* will work?"

In two short strides, he had me by the back of my neck and jerked me to the window panels, my heels slipping across the squeaky clean floor. Catching myself with my palms slamming against the glass, I was forced to finally look down.

Rows upon rows of beds were aligned two floors below. A child lay in each one, hooked up to a bag of glowing blue liquid.

The chimera agent.

A sob bubbled up in my throat as Brocker whispered next to me, "You ask me why? Then I will answer it with a question of my own. What does every king need?" His hand curled around my shoulder like a claw, worse than any other demon's touch I could imagine.

I stared at the rows of children ready and prepped to become monsters.

"An army," he whispered in my ear.

My knees buckled and I slid down the glass, silent, heavy tears rolling down my cheeks.

No, please no.

I felt his hand pet the top of my head. Like he would a dog. "Don't think for a second that they are important to me. Orphans—unwanted children—are a dime a dozen. I don't think I need to tell you what will happen if you don't do as I say."

"*Let them go,*" I said.

Brocker flinched, but then he exhaled, threw his head back, and laughed. "Yes, an order does make a difference, doesn't it? And I thought merely your emotions were strong. No, words are indeed more powerful. But that won't work, I'm afraid. You see, I've built up an immunity to your voice. When you were young, first experimenting with your pearl, I would listen to you talk and build up a tolerance to your voice." Brocker cocked his head thoughtfully. "Come to think of it, that's probably how your dragon boyfriend was able to resist you. I'd heard the BOI had recordings of a siren's voice. How convenient for them, and how very cruel for him."

"It hurts, Eris, to resist the pull of a siren. At least in the beginning. It's painful, like trying to carve out a bit of your soul. Your own will fighting against you."

He knew about Colt. Did he have BOI contacts that told him about Colt's origins?

"Now that you know what's at stake, Eris, perhaps you will be a bit more compliant to my plans. Tomorrow we will review them in detail," he said.

At that, the henchman strode over and picked me off the

floor. I could still feel Brocker's gaze crawling over me like spiders as I was led to the door.

It all felt so, so hopeless. How could I stop this? Wasn't there *something* I could do?

Then a terrible, awful idea struck me. It came with a memory that seemed like it was years ago. Colt, kneeling over the body of a manticore and saying, "*Many men choose death over being captured. That way they escape torture, and the possibility of giving up information to their enemies.*"

"Oh, and, Eris?"

I froze.

"Since I know you're thinking about it…consider this—if you choose to end your life there will be no one around to protect them"—he nodded downward, four floors below—"from my wrath at seeing you dead."

Chapter Thirty-Two

The Dragon

The building of Brocker and Kurtz Holdings was one of the largest private buildings I'd ever seen. It stood solitary among other older and shorter buildings, like a chrome sword stretching up into the night sky, the moon hanging above it in a hazy yellow glow.

"I can't believe I haven't heard of these people," I ground out irritably, rapping out a harsh rhythm on the door handle.

Jimmy took a sip of his joe and shrugged. "We're too busy looking at the underground, not the upside. Don't beat yourself up. Corporate crimes ain't part of the SOCD."

I shook my head, not trusting myself to speak. It had taken the better part of the day to drive all the way up from DC to New York. It hadn't helped that technically we were both on the run, since I hadn't really been pardoned and officially released.

I glanced at my watch. "When is McCarney showing up?"

"If you ask me that question again, I'm kicking you out of my car."

With a groan, I leaned my head back against the seat.

"Look, I know you want to rescue your princess, but you were right not to storm the castle alone." He gestured toward the lit-up skyscraper. "This place is locked up tighter than Fort Knox. McCarney and some of the SOCD have been casing it for the past week and we don't have much to go on, okay? So, keep a level head. I shouldn't have to tell you that. You're the best hunter there is, Clemmons. Act like it."

I blinked at Jimmy, making out his outline through the gloom in the car.

Silence stretched on for a while, and I decided not to point out that he'd just delivered me an actual compliment. He might take it back or punch me or something. Hiding a smile, I said, "Okay, what *do* we have to go on?"

Jimmy narrowed his eyes at the building a block away. "The past few days, there have been a lot of trucks and delivery workers coming in and out of the garage. I'm talking flowers and tables and chairs, food and, naturally, booze. Tons and tons of it."

"So, a party?"

Jimmy nodded. "A big fat one. The Moby Dick of parties."

"Do you know who's invited?"

Jimmy shifted, as if sitting on his ass for a good eight hours straight wasn't agreeing with it. "That's hopefully what McCarney has for us tonight. The guest list."

At the far corner of the street, a black car pulled to the side and idled.

I straightened. "That it?"

"License plate checks out," Jimmy answered as he started the car. Craning his neck over his shoulder, he checked the oncoming nightly Manhattan traffic and pulled out when there was a lull. We let the black car swerve into the traffic ahead of us, and then we followed it thirteen miles, all the way into Brooklyn.

Jimmy parked in front of an old brick house wedged between two others as the black car swung into the narrow driveway. Streetlights were positioned at either end of the street and silver garbage cans were left out front.

Jimmy and I got out of the car and headed up the steps. The door opened immediately, and I caught the screen door with my elbow as Jimmy ducked inside first.

The house was mostly bare with dusty wooden floors and drab walls. A brick fireplace sat in the corner and old furniture was pushed off to the side and covered in white sheets. Two men sat at a table full of papers and dozens upon dozens of photographs. My gaze homed in on my old boss sitting at the end, staring at the mess like it was a jigsaw puzzle he had to piece together.

The other man was Erickson, an agent and a manticore. I'd had his poison run through my veins every other night for five months before I built up an immunity to it. He was tall and in his late thirties.

Steps from the back alerted us to the arrival of the black car's driver. A woman stepped into the light of the living room. She walked in, pulling off a platinum blonde wig, revealing her hair of writhing emerald-green serpents. Threading her hands through her snakes like they were nothing more than locks of hair, the gorgon let out a deep sigh. "Next time someone else gets to scout. This wig is driving me batty."

Yet another one of my "torturers." Rita Sharpe. The only female hunter in the SOCD and a powerful gorgon. Like Jimmy, she'd been unaware that she'd been involved in my so-called "training." She'd just stared through two eyeholes for a few months. I'd fought against the lure of her magical stare until my muscles felt like they were melting. A gorgon's stare turned people immobile. If they stared at her long enough, their skin would turn to stone… I'd never gotten to that point.

"Colt." Her gaze softened as it came to rest on me. "It's good to see you."

"You, too," I said, trying and failing to return her smile. I kept glancing back to McCarney. The last time I'd seen him I'd been sitting across from him in an interrogation room, chained to the table.

Finally, McCarney looked up, but when he did, he looked at Jimmy. "Any trouble?"

Jimmy threw himself on the sheet-covered couch. "It was duck soup, bo*sssssss*."

"Good," McCarney grunted, then he shifted his gaze to me. "You look like shit," he said flatly.

I gave a harsh laugh. "Yeah, well, thanks for sicing the golem on me."

"Frankly, you deserved it," he grumbled. "You could've trusted me. Brought me into all this sooner and we wouldn't have to be here right now."

I stalked over to the table, slamming my fist down on it. The legs shuddered and the table rocked. "As if any one of you would've listened to me. The BOI would've taken Eris and broken her down—just like you did to me. And I'd do it all over again, too. Especially after I know what *really* happened in Boston. I only came to you because we have one enemy now."

McCarney's eyes narrowed. "What happened in Boston?"

"Don't play dumb," I growled. "The shootout. Through the hotel walls? At first I thought there were three groups after Eris. The BOI, her creator, and someone who just wanted her dead. But I had a lot of time to think about it while in the holding cell in DC. *You* were the only one who knew my location *and* you purposefully lured me out of the room to go get the car you sent."

McCarney tapped his fingers on the table, not looking remorseful. "And if you would've just gone to get the car—"

"She'd be dead!" I roared.

"Exactly!" McCarney bellowed back. "My superiors wanted her alive so they could use her, but the country is better off with her dead, Colt! Look at what's happening—someone else has her and God knows what they'll do with her!"

"This was a mistake." Burning with rage, I turned to go, but Rita was there with a hand on my chest.

"Colt, wait." She removed it quickly, surely feeling the heat of my fire breath. "It's like you said, we have one enemy now. We can work together to get her back."

"So McCarney can kill her," I spat.

"Then get there first," Jimmy said.

McCarney turned his head sharply to glare at him while Erickson and Rita looked over at their fellow agent in surprise.

"Use the SOCD, Colt." Jimmy's serpent-like eyes cut to mine, holding them. He kicked his right leg up to fold over his left. "Use us to storm the castle then escape with your princess when it's all said and done. This isn't a full-blown operation. We're rogue now." He gave me a crooked smirk as he tilted his chin up at me. "You can do whatever you damn well please."

McCarney stood. "That's insubordination."

"You used me to torture a kid," Jimmy snarled. "Fire me, I dare you."

Silence stretched on in the room before Rita patted the pile on the table. "Right. Time to focus. Erickson? Will you do the honors?"

Erickson leaned forward, moving a document out from under the pile. "James G. Brocker. He's an immigrant from Czechoslovakia, or at least that's what his birth certificate says, but it looks like it was forged. Basically, the guy popped up in tax records about twenty-five years ago. He started his company with a man named Robert B. Kurtz. Their holding company has boomed in the last decade and even more so after Kurtz mysteriously died. Brocker's known to be rich, but instead of making money off oil or railroads, he made money off other people's wealth." Erickson picked up a photograph from the pile and tossed it in the middle. It showed a man with graying brown hair, in a fancy suit and fedora, getting out of a Rolls Royce New Phantom automobile. "Rumor is, he's got a party two nights from now. Wednesday night, October twenty-third."

McCarney moved a sheet of paper forward with two fingers, cutting in. "The guest list is the who's who of Wall Street. The country's wealthiest men and women will all be present. They're calling it America's Royal Court."

My gaze jumped from photo to photo as I looked at different shots of the building and of the man who had Eris. His profile burned into my mind and my chest heated with anger.

"Unbelievable," Jimmy sneered. "We go from the top dogs of the criminal netherworld to the kings and queens of the United States? Will the arrogance ever die?"

Rita leaned her hip against the table and regarded Jimmy with a raised eyebrow. "Erickson managed to stun two of the waiters, and luckily their uniforms are roughly yours and Colt's sizes. Anyone with a special pin of Brocker's crest on their uniform is granted access to the building. You'll be going undercover."

Jimmy blinked at Rita. "No. No way. Why can't you go and be a maid or something?"

Rita smiled and winked. "I wouldn't fill out a man's uniform like you would, hon."

Jimmy's cheeks colored and he made a noise in the back of his throat.

I turned to McCarney. "Do we know what Brocker's play

is yet? Any word on that vial? Or Dr. Durwich?"

McCarney shook his head. "Your girl *just* arrived in Manhattan. Even if she still has the vial of blood there's not a chance in hell she would've been able to get it to Dr. Durwich yet. But he's on standby."

"What about more blood from Sister Adaline?"

"Tried that. Apparently the virus is different than before. She used the term *mutated*." He scratched his chin. "Unfortunately, the original strand in that blood is what we need to develop an antidote that will counteract the virus in its early stages, which is when it's the most contagious. As for Brocker's plan..." McCarney jerked his thumb back at Erickson and the manticore nodded.

This time, he withdrew papers full of charts, graphs, and tables with numbers. "Got a friend of mine to look into BKH's financials and what he found was...alarming."

"In what way?" I asked.

Erickson pulled out a pack of Lucky Strikes and tapped the end, sliding one out and fixing it between his lips. He lit it with his Banjo automatic lighter, clicking the side button with his thumb and letting the flame catch on the butt of the gasper. He took a drag and I wanted to grab it from his mouth and stamp it out. He was taking too long.

"Ever seen a house of cards?"

We all nodded.

"That's what this fella's financials are like. A house of cards. Everything is built on one another. People's shares and investments and money all carefully placed precariously." Erickson took another pull from his gasper and blew smoke into the air. "One blow could knock this house of cards down. If any of these companies were to hand over even one more share to Brocker, he could actually be named as the main shareholder and, using his own money, he could buy the rest out."

We stared at him.

He sighed. "I'm *saying* all these companies would be owned by Brocker. You'd be looking at the wealthiest man in the country. In the whole damn world."

"And all he would need is one more share from each of his companies?" Rita asked. "The owners of the companies would have to know that, though. There's no way they would do it."

My blood turned to ice, a direct opposite of the intense heat that had been radiating from my chest and throat.

I pictured Eris's face as she sat on the bed of the hotel room that night before the tommy gun's bullets blasted through the wall. Her words drifted through my mind in a soft whisper.

"*They'll either kill me or use me for evil. I don't want to be evil, Colt. Please.*"

Closing my eyes, I swallowed. "Not unless a certain someone told them to do it."

Chapter Thirty-Three

The Siren

The morning sun filtered through my white silk curtains and shone between the gaps, making me squint. Flipping onto my back, I threw an arm over my eyes. For just a moment, in the darkness I had created, I could imagine that I was back in my small room at Madame's apartment above The Blind Dragon. I could hear the kettle's whistle going off, screaming at her that the water was boiling for her afternoon cup of Earl Grey. I could smell the thick Ethiopian coffee blend that Stanley put on when he came in to unload liquor for that day's bootlegging shipment. And the sounds of Manhattan were similar to the sounds of Boston. Sirens, dockworkers, cars honking, thousands of busy footsteps across pavement—all blurring together into a background symphony of which I knew every note.

All last night I'd tried, and failed, to come up with a plan. But no matter what scenario I could think of, my conscience kept going back to those children. If I somehow escaped, then Brocker would kill a child, or however many he chose until he had me once again.

A light knock on my bedroom door had me flinching, throwing my arm off my face to see my visitor, praying to God it wasn't the devil himself.

The cyclops woman stood in the door. She wore a maroon day dress with a cloche hat pulled low over her brow to conceal her third eye. It had peacock feathers embedded into the velvet ribbon trim. "The maids told me you didn't eat dinner or breakfast."

I turned away from her to stare out the bedroom window at the crawling expanse of New York City. "If you just saw the only mother you'd ever known get her head blown off, would you be peckish?" I replied.

Footsteps on carpet, then a gentle touch on my arm. "I'm sorry about Helena Kurtz, Eris. I really am."

Disgust rolled through me and I jerked away from her, pulling myself out of bed and stumbling against the window. I hadn't realized how weak I was—I hadn't eaten for almost twenty-four hours and I'd cried most of the night. My back against the cold glass, I glared at the monster. "You used your power to find me and bring me in. Why should I believe anything you say?"

Her red lips turned down into a frown. "Haven't you considered I'm his prisoner, too?"

I opened and closed my mouth. No, I hadn't. But I should've. She had been the one to tell me yesterday that there was more at stake than just my life. She'd known about the children and wanted me to help protect them.

Digging my hand into my messy curls, I sighed. "Okay, I believe you. But who are you? I don't even know your name."

She sat down on my bed, twisting her hands in her lap. "My name is Marjorie. Sister Marjorie," she added.

Sister?

"I had come to St. Juliana a few months before you

were adopted by Brocker and you received your pearl. We hadn't known each other for very long, but still, you'd left an impression on me. I'd never liked the man who adopted you. A year after you left the orphanage, I went to look for you… to see how you were doing. I entered Brocker's building, and…and never left."

Raising a trembling hand to my mouth, I tried to repress a choking sound. She'd come looking for me? To check on me?

"At first, he kept me because he thought I might have something to do with your kidnapping, but then he decided he wanted to use me. Pumped me full of chimera agent and gave me this eye." She tugged the brim of her hat a bit lower, her painted lips twisting to the side in revulsion.

"Then that means…because of me…you…" I couldn't finish my sentence. How many more lives was I destined to destroy?

Marjorie pushed off the bed and grabbed my shoulders, giving me a gentle shake. "No, Eris. *None* of this is your fault. It's all Brocker's. But we have to think of those children. In fact, the truth is I'd suspected you were in Boston for quite some time. You'd spoken two years ago—something small—but I ignored it. I didn't want Brocker to have you. And then he kidnapped all these children and threatened their lives if I didn't find you, and soon. So when you started talking again, I traced you all the way to that hotel. Don't you see? I had no other option. We need to do what he says and maybe—"

"But if we do what he says, they'll turn into monsters!"

"Better than one hundred and twenty children dead. Turning into a monster doesn't condemn you to hell, your actions do."

"But then they'll be made to fight!" I fisted my hands in my hair. His words haunted me. *What does every king need? An army.* "He's got some bonkers idea to become king of the United States. Like he can march on the capital with an army of monsters and just…" It sounded crazy and yet…what would the government do against a slew of monsters storming the Capitol Building? They might just be children now, but they would grow up and their powers would only get stronger with them. They could be unstoppable.

But I couldn't let it get that far. I *wouldn't.*

I glanced at Marjorie and the resigned hopelessness in her expression. She'd been Brocker's prisoner for so long that she saw no other way out. Even with three eyes.

"You learned how to control your powers and find me," I said slowly, the wheels in my head slowly picking up speed.

Marjorie nodded. "Eventually, with practice, I was able to control the eye."

For so long, I'd been desperate to control my voice. To learn what I was able to do, and of course, how to suppress it. Colt had once said I was the most powerful weapon in the country. If that was really true then there had to be something, *something* I could do that didn't involve taking my own life.

I'm ready to fight.

I wasn't sure what I could do yet, or how to get the vial of blood to Dr. Durwich, but I had to start somewhere, and I'd been ignoring this great power for far too long.

Picking up Marjorie's hands, I squeezed them. "Teach me what you know. *Please.*"

First, Marjorie walked me through her early training days as a cyclops. She'd told me how she pushed through the hours of migraines to shut off all other senses and focus on the magical trace that monster parts produced. She used her eye to follow the trace and home in on certain ones, flexing her ability to stretch across great distances. While everything she'd told me had been fascinating, I wasn't sure how helpful it was. My power just came out no matter how hard I'd tried to suppress it. Hers had to be used and exercised, like a muscle. But how could I exercise my own emotions when they flowed out with every word I spoke?

It felt like we'd barely scraped the surface of how Marjorie's powers worked before one of the henchmen arrived at my suite to fetch me for lunch with Brocker. Marjorie helped me get ready and then sent me off with a supportive smile and a squeeze on my shoulder.

The man took me to a grand ballroom that occupied most of the entire floor. It went on for what felt like ages with high, high ceilings that easily displaced another floor above. The western wall was all glass, likely designed to watch the sunset. Crystal chandeliers hung in a grid, lighting up every deep corner with a yellow glow and rainbow light bouncing on the sleek marble floor. On the left and right sides of the ballroom were large round tables covered in white silk tablecloths and clear vases awaiting expensive floral arrangements. There was also a large oak bar that appeared eager to fill patrons' glasses with giggle water in sparkling glasses.

And to my never-ending horror, at the very opposite side of the ballroom was a stage. Along with a grand piano, instruments and chairs that were all aligned, ready for a big jazz band. A spotlight hung from the ceiling, awaiting its next performer.

I had an idea I knew who it would be.

"Eris." My name traveled across the expanse of the ballroom, and it was only then that I noticed a single man sitting at a table not far from the stage.

Stiffly, I made my way down the middle of the large marble aisle meant for future dancers and wove through the tables until I reached the one where Brocker sat.

He lifted a white mug of coffee to his lips. "I thought we'd have lunch together."

"It's awfully big for just the two of us," I commented, making a point to glance around at the ballroom again.

He patted the seat next to him, a ghost of a smile on his lips. "So it is. Come, sit. Let's eat."

Every inch of me wanted to dump that scalding coffee into his lap, but I took the seat and the moment I did, a waiter came up, bearing an entire tray of food. Silently, the waiter set down the dishes and my jaw nearly dropped at the wide array. Just before he left, he arranged two plates of fine china, silverware, and two carafes—one of ice water and one of iced tea.

Brocker spooned food onto my plate. "A bit of Waldorf salad. Breast of chicken, a la rose. Try the roast duck broiled potatoes. But leave room for dessert because Chef Andre has prepared some delightful biscuit tortoni angel cake bonbons."

It was far too much. I longed for the simple pastrami sandwich back in Philly, and of course, the man I'd eaten it with. Swallowing back a fresh wave of pain, I picked up my fork and stuffed a few bites of Waldorf salad in my mouth. The dressing was light and flavorful and the fresh green apples and almond slices provided the right crunch to the leafy mix.

Brocker spoke at length about all the luxuries I'd be afforded while living with him. He described all the jewels and the fancy dresses I could expect. He even wanted to personally take me to Bergdorf's the following week. I responded when it was polite and pushed the food around on my plate just enough to make it appear like I'd eaten more than I actually had.

"All this and more will be yours if you simply do as I ask," he said at last, wiping his mouth with his napkin and dropping it to his lap, "Eris, you will be useful to me in many ways in the next few years, but you will perform no single action that is more important than what I require from you tomorrow night."

"What am I to do tomorrow night?"

Brocker took another sip of his coffee. "Something you've been doing almost every night for the last eight years."

"You want me to sing."

"Yes."

"What song?"

"It doesn't matter what song really, so long as these lyrics are inserted somewhere in the midst of it." He removed a folded sheet of paper from the inner pocket of his jacket and placed it on the table, sliding it toward me.

I scanned the lyrics. "They don't even rhyme."

"They don't have to. You just need to sing them in your beautiful, powerful voice."

I read them through again. "What happens once these men sign over these shares to you?" I remembered reading about Brocker's holding company, and the fact that he held the shares of many businesses, but I wasn't sure why I needed to order these people to sell over even more of their stocks. Were they so difficult to convince or would something nefarious happen once they did?

His smile turned brittle. "Don't you worry about that, my pet. Now, I hope you have room saved for those angel cake bonbons." He snapped his fingers at a nearby waiter as I reread the lyrics.

It was then I remembered Marjorie's words from yesterday. "*You have to agree to his heist.*"

This was his heist. Signing over the rest of their shares meant Brocker wouldn't just control a piece of all these companies, it meant he would control them all. He wasn't just stealing money, he was stealing entire corporations, and all their profits.

While I was still wrapped up in the piece of paper before

me, a familiar scent tickled my nose. A gloved hand set down a teacup full of steaming orange pekoe.

My heart stuttered.

I jerked my gaze up to the waiter. The man had dark hair, smartly styled, and sharp green eyes with narrowed pupils... almost reptilian.

He gave me a smile. "Thought you would like some tea, miss," he said smoothly.

"Tea will go well with the cakes," Brocker commented absently as he turned to a stack of papers set by him.

The waiter offered another polite smile. "If the miss doesn't like orange pekoe, I'm happy to get her something else."

"No," I said quickly, trying to keep the desperate panic out of my voice. "This is perfect. I love orange pekoe."

The waiter nodded and gave a short bow, backing away from the table.

For a long minute, I stared at the cup of tea, hopeful, yet with hopeless possibilities racing through my mind. Clenching my fists, I searched for the waiter. He leaned against the doorframe of the ballroom, staring right at me. Intensely.

It could just be a coincidence, but I'd never forgive myself if I lost all hope for him.

"Sir?"

"Hmm?" Brocker flipped to another page in his stack.

"May I go back to my room?"

At that, he looked up, inspecting me intently. "We will have to move past this, Eris. It will be much easier if you didn't hate me forever."

I returned his stare. "After seeing all that blood yesterday I wasn't able to eat anything. This rich food on an empty stomach has made me unwell."

Brocker set down his papers, actually looking concerned. "I see. Then yes, you may go." He made a gesture for one of his men in suits to come get me, but I laid my hand on his arm, stopping him.

"Sir, I can find my own way back."

He said nothing, still watching me. Perhaps considering whether or not he could trust me.

"If I am to live here happily, I cannot be treated like a prisoner," I added.

A slow, cruel smile started on his lips. "Very well, Eris." He picked his documents back up and tapped their edges on the table. "I trust you. At least, I trust that you care very much about the well-being of those children."

Shards of glass pricked my throat as I swallowed and stood from the table, the chair scraping across the marble. Brocker made no move to stop me, or gave any indication that he worried I would disobey him. He knew his threat was sufficient.

At the same moment, the waiter with the orange pekoe disappeared through the door, with one last piercing gaze right at me. My heels clicked across the marble as I wound through the tables and escaped through the ballroom door. Catching just the profile of the waiter as he rounded a bend, I picked up my pace.

I turned the corner and found the short hallway empty. *Rhatz!* Had I lost him? I rounded the next bend and an arm wrapped around my waist, quickly followed by a large hand tightening over my mouth. With a muffled gasp, I was pulled into a hallway closet.

The hands dropped away and went to the closet door in front of my nose, closing it and locking it with a click. Now free, I spun around, expecting to see the strange waiter I'd been following and...

Found Colt instead.

His thick hair, the color of wheat, was slicked back and styled like a fancy gentleman's. He wore a waiter's uniform and a nasty-looking bruise on his cheek, but other than that he hadn't changed much at all. His dark eyes traveled over my skin, from my legs, to my arms, to my neck and coming to rest on my face.

"They haven't hurt me," I breathed, answering his inspection.

He cupped my cheeks, his brow furrowing, eyes searching mine, and seeing something there that was maybe visible to only him. "Yes, they have," he whispered back.

Trembling, I reached up and felt his face. My fingers traced the planes of his cheeks, careful to avoid his bruise, then dropped to the line of his jaw and skimmed across his neck.

I choked back a sob at the familiar feel of him. "You're really here."

He took my hands from his face and kissed my palms—like he had back at the Cerberus Club. His lips lingered as he whispered, "I told you I'd find you."

While I was still reeling in the euphoria of his mouth on my skin, his arms enveloped me, holding so tightly it felt like he was trying to fuse all my broken pieces back together.

"I thought maybe I lost you," I murmured as silent tears rolled down my cheeks. The smell of burning wood filled me up and my heart seemed to absorb all that smoke and pump it through my veins, infusing me with his essence.

"You can't shake me that easily, doll," he whispered into my shoulder.

I pulled back and wiped at my damp cheeks. "And thank God for that."

Colt leaned in, pressing his forehead against mine. His hot breath fanned across my lips. "Don't bring Him into this."

Ah. There it was. My sweet taste of sin that I'd give my soul over to. I tilted my chin up and pressed my mouth to his. A moan escaped from the back of his throat as his strong hands cupped my neck, fingers digging into my perfectly styled waves. When his teeth raked across my bottom lip, I responded willingly, already eager for that deeper kiss he'd shown me in the shade of the chapel.

Somehow, it was all hotter and faster than before. His tongue and lips were demanding, and yet not demanding enough. Precious, blissful clouds of pleasure filled me as everything but our bodies and breaths ceased to exist. He pressed me against the closet door while the knob dug into my lower back—a delicious pain that I blatantly ignored as I tugged him closer.

His lips left mine to drop searing, tantalizing kisses along my jaw and down my neck. I bit my bottom lip and closed my eyes, my hands roaming over his strong shoulders and down his pressed white shirt. My fingers slipped under his jacket lapels and hooked around his black suspenders. He let out a growl against my skin and I realized that it was my name—said more like a warning. "*Eris.*"

Please. More. Nothing but you.

His kisses trailed back up to my mouth and my mind spun out of control. I wasn't thinking. There was wonderfully nothing *to* think about. Only him, alive, with me and kissing me.

As our tongues tangled, my hands turned greedy, and before I could stop myself, I was tugging his shirt out of his pants and sliding my fingers across his smooth, muscled stomach.

Colt tore his mouth from mine, panting, just like me, and caught my hands, removing them from his skin. "Hold on, baby, hold on."

I almost whimpered with the loss of him. "Please, Colt. I don't want to stop."

"Listen, doll," his breath was labored and shallow as he murmured in my ear, "when we're out of this mess and you've got a manacle on your left hand, I'll *never* stop. But right now, we can't."

His words were beautiful and yet lost on my frazzled, grief-stricken mind. "But when I'm touching you, everything bad goes away and I just—" My throat tightened and I couldn't breathe through it.

Colt wrapped one arm around my back and used his other to tuck my face into his neck as he threaded gentle fingers through my hair.

"I know," he whispered into my temple as he kissed it lightly. "I know."

"He killed Madame."

Colt stiffened for a moment, then squeezed me tighter. "I'm sorry."

We were quiet for a long time, him just holding me in the little hall closet.

"We could run," Colt said, breaking the silence.

I leaned back to look him in the eyes. His gaze was serious and dark.

"I could get us out of here and we'd be out of the state before Brocker is done with his cup of joe. *Eris*"—he took both my hands in his once more and kissed my fingertips—"run away with me."

Over the years, I'd lost count of how many men had asked me that. How many had grabbed my elbow after a set at the Dragon and promised me the world.

For just the tiniest moment, I let myself imagine what it would be like if we actually did run.

Golden California with its giant Redwood trees, rolling hills, and rocky coastline—all of it, with Colt.

Delicious, sweet temptation.

"I can't." My heart crumbled and cracked. "If I ran, more innocents would die."

To my surprise, Colt smiled. "That. Right there."

"What?"

He brushed his thumb across my cheek. "That's why I fell in love with you."

I let out a shaky laugh, my heart tap-dancing the Charleston at his confession. "Anyone would do that, Colt."

His brow furrowed. "Not everyone, doll."

"You would," I argued.

One side of his mouth quirked up in a half smile. "Being with you has its side effects."

Side effects. The virus. Pulling away from him, I quickly turned back to the door.

"Eris?"

I dug under my dress to pull out the vial of blood then whirled back around, pressing it into his palm. "I was trying to figure out how to get it to the doctor, but maybe you can now."

Colt curled his fingers around the vial. "I'll take care of it. Now what were you saying about more innocents?"

As fast I could, I told him about all the children being pumped full of chimera agent on the floor far below us and Brocker's cruel plan to use them for an army. "It's like he has his own little hospital ward set up. Colt, if I don't sing these lyrics at this ridiculous party tomorrow, he'll probably kill them all. He's threatening me with them and also using them for his own gain. It's..."

"Monstrous." Colt shook his head. "Are the lyrics about telling CEOs to sell their shares to Brocker?"

I blinked. "How did you..."

"Long story. You can't sing those lyrics."

"But the children..."

"If we can get them out safely, we can expose Brocker. Put him behind bars for kidnapping all of them."

"If I remember correctly, the children are below the thirteenth floor–I would try the eleventh. But Colt..." I nibbled on my bottom lip. "Do you have the rest of the BOI with you? Was that an agent I followed?"

"Yeah, Jimmy Sawyer. Good guy."

"How did you two get in here undetected?"

Colt gestured to his waiter uniform. "We've got a manticore on our team who knocked out some other waiters and stole their uniforms. Apparently if you have this"—he nudged a small silver crest that acted as a pin on his lapel—"it's duck soup getting in."

"How many of there are you?"

"Four."

He read the devastation on my face and took my chin between his forefinger and my thumb, tilting my head up to meet his gaze. "Don't worry about us, Eris. Just focus on your song and make sure they don't hand over their shares to Brocker. We'll get those kids out some way."

Icy fear gripped my whole body. I pictured Brocker's cold indifference as he pulled the trigger on the gun against Madame's temple. "Colt, I don't know if I can do this. I…I'm not strong like you."

Colt was quiet for a moment as I felt his eyes rake over my face. I couldn't look at them. How could I tell him that I was scared to go up on that stage and sing the wrong lyrics and then have Brocker gun me down where I stood? I was a coward. Every time I protected others it was because I knew they were forbidden from actually killing me. But now Brocker was here, needing me for this one important thing. If I failed, and all his collateral was gone, then why *shouldn't* he kill me?

"Then I'm not sure you know what strength is."

My gaze shot back up to him, and he was staring down at me, something in those dark irises holding me captive.

He placed two fingers into the hollow of my throat, ever so lightly. "Strength is acceptance. It's forgiveness. It's doing what's right. It's sacrifice. It's not speaking for seven years to ensure that others around you can keep their free will. It's not running away with a handsome scoundrel who wants to marry you when others need you. Eris, strength *is* you. You might be terrified to get on that stage, but you would anyway. To save whoever you could. Being scared doesn't mean you're weak. It means you're human."

And just like that, all those broken pieces inside me started to heal, threading themselves back together again. Bit by bit. My voice was thick as I muttered, "You're such a smooth talker."

"I've never lied to you, Eris." Colt pulled me flush against his body. My heart pounded and my stomach flipped as I felt the hard planes of his chest against my own. "Even at The Blind Dragon. You ensnared me before I even heard your voice." My knees buckled as I laced my fingers through his hair, his head dipping to kiss my neck and then collarbone…

The closet door I'd been half leaning on was wrenched open, and Colt grabbed me to keep us both from falling.

The waiter I'd been following stood in the door. "Oh, for God's sake, Clemmons. Bank's closed! We don't have time for any petting in the hall closet."

Blushing from head to toe, I pulled away from Colt and smoothed down my dress, patting my hair even though there was no recovering from that.

"We were almost done, Jimmy," Colt snapped.

I swallowed. "Brocker thinks I went back to my room. I should go in case he sends someone to check on me."

Colt snatched my hand before I could disappear. "Eris, this guy won't go down without a fight and this place *is* a fortress. Getting kids out of here will require something big."

"You mean a distraction," I said slowly. "Something that will cause chaos. Like…thinking the building was…on fire maybe?"

Colt grinned, already catching on to my plan.

With a chuckle, I leaned forward and pressed a finger to my dragon's lips. "If only *someone* could produce some high-quality smoke."

Chapter Thirty-Four

The Dragon

"I can't believe you didn't think of that," Jimmy muttered as we stripped off our waiter uniforms back at the BOI safe house in Brooklyn.

I tried to give a reasonable explanation, but I couldn't. The last day we must've gone over seven different plans of getting Eris out, but driving everyone out of the building with signs of smoke had never crossed my mind.

"I've had a one-track mind lately," I admitted, thinking about my brief time with Eris in the closet. *Maybe I should start believing in God*, I thought. Because something truly divine had intervened when I stopped her from undressing me.

A bang on the door made Jimmy and me jump. Rita's voice came through the wood. "Hurry up, gents."

"You don't rush Italian tailoring, Rita," Jimmy snipped as he finished buttoning his shirt.

Muffled laughter. "And yet you have no problem taking them *off* fast," Rita called back.

As Jimmy's face went a deep shade of red, I ducked my head to hide a smirk, wrenched the door open, and headed to the living room.

Taking a seat, I addressed Rita. "Does Dr. Durwich have the vial of blood?" As soon as Jimmy and I had stepped out of Brocker's building, I handed the vial off to Erickson and he'd personally delivered it to the good doctor. From there, we headed back to the Brooklyn safe house to brief McCarney and strategize for the following night. It had been over an hour since I'd seen Erickson and I was eager for an update.

Rita nodded. "Erickson just called to confirm. Durwich is in a BOI lab as we speak, working on an antidote. If he can extrapolate the chimera agent strand from it, he may even be able to produce a serum that could reverse its effects."

"You mean stop someone from becoming a chimera altogether even once they're injected with the serum?"

The gorgon shrugged. "Once a monster part is attached, there's no reversing it, but just removing the agent itself might be possible."

I shot McCarney a look. "Why wasn't this looked at before?"

"Gin's scientists appear to be better than ours," Rita continued. "There's something in the virus she's manufactured that is active and volatile, which is changing the chimera's blood itself. I'm not saying it can be done overnight...but this is major headway. If we can reverse the chimera blood altogether, we can stop monsters from ever being produced again."

"So, you're saying that in an effort to mass produce the chimera blood they gave us a way to stop it entirely?" Jimmy asked.

Rita nodded again.

Jimmy tossed his head back and laughed. "That's rich!"

McCarney rubbed his three-day-old beard. "Did you get

more uniforms?"

I nodded to the bag sitting on the sofa draped with a sheet. "One for Erickson and one for Rita. They'll be able to go to the party, too."

"Good. All right, let's review. After all"—he moved his light gray eyes to each of his agents—"this may be your most important hunt yet."

I'd never seen more hooch in my life.

Erickson and I were in the storage rooms below the grand ballroom where the party was already in full swing. Wine, champagne, whiskey, scotch, vodka, bourbon—all of the finest brands likely smuggled from across Europe to get here—tucked below in their great storeroom. There was no panther piss or homemade booze in sight. Clearly, only the finest liquor for "America's Royal Court."

We'd arrived at Brocker's building, along with the rest of the staff, at six in the morning. The early hour actually gave us more time to explore and find the "hospital ward" that Eris had mentioned. It was in fact the eleventh floor, because when Rita tried it she was turned away by two guards stationed in front of a nondescript door. But they would be easy enough to overpower.

I picked up my tray of champagne flutes and headed back up to the party. I hadn't found Eris, but the night was still young and guests were still arriving.

No need to panic. Yet.

Looping around already intoxicated guests wearing their finest, I made my way through the ballroom.

Even I had to admit, Brocker knew how to throw a party.

The sunset rays of gold, lavender, pink, and orange stretched across the sky, outlining the Manhattan skyline like a steel mountain ridge. The colors cascaded into the ballroom, hitting the crystal chandeliers and throwing a spectrum of sparkles across the lavish place settings and overdressed guests. The jazz band played in the background, their stylings only meant to enhance the atmosphere, not overpower it—the complete opposite of the band at the Cerberus Club.

One guest, two guests, three guests, plucked champagne flutes off my tray as I moved through the crowd.

Then I saw her.

Tonight, she wore a dress that mocked the sunset. It was red at her shoulders and neckline and then fanned out into gradients of orange, gold, and pink. It shimmered with the slightest movement, and around her neck and dangling from her ears were big rubies. In this light her chestnut hair looked more auburn and it was twirled and bunched just below her ears in the latest bobbed fashion. Across those red, red lips she wore a pleasant smile, as a fat older gentleman with white hair and a handlebar mustache gestured animatedly. Her hand was threaded through Brocker's arm and my chest heated at the sight of her touching the madman.

She must've felt my searing gaze on her, because it was then that she noticed me. Her smile faltered as those blue eyes locked with mine. The fire in my chest roared and I pressed a hand on my heart to quell it.

Swallowing, I tore my gaze from her. If I looked at her a second longer, I'd lose my composure and forget the plan entirely. Not to mention that I needed to avoid Brocker if I could. I hadn't actually met the man face-to-face, but it was possible he knew what I looked like. Maybe through photographs or descriptions from his many monstrous henchmen that had been sent to capture Eris. Luckily, my saving grace was that he thought I was dead. Shot, and tossed over a boat in Lake Michigan. Even so, styled hair with a crisp uniform could only hide a dead man so much.

Once I wandered back into the crowd, I waited a few minutes, then went to the corner near the bar where waiters were mixing drinks. Jimmy was tending to the bar and doing a damn fine job, too. He gave me a tight nod then turned back to a fancy brunette to make her cocktail.

A minute later, Eris was standing in line for the bar, and I positioned myself to be just behind her.

"How are you?" I muttered out of the corner of my mouth.

"Don't worry about me. Did you find the floor?"

"Yes, you were right. It was the eleventh. Everything is all set."

The line to the bar inched forward and time seemed to slow down. I was hyper aware of her next to me, and all the things I still wanted to tell her but had no time to. It would just have to wait until next time. There would *be* a next time.

The band changed their song and Eris glanced back toward the crowd, where she must've left Brocker. "I should go."

I caught her fingertips. "Join the crowd heading for the stairs and get out. Run, don't look back."

She finally met my eyes. They seemed to burn right through me. "Back in the hall closet, I forgot to tell you something."

My brow furrowed. "What?"

She slipped her fingertips from my hold—"I fell in love with you, too"—and disappeared back into the crowd.

I wasn't entirely sure how long it was before I could move again. And it took many steadying deep breaths to control the hot desire burning its way through me.

Half an hour later, the sun was gone and the view of New York City at night was even more breathtaking than the twilight hours. Lights lit up the skyline in shining orbs that made the city look like a sea of stars on earth.

I scanned the crowd until I found Eris and Brocker at the bottom of the stage's steps. He was whispering something in her ear and her gaze was downcast, her jaw tight. With a nod, she climbed the steps.

The music of the jazz band faded and then went silent. A hush fell over the crowd as she walked up to the mic and the spotlight swung on her. Her dress glittered and standing there in the golden light she looked like a candle's flame.

The piano cut through the silent ballroom. Calm, slow notes wove through the air like a breeze through the buildings of Chicago. It swept you up and carried you away. Then it was joined by a cello, then a sax and clarinet.

And then, finally, the voice of a siren.

Eris opened her mouth and began to sing one of the most popular songs on the radio. The song that seemed to have the whole country ensnared.

"*I'm just a woman, a lonely woman. Waiting on the weary shore.*"

Magic wove through the very oxygen with her song. People seemed to forget how to breathe.

"*I'm just a woman who's only human. One you should feel sorry for.*"

Her crimson lips brushed against the mic as she wrapped delicate fingers around its metal stand. Those blue eyes slipped closed as she stepped further into the spotlight, singing with all her heart. All her soul.

"*Am I blue. Am I blue. Ain't these tears in my eyes tellin' you…*"

I thought she would skip over them, finish the song and not sing them period, but Eris sang her own lyrics.

"*And now I stand here and pray…that you do as I say…*"

I winced as someone pinched my arm. Rita.

Right. The children.

With one final glance at the siren who had the whole

room in rapture, I exited the ballroom and tore off my waiter jacket, sprinting down the hall to the elevator where Erickson and Jimmy were already waiting.

There were two guards in front of the door, easily taken out by Erickson's stingers that he let fly from the center of his palm the moment we stepped off the elevator.

In addition to his manticore talents, Erickson was also a very skilled yegg. Complicated safes were his specialty, so it took him no time at all to pick a simple lock and open the door. Once he did, Rita gasped.

It was exactly as Eris had described. Rows of hospital beds each containing a child, aged between eight and fifteen, hooked up to an IV of glowing blue liquid.

"How are we even going to move them?" Rita asked. "They won't be able to walk."

"Just focus on getting those IVs out," I ordered, already running to the first bed.

There was no time to be gentle. I slipped the needles out of their arms and moved from bed to bed. There was no time to bandage, so trickles of blood oozed down their thin, emaciated arms. Kids groaned, some of them rubbed at their eyes, but most of them barely stirred.

When we were halfway done, Jimmy yelled at me from two rows over. "Better get the smoke going, Clemmons!"

Cursing under my breath, I dashed out of the ward and down the hall back to the elevator. I took it up to the floor right below the ballroom where I knew there was an air vent. Barreling past staff, I came to the metallic grate hanging on the wall. Taking one deep breath, I summoned the heat in my chest…and blew.

Smoke poured from my mouth and nose, curling

through the vent in thick dark gray plumes. I kept blowing and blowing, pouring as much smoke as possible into the air ducts until it would fill the vents with it. I pictured the smoke seeping through into the ballroom where people would smell it, see it, and then think the worst.

I didn't have to wait long to hear the sound of footsteps racing down the stairs.

Hearing all those feet—the power of a thundering crowd—an idea hit me like a pug's right hook.

Despite most of the guests being half-seas over, they were still able-bodied adults. At least half of them had to be strong enough to carry a child. I charged toward the staircase, threw open the door and roared at the surging crowd.

"*HELP.*"

It was the perfect cocktail of chaos.

The men—and some women—who were young enough, strong enough, and sober enough to carry a child rushed out of Brocker and Kurtz Holdings and into the street. In the midst of the confused guests rescuing children from what they thought was a burning building, I caught glimpses of Brocker's henchmen. They merely watched, helpless, as America's Royal Court escaped with their arms full of Brocker's treasure.

The only possible way the panicked mob could've been stopped was if the doors were locked, but by the time the staff realized what was happening, it was too late. Everyone milled around in the street where police cars and fire trucks waited.

All part of the plan. With regular law enforcement present, there was less chance of a monster rampage. Brocker wouldn't dare reveal his involvement with monsters in such a public setting.

During the entire ordeal—the mess of bodies and crying children—I looked for her.

Eris, where are you?

Just when I was sure I'd scanned every face coming out of the building, an explosion went off, forty-five stories up.

Red, orange, and yellow flames lit up the black sky. People gasped, pointing upward as the plumes of smoke mixed with the wispy clouds of the October night.

For the second time in my life, I wished I had my wings.

Chapter Thirty-Five

The Siren

Under this single spotlight, for three long minutes on this one night, I am a monster.

The song flows out of me, restrained and sour and rageful. Terrible and unmemorable. Cheap and harsh as a glass of panther piss.

Keep singing, Eris.

Don't.

Stop.

Singing.

When I opened my eyes on my last wavering note, the first thing I saw was a sea of faceless silhouettes. In the bright light of the spotlight, it was all I could discern. The nausea and fatigue that I sometimes felt when using my voice too much was worse than ever before, but somehow I remained standing. Maybe through sheer force of will.

Then movement caught my eye at the edge of the stage.

Brocker had climbed the steps and he was stomping

toward me with murder in his eyes. My head still dizzy from my song dripping with magic, I could do little other than stumble after him as he jerked me off the stage and through the mystified crowd. Slowly, they came to, whispers erupting around us as the effects of my enchantment began to fade.

I couldn't believe I'd done it.

Seeing Colt had breathed new life into me. New clarity. *New strength.* Night and day I'd worked with Marjorie, writing the new lyrics, rehearsing them, while simultaneously trying to control the magic in my voice. Frustratingly long hours went by as I spoke nonsense words, trying and failing to keep my emotions from bleeding through. We had to stop every few hours so I could take a break before I passed out from exhaustion that my magic brought, but then each time we went back to it, I felt just a little bit stronger.

Marjorie was my willing test subject, but by the time the morning came, she was a wreck of emotions, feeling every bit as tired and frustrated as I was.

"It's not something that can be mastered overnight, Eris," she'd said to me, wiping at the corners of her eyes. "It will take training."

She was right. It seemed so simple, and obvious, but I'd never thought of my voice like that before.

Chorus girls, jazz singers—every singer went through some kind of vocal training. I'd never had the luxury of being trained. I'd relied so much on my power and simply followed the melody that I'd heard. But the vocal cords were muscles. They required tension, release, and coordination just like the muscles of an athlete.

Maybe it wasn't so much about controlling my emotions as it was controlling the muscles that allowed the pearl's magic to pass through. If I could learn to separate my real voice from the power of the siren's pearl, would that give me the control I needed?

But that was for another time. Maybe in the future when I could walk free, without Brocker or the BOI chasing me, I could have normal conversations with people. I could finally, *finally* be heard.

Tonight, however, I needed that siren's magic. And if it was attached to my voice, then I just had to warm up those muscles and give my best performance yet.

And if the entire ballroom's enchanted silence had been any indication, I had succeeded.

Dimly, I smelled the signature scent of smoke wafting through the ballroom as Brocker hauled me through its doors. The crowd's murmuring escalated to shouts of alarm. If I hadn't been so worn out from using my magic to ensnare a ballroom full of people, I might've been able to tear from Brocker's grasp and join the escaping mass. But I hadn't expected to be so worn out. It was probably thanks to my night of practicing as well.

In the elevator, I tried to pry Brocker's iron grip from my arm, but my hands were weak.

He shook me so hard my teeth knocked together and then he tightened his hold, like he was trying to grind my bones to dust. "Do you realize what you've *done*?" he seethed.

"Hopefully stopped you," I bit back.

With his other hand, he grabbed a fistful of my hair and yanked, causing me to fall to my knees with a cry of pain.

"No," he hissed in my ear, bending low, "you have no *idea*."

The elevator stopped at his office floor and he wrenched open the iron grating. He shoved me out of the lift and I fell on my back. Fighting tides of fear, I scrabbled backward like a crab on the ocean blue carpet, staring up at the enraged man before me.

He advanced on me. One step, and then two, his eyes burning gold in the gloom of his office. *Gold?*

"My army would've been the start of a new age, Eris." He let loose a laugh that had a mad edge to it. "But now..." He stopped, towering above me in his black tuxedo, and everything seemed to hold its breath. Then he crouched, hooking his hand around the back of my neck and squeezing it so tightly that I gasped.

"You hurt me, Eris. Deeply. And now I wish to return the favor. I wasn't going to show this to you because, truly, I never wanted to hurt you. But now..." His gold eyes roamed across my face. "Now...an eye for an eye."

I flinched, but no strike came. Instead, he stood and heaved me to my feet. Terror had me stumbling after him through a side door and up a short flight of stairs. Terror had me back to my feeble self. Gone was the bold girl who disobeyed the man who had the power to take away everything—and did.

Up on the roof, the October wind threatened to knock me down. My dress rippled against my legs and locks of hair escaped the delicate pins, blowing curls around my cheeks and sticking to my rouged lips. Brocker dropped my wrist, strode across the rooftop, and stopped a foot away from a hulking silhouette that had chains scattered around it. Iron manacles bound its wrists and ankles.

Good God.

It was a human.

Or it had been.

The creature lifted itself off the ground using its boxer-like arms with barrel-sized biceps covered in scales and hands that ended with sharp metal claws. Horns attached to its temples shone under the light of the moon. Great leathery... *wings*...flapped on its back.

And then its face...

"Do you see him, Eris? Isn't he beautiful?" Brocker called over the night wind. "The world's first *real* human chimera. Scales of a basilisk, claws of a werewolf, horns of a minotaur, *wings* of a dragon…took me a long time to get my hands on those."

Brocker's voice faded into the roaring wind as I traced the lines of a face I knew so well. The face of a man who took me to a Red Sox game, who taught me how to mix an old-fashioned, who crafted me my own little stage made of whiskey crates…

"Stan?"

Chapter Thirty-Six

The Dragon

I barreled past the throng of people, their shouts of confusion and panic filling the air while firemen unrolled their hoses and coordinated teams to go after the giant explosion above. What had caused it? A bomb? Nitroglycerin? A gas main?

No, a madman.

I was just about to charge back through the doors when a hand gripped my arm. Twisting around, I found myself staring into a familiar face. It was a woman with raven hair and high, sharp cheekbones. The image of her in a maid's uniform came back to me, and I knew then that she'd been the one who'd found us in Boston. She had to work for Brocker.

Instinctually, my hand went to her throat, slamming her against the side of the building. "*You,*" I rasped, smoke pouring from my mouth as I fought to keep my anger in check.

She tried to pry my hands away. "E-Eris," she squeaked.

Instantly, I let go and she leaned her head back, coughing, rubbing her throat.

"Did Brocker take her?" I asked, but already knowing

the answer.

"Yes, you have to stop him. What he's created...it's an abomination. Not even Eris knows—"

"Where is she?"

The woman ripped off her headband and a cyclops eye stared up at me. It glowed blue in the darkness of the chaotic street. "The roof."

I tore through the entrance and into the stairwell. My leg muscles pumped as I propelled myself up the steps, taking them two—sometimes three—at a time. Thoughts like *I never should have left without her* and *if she's dead I'll never feel alive again* spiraled through my head.

My breath was shallow and the only thing I could hear besides my endless footsteps as I climbed higher and higher.

The sixth floor...the twenty-first floor...the forty-fourth floor. Hold on, Eris. Hold on.

Chapter Thirty-Seven

The Siren

"Stanley?" My voice cracked as I stepped toward the creature.

No, not creature, my best friend in the whole world.

The man who'd made me laugh till tears rolled down my face when he stuck straws under his lips and pretended to be a walrus. Who would play checkers with me until the bar opened. Who never ever begged me to talk to him because he knew how badly I wanted to.

My fierce protector for seven years.

My Stanley.

A monster. *Because of me.*

I fell to my hands and knees, unable to remain standing. "No, no, no, *please.*" Heaving sobs racked my chest as Brocker went around the creature, unlocking manacles.

"Yes, yes, boo-hoo. The man came looking for Helena and I thought it would be a good opportunity. Gin is not the only one who likes to experiment. Unfortunately, the children I'd tried this on—their bodies weren't strong enough to maintain multiple monster parts. Sometimes you just can't beat strong, able-bodied soldiers."

My stomach heaved at the knowledge that Brocker had attempted this horror on children, too. *And he failed. Oh God.*

The clinking of chains traveled across the vacant rooftop, and I could hear Stanley's labored breathing, growls from deep within his massive chest.

"You've set me back, Eris. Many years. And I will not forgive this. But there will be other pearls. Other sirens." One more manacle dropped, hitting the concrete with a kind of echoing finality. "*Get her.*"

With a flap of wings and a growl, self-preservation kicked in.

I scrambled upward and ran across the rooftop and down the stairs. A presence chased after me—large and inhuman and impossibly powerful. Claws swiped with a metallic scrape as I dodged away and into the office. Slamming the door on scaly fingers, I locked it and kicked off my heels, sprinting across the stretch of carpet toward the elevator.

Like a nitro bomb going off on a safe, fire, sparks, and intense pressure exploded the door open and burst through the window in great billows of flames and smoke. I turned, unable to look away as dragon breath came out of the lungs of the creature who was once my bartender.

Now free from the roof stairwell, Stanley swung his head toward me and snarled, smoke still curling from his nostrils like he'd just taken a long drag on a gasper.

How ironic. My Stanley had never smoked in his life.

"Dear God," I breathed as the chimera stepped over the charred remains of Brocker's desk and his kingly chair. The leather wings *twitched*. "What has he done to you, Stan?"

"Given him powers that no human could ever dream of."

Brocker stood in the smoldering ruins of the doorway to the roof. He clasped his hands behind his back, surveying the destruction of his office and looking…satisfied?

At the vibrations of Stanley's footsteps, I tore my attention away from Brocker to watch the monster trudging toward me. Like every inch of movement hurt him.

Seeing him advance, slowly and painfully, half his face in shadow and the other half lit by the flicker of flames growing across the carpet, I realized I wasn't going anywhere.

I *would not* leave Stan. He came here looking for me. Looking for Madame. I wasn't going to turn my back on him. Because he would never turn his back on me.

This is what strength is, Eris. It's never turning away from someone who needs you.

"Stanley? Stan, it's me, Eris," I said, forgetting about the magic in my voice and my own emotions of desperation and despair. I just wanted to reach him. However I could.

The monster continued to move toward me, each of his steps shaking the floor. *Thud. Thud. Thud.*

Brocker's laugh echoed through his office. "Even *your* voice can't reach him. His mind was lost a few days ago."

I ignored Brocker. I had to or I'd lose my best, oldest friend. "I know this isn't you, Stan. You're in pain. But…" I took a breath. "We can take it all away, if you just let me help you."

Stanley stopped and blinked blearily in confusion, but then his wings twitched and he recoiled, wincing as he groped at his shoulders with his massive clawed hand.

Those wings…they're really driving him mad…

How had Colt survived with them? Even just a week?

Stanley fell to his knees as his wings unfolded and stretched, giving me the full breadth of his agony. They were tipped with sharp claws and were so red that the edges faded to black.

Swallowing, I took a few tentative steps toward him. When he didn't move, I summoned the final bit of my courage and crossed all the way to him, stepping over to cup his unshaved cheeks in my small hands. My thumb swept over the remnants of a black eye he'd gotten at an underground boxing match a few weeks ago. It had taken longer than usual to heal. I remembered icing it when he came home.

His eyes were glazed over with pain and hopelessness. I smoothed my hand along his jaw and there was some kind of flicker there. Maybe of recognition. Maybe of more pain.

"Don't just stand there! *Kill her!*"

With a thick sob, I threw my arms around Stan's neck. I was scared. I was so, so scared, but I was even more scared of losing him. I had to be strong.

Colt was right. This was what strength was.

Stanley was like a marble statue under my arms, but at least he wasn't trying to bite me or claw me, or burn me to death. My Stanley was still in there somewhere.

Feeling his pain like it were my own, I skimmed fingers across the scales on his arm. Freshly attached. I took a deep trembling breath. "Don't worry, Stan. I'm not leaving you. I saved you once, I'll do it again."

"Oh, for the love of..."

The sound of a gun clicking and firing ripped through the silence of the office.

In that same second, the massive leathery wings swept across the carpet to surround me in a cocoon. I fell on my back as their force knocked me down. The spray of lead hit the wings, but did not pierce them. Stanley roared in agony as more bullets struck and he staggered to his knees, blood dripping down his arms and legs. The wings unfurled around me, sweeping to the side as they spasmed with what must've been blinding pain from the storm of shells.

"I should've known that Beauty would tame the Beast," Brocker's voice boomed. As the fire spread across the carpet and up the walls, I could see his silhouette standing over the burnt pieces of his desk. "Ah, well…"

He lifted his tommy gun.

Before my brain caught up to what was happening, another gunshot pierced the air. But this time, it came from the stairwell. Brocker cried out and twisted to the side as a bullet caught him in his left arm. Another figure emerged from the charred doorway holding a pistol.

Colt.

His hair shone like liquid gold in the firelight as shadows danced across his face and the black slacks and white shirt of his waiter uniform. "Eris!" He called over the growing crackle of flames, his gaze never wavering from Brocker.

My heart soared at seeing him.

"Colt! I'm here!" I yelled back.

Brocker whirled around, but instead of aiming the tommy gun at Colt, he fired another round at Stan. The Chicago lightning was far worse this time, and even the strength of four monsters was not enough. Stanley thrashed on the floor, roaring and swiping with his claws. Before I could roll away, they raked across my stomach and pain exploded through me. I screamed, hunching over as warm liquid blossomed through my dress.

"ERIS!"

Colt raced for me and I reached out to him, my vision now bleary, threatening to blacken. Beside me, Stan continued to writhe in pain from so many bullet wounds.

No more fighting. Please. No more.

Colt dropped to his knees next to me, placing pressure on my open wounds with large, strong hands. "They're shallow," he panted. "It'll be all right."

"No," Brocker growled, hefting his tommy gun for yet a third time. "No, it won't."

"Stay back," Colt breathed, guiding my hands to maintain pressure on my own stomach. He inhaled deeply, his chest expanding to hold the full brunt of his dragon breath.

Brilliant, blinding columns of fire burst out of Colt's mouth, rolling toward Brocker in a volcanic tidal wave. When the flames cleared, catching on the walls and ceiling, Brocker still remained standing.

Completely untouched.

How…was that possible?

Much of Brocker's clothes began to crumble to ash as he walked toward us, backlit by the fire. "You know," he said. "I'd always lamented not having many powers. And yet, I do have to admit, when you're fighting a dragon…it helps to be a phoenix."

Chapter Thirty-Eight

The Dragon

A phoenix.

The legendary monster bird of fire. A bird known to be immortal, reborn in flames.

I'd heard of such creatures existing, but never being fused with a human.

But then again, who knew how Brocker had come to be. Erickson had said the man had damn near manifested into existence twenty-five years ago only through tax records. Clearly, the man held more mysteries than just a few background checks could uncover.

The more pressing issue, of course, was that my fire breath hadn't worked on him. And yet…my gaze jumped to his left shoulder soaked with blood from the bullet I'd managed to sink in him. The man could bleed. Just because he didn't seem to age didn't mean that he couldn't be destroyed… somehow, some way.

Pulling out my own gun from my jacket pocket, I watched while Brocker slid open a door to the left and pulled out another box of bullets. He fed the shells into his tommy, quickly and expertly. Like he'd done it a thousand times.

When Eris squeezed my arm, I glanced back at her, terrified that her wounds had worsened. But instead of watching me or Brocker, her gaze was glued to the creature at our feet.

Brocker was indeed a demented soul. He'd created an actual live chimera, out of Eris's bartender no less. Not to mention…he had my wings on him. I'd never thought I'd have to see them again, and yet, here they were. Perhaps to end me because they hadn't been able to the last time.

Human, phoenix, monster…Brocker was none of those things. He was a true demon.

In the near distance, I heard him feed the last of his ammunition.

Standing up to a phoenix with a submachine gun…I didn't like my odds…and I wasn't a gambling man, but I'd bet on her. On us.

Brocker swung his freshly loaded gun toward us.

"Eris," I said, pushing myself to stand over her as I pointed my own pistol at Brocker, "you've gotta run, doll."

Chapter Thirty-Nine

The Siren

One revolver against a tommy. *Impossible.* Colt would be dead before he even let fly a single round. Like that night a lifetime ago, in The Blind Dragon, with the Harvard boy pulling out his pistol, I pictured the next few seconds in my head.

Flashes of light going off every half second as a whole slew of bullets exploded from Brocker's tommy gun. Shells ripping through Colt's body as it danced above me like some macabre puppet.

Another future I wouldn't let happen. Somehow, I'd stopped the bullet in midair that night. I'd stopped everything.

I am the most powerful monster in the world.

Speak, Eris.

"JAM."

If one word could cast visible shockwaves through the air, then mine did. Everything seemed to slow. The flickering flames moved more like blades of grass in a lazy summer breeze. Smoke drifted through the air, caught in a current of a lake in the winter—nowhere to go and nowhere fast.

The tommy gun clicked and clicked but no bullets came out—jammed, just like I'd commanded.

As Brocker cursed and shook his gun, trying in vain to fire his rounds, I staggered to my feet, blood from the claw wounds seeping through my fingers as I clutched my stomach.

I glared at Brocker through the slow-moving smoke and embers drifting in the breeze. The man who'd lived so long as this legendary fire bird, consuming everything. Destroying lives. Hurting innocent children.

I wouldn't let him spread his hell anywhere else.

Wrapping one arm around Colt's middle, I rested my head against his shoulder and asked, "Do you have any bullets left?"

"Just one," Colt rasped.

My grip tightened on his arm. "*You won't miss.*"

Colt's body stiffened against me and his arm moved a centimeter to the left. His chest rose and fell in one deep, relaxing breath, then he pulled the trigger. The flint sparked, the bullet left the chamber, and Brocker's neck jerked back.

His body fell to the floor with a clean, perfect bullseye right in the middle of his forehead. Like his very own cyclops eye.

That's for Madame, I thought as my head grew heavy and thick. Dizzy with fatigue, loss of blood, and all the magic leaving me too quick and so fast, I felt Colt's arms tighten around me and it all went…blissfully black.

• • •

"*There's a saying old, says that love is blind.*"

A familiar, beloved melody wove through the air, gently prodding my sleepy head to wake up and appreciate it.

"*Still we're often told, 'Seek and ye shall find.'*"

Softly, I hummed along, keeping my eyes closed, lost in the sound of Gertrude Lawrence's voice coming through an old radio speaker. Maybe Madame had left the radio on in the kitchen. I'd have to turn it off soon, but not till this song was done.

"*So I'm going to seek a certain lad I've had in mind.*"

I knew the lyrics like the back of my hand—Marv would ask me to sing it often and, with just the two of us, we'd jive together. Me with my lyrics, and him with his soulful sax notes.

"*Looking ev'rywhere, haven't found him yet.*"

It was the very song that had prodded that Harvard boyo to stand up to Stanley that night.

Stanley!

With a gasp, I wrenched my eyes open, my heart pounding as my frantic gaze scoured the unfamiliar room. It looked like a hospital—white sheets, metal bed railing, soft cream curtains gently fluttering in the afternoon October breeze. Wincing, I closed my hand over the IV needle dug into my arm. A radio sitting on the window ledge continued to play my favorite song.

"*There's a somebody I'm longing to see…*"

The door opened and Colt strode in, a spoonful of applesauce halfway to his mouth.

He froze when he saw me, his brows raising in surprise.

"*I hope that he turns out to be someone who'll watch over me.*"

"Eris," he breathed. His fingers loosened around his spoon and applesauce cup and they dropped to the floor, some of the sauce spilling across his shirt. He swore under his breath, wiped at the stain, then crossed to the bed, dropping down to kiss me swiftly on the lips.

If I hadn't had a thousand questions, I would've held the kiss for longer.

"How are you feeling, doll?" he asked, kissing my temple then the top of my head. "Doctor said you probably wouldn't wake up till tonight."

"Stanley," I croaked. "Where is he? *How* is he?"

Colt nodded as if he knew that question would be my first. "He's alive. Stable. But he's got a long road to recovery ahead, Eris. They were able to remove the wings and the horns, and the claws, but those scales…well, we decided to leave them intact for now."

Alive. He was alive. That was all that mattered. He could get better. Scars would remain, but wounds would heal.

"I want to see him. Is he here?" I started to get up, but Colt placed a strong halting hand on my shoulder.

"Easy, tiger. You can't go opening your stitches."

Instinctually, my fingers feathered across my stomach to find bandages. "Stitches?"

"Your cuts were shallow enough not to hit anything crucial, but you're no dragon," he said, giving me a tiny smile.

"When can I see him?" I asked, reluctantly settling back into my pillows.

"When the doc says you can. Until then, I'm not letting you out of this bed."

I smiled back. My dragon was very cute playing nurse. "Has he woken up yet?"

"Sure has," Colt said with a nod. "I was there. First thing he asked about was you."

"Thank God," I breathed.

Colt took the lone wooden chair and pulled it closer to my bedside. He gave me a crooked grin as he picked up my hand and lightly ran his fingers across my skin, just enough to give me goose pimples. "You mean, thank *Eris.* God had nothing to do with what you did back there. That was your own special brand of miracle."

As the full events of the night washed over me, I curled

my body toward the side to face him—wincing just slightly. "So it's not true?" I asked.

Colt tilted his head. "What isn't?"

"That phoenixes are immortal? I think I'd read that in a book somewhere."

Colt shook his head. "He's still half human. The phoenix flames may have given him everlasting life, and maybe advanced healing, but a bullet between the eyes?" Colt tapped his forehead. "No contest."

I'd killed a man. Colt may have pulled the trigger, but I'd ensured that he wouldn't miss. I wasn't quite ready to face that fact yet.

"What about the children?" I asked.

"They're being kept at different hospitals right now. Dr. Durwich is almost done with an antidote to remove all traces of the chimera agent in their system. It may not prevent a virus, but it can heal someone infected with chimera blood. Prevent them from becoming a monster later."

"That's good, then."

"Yeah…" But Colt's gaze was distant, on the verge of staring off into space.

I knew that look. "What are you worried about?" I asked.

Colt frowned. "The monster parts," he confessed. "Brocker was so sure he'd get one hundred and twenty monster parts into the country. Usually when they're smuggled it's only been two or three at a time. Ten tops. But *that* many? I'm worried about how he thought he could get them into the country. We have agents on the East Coast who are all trained to find those kinds of things."

I grabbed Colt's hand, suddenly remembering my journey through the Great Lakes on Brocker's boat. "Chicago's pier."

Colt's brow furrowed. "Huh?"

"Brocker's yacht took me up through Lake Michigan into Lake Huron, and through Lake Erie and into the Erie

Canal and then the Hudson River," I explained hurriedly. "When I was on the yacht, I saw crates as if they were waiting to be offloaded at various docks. We stopped several times, too. What if they offloaded those crates at the docks because they knew they wouldn't be checked by the BOI? Those waterways could be how he's smuggling the monster parts into the country."

Colt's eyes widened, then a confident smile traveled across his lips. "I'll tell McCarney."

"Speaking of…" I peeked at Colt from under my lashes, almost nervous to hear what came next. "How is your old boss? Is the BOI still mad you deserted them?"

At that, Colt let out a booming laugh. "I think us saving the whole darn country gave us a president's pardon." Then he fixed me with a tender gaze, one full of hope. I knew because I had to be looking at him the same way. "You get it, right? We're free to go wherever we want, doll."

Something unspoken settled between us, and I knew right then that I had plans to make. He must've known, too, because then a comfortable silence settled over us in my little hospital room, filled only by the radio playing on in the background. I recognized the song as "Let's Do It, Let's Fall in Love" by Cole Porter.

Already there, I thought happily.

• • •

It was a whole two days before I was allowed to visit Stan. For complete privacy, he was kept in a top floor hospital suite while he healed through his difficult wounds.

Colt had escorted me to the gift shop and I had bought a bouquet of flowers—with Colt's money because I had none, of course—and then he took me up to Stan's room. Colt told me he'd wait outside, but even as he stood with me by the doorway, I couldn't bring myself to knock.

I was nervous.

"What if he hates me now?" I asked. "It's all my fault that this happened to him..."

"If I didn't know any better, I would've said you'd snuck a few rounds of giggle water. Eris, go." Colt nodded toward the door.

Taking a deep breath, I stepped into the room, ignoring the small pang of pain in my stomach that came with most movement. Colt shut the door behind me and I was left to face Stanley alone.

My bartender lay in his bed, pale, but alive. His wings were gone, but his hands were bandaged and I wondered if he'd ever have normal fingernails again instead of his werewolf claws. Three stitches were lined along each side of his temple where his horns had been and aquamarine scales covered his big arms.

A grin stretched across his face when he saw me. "Eris."

Dropping the flowers, I flew to his bedside and buried my face in his chest, breathing in his scent. Even now, after being away from The Blind Dragon for over a week, he had its smell. He wrapped his scaly arms around me and held. "I'm so glad you're all right," I breathed, my sentiment muffled against his chest.

He stroked my hair. "All thanks to you, my girl."

"But it would've never—"

Stan took me by the shoulders, pulled me away. "Now you listen to me." He stuck a finger in my face, shook it like I was a small child again. "Don't you dare. You start taking the world's evil on your shoulders and you'll stop seeing what's good in it. And there is plenty of that, Eris. *You* are good. That young man out in the hall...*he's* good. Heaven or hell. God or the devil. Monster or angel. None of that matters. You do what's right. Like you always have. Your heart has always been in the right place. Like protecting those women when they couldn't protect themselves."

I gaped at him. "You saw me do that?"

He nodded. "Course. Ain't nothing that goes on in my bar that I don't know about."

"But don't you think that was…wrong?"

Stanley's brows pulled together as he studied me. "I know you've lived your whole life thinking that you want to give people their free will. But sometimes, Eris, the hard truth of it is that there are evil souls out there in the world that keep the good ones down. And that just ain't fair. If you can stop that evil, then that's nothing to feel guilty about."

I couldn't help but agree. Perhaps I should've felt some remorse for taking someone's life. After all, it was God's greatest sin, but when I searched my soul for it, I couldn't find any. Not a shred. Brocker had left his humanity and his redemption a long time ago.

For whatever reason, the image of the stained-glass mural of St. Michael the archangel from St. Agnes came back to me.

I was no angel or warrior of God like St. Michael, but I knew right and I knew wrong. Brocker and everything he stood for had been wrong. Had it been right to kill him? I wasn't sure, but I would sleep better knowing that every one of those children would not serve as a soldier in his monster army.

"Now," Stan said, cutting through my morbid thoughts. "What's next for you?"

"Well, I want to make sure you're okay. And then we can go back to The Blind Dragon and close it up and—"

"No."

I blinked. "No?"

"That's my bar," Stan said. "My home. I'm not closing it up. And now that…that Helena is gone, it'll go to me."

Slowly, I nodded. "Okay, then I'll go with you and we

can..."

"No." He was shaking his head again.

"Stan—"

"Eris, what did we just talk about?" He tilted his chin toward the door. "Being in Boston, being in some drum for the rest of your life...is that what you really want?"

I bit my bottom lip. "I want to make sure you're okay."

"And I will be. A fellow came by, Agent Sawyer, I believe. Said he's a basilisk and can teach me how to hide my scales. Listen, honey, you'll always have a home at the Dragon." He took my hands and squeezed them. "But I don't think it's a home you ever wanted. I watched that far-off look in your eyes every time you sang or wiped down tables. You were dreaming of another place. It's out there. Go find it."

He was handing me the key to my freedom. *Are you ready to fight for your freedom, Eris?*

I loved that I didn't have to fight for it this time.

I smiled. "You won't find a singer better than me, though."

Stanley chuckled. "But a better waitress I'll bet."

I playfully whacked him on the arm.

After an hour of talking, I left Stan so he could rest. When I came out of the room, I was expecting the hall to be empty, but Colt sat there on the floor, waiting for me, his fedora tipped back as he stared out the hallway window. At my entrance, he looked up and gave me a smile.

"All jake?"

I nodded. "All jake."

He got up, dusting himself off. "If the doc says it's okay, we can go get some dinner. I'm starving for some pastrami. There's a deli around the corner..."

"Colt." I grabbed his jacket, jerking him close, and gave him a hard, steamy kiss. Our steamiest yet since the coat closet.

When our lips parted, he looked down at me, sporting a

small, confused smile. “Not that I’m complaining, but what was that for?”

“It was a proposition.”

“A proposition?”

“Yes.” I tugged at his tie, pulling his face closer still. “Colt. Run away with me.”

Epilogue

Somewhere Out West...

A small farmhouse stood in fields of corn and tomato plants. It had been standing for generations and would still stand even in the midst of America's worst economic crisis yet. It would persevere, though too many would not.

Off in the distance, about half a mile down the lone dirt road that led to and from the farmhouse, there was a cloud of dust, kicked up by the wheels of a jalopy, heading west.

The farmer of the residence stood on the porch, hands on his hips, watching the jalopy drive away.

"Jack?"

He turned at the sound of his wife calling him. She stepped out from behind the screen door and let it swing shut.

"Who was that?" she asked, lifting a hand to shield her gaze as she watched the cloud of dust get smaller and smaller.

"A couple. Newlyweds, I think. Wanted to ask about the property some fifty acres away."

"So they want to be our neighbors?"

Farmer Jack shrugged. "Maybe. The girl had the sweetest

voice I'd ever heard. She'd do well in our church choir."

"Well, are they coming back?" the farmer's wife asked.

"Said they might. But first they wanted to see the Redwoods out in California."

Acknowledgments

Thank you to my doting parents who encouraged my love of history and enrolled me in all the jazz and musical theater classes I could've ever wanted—they greatly inspired my love for the 1920s. Thank you also to my best writing buds, Melissa Jackson and Season Vining, and to Tiffany Brownlee with whom I edited the bulk of this book on our trips to book fests.

While I can't begin to describe the fun of weaving paranormal mythology into a decade of such wild cultural and social dynamism, I will say that I felt quite zozzled by the end of it. So thank you to my awesome editors, Lydia Sharp and Judi Lauren, and everyone else over at Entangled Teen—Curtis, Alexandra, Heather, Julia, and LJ. Cheers to you all.

About the Author

Lindsey Duga developed a deep love for courageous heroes, dastardly villains, and enchanting worlds from the cartoon shows, books, and graphic novels she read as a kid. Drawing inspiration from these fantastical works of fiction, she wrote her first novel in college while she was getting her bachelor's in Mass Communication from Louisiana State University. By day, Lindsey is an account manager at a digital marketing agency based in Baton Rouge, Louisiana. By night, and the wee hours of the morning, she writes both middle grade and young adult. She has a weakness for magic, anything classical, all kinds of mythology, and falls in love with tragic heroes. Other than writing and cuddling with her morkie puppy, Delphi, Lindsey loves catching up on the latest superhero TV show, practicing yoga, and listening (and belting) to her favorite music artists and show tunes.

Also by Lindsey Duga…

KISS OF THE ROYAL

GLOW OF THE FIREFLIES

Discover more Entangled Teen titles...

Smoke and Key

a novel by Kelsey Sutton

Key has no idea who or where she is. Or why she's dead. The only clue to her identity hangs around her neck: a single rusted key. Under is a place of dirt and secrets, and Key is determined to discover the truth of her past in order to escape it. Then the murders start. Bodies that are burned to a crisp. And after being burned, the dead stay dead. Key is running out of time to discover who she was—and what secret someone is willing to kill to keep hidden—before she loses her life for good...

Demon Bound

a *Crossroads Chronicles* novel by Chris Cannon

Meena's summer job becomes drastically different when she's suddenly bound to a demon as his soul-collector. Who knew that her boring, pageant-obsessed, bonfire-loving town was a hotbed for soul-sucking demons, demon-hunting witches, and vampires who just wanna have fun? Good thing she meets new guy Jake—who gets her and still hangs around. Jake never counted on staying, but Meena's bound to a demon who wants to destroy her soul—and Jake's finally found someone worth fighting for.

The November Girl

a novel by Lydia Kang

I'm Anda, and the lake is my mother. I am the November storms that terrify sailors, and with their deaths, I keep the island alive. Hector has come to Isle Royale to hide. My little island on Lake Superior is shut down for the winter, and there's no one here but me. And now him. Hector is running from the violence in his life, but violence runs through my veins. I should send him away. But I'm half-human, too, and Hector makes me want to listen to my foolish, half-human heart. And if do, I can't protect him from the storms coming for us.

The Things They've Taken

a novel by Katie McElhenney

Lo Campbell wants to be a normal teenager with a normal life. Instead she travels the country with her mother, chasing the "what else" that's out there... Until one day, the "what else" chases back. Rescuing her mom requires the skills of a Tracker. Shaw may be good-looking, strong, and utterly infuriating, but his help is desperately needed, even if his secrets plague them at every turn.

Made in the USA
Monee, IL
10 September 2020